HAWKS OF SORGA

THRICE BORN

By *Summer Hanford*

Martin Sisters Publishing

DEDICATION

To my parents, Karen and George Hanford. Thank you for a lifetime of love and encouragement.

THRICE BORN SERIES
MARTIN SISTERS PUBLISHING COMPANY

Gift of the Aluien
Hawks of Sorga
Throne of Wheylia
The Plains of Tybrunn
Shores of K'Orge (2017)

COMPANION SHORT STORIES
BY SUMMER HANFORD

The Forging of Cadwel
Hawk Trials for Mirimel
The Fall of Larkesong
The Sword of Three

ACKNOWLEDGEMENT

My gratitude, as always, to Martin Sisters Publishing for their continued confidence and support, and to Simply Marcella, the Baltimore Woods Nature Center and Sycamore Hill Gardens for allowing me to participate in their events.

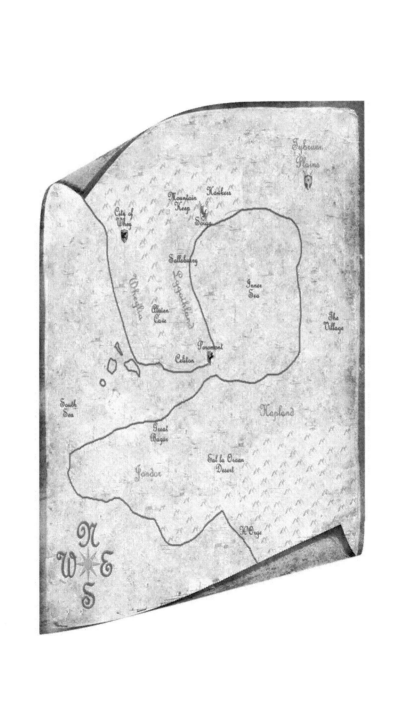

Chapter 1

Aridian stood in the middle of the tree-shrouded trail, unmoving, watching the farm burn in the clearing before him. Flames reached high into the night, their dire orange glow blotting out the moon and stars. A part of him knew it was a dream, knew he wasn't really there.

Still, he cried out, fear shooting through him at the assault of smoke and charred flesh on his nostrils. He drew the broadsword at his side, trying to take up an offensive stance. In all his nearly sixteen years, he knew he'd never witnessed anything like the blazing farmstead before him. Dream or no, Ari desperately wanted to help, but he couldn't uproot his feet from the rutted dirt path.

The upper story of the farmhouse was nearly gone, one dark wall left standing as a backdrop to the blaze. The lower story sprouted flames like giant feathers dancing to the jumbled music of the wind. There was an unearthly groan as the large barn crumpled inward. All about the yard, smaller outbuildings collapsed as they burned. The scorched ground was splattered with random patches of flickering orange as fire consumed anything it could.

But what tore at Ari's heart, what wrenched a cry from his throat, were the dead. Pigs, chickens, a cow and a goat were strewn through the yard, torn and burning, yet it wasn't just farm animals. Two unmoving human forms sprawled outside what was once the farmhouse door. They were face down in the dirt, charred black and red. Dark four-legged beasts circled them, nipping at their lifeless bodies, rending them.

Ari struggled against his own immobility, nearly mad with the desire to charge the beasts and scatter them, slay them. But he couldn't move from where he stood, and the beasts gave no indication that they heard his cries.

A man came out of the house, a palpable darkness surrounding him. It wasn't the darkness of the smoke that billowed in undulating waves into the night sky. The man's darkness was a clinging thing that moved with him, surrounding without obscuring. He was untouched by the flames.

The man tilted his head back. A screeching howl burst forth from his bloodied lips. Around him, the creatures answered in kind. Their cries were wolf-like, yet hollow. As one, they sped away across well-tended fields and into the darkness of the forest, the man as swift as his four-legged companions.

Still, Ari could not move from where he stood. He sheathed his sword, tears streaming down his face. He knew the man and woman were dead. He was sure of it. Even at a distance, he could feel the heat of the flames, see how the wolf creatures had mauled their bodies. Tearing his eyes away, he looked around the clearing, feeling he should recognize this place.

Light flickered in the forest to Ari's left, away from where the man and his wolves had gone. It was a pale shimmering glow, like the light cast by the moon. Across the field it came, silent and swift. It paused at the edge of the clearing, in front of the now unrecognizable barn. This creature, too, seemed not to heed the flames.

The light, almost man-sized, entered the blazing farmhouse. The shattered ruins of windows, hollow holes in the one remaining wall, offered Ari a view of the burning nothingness inside. A flame-licked staircase was all that still stood to bespeak of the second floor.

Ari watched through the empty windows as the being of light moved within. It went to the staircase, circling behind it and bending low. It seemed to disappear, and Ari called out, fighting against the dream-restraints that kept him from rushing to its aid. When the figure reemerged, it clutched something to its chest, its light dimmed.

The Lady, Ari thought, recognizing her diminutive form and delicate ancient features, now that her light no longer concealed them. The Lady was the magical Aluien who'd wrenched him back from death the spring before. Who'd changed him, making him something more than human. Making him the Thrice Born.

She hurried from the house, the bundle clutched in her arms. Ari could see that while the flames did not touch the Lady, the blankets she retrieved from below the stairwell were scorched as she bore them from the flames. She didn't return the way she'd come, but instead headed up the trail toward him. He called out to her and she looked up, eyes narrowing.

Ari wasn't sure if she could see him, but she held up the scorched blankets, revealing a mewling baby, his squashed face and bright pink flesh giving Ari the impression he was newly born.

"It is you, Thrice Born," the Lady said, her voice musical.

The baby let out a cry and she brought it back to her chest, cradling it, continuing up the path. Ari still couldn't move, and it seemed she didn't intend to go around him. As they collided, he awoke with a start, gasping, into the cool darkness of his bedroom in Sorga.

Wakefulness poured in, robbing his dream of details, but the voice of the Lady sounded clear inside his mind. "Beware the Caller, my Aridian, beware the called."

Ari stared at the ceiling of his bedchamber, trying to sort out the images of his dream. Was it the fate of his own parents he just witnessed, helpless to go to their aid? But how could he see that? He had no memory of that night. The man and woman who raised him as their nephew said he was a baby when his parents died, nearly sixteen years ago. They never told him of a fire. He wished he had a way to contact the Lady, or the Aluien bard Larkesong. They would know the answers to his questions.

The amulet the Lady had given him that winter rested on his chest, cool and solid. He reached for it, tracing the lines of its ever-changing twisting pattern with his fingers. He never took it off. The Lady told him it would keep him safe. No one, Aluien or vile Empty One, could use magic to find him so long as he wore it, or use their arts to beguile him, distorting his reality with their will.

Sighing, he shook off the grim mood his dream had left him in and glanced toward the curtained window, trying to guess what time it was. He felt it to be morning, but it was always difficult to tell because the heavy blue curtains hung over the tall windows, holding back any light that might try to get in. Ari liked the curtains, because embroidered on them was the brown hawk on blue and white that was the symbol of Sorga, but he didn't like them drawn.

His best friend and valet, Peine, insisted they stay closed tight against the chill spring air, even though Ari didn't get cold, not after the Aluiens had used their magic to change him. Ari would rather have the curtains and the thick leaded glass windows thrown wide, but somehow, Peine always got his way. It didn't seem to matter that Ari was almost two years older than Peine and heir to the dukedom.

As quietly as he could, Ari slid from beneath the covers and out of the massive bed that belonged to the Lord of Sorga. Ari wasn't the Lord of Sorga. Sir Cadwel, King's Champion and

Ari's mentor, was still the master of Sorga, but Sir Cadwel insisted Ari take the lord's rooms. Sir Cadwel's lingering guilt over not saving his family from murder kept him from ever embracing his role as lord of the keep. He seemed to view himself as a caretaker, waiting for the true lord to come. It was still a matter of stunning incomprehensible joy to Ari that Sir Cadwel deemed him that person.

Ari slid open a set of curtains, shooting a glance at the door leading to Peine's room. Ari thought it was strange that Peine's room was through his, but Peine said that was how valets' quarters were. If Ari had his way, Peine would have his own rooms. Ari still didn't like the idea of anyone being his servant, but especially not his best friend. There was no dissuading Peine, though, who always wanted Ari to act like a proper lord.

Dawn was touching the horizon. Ari smiled, well pleased. The earlier you start practicing each day, the more prepared you are when someone comes to kill you. That was what Sir Cadwel always said. Ari took things Sir Cadwel said very seriously.

Ari made an effort to push his dusty brown hair into order and splashed some water on his face. Pulling on yesterday's clothes, he grabbed his gleaming boots and belted on his sword, sneaking out of the room. If Peine woke and caught him, there would be a whole list of things Ari had to do before he was considered presentable enough to go about the castle. Take a bath and shave and select trousers and a shirt that looked proper with one another, whatever that meant. He didn't really have to worry, though. Peine had tiptoed in very late the night before, so he probably still slept quite soundly.

Ari rubbed at the soft stubble on his chin as he descended the broad staircase leading from the nobles' quarters to the central foyer. He'd started shaving that past fall. You couldn't even see his beard unless he went for days without doing it, but Peine never seemed to care. Ari supposed that was why gentlemen had valets. Otherwise, who knew what state most men would walk around in?

13

Opening one of the massive double doors leading outside, Ari sucked in a deep breath of cool air. He pushed the door all the way open, leaving it that way to let in fresh air. The castle, built as it was half inside the soaring peaks behind it, tended to get fusty during the winter. The inner rooms didn't even have windows.

"Good morning," Ari said to the two guards at the bottom of the steps. "I'm headed over to the stable yard to practice." He didn't think it was polite to walk by without talking to them or telling them what he was doing.

"Yes, my lord," one of the men said.

Ari went first into the stable to say good morning to his horse, Stew. The brown watched Ari approach for a moment before putting his nose in the air, affecting a look of indifference that would be comical if Ari didn't feel so guilty. Since Ari and Sir Cadwel returned from the capital in the south near the end of winter, Stew spent a lot of time in the stable, and he didn't appreciate it much. The grooms exercised him any day Ari couldn't, but Stew didn't find running in circles in the stable yard very entertaining.

From the stall next to Stew, Sir Cadwel's horse, Goldwin, glanced over before returning to his standing sleep. Goldwin seemed much more content with their enforced rest. Of course, Goldwin was a lot older than Stew.

"Good morning, Goldwin," Ari said as he passed the dun-colored destrier. "Good morning, Stew." Ari stopped to lean over the front rail of Stew's stall door. "How are you today? Would you like me to brush you before I practice?"

Stew shook his whole body, as if shaking off after fording a river, and turned his head away.

"I promise we'll go riding soon," Ari said, meaning it. "I need to practice right now, but in a few weeks, we'll ride back to Poromont for the royal wedding and the spring tourney. Then you'll get to travel and run the lists and everything."

Stew's ears swiveled toward Ari, taking in every word, but his head remained averted.

"Maybe after lunch today, we'll go for a ride," Ari said, trying to placate his horse. "I can't practice all day every day, after all."

Stew gave a whistling huff before turning around in his stall so his rump was in Ari's face. Ari left the stable, shaking his head. Stew obviously didn't believe him.

In the stable yard, Ari drew his sword, squaring off in front of a straw-stuffed dummy. He began one of the many offensive drills Sir Cadwel had taught him, starting out with slow controlled swings. He touched the tip of the blade to the dummy's neck, its chest, the vulnerable spot that on a man would be the hole in his armor under his arm. Ari concentrated, reining in his strength and focusing instead on increasing his speed and accuracy. Ever since he'd almost died the spring before and the magical race of Aluiens had used the power of the Orlenia to save him, he had more strength than a normal mortal. If he unleashed it, he would be stuffing a new practice dummy every other stroke.

He switched from offense to defense and back again, adding in more footwork, dancing around the practice dummy. Focusing, he whipped the heavy blade about faster and faster until it was a blur of movement. He sank into the moment, all cares leaving him. There was no Stew, no Peine, and no Lady Ispiria, although even thinking about not thinking about her threatened his concentration.

Redoubling his efforts, Ari forced even greater speed from his muscles, working himself into a state of concentration so deep, he could even set aside his normal disappointment that there were so few men he could square off against. In Sorga, only Sir Cadwel was good enough to test Ari anymore, and the old knight seemed less and less inclined to spar. It wasn't because Sir Cadwel couldn't still best Ari, for he could. Rather, since facing his own mortality that winter, Sir Cadwel took an increased interest in the legacy of his future.

To this end, the great knight planned a compilation of warfare, both gathered and composed, that would take years to complete. Some would think starting such a project late in life

15

was folly, but Ari and Sir Cadwel knew a secret. Sir Cadwel would never die. When his time came, he would join the ranks of the immortal Aluiens, scholars of the ages.

"Happy morning to you, Ari."

Ispiria's voice stabbed into his concentration and Ari careened toward the sound. Swiping his sword around with more force than intended, he sent the straw-stuffed head of the practice dummy sailing through the air to bounce off the rough gray stone of the stable.

"You won," Ispiria said, clapping.

Sweat streaking his face, Ari watched her walk over to the straw head. As was often the case, Ispiria wore a pale green dress that morning, the color a perfect backdrop to her creamy skin and wild red hair. The dress was of a childish style with its unrevealing bodice and high waist. It couldn't hide her beauty, though, nor the grace with which she moved. She bent to pick up the practice dummy's head and Ari looked away, realizing he was gawking.

Her green eyes and perfect lips both smiled as she came back with the head, jamming it down onto the hewn-through wood protruding from the trunk of the dummy. "There," she said. "He's well again and ready to fight some more." She turned her smile on Ari and he stood there, staring at her like a fool. Her smile turned into a frown.

"Thank you," Ari said, dropping his gaze to sheath his sword, as if he couldn't do it blindfolded. He wondered if she realized he'd been avoiding her. He cast about, looking for an excuse to leave. The last thing he wanted was to be anywhere alone with Sir Cadwel's grandniece, Lady Ispiria.

It wasn't that he didn't like her. It was quite the opposite. He loved her. He kept the kerchief she'd given him upon his departure from Sorga last winter folded under his pillow. The trouble was, he didn't know if she loved him back.

That winter, when Ari thought he and Sir Cadwel might die during their quest to save the kingdom from the evil Empty One, Lord Ferringul, Ari sent Peine back to Sorga with a message for Ispiria, asking her if she would agree to be

16

promised to him someday. It seemed like the right thing to do at the time, because he didn't know how long he'd be away and didn't want her getting promised to anyone else while he was off saving the kingdom.

But now, he didn't know what to do or how to act. Peine said that when he asked Ispiria, she started crying and ran away. Ari didn't know if that was a yes or a no, but it seemed more like a no. Did having Peine ask in Ari's stead make her so angry she couldn't even answer? What if having Peine ask didn't count? Ari feared that if he asked her about it, she would run away crying again, or worse, say no.

He had time to sort it all out, though, because while he would be sixteen at the start of the summer, Ispiria wouldn't be until fall. Nobles didn't get promised before they were sixteen, and didn't marry until they were seventeen. Ari figured he had until fall to figure out if they were promised or not, and if she felt the same way about him as he did about her.

"Why do you look like you ate something terrible tasting?" Ispiria asked, twining a lock of red hair around one finger and tugging on it. "You're head to toe sweat, Ari. Do you need some water? You could stick your head in the horse trough. I bet that water is really cold. How long have you been practicing? I bet you didn't even eat breakfast."

Her smile was warm and amused, her head tilted to one side as she regarded him. Was it a loving look, or a friendly look? Before he left last year, she'd kissed him, but she hadn't since. Of course, how could she kiss him when he was avoiding her?

Ari realized she'd asked him several questions. He squinted up at the sky, noting how high the sun was. She was right, he'd already been practicing for over an hour. Before he could answer, a brown speck caught his eye. "What is that?" he said, pointing.

"A hawk?" Ispiria said, looking upward. "A Sorga hawk, but he isn't flying right."

Indeed, the tiny brown speck grew at much too rapid a pace as it spiraled down from one of the high peaks of the mountain range on the northern border of Sorga. The spiral became tighter, the descent quicker, until Ari realized the hawk was aimed right at him. Doubting it could halt its rapid plummet, he stuck out his arms, dropping to his knees to cushion its fall as he caught it.

Ari heard Ispiria gasp. The little brown hawk was covered in blood. One of its eyes looked to be missing, gouged out. It shuddered and went limp in Ari's cupped hands, which were already slick with its blood. He could feel the pulse of its life flickering against the sensitive skin of his palms. He resisted the urge to clench his hands to try to hold that life inside it, knowing that would crush it.

"We have to get him to Master Rellus," Ispiria said, referring to the hawkmaster. "Hurry." She tugged on Ari's arm and he stood up, nodding.

Ispiria ran across the yard and up the castle steps in a flurry of red curls, holding her dress up so high to free her legs that Ari found himself blushing even as he strode after her. He knew he had to get the little hawk to Master Rellus as fast as he could, but he didn't want to jar it by running. He looked down at it, flat, limp and motionless in his cupped hands. When he looked up again, he couldn't help but notice that the two guards at the base of the steps were watching Ispiria and her too high skirts. He pressed his lips together, trying not to scowl.

He followed Ispiria across the vaulted foyer and up the narrow stairs leading to the majority of the rooms cut into the cliff face. Most referred to these passages as the common corridors, Ari knew, because the nobles all had their rooms at the top of the vast stairwell Ari came down earlier. Ari didn't care for the term. Having once been a commoner himself, he was sensitive to any implications that people not of noble birth weren't as worthy as those who were.

Taking the steps three at a time, Ari gained ground on Ispiria, who pelted up the stairs above him, skirts bundled in one hand so she could run the other along the wall beside her to keep her balance. Fortunately, their headlong journey met no one coming down, and soon Ispiria turned onto a landing. Ari reached the top in time to see her skid to a halt at the end of the corridor in front of the hawkmaster's door. Ari's long strides carried him to her. She dropped her skirts, pounding on the door with both hands.

"Master Rellus," Ispiria called. Her cheeks were flushed with color. Her green eyes sparkled in spite of the worry in them.

"You shouldn't run around the castle holding your skirts up to your waist like that," Ari said in a low voice.

"Pardon?" she said, looking over her shoulder at him, confusion wrinkling her brow.

"It's just . . . your legs," Ari said. "Everyone could see them."

She looked at him like he was daft. "It isn't as if they're a secret, Ari. Women don't really float around like clouds. Whatever have they been teaching you in the capital?"

Ari didn't think she understood his point. He shook his head. Peine was always cautioning him that Ispiria was wild. Before Ari could explain himself, the door to the chamber was thrown open.

Hawkmaster Rellus was a slender man, slightly taller than Ispiria, but he had a strong presence which filled the doorway, though his ire melted as soon as he saw who stood without. "My lady, my lord," Master Rellus said. "May I be of service to you?"

Ispiria stepped to the side, tugging Ari forward so Master Rellus could see the hawk. The hand she placed on Ari's arm was warm through his shirt. "He came falling out of the sky," she said. "Ari caught him."

"Bring him." Master Rellus's mouth pressed into a grim line.

They followed him through a neat chamber that combined both a room for sleeping and any other private occupations. A basin and a pitcher of water stood on a small table near the bed with a block of soap and a fine-toothed comb. There was one small plush-looking leather sofa near the fireplace and a round table with two chairs. The carpets under bed and couch were threadbare, but logs were piled high in the fireplace.

Ari realized he'd never been in any of the less ornate chambers in the castle of Sorga, or in the king's castle to the south. When Sir Cadwel took Ari into service as his page last summer, Ari went from sleeping in the attic of his uncle's inn to occupying suites of rooms as Sir Cadwel's servant, suites that grew larger once Sir Cadwel made Ari heir to the Dukedom of Sorga and the Protectorate of the Northlands.

They passed through the room, which had no windows, and into a tunnel hewn from the stone of the mountain. Ari knew, because he'd seen it from the outside, that the corridor must open to the aerie. As if to confirm his thoughts, they turned a corner to see light steaming in from a broad arched opening. Ari was surprised there was no door at the end, to keep out the weather, though the sharp turn in the passageway would be a fair deterrent.

They stepped out onto a large flat balcony, a walled shelf cut from the side of the mountain. Master Rellus strode past the rows of spacious cages, doors open whether occupied or not. He stopped before a table that was formed from rock left behind when the rest was chipped away. It budded up from the balcony like a giant gray flat-topped mushroom.

Master Rellus pulled supplies from a niche carved into the stem of the table. He unrolled a bundle of soft undyed wool and patted it, looking at Ari. "Place him here."

Ari slid the little hawk onto the table. It looked even smaller than Sorga hawks usually did, and they were already half the size of any other species. They lived in the cliffs of the Great Northern Range, at the southern base of which stood the castle of Sorga. For many generations now, the hawks served the dukes of Sorga as messengers. They gave the lords of Sorga the tactical advantage they needed to consolidate their hold over the lands surrounding them and form a strong and enduring dukedom. That was why the brown hawk was the symbol of Sorga.

"Did you see what did this to him?" Master Rellus asked, his keen eyes never leaving the hawk. The other hawks fidgeted in their cages, and several flew over to perch on rocky outcroppings to watch. "Was something fighting with him?"

"No." Ari looked down at the hawk, sorrow weighing on him. He didn't see how it could live, with so much of its blood now on his hands and its little body torn apart like it was. "We looked up and he was falling, struggling to fly."

"It's his good fortune he fell so close to you, at the least," Master Rellus said. He opened a jar of ointment, using a smooth wooden paddle to spread it onto the hawk. The hawk twitched, but didn't open his remaining eye. "You can wash up over there," he added, nodding to his right.

Following the hawkmaster's suggestion, Ari moved to a large barrel, drawing out enough water to rinse his hands in a nearby basin.

"It looked like he was aimed right for Ari," Ispiria said as Ari wiped his hands dry on his trousers.

Ari nodded, although their eyes were on the hawk. He looked out across the view of Sorga's dual external walls and the empty plain beyond before returning to the table. Why the hawk would come to him when the aerie stood so near, he had no inkling. It must have been chance. Only he, Ispiria, and the two guards at the base of the steps were even in the courtyard.

Master Rellus looked up as Ari rejoined them, leveling clear hazel eyes on him. "Aimed right at you, was he, young Lord Aridian?" he said. He dropped his gaze to the hawk. "Now, why would you go to the trouble, my tormented little friend?"

Master Rellus continued his work on the hawk, his movements a controlled sort of frantic as he tried to save it. Once the salve was smeared on, he began twisting long thin bandages about it. The little hawk never moved.

Ari racked his brain for something to do, some way he might help, but he didn't know much about treating wounds, and nothing about injured hawks. He clenched his hands at his sides, vowing to do some research in Sir Cadwel's books. Or perhaps he could ask Master Rellus to teach him. Ari didn't like being so useless.

"Should we clean his wounds?" Ispiria asked, her tone tentative, as Master Rellus continued to wind bandages.

"Not now," he said with a shake of his dark-haired head. "He's lost too much blood. It's going to heal quite the mess, but we can't be letting anymore seep out. We'll have a time sorting out the mass of scabs and feathers he'll become, but with so many wounds, there's naught for it."

"What about his eye?" Ispiria asked.

Ari thought she sounded like she might cry. He took a half step closer to her, wishing he dared to put his arm about her shoulders. She slid one hand, ice cold now, into his.

"His eye is gone." Master Rellus turned his attention from the body of the hawk to its wings.

"What do you think did this?" Ari asked, wondering what creature so savage dwelled in the mountains embracing their home.

"Seems like they are all glancing blows," Master Rellus said pinching his lips together, his forehead creased with thought. "Like he sped through closing jaws, barely escaping." He shook his head again. "But there are too many wounds for one near miss. Either there was more than one attacker, or he kept going back for some reason. I don't rightly know."

Ispiria shuddered, stepping closer to Ari until her arm was pressed against the length of his own.

"Not just what," Ari said, trying not to let Ispiria's nearness derail his thoughts. "But why. And why then did the hawk come here, to Sorga?"

"He must have come because he knew Master Rellus would fix him," Ispiria said, an idea that made good sense to Ari.

"Let us hope he was right," Master Rellus said, switching to the other wing.

Ari frowned down at the hawk, hoping he might be able to pick out answers from its bandage-swathed form. Even its talons looked injured. One had a toe bent out of place, looking broken, and the other was clenched into a tight ball. His beak and his remaining eye alone appeared unscathed. On the walls about them, the other hawks fidgeted, looking on with bright black eyes.

"That's about all we can do for him now," Master Rellus said after he moved from the second wing to the hawk's battered head, applying bandages.

"What about his talon?" Ari asked, pointing to the broken toe. "Should we straighten it?"

"We can try," Master Rellus said. "Good eye, my lord. I was so busy with the rest of him, I missed that. If he lives, he'll thank us for putting it right. Mighty inconvenient to have one of your feet not work."

Master Rellus rearranged the toe with a quick jerk, sending a shudder through the still unconscious-seeming hawk. He bound a small piece of metal, which looked as if it was made for the purpose, to the toe to hold it in place.

"Well," Hawkmaster Rellus said, straightening, "let's take him to my chamber. I don't want him out in the cold." He bundled the hawk into a clean blanket, tucking it into the crook of his arm. He looked up at the other hawks, all of them out of their cages now and watching. "I'll do my best," he said, and led Ari and Ispiria back inside.

"May you have good fortune in his recovery," Ari said, still feeling awkward under the weight of his uselessness. Ispiria's hand felt small in his and the terrible thought sped through him that if she was the one hurt, he'd have no better idea what to do for her than he did for the hawk.

Hawkmaster Rellus nodded, walking with them through his chamber. He stopped before the hallway door.

"Good fortune, little hawk," Ispiria said, reaching out with her other hand to touch its head.

"I'll do my best," Master Rellus repeated, tucking the hawk more firmly into the crook of his arm before swinging the door closed behind them.

23

Chapter 2

"We should report to Sir Cadwel," Ari said as they walked down the corridor. "Is it common for the hawks to be attacked?" In the brief time Ari had spent in his new home, he'd never before seen a hawk wounded from fighting.

"Sometimes they come in with hurt wings," Ispiria said. She didn't seem to be aware she was still holding his hand, and he wasn't going to say anything about it. "But I think that's usually because they got hurt flying. Once, a falcon attacked one and there was a big fight. All the other hawks in the aerie joined in. Master Rellus said the falcon was a young one looking for a new home, but the hawks don't tolerate any other birds of prey living around here."

Ispiria's hand was warm again. Holding it made Ari feel better. He would find some books about healing. Surely, with all the books Sir Cadwel was collecting about war, there would be some about healing too. After all, the one preceded the other. Ari snuck a glance at Ispiria. He was being silly about his proposal through Peine. He should ask her if they were promised yet.

A vision of himself saying those words formed in his mind. Ari didn't have much experience with women, but in his mind's version of things, asking her didn't turn out well. If she didn't think they were promised, it was a terrible way to ask, and if she did, he could only picture her being hurt by him not realizing they were.

Maybe he would wait until her sixteenth birthday that autumn and ask her again. A for real asking. With a betrothal gift and everything. He just needed a gift, which meant he needed money. Where would he get that?

Ispiria let go of his hand when they reached the top of the steps, gathering up her skirts so they wouldn't hinder her descent. With a mischievous glance over her shoulder at Ari, she held them much higher than she normally would to walk down steps, swishing them from side to side. As she rounded the corner to the next flight, he was sure he heard her laughing.

They found Sir Cadwel in his study. Even in the short time since they'd returned from Poromont, the knight's study had changed. After learning the Aluiens intended to offer him immortal life to forever preserve his vast store of martial knowledge, Sir Cadwel dedicated himself to the idea. Ari thought Sir Cadwel already knew everything there was to know about warfare, and the Aluiens' interest in the old knight seemed to confirm that, but Sir Cadwel wasn't as sure. He declared that if his immortal role was to preserve such knowledge, he didn't know enough. So now he studied, and requisitioned books, and studied more.

Already, all of the flat surfaces in the room were piled with books. Along one of the green walls, the dark wood wainscoting, decorative weapons and dead animal heads had come down and shelving was going up. If Sir Cadwel wasn't in the yard practicing with Ari, as he did with less and less frequency, everyone knew to seek him in his study.

Sir Cadwel sat in a large leather chair near the fire, reading. His gray mustache drooped over his upper lip, giving him the not altogether misleading appearance of a perpetual frown. The taut skin of the scar cutting through his eyebrow above his right eye gleamed in the firelight. He looked up at them when they entered, his finger on the page before him to mark his place. As they crossed the room to stand in front of him, he rumbled, "Ari, why aren't you practicing?"

"A hawk fell out of the sky," Ispiria said before Ari could answer. "Ari caught it."

"Why?" Sir Cadwel asked.

"Because he didn't want it to hit the ground?" Ispiria looked to Ari as if for confirmation.

"It was badly injured, sir," Ari said, unsure if Ispiria was making fun or not. "The hawkmaster said he thinks it was attacked by one or more long-fanged creatures."

Sir Cadwel frowned, his finger tapping on the page of the book. "That's all he could deduce?"

"Yes, sir." An image of the wolf-like monsters from Ari's dream flashed through his mind, but he didn't tell Sir Cadwel about them. It was only a dream, and Sir Cadwel hated it when people said they thought they knew something when all they had were shadowy half-knowledge and feelings to guide them.

"I think we should go investigate and warn the Hawkers," Ispiria said. "They should know something is attacking the hawks."

"Hawkers?" Ari asked. He'd never heard of such people.

"The people who live near the hawks and tend them," Ispiria said.

"I thought Master Rellus tended the hawks," Ari said.

"Here at the castle," Ispiria said. "Most of the hawks live in the mountains, and the Hawkers train and guard them. Most of the hawks don't even get to be messenger hawks."

"I'll send someone with the news and have them ask if there have been any other such incidents, although surely they would have sent me word," Sir Cadwel said. "How is your practice coming, Ari?"

"Well enough, sir. I think I should focus on archery tomorrow. You know it's my weakness."

"True, but you were to spend tomorrow with Peine, practicing your figures and learning Wheylian."

27

"I do not wish to gainsay you, sir," Ari said, although that was not entirely true. Sir Cadwel was determined Ari follow him in his studies, reading all the histories of Lggothland's many conflicts and learning Wheylian, the language of Peine's homeland, that he might pursue their martial exploits as well. Ari did find the work fascinating, but slow, and he'd rather be out in the spring air swinging a sword or shooting a bow. "I can learn Wheylian after the spring tourney, sir."

"I'll not have you neglecting your mind."

"Ari and I should go," Ispiria said before Ari could answer. "Ari and I should go tell the Hawkers. It's more important than shooting a bow or reading."

Sir Cadwel regarded her for a long moment, his finger resuming its tapping. "Why is that, Ria?"

"Because Ari is to be duke someday and he didn't even know there are Hawkers. He thought those few hawks in the aerie were all the hawks there are."

Ispiria gave him a pitying look and Ari fought not to blush. When she put it that way, it made him sound thick. He knew the two dozen or so hawks at the castle couldn't be all the hawks. He just never thought about it before today. He hadn't even lived in Sorga a full season yet, after all.

"Ari needs to know all about Sorga," Ispiria said, turning back to Sir Cadwel.

"I see, and why shouldn't I send him alone to the village?"

"Because I know the way," she said.

Ari found himself holding his breath. He liked the idea of him and Ispiria going together.

"And I haven't been since last summer, and I want to go." This last she said in a wheedling tone, leveling pleading green eyes on Sir Cadwel.

Ari knew he would say yes if those eyes were looking at him.

"I'll think on it," Sir Cadwel said.

Ari suppressed a smile. When Sir Cadwel didn't say no, it usually meant yes.

"Now off with you, Ria," Sir Cadwel said. "I have things to discuss with Ari."

"I love you, Uncle Cadwel," Ispiria said, her eyes merry as she leaned over to kiss his cheek.

Sir Cadwel scowled, but Ispiria's smile got bigger as she turned and walked to the door.

"My own fault," Sir Cadwel muttered to himself when she closed the door behind her. Sir Cadwel placed a strip of leather in the book and closed it, standing. He set the book on a small table beside his chair and turned to look at Ari with unreadable eyes.

"Yes, sir?" Ari said when the silence drew out to an excruciating length. Why was Sir Cadwel staring at him like that? Had he done something wrong?

"Ari." Sir Cadwel's voice was strained, increasing Ari's worry. "You know I trust you with my life, lad?"

Ari nodded.

"In fact, you've held it in your hands and it's never been safer, I'm sure of that." Sir Cadwel cleared his throat. "You're like a son to me, so I mean no censure."

"Yes, my lord." Ari was still confused, but he couldn't help but stand a little taller when Sir Cadwel said he was like a son.

"I know Ispiria is a beguiling girl, and I know you have certain feelings for her, but I'm afraid there's something I must ask of you."

"If it is in my power to give, sir," Ari said, but his insides twisted like a den of snakes. Was Sir Cadwel going to ask him not to be promised to Ispiria?

"I need you to swear to me, on your honor, that you will not take any liberties with my grandniece." Sir Cadwel's tone was very hard, his expression foreboding.

Ari sagged in relief. Of course he could promise that. He intended that already. He wouldn't sully Ispiria's honor like that, or disappoint Sir Cadwel, or allow himself to stumble so far from his own ideals of how a knight should behave. Not that Ari was a knight yet, but he intended to be, and he couldn't get there if he didn't uphold the ways of honor. "I swear, sir, to

29

guard Lady Ispiria's honor from everyone, including myself, or my life be given in the pursuit of that task," Ari said, invoking the formality of the ritual phrasing of a knight accepting a charge.

"Good lad," Sir Cadwel said, patting Ari on the shoulder. He sat back down, reclaiming his book.

Ari waited, unsure if he was dismissed. His mind turned over what he'd just promised. He knew it was the right promise to make. It was how he intended to behave all along. Still, a tiny little part of him, tucked in the back of his mind, sighed in disappointment, conjuring up an image of Ispiria's long white legs.

"Well?" Sir Cadwel said, looking up from his book.

"Your pardon, sir?"

"Are you going to return to practicing or would you like me to set you to learning Wheylian?"

"Practicing." Ari turned and hurried from the room.

Chapter 3

Ari woke early again the following morning. This time, Peine was already up. He had a steaming bath ready and was rummaging in Ari's wardrobe. With an exclamation of triumph, the dark-haired Wheylian boy held up a stiff blue doublet.

"Here it is," Peine said, his face breaking into a cheerful smile. "How did your best doublet get stuck all the way in the back of the wardrobe? I must remember to be more careful with it. Time to get up."

Ari shut his eyes. He enjoyed mornings, but sometimes it was too early for Peine's endless stream of chatter.

"I've a bath drawn," Peine said. "I shall have to run a hot press over this. I'll have it ready in no time. Never worry." He pulled out a pair of brown trousers and headed to the door, calling back over his shoulder. "Get up, Ari. We don't want to be late setting out to the Hawkers' village."

Ari sat up, recalling the mission of the day. No wonder Peine wanted Ari's best clothes. Ari didn't want them, though. The Hawkers' village was a fair ride into the mountains. He didn't fancy making it in hot uncomfortable brocade. Ari wandered into the bathing room, pondering the odds of getting Peine to let him wear something more comfortable.

He broached the subject when Peine returned with his pressed clothes.

"This is to be their first impression of you," Peine said, his face stern.

Ari eyed the doublet. There was enough silver thread on it to buy a horse.

"You can't show up dressed like a beggar, Ari. You owe it to the people you will someday rule over to look the part for them."

Ari sighed, letting Peine help him into the silly outfit.

"I had your breakfast sent up." Peine nodded toward the sitting room. "We're behind schedule. It's almost time for your sendoff."

"What do you mean, sendoff?" Ari asked, leaving the bedroom to take his place at the sitting room table. "We're just taking a ride into the mountains. It's only a three hour journey."

"You're riding out to inspect your future holdings," Peine said, coming around the table and squaring his shoulders. "And it will take more than three hours."

"How's that?" Ari conjured up a memory of the map Sir Cadwel showed him the night before. Even with the changes in elevation, it shouldn't take more than three hours. Ari was sure he and Stew could do it in half that time, were they alone.

"Because ladies are coming." Peine sat across from Ari. "And ladies are slow. Especially Civul."

"Civul? She's who Ispiria chose to accompany us?" Ari worked to keep the amusement out of his voice, wondering if Ispiria did it on purpose. Yet how could she know that out of all of her ladies, Civul was the one Peine least liked? Ari hadn't told her, and he didn't think Peine would have.

At fourteen, Peine was growing interested in the young ladies of the keep, and they in him. Wheys were not a common sight so far to the northeast, and what Peine lacked in robustness compared with the northern lads was made up for in angular good looks, jet-black hair and an overall appearance of cultured exoticness that the blonde-haired blue-eyed girls of Sorga seemed to find irresistible. Lady Civul found Peine as irresistible as the rest, but Ispiria's husky maid towered over Peine and Ari knew his friend didn't find her visage very agreeable.

Ari couldn't really blame Peine. Lady Civul was not a delicate flower of a maiden. Ari was relatively sure that each of the two thick braids she wore in her white-blonde hair had more girth than Peine's wrists.

"Yes," Peine said in answer to Ari's question. "Lady Civul." Peine frowned. "I'm surprised they can find a horse big enough. She'll probably squash the poor thing."

"She's only a little taller than I am," Ari said, shoveling porridge into his mouth. He followed it with some dried fruit, ignoring the half-congealed strips of last night's meat Peine also placed on the plate.

"It's just that Ispiria has so many prettier ladies." Peine eyed Ari's plate. "And Civul will stay taller than you if you don't eat properly."

"Don't prefer it," Ari said, glancing at the meat.

Peine rolled his eyes but resumed his chatter about their day. Ari finished his porridge while listening to Peine prattle on about which of the girls he did find attractive, a topic Peine didn't relinquish until Ari led the way down to the foyer and out onto the steps of the keep. Their horses, Stew and Charger, waited below, alongside two gentle-looking mares. Ispiria and Lady Civul stood near them and Ari recognized the white one as Ispiria's horse, Snowdrop. Each horse had a pack bundled to the back of its saddle, for they were to stay in the Hawkers' village three nights before returning. Remembering the inconvenient and elaborate lengths the ladies of the king's court went to in order to be comfortable while traveling, Ari was glad to see that Ispiria brought so little.

Catching sight of him, she came bounding up the steps. "There you are. Look, I have a new riding habit."

Lady Civul trailed Ispiria at, as Peine had predicted, a much slower pace.

Ispiria held out her skirts, sewn into something resembling two giant trouser legs, and spun in a circle. Ari raised his eyebrows. In its own way, the ridding habit was much more revealing than Ispiria's normal dresses.

"It's very nice," he said, trying not to stare.

She stopped twirling and took his arm, tilting her head back to put her mouth close to his ear. "I thought you would like it, since the way it's fashioned makes it almost impossible for me to hold it up and show my terribly scandalous legs."

Ari didn't know what to say to that, so he looked around instead. Sir Cadwel and Sorga's master steward, Natan, stood to one side of the steps, talking. Behind them was a set of serving girls who worked in the kitchen, weighted down with more saddlebags. A guard stood to each side of the steps. Ari was relieved to see it wasn't a large sendoff, although he wondered that Ispiria's great grandmother wasn't there. The old woman had seemed well enough at dinner the night before, if unusually dour.

"That must be our picnic," Ispiria said, turning toward the serving girls.

"Picnic?" Ari looked over at Peine, who shook his head. Ari shrugged. He didn't mind if the trip was a little slow if he got to have a picnic with Ispiria.

"Of course," Ispiria said. "We always have a picnic. Peine, can you help Civul with the saddlebags?"

"Yes, my lady." Peine waved over the serving girls, the younger of whom smiled at him.

Ari helped Ispiria to mount. In short order, they were all ahorse and the picnic things settled. The serving girls disappeared back inside and Sir Cadwel, followed by Natan, came over to bid them safe travels.

"You know the way, lad?" Sir Cadwel asked.

"Yes, sir," Ari said, having memorized the map Sir Cadwel showed him.

34

"I know the way by heart," Ispiria said. "I won't lead us astray."

"I know." Sir Cadwel gave her a smile. "I wish Ari to know it as well. Here's a message for the town elders." He handed Ari a folded parchment, the hawk of Sorga pressed into a blob of wax to seal it. "It's nothing of importance. A word about the hawk, some pleasantries."

"Pleasantries? From you?" Natan said, affecting a concerned tone. "Were you not feeling well when you penned it?"

"You could be leading this expedition if you don't take care," Sir Cadwel said.

Natan chuckled. "As if you would send me away. Who would do all the work around here then? I know you aren't going to."

Sir Cadwel scowled at Natan. Ari always wondered at how well Sir Cadwel put up with Natan's teasing. True, the master steward did tend to many of the day-to-day matters of running the keep, but that was his job. Sir Cadwel always saw to his duties as lord, if he was in Sorga. It wasn't his fault that, as King's Champion, he often had to be away. Maybe that was why the knight ignored Natan's jabs, because Natan was indeed good at overseeing Sorga when Sir Cadwel had to be absent.

"Have a safe journey," Sir Cadwel said, looking past Ari to include all four of them. "I'll expect you returned in four days' time. Leave early enough to be back before dark settles in. I don't want you on the mountain paths without enough light."

"We will, sir," Ari said. With a nod to Sir Cadwel, he turned his horse, the clip of hooves on cobblestones telling him the others followed.

"Send a hawk so we know you arrived safely," Natan called.

Ari led the way through the tall gates and into the empty area between the inner and outer walls of Sorga. Built in the embrace of two arms of the mountains, Sorga was impenetrable except from the south, which meant an enemy would have to conquer the outer wall and then the inner. In between, they must cross a broad empty expanse. A killing zone, framed in on two sides by the sheer cliffs of the mountain's arms and ending in the inner wall. In Ari's studies of the history of Sorga, he'd already read many accounts of how approaching forces were trapped there and slain. The most gruesome technique, by his thinking, was when the ground between them was soaked in oil so that once an opposing force entered, the whole of it could be lit like a torch.

Ari kept his eyes on the gate in the second wall, open in this time of peace. He knew sometimes men had to die, especially if they were trying to kill those you loved and take what was yours, but he didn't like to look around the vast empty space and think about how many men and horses had been slain there in times past. He was glad the dusty ground couldn't tell him its tales.

Once free of the walls of Sorga, they turned north to ride up steep trails and along narrow pathways. As they journeyed, Ari was glad that Ispiria knew the way. What seemed simple enough drawn out on a map had a way of becoming rather tricky in the precarious terrain of the mountains.

"How do you know the way so well?" Ari asked Ispiria as they reached a broader section of trail where they could ride side by side. He could hear Peine chattering away to Civul behind them. Even if Peine didn't think Lady Civul was pretty, it appeared that he still couldn't resist talking to her. Peine would carry on a conversation with a stone, given half a chance.

"My family is from the Hawkers' village," Ispiria said, smiling. "My great grandmother and I used to spend every summer there, until a few years ago. That's when her last sister died, and her eyes were already getting quite bad. You can't make the trip in a wagon."

"No, I'd think not," Ari said. "I didn't realize you had any family." His comment sounded silly to him, but he pressed on. "I mean, if you did, why didn't you go back to live with them? You know, after . . ." He trailed off. This was why he always let Peine do all the talking. In the space of three heartbeats, he'd managed to suggest that she had no family and bring up her mother's death.

"No one's told you the story?"

Ari shook his head, wondering who she thought would tell him, if not her.

"You know that my great aunt married Sir Cadwel when they were both young, but she was killed the day that old lord who hated Sir Cadwel took the keep, like the rest of the family? That lord must have been very evil to murder everyone. He even killed Sir Cadwel's mother and sisters, and they say my great aunt was heavy with child. Only a monster would kill a woman about to bear her child."

Ari nodded. He knew that part. Even though they were far into the mountains, he cast a nervous glance over his shoulder toward Sorga. Ari knew Sir Cadwel blamed himself for not saving his family. It was nearly worth a man's life to bring it up within the old knight's hearing.

"After that, my great grandmother and grandmother came to help Sir Cadwel. They say he was in quite the state."

Her voice caught with sorrow and Ari racked his mind for something less distressing to talk about. He hadn't meant to spoil their ride. To his left, the mountain dropped away, exposing a deep valley before ancient stone spiraled upward again toward another formidable peak. It was an impressive view, but offered him no quick change of subject.

"My grandmother married a man of the keep and bore my mother and my aunts and uncles," Ispiria said. "They all went back to the Hawkers' village as they grew up, as did my grandmother and great grandmother, but Mother stayed. They say she didn't care for the trials of village life. She wished to marry a lord and stay in the keep. Some say she had her eye on Sir Cadwel."

Ari tried to picture Sir Cadwel giving up the memory of his lost wife and marrying her niece instead. He shook his head. It was inconceivable, but Ari sort of wished he had. He hated to think of Sir Cadwel alone and grieving for so many years. "Who was your father?" he asked, realizing he didn't know. Ispiria had her great grandmother and that was all he'd known about her family, before now.

"They say he was a soldier of the keep. I never knew him. My mother never did find a noble to marry. She only found trouble. Then she died bearing me, which I've heard people whisper was fitting, since she wouldn't even admit who my father was."

"Well, those people are wrong." Ari felt anger rise in him. "There is no way bringing you into the world would ever make anyone deserving of death."

"That's very sweet of you, Ari." She smiled at him. "When my mother died, my grandmother returned to look after me. Then, when I was eight, my grandmother caught a sickness and she died." Ispiria cleared her throat. "It happened very sudden. So, my great grandmother returned. She came back to the place where she lost her second youngest child, and her youngest, and a granddaughter, so that she could raise me."

"Why didn't they take you back to the Hawkers?" Ari asked. "I'm sorry," he added, realizing he should be less curious and more sympathetic. "I'm sorry that your mother and grandmother died."

"It's not as if you killed them," Ispiria said with a toss of her red hair, but Ari could hear the sorrow in her voice. "I was more sorry when my grandmother died. I loved her. I never even knew my mother. People say I look like her. Sometimes they say I act like her, and I don't think they mean it well."

"You act perfectly," he said, wondering who those people were.

"Even when I run up steps?" she asked, but she smiled.

"Uh, well . . ." He floundered, unsure how to answer that.

"Oh, Ari." Ispiria giggled. "You look like a fish." Her smile grew wider. "And I don't know why they didn't take me back. I think it's because Sir Cadwel wanted me to stay. I don't think he liked being so alone in that big empty hallway of nobles' rooms. He always had my family stay there whenever they lived at the castle, even if we aren't strictly nobles. Hawkers don't have any nobles. The only reason Sir Cadwel was allowed to marry one was that he wasn't the eldest son."

"He gave Natan rooms in the nobles' wing, too" Peine said.

Ari glanced back. He hadn't realized Peine and Civul were listening.

"And Natan isn't a noble either." Peine sounded offended.

"He must be of the noble class," Ari said. "He was a knight." By the king's decree, only members of the nobility could become knights in Lggothland. Ari didn't care if he was a noble or not, but he wanted more than anything to be a knight and someday, when Sir Cadwel retired from the position, king's champion. Fortunately, when Sir Cadwel adopted Ari as his heir, Ari was elevated into the noble class.

"But the king stripped Natan of his titles and rank before he banished him to Sorga," Peine said. "So now he's just Master Steward Natan and not a noble at all, although normally master stewards are selected from the ranks of lesser sons of the nobility."

Ari knew Peine was a lesser son and that was why he'd been sent away to be a valet. There was only enough land for the eldest son in each family to inherit.

"I think nobility is something you are," Civul said. She spoke in a slow, thoughtful way. "It's not something a king can truly remove. And Master Steward Natan is very handsome."

Ispiria giggled.

Ari wondered what handsome had to do with anything and how Civul could think such thoughts about a man who was old enough to be her grandfather.

"It's time for our picnic," Ispiria said, pointing ahead.

Ari turned, taking in a magnificent waterfall across the gully. It cascaded from a cleft high up in the top of the peak to his left, full and verdant with spring's thaw. Seeing it made him aware of the endless rumble of water, as if his eyes, not his ears, drew sound. "There's a way across?" he asked, surprised. The gully looked impassable to him.

"Oh no," Ispiria said. "There's a nice clearing around the next bend where the trail becomes wide and we can stop and rest. The waterfall is loud enough from this side. I shouldn't think we'd want to get any closer, especially in the spring. By the end of summer, there's almost nothing left of it. Just a trickle."

The clearing was a flat area about the size of the keep's foyer, cut back into the side of the mountain. There was a place for a fire, looking from the scorched earth and carefully arranged stones to have been used many times before, but they didn't light one. A large boulder with smaller ones rolled up to it made a passable table and chairs, and soon they were all seated and eating.

Peine and Ispiria filled their lunch with happy chatter, Lady Civul offering the occasional comment. Ari was content to sit beside Ispiria, letting Peine do the work of talking while he daydreamed about the spring tourney. He and Sir Cadwel would leave soon. He wished Ispiria could come watch him, but there wasn't time for her to travel to the capital. At one point there had been talk of her going, but that swelled into talk of her escort and her ladies and when it was proper for her to meet society, whatever that meant, and it was deemed there wasn't enough time available for her to go that spring.

Ispiria would be so proud of him and Stew if they won. Ari felt it was wrong to be boastful, even to himself, but he didn't see any reason he wouldn't win. He'd won the fall tourney, and with a fair amount of ease too. He was sure he would win that spring.

"Let's go look at the waterfall, Ari," Ispiria said, capturing his attention. "Do you mind packing up?" she asked, looking at Peine and Civul.

"Certainly not, my lady," Peine said. "It's our place to."

Civul gave an unladylike snort at that.

"Oh, Peine," Ispiria said, her tone fond. She stood, holding a hand out to Ari.

He got up, clasping her warm fingers in his own. He loved how delicate and soft her hand was and how his, strong and callused, seemed to keep it safe.

Leading the way, she strode across the clearing to the trail, stopping a bit closer to the drop-off than Ari would have, tugging him up beside her.

"I've never seen the falls so full," she said. "I don't normally make the trip until the beginning of summer. The journey takes longer, with all the mules to carry my things for the whole season. I'll have to go later now than ever, of course, because the start of summer is when we celebrate your birth. I wouldn't want to miss it."

Ari was pleased she knew when his birthday was. He didn't recall telling her. She must have found out from Peine. That meant she'd been asking about him.

Ispiria glanced toward where Peine and Civul were packing up their lunch. She looked up at Ari, reaching to take his other hand and tug him toward her. "I think you should kiss me, Ari."

Ari went still, his mind blank of any thought other than complying. He looked down at Ispiria, her head lilted back, her lips near enough his own that he only had to lower his head slightly to touch them. Her green eyes were bright and the updraft from the waterfall blew her red curls around her face.

"They might see us," he said. "You know it isn't proper." He forced himself to say it. He intended to sound resolute, but the words came out as more of a whisper. He found himself lowering his head toward hers.

They shouldn't, he knew, but he very much wanted to. He remembered when she'd kissed him the night before he left last winter. He knew what he'd promised Sir Cadwel, but he couldn't bring himself to think of kissing Ispiria as being dishonorable.

"Oh bother with proper," she said, her voice low. "We're promised, after all. There will come a time when we'll do a lot more than kissing."

41

Ari felt tension drain from him at her words, easing away weeks of worry. They were promised. She wasn't angry, or upset he had Peine ask, or waiting for him to make some sort of grand gesture he didn't know how to make. She was his, promised.

He lowered his lips to hers, his elation at knowing she loved him giving their kiss an intensity he'd never felt before.

"Ehem."

Ari's head snapped up. Peine and Civul were there, each holding the reins of two horses. Lady Civul looked angry. Peine shook his head. Stew, Ari was relatively sure, was laughing at him. Sometimes Ari didn't know if it was such a lucky thing to have a secretly-intelligent somewhat-magical horse.

Ispiria sighed, letting go of Ari's hands.

"Lady Ispiria," Civul said, her tone hard.

"You two are spoiling things," Ispiria said with a toss of her head. She went to her horse, leaving Ari standing where he was.

"Your great grandmother would be horrified," Lady Civul said, sounding much older than her sixteen years.

Ispiria mounted and turned Snowdrop up the road, Lady Civul's tongue-lashing fading into the rumble of the waterfall as they headed up the trail. Peine stood holding the reins of his horse and Stew, looking disappointed.

"What were you thinking, Ari? We leave you two alone for a moment, and that's what you do?"

"I wasn't . . ." Ari stammered. "That is, we weren't . . ." His voice trailed off. He didn't have a good answer, because he was and they were.

"Ari." Peine lowered his voice, though the roar of the falls had already swallowed up Lady Civul's words so it was unlikely they could be overheard. "If you really can't restrain yourself, go into town and find some obliging girl at a tavern, or ride out to inspect the farms and try your luck. Don't go sullying noblewomen. It's very frowned upon. You'll end up stripped of your titles and exiled, like Natan."

Peine turned away, tossing Stew's reins at Ari. Ari caught them even as his mind struggled with what his friend had just told him. Go into town? Tavern girls? He knew men did that sort of thing, but had never pictured himself doing it.

He recalled the last time his aunt and uncle, or rather, the man and woman he once thought were his aunt and uncle, had a girl working in their tavern, where he'd grown up. She was a nice girl, and pretty. Ari was nine then and he liked her very much. When the man and woman who'd raised Ari had fired her, he'd asked them why. Everyone who came to the bar had seemed to like her. He recalled them looking at each other, their faces tense. Finally, his aunt May had said, "She had trouble keeping her skirts down so we had to let her go."

Ari's mind flashed to Ispiria holding her skirts high as she ran up the castle steps. He frowned, pulling his mind back from the comparison. Ispiria was not like that. She liked Ari, and she was a little wild, but she wasn't a tavern girl. She was Sir Cadwel's grandniece and a lady. The lady Ari intended to marry someday.

Looking around, he realized the others were well ahead of him on the trail. Stew stretched out his neck and touched Ari's shoulder with his nose. Struggling to put thoughts of imaginary tavern girls and Ispiria's legs out of his mind, Ari pulled himself into the saddle and let Stew canter.

Chapter 4

Ari lagged behind the others, the turmoil of his thoughts blotting out the beauty of the day. Surely, he hadn't done anything to besmirch Ispiria's honor. Did kissing even count as besmirching? He knew it was a bit improper, but he didn't think it would hurt anything. And they'd kissed before, so if kissing counted, the damage was already done. Of course, they would have to be more careful not to be seen in the future. He didn't want to sully Ispiria's reputation or give people reason to think she was like her mother.

As for Peine's suggestion, it was unthinkable. Ari was amazed his friend would even proffer such a path. When Ari used to be a commoner, he would have been more than happy to try his luck with the girls of his village, and eventually find one to marry as his older cousin had. Now that he was a nobleman, though, he would be taking advantage of them. Ari didn't think that was right at all.

Stew was restless as they drew near the village, shaking his mane and snorting. Ari patted him on the neck, but the destrier picked up his pace. Ari looked around, seeking the source of Stew's agitation. Higher up the last hill between them and the valley the Hawkers lived in, Ispiria urged her horse into a trot. Ari strained to see what was ahead, but from the dip below the rim of the valley, all he saw were the streams of smoke from many hearth fires rising up into the noon sky. He realized it must be a large town to have so many fires burning.

Ari sniffed the air. Something smelled odd. Maybe that was what was upsetting Stew. Breaking into a gallop, Stew sped up to the top of the hill as the others crested it, ignoring Ari's startled attempt to slow him to a reasonable pace.

Ispiria's scream broke the afternoon silence as Ari drew alongside her. His gaze plunged down into the valley, following her horrified stare.

The village of Hawkers was burned. Even from the crest of the ridge, Ari could see bodies strewn everywhere, torn and charred. He swallowed against the sudden dryness of his mouth, then coughed as the act brought the acrid odor of scorched flesh down his throat. It was his dream all over again, amplified a hundred-fold.

Sobbing, Ispiria kicked her heels into Snowdrop, but Ari caught the white mare's reins before she could run, wrenching her around. Ispiria slithered from her horse, dashing down the hill.

Ari tossed Snowdrop's reins at Peine, who sat stunned and motionless on Charger, and galloped after Ispiria. He overtook her halfway down the hill, turning Stew in front of her so sharply, she almost collided with them. Ari slid from his saddle, catching Ispiria in his arms before she could run again.

"Let go of me," she cried, but her struggles were nothing compared to his strength. He held her against him, being careful to contain his strength so he wouldn't hurt her, and turned them so she was facing up the hill where Peine and Civul still sat on their horses. Looking over Stew's back, Ari took in the devastation of the village. The ruin below assailing him, leaving him only half-aware of Ispiria's continued struggles.

Every building was burned. Every once living thing Ari could see, be it man, child, hawk, horse or dog, was dead. The fires no longer blazed, but charcoal and ashes smoldered, filling the valley with smoke.

He heard a noise behind him and whipped his head around, but it was Peine, Civul, and the horses coming down. The horses balked and had to be coaxed forward at a trembling pace.

"Please let me go, Ari," Ispiria said, her voice small. She wasn't struggling anymore and he loosened his arms, but didn't let her out of their protective circle. He kept himself and Stew between her and the valley. "I have to go down there. I have to see if anyone is alive."

Ari didn't think anyone was alive. In his dream, the Caller and the wolf creatures didn't leave anyone alive. Except the baby. He glanced back down into the ruined valley.

"We must leave immediately," Ari said as Peine and Civul reached them. Peine's fair skin was nearly translucent, his mouth pressed into a thin line. Lady Civul had tears streaking down her ruddy cheeks.

"No," Ispiria said, renewing her struggles. "We have to go down there. There might be people hurt down there."

"Ispiria." Ari tried to make his tone soothing. "Whatever did this could still be near. From the amount of damage done, I don't think I can protect you. We are not adding your life to the grievous loss below."

"But they could be hurt," she said, sobbing.

"The fires are almost out," Ari said. "I think this thing took place more than a day ago." When he was having his dream, he realized. "I have little hope anyone is alive down there, but many may have fled. There's that to hold onto."

"Listen to Lord Aridian, my lady," Lady Civul said, her voice catching. "It is most unsafe here."

"No." Ispiria started pounding her fists against Ari's chest. "These are my people. I won't abandon them. You'll have to tie me to my horse. You'll have to knock me unconscious."

"I'll stay," Ari said. He didn't like idea of sending them back without his protection, but nothing had menaced them on the mountain trail. "I'll stay and search, but you must go back with Peine and Lady Civul. You must get Sir Cadwel and the soldiers of the keep."

She stopped fighting his hold and looked up. Her green irises swam in a sea of bloodshot tears. "What if something happens to you? What if they come back?"

"Then I'll be better able to protect myself without you here," he said. He saw her flinch. He knew it was a mean thing to say, but it was true, and he felt a keen urgency to get Ispiria away from the valley and back to the safety of the keep.

She sagged, the last of her resistance spent. "Be careful, Ari," she said, her voice cracking. "Search everywhere. There must . . . there must be someone."

She started sobbing again, but Ari let go of her as she turned away, stumbling to her horse. He took a step to follow, to help her mount, but she pulled herself into the saddle before he could assist her. Lady Civul nudged her mount to Ispiria's side, speaking in soothing tones as their steeds trudged up the hill.

"Take care of them," Ari said to Peine, who was still looking down at the valley with horror-filled eyes. "Keep them safe. Ride as hard as you dare."

"Yes, my lord," Peine said, nodding. His movements jerky, Peine turned Charger to follow the ladies.

Ari watched them go with trepidation. Maybe he should follow after. For a short way. No one could have survived the onslaught that struck the village. Looking for people down there seemed a futile thing, hardly worth any risk to Ispiria. He could stay far enough back that she wouldn't see him, yet close enough to help if need be.

He heard their mounts break into a canter at the top of the hill. His mind made up to follow them, he turned toward Stew, but his horse was already down on the valley floor, stepping gingerly into the village. "I hope you're right," Ari muttered, knowing Stew couldn't hear him from there.

Swallowing hard against the nausea that twisted in his gut, Ari descended the hill to follow Stew. His horse seemed to have a particular destination in mind, picking his way through the rubble and around the bodies. Above, dark birds circled. Ari shuddered. Those were not the hawks of Sorga.

Stew led him to the center of the town, to a home that looked much larger than the rest, reminding Ari of the now useless letter of greeting he carried. Ari sighed at the sight of the bodies in what must have once been the front yard. People Ispiria knew and loved. People he would never meet.

He didn't turn from their twisted forms, their teeth and bones exposed where their flesh was charred away. Gruesome as they were, they were deserving of his regard and respect, not his disgust. He nodded to them as he followed Stew around the side of the house, a crumbled shell now, silently promising them that he would do everything in his power to bring justice upon the one who did this.

Stew stopped in the backyard in front of what had once been a large shed. Ari took in the dead hawks strewn about and realized it must have been an aerie. The little brown hawks were burned, but Ari could make out that they'd been mauled, much like the one who'd dropped from the sky the morning before.

He shook his head. The hawk hadn't come to Sorga to get help for itself. It had come to get help for the village. It came to Ari because he was in the practice yard, fighting, and it needed men who could fight.

Stew nudged his shoulder. Ari wondered what his horse wanted him to do. He surveyed the rubble. Nothing was left except a vast stone tabletop, the legs probably burned away. It rested almost flat on the ground amongst the charred debris.

Ari bent down to look at it more closely, seeking anything to explain its significance to his horse. He heard the faint chink of metal hitting stone, as if somewhere in the ground, something was trying to chisel through the stone slab.

He straightened. There must be a cellar. Who would build a cellar for an aerie? It didn't matter. Ispiria was right. Someone had survived.

The stone tabletop was one pace wide and almost three long, and at least four fingers thick. Ever since his time among the Aluiens, Ari was much stronger than a normal man, but he wasn't sure if even he could lift it alone. He looked about, but no wood remained with enough integrity to use as a lever. He considered tying Stew's reins to the slab, but they weren't long enough.

Ari shrugged. He had to try. If he couldn't lift it, hopefully help would arrive in time for whoever was trapped below. He squinted up at the sun through the miasma of smoke. It was past noon. It would take Peine and the ladies at least two hours to return to Sorga, for they could only dare to ride so fast on the mountainside trail with its steep drop-offs and winding turns. Then they would report to Sir Cadwel. Men would need to be mustered. Ari couldn't expect any help until almost dark.

He crouched on the long side of the slab, wiggling his fingers under it. Maybe he could tip it over. As he worked, Stew wandered away, nosing around in the rubble. Ari wondered if Stew was seeking more survivors. He hoped anyone else Stew found wouldn't be under anything this heavy. Bracing himself, Ari pulled.

At first, it seemed the slab was welded to the earth, but as Ari strained to lift it, a crack appeared between it and the charred ground. There was a startled squeak from beneath. Ari almost dropped it in surprise.

"Hello?" a girl's voice called.

Ari didn't waste his breath answering. He wrenched the slab higher, every muscle straining. With an inarticulate yell, he surged to his feet, toppling the heavy stone. He fell backward to the ground, landing in a puff of ashes, panting.

From where he sat, Ari could see the first few steps of a staircase. An orange curly-haired head appeared, followed by a pair of cautious blue eyes. Though she was a few years older, her hair more orange and her eyes blue, the girl bore such a strong resemblance to Ispiria that Ari knew they were related. She held a hunting knife in one hand and had her other arm wrapped about a Sorga hawk.

She stopped halfway up the steps, poking the broad blade at Ari. He was surprised to note that she wore a bow on her back. "Who are you?" she asked, eyes narrow as she peered at him. The hawk cocked its head to one side, looking about.

"I'm Ari," he said, trying what he hoped was a reassuring smile.

She didn't seem to hear him, her gaze taking in the destruction in which he sprawled. Ari wanted to get up, to offer her his hand, but he didn't want to startle her. Tears formed in the corners of her eyes and her lower lip began to tremble. The hand holding the knife lowered, but she didn't drop it as Ari expected, instead sheathing it at her side.

"Is there anyone else?" she asked, her voice a whisper.

"You're the first I've found," Ari said. She turned stunned eyes to him. "But I haven't looked anywhere else," he added.

"Then we best start looking," she said, pressing her lips into a firm line, but as she blinked, tears trailed down her cheeks.

"Can that hawk fly?" Ari asked, realizing here was a quicker way to rouse the keep. Or was it? He had nothing to write on.

"Yes," she said, her eyes once again roaming across the ground before her. From where she stood half inside the cellar, she handed him the hawk.

Ari set it on the ground by his side, knowing a Sorga hawk wouldn't fly away. He retrieved Sir Cadwel's message from where he had it tucked inside his tunic, spreading it out on the ground, written side down. Taking up a piece of charred wood, he wrote as neatly as he could, *Hawkers attacked. Burned. Send help now. Ari.*

"I don't have any way to tie it to him," Ari said, looking around. The girl pulled a green ribbon from her sleeve. It was so similar to the one Ispiria always wore that Ari stared at it in surprise for a moment before taking it and using it to tie the bulky parchment to the hawk. Normally, they used smaller and thinner pieces of parchment rolled into little tubes and tied between the hawks' shoulders. "I hope you can manage it," he said to the bird. "I don't have anything better. Take it to Sorga, please, fast as you can."

The hawk dipped in a motion almost like a bow and leapt into the air. It didn't even circle as it sped away. Ari lost sight of it in the murk cloaking the village.

The girl gasped, pointing. Ari turned, following her outstretched arm to see a plume of smoke rising from the mountainside behind him, south of the village. Before he could ask her what it was, she was charging up the steps. Ari was taken aback to find she wore trousers and a tunic, both of green dyed leather. A quiver of arrows hung from her belt.

"They attacked the grand aerie," she cried, racing away.

Ari jumped to his feet, running after her. She sped through the village, surprising Ari with her swiftness. She dodged around smoldering wood and bodies alike, not lowering her gaze from the smoke high up on the mountain face.

Free of the ruins of the village, she was faster than ever. Ari lengthened his stride, as they were now on a dirt pathway, worn smooth by generations of feet. He drew alongside her as she reached the side of the mountain and started up a steep trail, almost a staircase cut into the rock.

They scrambled upward, using their hands as much as their feet as the way grew ever steeper. Ari didn't try to stop her, didn't shout any questions. He was caught up in the urgency of their climb.

Near the peak, she pulled herself up onto a flat area with stones piled into low walls about the edges. There were dead hawks everywhere. Ari had to catch himself, keep himself from falling backward as his body tried to reel away from the bloody massacre of entrails and feathers. The girl ran to the back of the ledge, falling to her knees in front of a smoldering mound of toppled nests. Smashed eggs littered the ground, partially formed little bodies spilling out. She let out a ragged sob.

Ari followed after, trying not to tread on dead hawks. He crouched down beside her, wondering what he should say.

"They must have come for the stone," she said, pointing upward.

All Ari could see were ledges. Ledges that must once have been covered with nests.

"They always hide it in the nests," she said, wiping at her eyes with her hands.

"What stone?" he asked, confused. He thought her concern was for the hawks, not a stone. Indeed, even now she reached out and straightened a half-burnt little body, patting it as if to comfort it.

"It's just a stone," she said. "A stupid little white stone, but people believe it's magical. Some say that with it, others could control the hawks. As if we control them now. We don't. We're their friends, not their masters."

"If it doesn't do anything, why would anyone want it?" Ari couldn't imagine killing a whole village full of people for a stone that didn't do anything.

"The hawks think its special," she said. "We don't know why. They take it out once a year, in the autumn, and pass it around. Then they hide it in one of the nests until the next year. No one understands it. It's just what they do. Every once in a while, someone will show up, asking about it, with some crazy theory. We always send them away."

"You really think all of this is because of a stone?" Ari gestured around them, sweeping his arm out to include the village behind them.

"I don't know," she said. She looked up at the naked ledges. "Why else destroy the nests? Those hawks weren't hatched. They couldn't fight back or even fly for help."

"Why destroy any of it?" Ari wondered aloud. He sat back on his heels, recalling his dream. It must mean something, him dreaming about the Caller and the wolves the same morning someone, something, was ravaging the Hawkers' village. The destruction looked so similar to the farmhouse in his dream. All the fire, and the torn bodies, as if the wolf creatures were ripping people up. He suppressed a shudder, the Lady's words of warning ringing in his mind. Beware the Caller, she'd said, beware the called. Was she trying to rouse him to help?

"We must go after them," the orange-haired girl said. "I will take retribution." She sounded fierce, but tears streaked through the soot on her cheeks.

"We should wait for Sir Cadwel," Ari said, shaking his head. He couldn't take this girl, who looked so much like Ispiria, out into the mountains, chasing who knew what. It wasn't safe. She could be killed. "Did you see who they were? Who did this thing?"

She gazed down at the dead baby hawks. "They were as shadows before the dawn, light and swift," she said, her voice soft. "They poured over the valley walls and down into the village, a vast pack of howling wolves, but bigger and stronger than any wolves I've seen. Behind them came a man. He spoke words in a language I do not know, and fire burst up before him. If he took the stone, we must get it from him. I do not know much about magic, or those who wield it for evil or good, but I know a being like that cannot be allowed to have his way."

"You are correct, of course," Ari said, having no intention of letting her run off after a pack of demon wolves and a fire-wielding madman, whether it was the same one from his dream or not. "But Sir Cadwel will be here soon. Then we will have many men to search out this fire-wielder and his wolves."

She regarded him with serious eyes. Scrutinizing her face, Ari thought she was maybe seventeen years to his almost sixteen. She looked very brave. Her eyes were hard with anger, even if tears still trailed down her cheeks. Ari didn't know what to make of her at all, with her men's forest garb and her bow, her worry for the baby hawks that overshadowed the devastation of the village.

"It's Ari, right?" she said, pausing for him to nod. "Thank you for getting me out of that cellar, Ari, but I'm one of the guardians of these hawks." She cleared her throat. "Maybe the last one. It doesn't matter what you think of my plans. I'm going after the man with the wolves. It is my duty to my village, to Lord Cadwel and to the hawks of Sorga."

Ari realized she had no idea who he was. As Sir Cadwel's heir, he could order her to stay. Maybe they hadn't heard of Lord Aridian here yet. Or, more likely, she didn't realize that Ari and Lord Aridian, heir to Sorga and the Protectorate of the

Northlands, page to Sir Cadwel and the youngest man ever to win the king's tourney, were the same person. He knew he should tell her, but he always felt a little ridiculous proclaiming his titles to people. That was Peine's job.

Ari twisted his head to look over his right shoulder, taking in the lowering sun. He knew Ispiria and Peine hadn't reached the keep yet. Pushing away any thoughts of them being attacked on the way home, he tried to calculate how long it would take the hawk to reach Sorga, how close Sir Cadwel might be. He needed to keep this girl safe until then. "Our first duty is to search out the injured and offer them our aid, man and hawk. I'm sorry, Lady . . . ?"

"Mirimel," she said, holding out her hand, palm up, like a man would. Ari clasped it, finding it firm and callused. "Hawk Guardian Mirimel." She paused, appearing to size him up, like he'd seen Sir Cadwel do to new colts at the keep. "And you are wise, Ari. We shall search out survivors, as you say. I'm afraid I was letting anger cloud my sensibilities."

He scrutinized the hard line of her mouth, the slight furrowing of her forehead, realizing these were subtle signs of emotions in a face not used to expressing any. Indeed, the extreme sorrow she must feel did little more than bleed tears from her eyes. She might resemble Ispiria, but they were not alike. He rarely had any trouble knowing how Ispiria felt about something.

"Where do you hail from, Ari?" she asked, standing.

"I'm from the keep," he said, realizing as he rose that he'd doubly missed his chance to tell her he was Lord Aridian when he didn't reply to her declaration of title in kind when they clasped hands. "From Sorga."

"Then you must know my cousin, Lady Ispiria," she said, the grim lines on her face easing, but not enough to reveal a smile.

"I do," he said, feeling his skin heat. "Do you know where the Caller and his wolves went?" he asked, trying to distract her from his reaction to Ispiria's name.

Mirimel regarded him with knowing eyes. "She's very pretty, my cousin," she said. Before Ari could form a reply, she turned and looked out over the valley. "I do not know which way they fled, for my father tricked me into the cellar before collapsing the table on it. The hawk you sent to Sorga, she is late to clutch and heavy with eggs. Father wanted her, at least, to be safe." She turned back to him. "Why do you call him the Caller? Do you know the one who did this?"

"I'm not sure," Ari said. Her slight frown told him that wasn't a satisfactory answer. "I had a dream about a man with fire and wolves, destroying a farm. In the dream, I was told to beware the Caller." Ari shrugged, thinking he sounded a fool. He was sworn to secrecy about the Aluiens and the Lady, though, so he couldn't tell her any more than that. "I didn't know the hawk was near to clutching," Ari added, looking southwest, the direction of Sorga. He hoped she would be safe. He hadn't even realized she was female. "There are others, in Sorga," he said, to reassure Mirimel that not all of the hawks were dead.

"Are you prone to these prophetic dreams?" she asked.

"Not that I know of," he said, still feeling foolish.

She stared at him for a long moment before turning back to the destruction in the valley. "We should scout the perimeter of the village and note their trail before Sir Cadwel arrives. His men may trample it." Ari saw pain flash across her face as she looked out over her home. "Even a day old, I doubt signs of their passage will be difficult to find. Then, we can wend our way inward, searching for those in need."

"Should we check these hawks first?" Ari asked as she started across the plateau of the grand aerie.

"I would be able to sense if any here were alive." She didn't turn to look at him, but he could hear the strain in her voice. "Let's hope they were less thorough below."

With that, she started back down the steep stairs, Ari hurrying after her.

Chapter 5

They made their way around the perimeter of the village. There were tracks everywhere. Too many for Ari's poor skills to sort out. He could tell the ground was trampled and discern the occasional foot or paw print, but he couldn't begin to organize what his eyes saw into any semblance of what might have happened. He stayed alert to new danger, following in Mirimel's wake lest he trod on any important evidence.

Mirimel straightened from where she crouched low to the ground. "Many of my people fled," she said, her tone betraying her relief. "But the hounds have pursued them."

"Is there any way to signal they should return?"

"I can think of none save smoke, but a signal fire would hardly distinguish itself at this point. Best not to try until Sir Cadwel arrives, though. We'll only signal the enemy as well."

They reached the bottom of the hill leading up to the trail from Sorga. They weren't even a third of the way around the village, but Ari saw no point in continuing if it would reveal more of the same. They could not find which way the Caller and his wolves had gone because they seemed to have gone many ways. Mirimel's thoughts must have traveled a similar line, for she stopped, turning to face the smoldering village. Ari wondered where they should start. It seemed a daunting task to search it all. They would have to plan their course to be sure they covered each area, yet didn't lose time going back over what was already done. He saw Stew wandering about in the northeast corner of the village and wondered if his horse was having any luck finding more survivors.

"Is that your horse? Shouldn't we catch him?" Mirimel asked, peering through the smoke at Stew.

"He's looking for survivors," Ari said before realizing how ridiculous that sounded.

Mirimel turned to him with a questioning look.

Hooves pounded behind them and Ari whirled to face back up the hill, his hand going to his sword. He noted Mirimel turned almost as fast as he did, her bow already in her hand. A lone rider was silhouetted against the afternoon sun before plunging down the hill toward them. Once they left the bright backlight of the rim, Ari could make out that it was Peine on Charger.

Ari's hand clenched on his sword hilt, his insides twisting as he ran up the slope to meet Peine. Why was he here, alone?

"Where's Ispiria?" Ari demanded as soon as he was near enough for Peine to hear. "What happened?"

"Happened?" Peine looked confused as he slid from his mount. "Nothing. Sir Cadwel sent her back to the keep. He got your hawk. We met him on the way back."

Ari's ability to breathe returned to him. For a moment, he'd been ready to grab Peine's horse and race up the trail. Mirimel drew alongside them, returning her bow to her back.

"I'm sorry, Ari," Peine said. "I should have realized how it would seem. Ispiria is fine. Well, not really. She's very upset, but she's safe."

"How far behind you is Sir Cadwel?" Ari asked.

"Less than an hour, but not by much," Peine said. "There are too many of them to travel with any speed on the narrow trail."

Peine must have ridden fast, Ari realized. Indeed, Charger looked ready to collapse. "You best brush down Charger. Is there a well, Mirimel? You shouldn't abuse him like that, Peine. If your horse is exhausted, he'll fail you when you need him most."

"I'm sorry, my lord," Peine muttered, looking down.

Ari winced, realizing how he sounded. He and Peine were friends, not master and servant. Ari shouldn't speak to him that way. He'd said the words he knew Sir Cadwel would say, were he there, but people were accustomed to such bluntness from the knight, not from Ari. "No, I'm sorry."

"My lord?" Mirimel interrupted before Ari could finish his apology, her tone questioning. "Are you? A lord? One without enough manners to introduce yourself properly, or your friend."

Ari's face heated.

Peine looked up, his embarrassment replaced by a smile. "He has no manners at all. I do my best, but sometimes I think he's hopeless."

Ari was sure he should say something to refute that, but he didn't know what.

"I, my lady, am Peine, valet to Lord Aridian, heir to the Dukedom of Sorga and the Protectorate of the Northlands, and the youngest man ever to win the king's tourney. May I present to you my master, Lord--"

"I think once was enough," Ari said, breaking in. "The lady is Hawk Guardian Mirimel. She's Ispiria's cousin."

"It's an honor to meet you, Guardian Mirimel," Peine said, bowing.

"And you as well, Valet Peine." Mirimel turned to scrutinize Ari. "That explains the doublet, but not the sword. I assumed from the fancy dress that you were a poor noblemen striving to look wealthy, not a wealthy duke with a strangely utilitarian blade. I've seen soldiers with nicer looking weapons than that."

"This?" Ari said, pulling his sword halfway out of the sheath to look at it. "It works." He shrugged. He'd borrowed the sword from the stacks of reserves in King Ennentine's armory. It was well balanced and strong. What more did he need from it?

Peine seemed about to comment, but Ari hardly thought it the time or place to digress into one of Peine's favorite subjects, Ari's lack of lordliness. "I thought you were going to rub down Charger while we seek out a usable well."

Peine rolled his eyes, but turned to unsaddle his trembling mount. Ari would have to teach his valet more respect for the animal. Charger was a solid horse. A trifle past his prime, but Peine would have him for years if he cared for him well.

"Shh," Mirimel hissed before Ari could start toward the village.

Behind them, Peine went still. Ari turned, his gaze following Mirimel's outstretched arm.

To the north, something moved among the rocks and small shrubs filling the space between the village and a swath of the hearty pines that banded the mountains. Mirimel reached for her bow but Ari raised a hand to stay her. His eyes picked out a blonde head among the boulders.

"It's safe," Ari called, cupping his hands to make his words carry while trying to modulate his voice into a reassuring tone. "They're gone. You can come out."

A girl in a soot-smudged tunic emerged from the rocks, hurrying toward them. At first, Ari thought her quite young, but as she neared, he realized she was only a little younger than he was. She was just slight for her age. She was garbed as Mirimel, in forest green, though covered with a lot more grime and, Ari realized, blood.

"Kimmer," Mirimel cried, hastening toward the other girl.

Ari followed after at a slower pace, leaving Peine to tend to Charger. The girls hugged, the action made a bit awkward by the hunting knives, quivers and bows they both wore.

"We can't stay here," Kimmer said. "They're hunting me. We have to save the hawks."

"The hawks?" Mirimel repeated.

"I saved some of the fledglings. I put them in a tree. I didn't want to leave them but I couldn't travel fast enough with them." Concern marred her otherwise comely face. "I don't know if the wolves still chase me or if they're trying to get the hawks. Come." She tugged on Mirimel's arm.

"Can't they fly away?" Ari could hear Peine walking toward them and he frowned, sure Peine hadn't had enough time to take care of his horse.

"They're fledglings," Mirimel said. "They can't fly well yet. Kimmer, this is Valet Peine and Lord Aridian, from Sorga. This is Hawk Guardian Kimmer."

"My lord," Kimmer said, bowing. "Please excuse us, but we can't tarry."

"I'm coming with you," Ari said, his tone firm. He didn't care if they were some sort of hawk guardians. He wasn't letting the two of them go running off into the woods alone with the Caller and his wolves hunting them.

Kimmer looked to Mirimel, who shrugged.

"And me," Peine said.

Ari's first instinct was to say no. Peine, for all his good qualities as a friend and valet, wasn't very useful in a fight. He was also squeamish, not just about blood, but anything to do with the out of doors, since he'd always lived in a city. And he needed to tend to Charger.

But Ari could see the fear in Peine's eyes and realized his friend didn't want to be left there alone in this charred village full of the dead. Especially not when the wolves still hunted nearby. In good conscience, Ari couldn't leave Peine. He didn't have much of a chance of defending himself. It was true Sir Cadwel must arrive soon, but what would happen if something dire arrived before Sir Cadwel and his men?

"That horse will never manage among the trees," Kimmer said, pointing at Charger, who regarded them with tired eyes. "We must go now. Will you two be able to keep up?"

"Of course we will," Peine said, looking halfway between blustering and chagrin.

"One moment," Ari said. He whistled. Stew looked up. Ari waved and Stew trotted over. Ari was aware of the impressed looks the hawk guardians were giving him.

"How did you train him so well?" Mirimel's tone was impatient but tinged with curiosity.

"He was a gift," Ari said, which was true. He hoped that would suffice. He had no intention of revealing the secret of the Aluiens' magical horses.

Stew stepped from the rubble of the village, stopping before Ari with a shake of his mane.

"Stew, keep Charger safe until Sir Cadwel comes," Ari said. He didn't know how Stew could accomplish that, but it was the best he could think of. "I need to leave a note," he added, looking around. He had, lamentably, plenty of charcoal to write with, but nothing left to write on.

His gaze fell on Charger and his cooling flanks. Ari hoped the horse didn't cramp but there wasn't time now for Peine to rub him down. Picking up a piece of charred wood, Ari walked over, writing, *Gone to save hawks – Ari*, with large strokes on Charger's side. He hoped someone would notice. Charger was the only thing around not already too covered with soot. Charger nuzzled him, pleased with the attention. Ari patted him on the neck.

"We're going to go rescue some hawks," Ari said, turning to Stew and patting him as well. "If we aren't back soon, be nice to whoever unsaddles you."

"You do know he's a horse?" Mirimel asked from where they stood waiting for him. She sounded annoyed and Kimmer clicked a nail on the hilt of her hunting dagger in a rapid staccato of unconcealed impatience.

"Lord Aridian always talks to his horse that way," Peine said, sounding a little stiff. He put an emphasis on the word lord.

Ari frowned.

"Then Lord Aridian is going to get a reputation for being batty," Mirimel said. She nodded to Kimmer and they turned and headed up the rocky slope.

Ari's long legs quickly brought him alongside Peine and they followed the girls into the woods.

Chapter 6

It was dark in the pinewoods, and cool. The lowering sun barely penetrated the deep boughs. The evergreens weren't the thick fluffy kind that dotted the forests farther south. They were tall and gnarled, their lower branches long since fallen away in the darkness they created. Their tall spiny tips and upper limbs twisted toward the sky. Ari found it easy to move with near silence, the bed of needles on which he trod a deep cushion. He inhaled, pulling in the fresh earthy scent of trees to drive the scorch of fire and death from his nostrils.

Kimmer set a rapid pace, one hand resting on the hilt of her knife. Ari wondered how skilled she was with it, and how skilled Mirimel was. How good were they with their hunting bows? The bows had little range, Ari knew, but were deadly. In these woods, range provided no real advantage, for you could only see so far between the endless dark trunks.

Ispiria had never mentioned the hawk guardians, but then, they hadn't had much opportunity to talk of her ancestral home. Ari wondered if all of the guardians were women. He would have assumed the position honorary, if not for the sureness of the two girls, the aura of competence they gave off, and their obvious dedication to the hawks. He recalled what Mirimel had said, that she would sense if any of the hawks on the ledge still lived.

There was a loud popping sound behind Ari as Peine stepped on a twig, snapping it in half. Ari winced. Kimmer and Mirimel both looked back, their expressions hard, but neither of them issued a reprimand. One look at Peine's embarrassed face assured Ari it wasn't needed.

"Sorry," Peine said, his voice loud beneath the pines.

Kimmer shot him another quelling look, her straight blonde hair framing a frown.

They crept through the woods as the sun dropped low. Ari's every sense was alert, seeking danger. Time stretched out in the ever-darkening silence. Eventually, they came to the edge of a wide brook. Kimmer looked from side to side, as if seeking a way across. The water wasn't deep, but it bubbled with the vitality of spring. Ari spied several rocks they could use to cross, if they were surefooted enough. He glanced at Peine, wondering how his friend would fair should they try.

"Enough," Mirimel said, startling Ari. "Where do you lead us, Kimmer? I've seen no sign of your tracks, nor of the wolves. If you came from a tree where you left the hawks, then take us there."

"Shh," Kimmer hissed. "What if they pursue us?"

"I have also detected no sign that any follow us," Mirimel said. She looked at Ari. "What think you, my lord? Does danger draw near?"

"I've heard nothing but our passing." Ari pushed a hand through his thick brown hair. "Nor seen anything to indicate we're not alone."

Mirimel folded her arms across her chest, turning back to Kimmer, who looked younger than ever now, her competence melting into confusion.

"You're right," Kimmer said. "I'm lost. You know I am. I thought to take us a quicker way back, for my route to the village was twisted as I could make it, to confound them if they chased me."

"Why did you not say so already?" Mirimel's tone was hard. "How long did you intend for us to wander? Do you even know how to find the village now, Kimmer?"

"Not all of us can be like you, Mirimel," Kimmer said. "Not everyone is made for all aspects of our duty. So I'm not a good tracker, or a perfect shot, or an accomplished fighter. Some of us get chosen for being nurturing and caring, not . . ."

"Not what?" Mirimel said when Kimmer stopped.

"Nothing," Kimmer muttered, looking away.

"What do you mean, get chosen?" Ari asked. He asked it to defuse the situation but also out of interest. If they weren't going to sneak anymore, he wanted to know some things.

Mirimel kept her icy gaze on Kimmer for a long moment. "The hawks choose who shall serve them," she said, turning to Ari. Her arms uncrossed, falling back to her sides. "Each fall, we hold games. Competitions between everyone coming into their fourteenth year. Those who prove their worth are presented to the hawks. So, in spite of this display of inadequacy, Kimmer does know how to track, shoot and fight."

Kimmer scowled.

"How do the hawks choose?" Peine, who was fourteen, sounded very interested.

"How long do you serve?" Ari asked.

"You go before the hawks," Mirimel said. "If they want you, one will come to you. That's when the connection is supposed to form. They come to you and from then on, you can sense them. Their feelings."

"That's how it's supposed to work," Kimmer said. She started tapping her finger on the hilt of her sword again. "It never does. I don't know anyone who can actually sense the hawks. I'm not sure it's even true."

Ari glanced at Mirimel. She looked away, her lips squeezed into a thin line. She could sense the hawks. Why wouldn't she tell Kimmer?

"You serve for as long as you wish," Mirimel said. "It's an honor, not an obligation."

"I'm only serving one year," Kimmer said. "I was chosen last fall. I don't want to spend all my time sitting around with birds. I like people."

The two hawk guardians locked eyes. Mirimel kept her gaze level and unconcerned, her face unreadable. After a moment, Kimmer looked away.

"I suppose now we'll have to camp out here," Kimmer said. "It grows late."

"In the forest?" Peine sounded worried. "We don't have a tent, or cloaks."

"I'll make you a fire." Kimmer's expression lightened as she smiled, revealing dimples.

"It is getting rather dark," Mirimel said. "What say you, my lord?"

"Can you lead us back to the village?" Ari asked. "What of the hawks?"

"I could lead us closer before full dark. We would have to strike out in the direction of the village and hope we hit no insurmountable obstacles. It would take too long to follow our own trail back and I'll admit that the journey here was circuitous enough to test me in poor light."

Kimmer snorted.

"As for the hawks," Mirimel said, giving no indication she'd heard. "If the wolves had a way to get to them, we're already too late. Once we return to the village in the morning, I should be able to follow Kimmer's trail back to the tree she left them in so that we may discover their fate. It could be," her voice took on the faintest note of hope, "someone has already followed her trail or follows ours. Sir Cadwel must have reached the village by now."

Ari squinted up through the trees. One of his gifts from the Aluiens was the ability to see in any light, usually a blessing, but it made it difficult for him to guess how well his companions were able to see under the forest canopy. "If we cannot gain the village by full dark, or guarantee we shall be near, then I propose we camp here." He saw Peine grimace. "It seems to me that wandering blind through the forest at night would prove more dangerous than choosing as defensible a spot as we can and taking turns at watch."

It took them little time to find a location both Ari and Mirimel agreed on. Up the stream a short distance, a steep cliff rose from the forest floor and a waterfall rained down. The cliff to their backs and the falls beside them would shield them from enemies on two sides, so at least they couldn't be surrounded.

Ari looked up at the flora-draped wall of striated stone. It was exactly the sort of thing he didn't want them blundering off the top of in the dark, something he could envision them doing as he gazed up at it. This image, coupled with Mirimel's acceptance, reassured him that he had made the right choice.

"I'm going to see if I can shoot us something to eat," Kimmer said as Ari began gathering wood. Mirimel started scuffing away layers of pine needles, working to clear a space for their fire.

"Is that wise?" Ari asked. By now, even he could tell it was getting fairly dark.

"As Mirimel so generously allowed, I do have some skills, Lord Aridian," Kimmer said, squaring her shoulders. "Besides, I'm the one who led us here. It's only right I find us food."

"Just fish," Mirimel said, pointing at the stream. "You've no need to go far."

Kimmer pursed her lips. "It's almost too dark to see them, and they're probably terribly small," she said, but she dipped a hand into the pouch at her waist and pulled out a slender rope. She didn't attach a hook to it. Instead, to Ari's surprise, she drew an arrow from her quiver and secured the rope to that. "I'll let Mirimel make you a fire tonight, Valet Peine." Kimmer showed Peine her dimples. "Once I catch us a few fish, you should come help me clean them," she added, heading for the stream.

Peine stared after her for a moment before turning to help Mirimel. Ari hid his grin. Apparently, the young ladies here were no more resistant to Peine's looks than those at the keep.

They built their fire near the cliff, in the embrace of some sheltering boulders, and kept it small. Ari was painfully aware that it shone like a beacon but the night was cold and they would need to cook whatever Kimmer brought back. He didn't think light would travel too far through the thick pines, and, he admitted to himself, he wasn't sure the Caller or the wolves needed anything as mundane as fire to guide them. They would have other means.

Peine did help Kimmer clean the fish, although he came back looking a little queasy. From what Ari could see from where he sat by the fire with Mirimel, Kimmer had to carry the bulk of the conversation, all the while hacking into the fish with her hunting knife. Ari was very impressed with the way she shot them out of the water.

They ate their fish, cooked in the fire till the scales were nicely burnt. Then, once they agreed on an order for watch, everyone but Ari went to sleep.

Ari let Peine sleep through his turn at watch. He considered not waking Mirimel for hers, but he worried she would take offense and he was rather tired by then. He touched the copper-haired hawk guardian on the shoulder, unsurprised when she woke instantly. Her blue eyes were leached of color by the starlight, taking on an odd silver glow even to Ari's enhanced vision.

She sat up, her gaze going to Peine, who slept curled into a ball between Kimmer and the cliff face. Mirimel turned her eyes back to Ari, raising her brows. Ari could tell she was curious why he'd woken her up when it was Peine who should have. Ari shrugged.

He knew it was better to let Peine sleep. Peine very well may have drifted off anyhow. If he stayed awake, it would have been because of constant fear. Ari knew his friend would have found the dark forest disconcerting. Leaving Peine to watch would probably have resulted in them all waking up when he roused them from their rest the first time a skunk paused in its evening wanderings to peer with fire-brightened eyes into their little camp.

Mirimel stood and stretched, going through a routine Ari recognized from Sir Cadwel's teaching. It was a series of movements designed to bring you fully to wakefulness so you wouldn't return to sleep as soon as you settled into watching. It worked almost every muscle and she performed it in flawless silence. When she was done, she nodded to Ari.

He took off his sword belt and his fancy doublet, pleased he had it to use as a pillow and that he wore a light tunic underneath. He unsheathed his sword and settled into the spot Mirimel had vacated by the fire, laying the blade on the ground next to him. He hoped she hadn't noticed him staring.

Ari woke near dawn to find Mirimel stirring up the fire and Kimmer gone. Peine still slept. Ari stood, nodding to Mirimel when she glanced up. He gathered his things and headed downstream, following the river in a wide curve until he was out of sight so he could wash up. He wondered where Kimmer was. He'd half-expected to see her shooting at fish again.

After he was through at the stream, Ari stood for a moment in a patch of morning light filtering through the trees, waiting for his face and neck to dry before putting his tunic back on. He belted on his sword, wondering what he should do with the doublet. He preferred to wear only his tunic. Would Peine have the presence of mind that morning to notice? Folding the expensive doublet carefully, Ari set it on a rock by the stream. Maybe some animal would make a nest out of it.

He dropped his tunic over his head, doing up the laces. His fingers brushed up against the amulet the Lady had given him and he was struck by how cold it felt. It was colder than getting dunked in a stream on a cool spring morning warranted. A strange fear invaded him. He had the dreadful feeling that something was wrong.

Abandoning his laces, Ari raced through the pines, forgoing the curve of the stream. He heard Mirimel shout and Peine's startled cry. Ari pulled his sword from its sheath as he burst from the trees near the base of the cliff.

Four creatures formed a semicircle around Mirimel and Peine, pinning them against the rock face. At first glance, they were wolves, but they had a sinewy grace that surpassed that of natural animals. A grace made obvious by the blinding speed at

71

which they spun to face Ari. He didn't know if the others could see it, but to him the beasts were draped in undulating darkness. A pall of evil that did not obscure them, yet enshrouded them entirely.

Ari didn't slow. Mirimel seemed competent enough, but these were not ordinary wolves. Only Ari had the strength and speed to stand against them. Not knowing any other way to protect his companions than by making sure all four of the creatures were attacking him, he waved his sword, crying out a challenge.

They hurdled toward him. With an inarticulate yell, Ari launched himself into the air, coming down almost on top of one of the center two. With both hands on the hilt, he drove his blade downward, cleaving through fur and bone alike. The wolf creature's skull burst open, split in half. It fell with little blood, seeming to shrivel away from Ari's blade even as he wrenched it free.

Ari had seen rapid decomposition of this sort before, but never in a beast. It was the way vile Empty Ones, the evil opposite of Aluiens, died. He'd never had any thought that animals could be made into Empty Ones, but he didn't have time to ponder it now.

Pulling his eyes from the fascinating way the dead wolf deflated, Ari jumped back, sweeping his sword left. The wolf he was aiming for, a giant black-furred beast, turned its head as he swung. Ari grazed it, slicing off part of its upper jaw. It reared away, knocking into the dirty gray wolf next to it just as that one leapt at Ari.

The colliding wolves sprawled in a confusion of snarls and limbs, but the fourth one launched itself at Ari. It came from Ari's right, jaws open wide. Not having time to bring his sword back into a defensive position, Ari swung the blade hard, slamming it into the side of the wolf, knocking it from the air.

The creature landed on its feet, shaking its head. Ari didn't wait to see how hurt it was, for the other two had regained their footing. Far from being slowed by the chunk Ari had cut from its face, the black one only seemed more enraged. Saliva oozed from its partially rent jaw, but no blood flowed. It leapt at Ari, mangled mouth wide.

Ari dove forward, impaling it as he rolled to the side, brutally aware that there were two remaining. He saw the flaw in his strategy now, at attacking the ones in the middle first. He'd left one to each side. No matter which way he turned, his back was still vulnerable.

His sword protruded from the black wolf's back, his refusal to relinquish the hilt trapping them together as they rolled across the pine needle covered ground. Ari struggled to his feet, its teeth and claws flailing at him. He wrenched his sword up the length of its body, using his strength to rip through muscle and bone. If they were Empty Ones, he knew he must do more than injure. When only wounded, they would simply heal.

Ari pulled his sword free of the disemboweled corpse, the sticky scent of decay filling his nose as it started to crumble. He whirled to the left, to face the gray wolf he hadn't yet struck, hoping the blow he'd given to the other would slow it down enough for him to dispatch the one he faced.

To his right, Ari heard three loud twangs in rapid succession, followed by three corresponding thumps behind him. The gray wolf leapt at him. Ari jumped to the side and swept his blade up, half-braced for the blow from behind that he knew would come.

The wolf twisted in the air, trying to avoid Ari's sword, its jaws snapping toward his face. Ari swung his blade higher, cleaving it into the wolf's jugular. The creature opened its mouth, but no sound emerged. The weight of it on his extended blade dropped Ari to his knees. Straining, he pushed himself up, dragging the sword with him, right through the wolf.

Pulling his sword out of the already decomposing body, Ari whirled around, only to find the final wolf dead. Three arrows protruded from it. As far as Ari could tell, since it was decaying as fast as the other three, one had stuck in its throat, one in its eye and another in what must have been its ear.

There was a deafening howl. Ari raised his blade along with his eyes, spotting a large gray wolf atop the cliff above their camp. Its howl broke off and it locked eyes with Ari. It turned and bounded away.

Ari lowered his blade, wrinkling his nose at the stench of decay emanating from the wolf bodies. Mirimel eased the tension of her drawn bow as she turned to face him.

"No shot," she said, sliding the arrow back into the quiver at her waist.

"What was that howling?" Kimmer asked, charging into their camp from the direction opposite the river. She had her hunting knife in one hand and two dressed rabbits in the other. She slid to a halt, her face paling. "What happened? What are those?"

Her eyes were on the wolf corpses, unrecognizable lumps of half-liquefied fur. Like all Empty Ones, once killed they decayed rapidly. How fast their kind decomposed seemed to Ari to be proportionate to the length of their time as an Empty One. Ari was still shocked that animals could be turned, but it must be so. The evidence was before him.

"Lord Aridian was just demonstrating for us why he's the youngest man to ever win the king's tourney," Mirimel said in her matter-of-fact tone.

In spite of the carnage around him, Ari felt a smile tug at his lips for a moment before seriousness overtook him. "Were those the same beasts that attacked your village?" he asked Mirimel and Kimmer, although he already knew the answer.

"They looked it," Mirimel said.

"And now they're dead," Kimmer said. "Thank you, my lord." She bowed slightly to Ari. "We Hawkers are forever in your debt. I shall repay you with rabbit stew."

"Don't be ridiculous, Kimmer," Mirimel said, her tone sharp. "There are sure to be more of them. Hundreds came baying over the hill when--" She broke off, stomping away.

Kimmer's face crumpled. "I guess I am ridiculous."

"Save the rabbits." Ari patted her on the shoulder. "I think it best we head back as soon as we put out our fire. If you could take charge of that, I need to wash up." He turned and started for the stream. He hadn't noticed during the fight, but he'd taken quite a few gashes and nicks. Nothing serious, but enough to draw blood.

"That was amazing," Peine said, hurrying after him. "You chopped those wolves right in half. I bet even Sir Cadwel isn't strong enough to do that."

Ari winced. He hadn't meant to make such a show of his enhanced strength. He'd been rather carried away in the moment, wanting the wolf-monsters dead.

"Why did they shrivel up like that?" Peine asked. "They smell awful."

Ari shook his head. He would have to think of a plausible explanation. He wasn't allowed to tell anyone, not even Peine, about the secret race of the Aluiens or the Empty Ones. The only other people who knew were Sir Cadwel, King Ennentine, his son Prince Parrentine, and the prince's wife, Princess Siara. Maybe Ari should just lie and say he didn't know why the wolves had decayed. Was it acceptable to lie to uphold a vow? Ari didn't know, but the situation wasn't helped by the fact that he was terrible at lying.

"You're hurt," Peine said. "We should bandage you. We can shred your tunic. It's a good thing you didn't have your doublet on. It would be ruined. Where is it?"

"Why, he must o' left it downstream in his haste to be savin' you," a musical voice said.

Ari turned to see the long form of Larkesong, the irrepressible Aluien minstrel who masqueraded through the lands as the bard Larke, striding upriver toward them. More garish than ever, Larke had on a multi-colored tunic of bright yellow and blue, with blue hose to match. His wide brimmed hat was blue as well, with yellow feathers. His ensemble was completed by a short yellow cloak and a thin rapier Ari knew he never drew. His lute hung across his back. He was also, to Ari's despair, cheerfully waving Ari's heavy brocade doublet in one hand.

"Larke," Peine said, his eyes wide with surprise.

"Minstrel Larke?" Mirimel called, striding over from where she'd been stomping out their fire. "Whatever brings you here?"

Kimmer followed her, rabbits dangling from one hand.

"You know him?" Ari asked, surprised. Aluiens mixed with humans as little as possible. Though their existence depended on augmenting their ranks with carefully chosen humans, every Aluien swore a binding vow to avoid influencing the course of mankind.

"Certainly," Kimmer said. "He comes through the village yearly."

"Did ye think a minstrel of my renown could find no other work than at that grim keep in Sorga?" Larke asked Ari, winking. "As for my being in the woods, as it were, I've come seeking you all, for I arrived at the Hawkers on the heels of the good knight, Lord Cadwel himself."

There was a moment of sad silence as they were again reminded of the state of the Hawkers' village. Mirimel and Kimmer began questioning Larke, asking how the search was going for survivors, if anyone had returned, and if he'd seen any hawks.

Ari was only half-listening. He wasn't fooled for a moment. If Larke went to the Hawkers' village every year, Ari was sure it was to check on the hawks and the mysterious stone Mirimel had spoken of. Ari was relieved Larke had chosen to come, for he'd missed the bard after their travels the past autumn and valued Larke's knowledge and advice, but it also made him nervous. To stir Larkesong from the secret caverns of the Aluiens' their troubles must be even more serious than Ari had thought them, and he'd already thought them serious indeed.

Chapter 7

Larke answered several of the hawk guardians' questions before cutting them off with an arcane gesture. Ari could see the glow of the Orlenia, the earth magic that flowed through Aluiens' veins like blood, surrounding Larke's nimble-fingered hand as he drew a glowing symbol in the air before them.

"That fire isn't all the way out," Larke said to the others, pointing toward the cliff face. "I daresay you three should see to it, and not attend to a thing we two are saying. It won't be doing to burn down Sir Cadwel's forest."

Kimmer broke off mid-word. She and Peine nodded. Their eyes a bit glassy, they turned away. Mirimel opened her mouth as if to protest but at a second gesture from Larke, she shut it and followed them.

Almost more than anything else that had happened since they'd arrived at Hawkers, Larke's blatant use of magic disturbed Ari. Usually, the bard subterfuge to enchantment. Ari had traveled with him for a whole season without even realizing Larke was using magic on him every day.

"Did the Caller take the stone?" Larke's tone was low and intense as he turned to face Ari.

"I don't know," Ari said, wondering if now was the time to tell Larke that he had a dream about the Caller the same morning the village was burned. "The grand aerie was destroyed and all of the nests pulled down, but the wolves still hunt." He made a vague gesture toward the rotten wolf corpses. "Would they stay if they had what they wanted?"

Larke frowned, an unnatural expression for his normally cheerful countenance. "It seems unlikely. Maybe there is yet hope."

"Larke, who is this Caller?"

"An Empty One," Larke said, confirming Ari's suspicion. "He is old, and powerful, but as happens to those of his kind, his mind is almost gone. We hadn't seen him in nearly sixteen years. We'd hoped, perhaps, he'd lost his mind, faded away." Larke shook his head. "But now something about the stones has drawn him forth again."

"Why this stone? Why is it so special? Mirimel said it's just a small white stone."

"Alone, it's not very special, lad. It's part of a set. One for each, they link the heart, mind and deed of the wielder, that his abilities may be magnified and his intentions carried out as quick and clear as his very thoughts."

Ari didn't bother trying to sort out what that might mean. As Mirimel had said, if a being such as the Caller wanted the stones, the most important thing was to stop him. Once that was accomplished, there would be time to ponder his motives. "So there are two more? Where are they? Has he already taken them?"

"One is with the Questri, Stew's race, on the endless plains beyond the Northern Range," Larke said. "Warning was sent to them to beware. The other is lost. It was entrusted to a third magical race, one that dwelled beneath the sea."

"A third magical race?" Ari hadn't even known there was a plain beyond the Northern Range in which they stood, let alone an endless one. He knew Stew wasn't a normal horse, though. He was like Sir Cadwel's horse, Goldwin, and Larke's silver-gray mount. "Do you mean the Sorga hawks are magical?"

"Lad, it isn't that I don't love telling a grand tale, you know I do, but my compulsion wears thin. The others will be tricked into trying to put out an already dead fire for only so long, and we should quit these woods and seek the greater safety offered by Sir Cadwel's forces."

Ari knew Larke was right. Already, Mirimel was staring at them, though Kimmer and Peine still scuffed at where the fire had been. Ari nodded. He was frustrated to have Larke and all his knowledge so near, yet be unable to learn more, but he had to get Peine and the hawk guardians safely back. As Mirimel had said, somewhere there were a lot more wolves.

"Are you two finished?" Mirimel called. At the sound of her voice, Peine and Kimmer stopped scuffing, blinking as if waking up. Larke was correct. His spell had worn thin. Grimacing, Ari pulled off his shredded tunic and donned his heavy doublet. Without the tunic as padding, the silver threads bit into his flesh. He only hoped that the blood from his wounds, which he hadn't found time to wash, would ruin it.

Mirimel took up the lead, heading without hesitation in a different direction than the one they'd arrived from the evening before. By the stream, Ari could see enough sky to know which way was east, but he didn't have a strong sense of what course would take them back to the village, rather than north or south of it. Once they were under the thick conifers, Ari lost even the surety of his compass points. He was impressed with Mirimel's unfaltering course.

They hadn't traveled far when Kimmer stopped and cocked her head to one side, the others halting behind her. "Mirimel," she said.

Mirimel turned back, raising an eyebrow.

"Shouldn't we go that way?" Kimmer asked, pointing to their left.

"Don't be ridiculous," Mirimel said, setting off once more. "Where have you put your skills, Kimmer?"

Kimmer scowled, her fists clenched at her sides. For a moment, Ari thought she might storm off in the direction she'd suggested. He was racking his brain for something to say when she turned to follow Mirimel.

Ari looked over to Larke to share his relief that the situation hadn't digressed into a shouting match, but the bard's face was folded into a distracted frown. As far as Ari could tell, Larke hadn't even noticed the pause in their progress. Shrugging, Ari trailed after the two hawk guardians, hoping Larke would say something if they weren't going the right way.

Mirimel's path proved true and much shorter than Kimmer's circuitous route the night before. Despite their slow start, they reached the edge of the woods about four hours after dawn's first light. As they wended their way through the large boulders strewn over the hillside between the pinewood and the village of the Hawkers, Ari was amazed at how much Sir Cadwel had already accomplished.

The fires were out, save cooking fires. An encampment for the soldiers of Sorga stood at the base of the hill over which the roadway ran. A second camp, for villagers, was set up at the bottom of the hill Ari and the others walked down. It was a distressingly small city of tents, dashing Ari's hope that more people had survived than he'd first assumed. Beside it was a lone tent that looked to house those few who were wounded, yet hadn't perished. The horses were picketed near the soldiers' encampment. Ari could make out Charger and Stew standing beside Sir Cadwel's Goldwin.

They were spotted as soon as they left the shelter of the woods, soldiers in the brown and blue of Sorga coming forward to meet them. Ari waved and they stood down. He could see men from Sorga and a smattering of Hawkers working in the ruined village and up in the grand aerie.

In spite of how pleased he was by the obvious progress, Ari felt a growing sense of disappointment in himself, one that was rapidly boiling into anger. Everyone was working hard to put things right and all he'd done was spend the night camping in the woods.

Below, Ari caught sight of Sir Cadwel supervising from the open space before the village. Without a word, Mirimel quickened her step and turned aside to wend her way toward the Hawkers' tents. Kimmer waved, smiling, before following Mirimel. Ari looked after them as he, Larke and Peine made their way to Sir Cadwel. He shook his head, worried the hawk guardians wouldn't find those they loved. Mirimel in particular he feared would meet anguish, for he recalled the bodies in front of what had once been a house, near where he'd freed her.

"I see you found them," Sir Cadwel said to Larke as they neared.

"Aye, and them only a touch worse for the wear."

Sir Cadwel looked around, as if something was missing. "Your note said you went after some hawks? Report."

Ari clenched his jaw, his shame at not finding the hawks doubling. "Yes, sir, but we couldn't find them. Failure is all I have to report." He thought about adding that Kimmer had lost their way, but it sounded too much like an excuse.

"We'll send out another team." Sir Cadwel's even tone was at odds with the surprise on his face when Ari had admitted their lack of success. "I daresay the way will be easier by daylight."

"It was still daylight when we left yesterday, sir," Ari said, disgrace and anger making his temples throb.

"I'm sure you did your best, lad."

"Ari slew four wolves all by himself," Peine said, his tone excited. "He chopped them right in half."

"Hawk Guardian Mirimel killed one," Ari corrected. "With her bow." The one weapon Ari couldn't seem to master.

"Did she?" Sir Cadwel lowered his voice to a low rumble. "They've taken several of our men already and we've found quite a few remains out there in the forest. Particularly in the direction you approached from. It's a lucky thing for the hawk guardians who came out of the pinewoods with you that you were along. So far, the most we've been able to accomplish is to drive them off."

"I'm sure you could slay them, sir," Ari said.

"These wolves--" Sir Cadwel paused, his worried eyes traveling from Larke to Ari and back again. "They don't strike me as natural. I'd not expose my men to them, but I must send out search parties. After the first few didn't return, I raised the number in each party to a score."

"What do you mean, not natural, my lord?" Peine asked, looking confused.

Ari stared at his friend in surprise, ready to remind him of the wolves' accelerated decay. There was a light touch on his arm. He turned to see Larke give a quick shake of his head. Magic, Ari realized. Larke had already used his magic to make Peine, and most likely Kimmer and Mirimel, forget the details of what they'd seen.

"Unnaturally well-trained to travel in small groups and seek people out," Sir Cadwel said, his voice returning to its normal volume, a near-bellow long accustomed to giving orders. "When I meet the man who trained them, I'll give him my sincere compliments on his skill. Right before I kill him."

"What can we do to help, sir?" Ari said, looking around. He should use his strength, subtly of course, to help clear up the wreckage of the village.

"In a moment," Sir Cadwel said. He turned to face Peine. "When we arrived, Charger was in a highly disreputable state, Valet Peine. You should know better. If you exhaust your horse and tend him poorly, he'll fail you when you need him most. And I don't recall giving you permission to turn and ride back to Lord Aridian, after you and the ladies met our troop."

Peine looked down, clearly abashed. "I forgot to ask for it, my lord," he mumbled.

Ari winced, feeling bad for Peine that he'd incurred Sir Cadwel's wrath. Ari hadn't thought to ask Peine how it was he'd come back so soon when another messenger, on a fresher horse, would have been better.

"As I recall, you called out that you would go tell Lord Aridian we were coming and immediately headed back down the trail, not giving yourself very much time for propriety." Sir Cadwel's gravelly voice was hard with censure.

There was a drawn out silence, painful to watch, as Sir Cadwel glared and Peine stared at the ground. "What do you have to say for yourself, Valet Peine?"

Peine looked up, his face squished into lines as he held back tears, reminding Ari that Peine was only fourteen, no matter how hard he tried to run things and to seem grown up. "It's just, last time I missed everything," Peine said. "No one will even tell me exactly what happened with Princess Clorra, or where you two went to all winter, or anything. You sent me back to Sorga to wait and worry. I didn't want to be sent back to Sorga again, my lord."

Sir Cadwel considered him for a long moment. Ari hoped Peine wouldn't be sent back to Sorga now, even though he deserved to be. Ari could understand Peine's desire not to be left out, but it wasn't a good reason for not behaving well.

"That's no excuse for insubordinate behavior, Peine," Sir Cadwel said, but his tone was kinder. "As I can't spare the men to escort you back to Sorga, your punishment will be caring for everyone's horses while we are here. It should take you most of each day. Perhaps after a week or two, you'll wish I had sent you back to wait."

"Yes, my lord," Peine said, looking down again.

Ari suppressed a smile. The punishment was fitting, and would torment Peine sufficiently since he didn't care much for horses. Ari just hoped it wouldn't be a punishment for the animals too. He'd keep an eye on Peine, though, for the horses' sake and his friend's.

Sir Cadwel and Larke both turned toward the hilltop over which the mountain path came. Ari followed their gaze, realizing that he too could hear someone approaching the ridge above. As one, the three started toward the roadway, leaving Peine staring down at his shoes.

Soldiers crested the hill, presumably some of the guards Sir Cadwel must have stationed up the path. They held someone between them. At first, the billow of fabric made Ari think it was a prisoner in a long cloak but as they neared, he realized they were supporting the person. A woman, in a dress.

Before the thought could fully register, Ari was racing forward. He skidded to a halt in front of the men as they reached the bottom of the slope, Lady Civul suspended between them. She would have fallen to her knees if they weren't holding her up. She swayed, her head lolling to one side. The left side of her face was covered in dry blood and half of her hair was torn free of its braids.

Ari sucked a deep hissing breath between his teeth, clenching his hands at his sides. He was almost overcome by a desire to shake her and demand to know where Ispiria was. He took another deep breath, trying to gather words to his lips that didn't sound like he was accosting a woman already attacked. "Ispiria?"

She looked up at him with glazed eyes.

"Get a sawbones over here," Sir Cadwel roared from right behind Ari. If every muscle in Ari's body wasn't already so tense it had forgotten how to move, he would have jumped. "And a blanket."

"Sir Cadwel," Civul said, her voice cracking. "He said, tell Cadwel the girl for the stone. Tell him."

"Get some water," Ari heard Larke say.

Someone scurried off. Maybe Peine. Ari couldn't turn his head to look. He couldn't take his eyes off Civul. "Ispiria?" he repeated.

"Who gave you the message, Civul? What happened?" Sir Cadwel said, his tone soft. The knight came into Ari's view, moving to take Lady Civul from the guardsmen. He wrapped one massive arm about her, holding her up. She didn't look as if she'd heard him.

"She came down the road, sir," one of the guards said. "We went to get her as soon as we saw her. She kept coming, even though we called to wait. She kept getting up, then falling over." He shook his head.

A healer arrived, moving to Civul's other side to start examining her while Sir Cadwel helped her to sit on a blanket. Peine raced up with a bucket full of water and a metal cup. Ari stood where he was, fists clenched, glaring down at them as they huddled around Civul.

"Where," Ari said, struggling to keep his tone even. "Is." He tried to take a breath, to stop the swarming darkness around the edges of his vision. "Ispiria."

Everyone looked up at him. For all he knew, everyone in the whole burned valley was looking at him. His eyes were locked on Civul's face.

She lifted her head from the cup Peine held to her lips, her expression unfocused. "He took her. He took Lady Ispiria and killed everyone else. We never left the mountains. They attacked before we could. The guards who were taking us back, they're all dead." She choked back a shuddering sob. "But Lady Ispiria isn't. I saw her." She raised a shaking hand to her bloodied scalp. "He had me by the hair. His face was so close. He said, tell the Thrice Born the stone for the girl, but I don't know who that is. I told him so. He said, tell Cadwel, then. I couldn't look at that horrible face, with his mad blue eyes and red teeth. I looked away, and they had her, his wolves. A giant black wolf was standing on top of her, holding her down. I begged him to take me instead, my lord. I begged him." She started to cry.

Ari plunked down on the ground in front of her, his muscles releasing. The Caller had Ispiria. The Caller and his wolves. What honor had they? The girl for the stone, he said, but she could already be dead. Dead because an Empty One thought Ari could give him a stone.

Ari reached out and took Civul's hand. "I'm sorry," he said. He didn't know if he meant for yelling or for her ordeal. Mostly, he was sorry he hadn't stayed with Ispiria.

Ari let his hand fall. He sat in a numb haze while they tended Lady Civul. His mind ranged over the choices he'd made the day before. All of them seemed wrong.

"He hit me on the head," Lady Civul said. "I didn't wake until almost dawn. I came as fast as I could, my lord. As fast as I could."

Ari realized she was talking to him. He forced himself to listen. He wasn't going to do Ispiria any good sitting around in the charcoal-smeared dirt, feeling sorry for himself.

"I'm sorry, my lord. I'm sorry." Her tears made a trail through the dried blood on her cheek.

"You did your best," Ari said, standing.

Sir Cadwel rose as well, patting Lady Civul on the shoulder. "They'll take you to the healers' tent to rest," he said. "You've been very brave." He nodded to the two guards, who still hovered behind Civul. The guards and the healer led her away.

"We need to send out a search," Ari said to Sir Cadwel. "I will lead it."

"Aye. We do and you shall."

Ari turned, his eyes seeking Stew. It would be best to ride back down the path until he found the bodies of the men who'd been guarding Ispiria and Civul. Then he could pick up the Caller's trail.

"But first, we need at least half a plan." Sir Cadwel's sharp tone stopped Ari from running for Stew. "And I need some answers."

Ari spun back. "But the Caller--"

"Is already well away, holed up somewhere, and undoubtedly aware you'll be coming after her," Sir Cadwel said. "First there are answers I need. In private."

Sir Cadwel locked eyes with him. Ari forcibly relaxed his muscles, nodding. Sir Cadwel would need to know the same things Ari did. What weaknesses did this Caller have? How many wolves were there? Larke would tell them, but not where everyone could hear. Then Ari would go find Ispiria, armed with knowledge and a proper plan. It wouldn't take long. They would be leaving soon.

"We'll discuss this in my tent." Sir Cadwel turned to Peine. "Have you eaten?" Peine shook his head. "Find some food for Larke, Ari and yourself."

"Food?" Ari said, his anger and impatience springing back to life. "How long do you expect me to wait? I have to find her. I don't want to be too late to save her."

The moment Ari heard the words leave his mouth, he flinched back, half-expecting Sir Cadwel to hit him.

The old knight's eyes went dark. He bared his teeth at Ari, the words that came from between them hardly discernable from a growl. "My tent. Now." Tension clear in the stiffness of every movement, Sir Cadwel headed toward his tent.

"I didn't mean it," Ari said, his voice small. He wasn't sure Sir Cadwel heard. "I didn't mean it like that."

Everyone knew that in his youth, Sir Cadwel did arrive too late. Too late to save his family, including his pregnant wife, from the wrath of his greatest enemy. Ari couldn't believe that he'd let himself say something like that.

Next to him, Larke sighed. "Ari, lad," the bard said, his disappointment clear.

"I didn't mean it like that."

Peine shook his head at Ari, then scurried away.

"Let's not keep him waiting," Larke said. "No reason to pour cold water on an angry badger."

Normally, the bard's light tone and nonsensical saying would have made Ari smile, but he was too wretched for even Larke to help. Larke's voice wasn't as light as it should be, anyhow. Ari knew his humor was forced. They crossed the distance to the tent in silence.

Ari pushed the tent flap aside with trepidation. It was a pavilion, meant for longer stays, not the small portable tent Sir Cadwel used on the road. The knight stood in the center with his back to them. Larke nudged Ari forward.

"Sir?" Ari said, his worry for Ispiria momentarily subsumed by the anguish he felt over his words to Sir Cadwel. "I wasn't thinking, sir. I spoke in anger. Please . . ." He stopped, unsure what to plead for. Sir Cadwel's forgiveness for Ari's rash words? If Ari could have a plea answered, he would plea for Sir Cadwel's forgiveness of himself, even if he never forgave Ari. The knight had never remarried after his wife was killed, living under the burden of his guilt for over twenty years.

"Who is the Caller?" Sir Cadwel said into the silence, his voice almost normal. He turned to face them, scrubbing a thick-fingered hand through his gray hair.

Ari dropped his gaze from the haunted look in Sir Cadwel's eyes.

"An Empty One," Larke said. "He's called the Caller on account of how he communicates with his wolves."

"And they are Empty Ones as well?"

"Aye."

"How is that possible? Can you make animals into Aluiens too?"

Larke nodded. "Aye, but it's not a thing that's much encouraged. An animal is still simply that, an animal. Endless life is usually a bit lost on it."

"What is this stone the Caller seeks?"

Larke repeated what he'd told Ari earlier about the stones, for heart, mind and deed, adding before Sir Cadwel could ask that he didn't know why the Caller had attacked, since one stone was lost and all three undetectable.

"One is lost? You'd best give me the details," Sir Cadwel said. "And spare me both your theatrical embellishments and Aluien evasiveness."

Larke nodded, looking a little hurt. "Theatrical indeed," he muttered under his breath, before continuing in a more strident tone. "There were three stones, guarded by earth, sea and sky. One was entrusted to the horse lords, Questri true and fleet. One placed high above the mountains, with the Sorrecia soaring and brash. One lost, hidden deep below, in the sea's endless embrace."

Sir Cadwel scowled. "You've sent warning to these horse lords?"

"My people have."

"What, no poetry in your answer?"

"What can I say?" The bard heaved a dramatic sigh. "My skills are not what they once may have been."

"If these rocks are undetectable, how is it this Caller knew to attack here? It's my dukedom, and I knew nothing of this stone."

"But people knew," Ari said, recalling Mirimel's words. "Hawk Guardian Mirimel said that sometimes people would come looking for a magic stone, chasing stories, and they would send them away again, and the hawk guardians knew."

"To attack on a rumor?" Sir Cadwel shook his head, not looking at Ari. "No, there must be more. Does having one stone help you in seeking the others? The Caller may possess the lost one. It could be that's what spurred this attack, for my next question is, why now?" He was silent for a moment, his brow furrowed as he thought. "And we don't know where the stone the hawks guarded is, correct?"

Ari restrained himself from pacing. That morning by the stream, he would have had Larke tell him all he knew of the stone, but now Ari didn't care. He didn't care why the village had been attacked or how the Caller had known the stone was in the aerie. He only cared about going after Ispiria.

"No," Larke said. "Nor can I seek it. The stones are wrapped in enchantments that keep them from being scryed out. But we can guess the Caller doesn't have it. We wouldn't be trading it to him if we did, so we're at no real disadvantage."

Ari winced, realizing that he very well might trade the stone, if he had it and had any reason to believe the Caller would return Ispiria unharmed. After all, there were two more stones and you needed all three to do anything.

"I would prefer we find it," Sir Cadwel said.

"The hawks may know where it is," Larke said. "When they come out of hiding, for I doubt all perished, I'll ask them."

Ari wasn't sure if Larke was joking or not. If it was a joke, it wasn't funny.

"If that's all the knowledge we have, it's what we work with," Sir Cadwel said.

"And here I thought I was being helpful," Larke said.

"Do we send a large group or small?" Sir Cadwel mused.

Ari thought they should send the whole army of Sorga, but he was afraid to demand it. He was worried Sir Cadwel would refute him. Or worse, look at Ari again with the pain of the past in his eyes.

"I would rather stealth and cunning over brute force," Larke said.

Sir Cadwel turned to him, eyebrows raised.

"Eloquent as always, old friend," Larke said. "If we bring force, he will bring greater. If we muster an even greater force than he can, he'll disappear. Don't mistakenly think we haven't tried to draw this Empty One out and dispose of him before." Larke raised a hand when Sir Cadwel would have spoken. "I have many assets to offer this venture that I can't, in good conscience, put on display to the general populace."

"So your help is contingent on secrecy?" Sir Cadwel said, scowling.

"You know that in this, my will is not the deciding factor," Larke said, referring to the Aluien vow not to expose themselves to mortals or interfere in mortal affairs. "It is only the involvement of the stone that allowed me the laxity to come here."

"A reconnaissance then," Sir Cadwel said. "As soon as you find this Empty One, come back and we'll attack him in force."

"I'm going with Larke," Ari said, not liking Sir Cadwel's phrasing. Did he mean for the bard to go alone?

"Yes, you are," Sir Cadwel said, the eyes he turned on Ari still cold. "You'll be useless to me here. I have every intention of putting you in command of this venture, succeed or fail."

Ari swallowed. He wanted to go. If Sir Cadwel told him not to, he would still go, but the knight's words were almost a threat. Ari heard the undertone. If Ispiria died, Ari would live with it. "If I'm leading, what will you be doing, sir?"

"Insuring the survival of the Hawkers," Sir Cadwel said. "I love Ispiria, Ari. She's like a daughter to me. But I can't leave my people. You will find her. You have my complete faith."

Ari nodded. It almost seemed wrong to go on a quest without Sir Cadwel but as much as he wanted his mentor's experience and battle prowess, Ari knew the knight had to stay and manage his dukedom. Protection had to be organized for the remaining Hawkers. Search parties needed to be sent out, food and supplies brought. The people of Sorga were scared. The hawks were missing or dead. They needed Sir Cadwel to lead them.

Not to mention the normal affairs of the dukedom which Natan, as master steward, always helped with, but which would be hindered by having half the able-bodied men of Sorga taking up temporary residence in the Hawkers' village. Not only Sorga's guards, but craftsmen as well, and additional supplies for them to work with. How would Sir Cadwel pay for it all? Ari hadn't had time yet to learn about the financial side of running a dukedom, although he knew the people tithed to Sir Cadwel. How deep did the coffers go and how much could they afford to give the Hawkers when there was no way to know what disaster might strike next?

"I have your food, my lords," Peine called from outside. He waited a discreet moment before ducking into the tent. He held two bowls of stew. "I'm sorry it took me so long. It wasn't quite ready yet. I should warn you, Hawk Guardian Mirimel is on her way over. She heard about Ispiria." He lowered his voice, his tone grave. "And I don't think things went well for her at the Hawkers' tents."

He held out the bowls. Ari didn't feel like eating and from the look on Larke's face, he didn't either. Ari took his, afraid Sir Cadwel wouldn't let him go after Ispiria until he ate. He spooned some into this mouth.

Mirimel pushed aside the tent flap without warning. Her face was white, save for a splotch of red on each cheek. Her lips were pressed into a hard line. "How can you stand around eating when that monster has my cousin?"

Ari resisted the urge to throw his stew bowl at her, his anger flaring up anew. Instead, he shoved another spoonful into his mouth.

"Lord Aridian will be leaving to pursue the Caller shortly," Sir Cadwel said in a mild tone that Ari knew meant the knight was controlling his temper.

"I'm going with him," Mirimel said.

"That's up to him. I'm sending a unit of men to collect the bodies and restore them to their loved ones in Sorga, but finding Ispiria is Ari's command."

Mirimel turned her glare back to Ari. He held out his bowl, trusting Peine to take it. Looking Mirimel up and down, Ari assessed her worth, wanting her to know he was doing it. He recalled how steady she was at the top of the grand aerie, in spite of how upset she must have been. He thought about how well she'd led them out of the woods and how Kimmer had said Mirimel was the best tracker. Most of all, he remembered how she'd killed one of the Empty One wolves with her bow.

"I will be taking Larke," Ari said. He saw anger flash in her eyes and, he thought, hurt. "And Hawk Guardian Mirimel."

"And me," Peine said. He stood up straight and squared his shoulders. He was still shorter than Mirimel.

Ari turned to him, surprised Peine would try to go after the reprimand Sir Cadwel had issued him earlier.

"No," Sir Cadwel said, saving Ari from saying it. "You will stay here and serve out your punishment. Perhaps next time you're inclined toward rebelliousness, you'll recall that such behavior leads to less inclusion, not more."

"Yes, my lord," Peine said, looking hurt. "I'll go ready a pack for you, Ari, and ask someone to saddle Stew." He stomped out.

Ari wasn't pleased his friend was in trouble, but he was relieved Peine wouldn't be going with them. In the forest, Peine was more of a hindrance than a help. "You should have someone check on the horses each day when he's done, sir."

"I was planning to." Sir Cadwel frowned. "Perhaps I allow him too much laxity for one so young. He's never shown any inclination toward unruliness before. How old is he now, Ari?"

"He saw his fourteenth birthday this winter, sir," Ari said, glad that Sir Cadwel's tone was nearly back to normal.

Sir Cadwel nodded, his face thoughtful.

"I'll need only a moment to make ready," Mirimel said. "I assume we're leaving soon."

"Is your horse near?" Ari asked Larke, his anxiety for Ispiria springing back to the forefront of his thoughts.

"Aye, lad. Should I step outside and call, I warrant he'll come."

"Better start calling," Sir Cadwel said. "You need to be off, and I don't recall that horse being very obedient."

"On the contrary," Larke said. "Last time, he played his role to perfection." Larke left, the long low whistle he used to call his horse drifting back to them.

"You'll ride with me on Stew," Ari said to Mirimel.

She looked confused by that, so Ari glowered at her. He didn't like to seem unreasonable, but unlike normal horses, they could leave Stew and Larke's horse alone if they had to seek the Caller in the forest. Ari couldn't explain that to Mirimel, so he would have to settle for appearing arbitrary.

She frowned, but nodded. "I'll meet you by the picket line, my lord," she said, departing.

Ari turned to Sir Cadwel. Before he left, he wanted to apologize for his ill-chosen words earlier, but he worried that would create more awkwardness between them. The knight watched him without expression.

"Lad," Sir Cadwel said, just as Ari was about to leave in silence. "I meant what I said. I trust you completely. You will find her. Come get me when you do. We'll gather the full force of Sorga. This Empty One and his hellish beasts will face retribution such as they've never known."

"Yes, sir," Ari said. He wanted to say more. Thank you for your faith in me. Thank you for taking me in and making me your heir. Thank you for becoming the father I never had. Ari didn't know how to say any of those things. Instead, he said, "I'll bring her back, sir," and pushed open the tent flap, walking out into the midday light.

Chapter 8

Ari found it odd to have Mirimel riding behind him. The only other woman who ever had was Princess Siara, but there was no parallel there. Riding with Siara was both more enjoyable and more awkward. Ari could admit now that he'd once held the brief hope he and Siara might be more than travel companions. That hope had been crushed by her unwavering and magically sealed love for Crown Prince Parrentine, and made irrelevant by Ispiria. Ari and Siara were friends, and now that he had Ispiria, he realized his short-lived infatuation with Princess Siara had been nothing even remotely close to love.

But for all of his love of her, Ispiria had never ridden on a horse with Ari. Not once. She would, though. He would find her and get her back. It was impossible to think of things coming out any other way.

Having Hawk Guardian Mirimel riding on Stew with him was like cantering down the trail with a hot ball of anger on his back. He could feel her rage. It was so palpable, it amazed him she could appear so outwardly calm. Her face and crisp tone had seemed nearly devoid of emotion when he'd helped her onto Stew.

She could be angry. Ari didn't care. He was angry too. Furious and, he admitted in the silence that raged in his head as the trail seemed to stretch out forever before them, scared.

Almost a day. That was how much of a head start the Caller had. And they still hadn't found the spot of the ambush. Stew's hooves pounded almost as fast as Ari's heart as they sped through the mountains.

Stew was going as fast as was prudent, Ari knew. They dared not try for more speed on the steep mountain trail with its endless drop to Ari's right, yet they still hadn't reached the scene Ari knew would come. The bodies of the guards. The blood-soaked ground. The clues that would tell Mirimel which way the Caller had gone.

Stew skidded as they careened around a tight bend in the trail. They were almost out of the mountains, but the drop off was still a deadly height. Ari grabbed onto the saddle horn, but Stew wasn't sliding over the edge. He was stopping, keeping himself well back from the still forms that came into view as they rounded the turn. Ari wondered if Stew was afraid to go near the dead, or if his horse was actually smart enough not to tread on any tracks.

Mirimel slithered down as Larke pulled up behind them. The bard jumped from his saddle, hurrying forward. Mirimel glanced at him sharply, but Larke appeared to step with care and she issued no complaint as he flittered from body to body on the dusty mountain trail, checking each. Ari dismounted, standing beside Stew with one hand resting on the brown's neck.

As if their terrible wounds didn't say enough, Ari could tell by how little time Larke spent at the side of each of the eight men that there was no hope any yet lingered in the living realm. From where he stood, Ari could see two of them weren't even identifiable, their faces were so badly mauled.

He turned his head away, eyes tracing the trunks of the tall pines growing on the steep slope to his left. Sorrow washed through him, and the anger that followed hard upon it couldn't completely block out the queasiness in his gut. He didn't know why this seemed so much worse than the village. Maybe it was because he knew these men. They dined in the great hall alongside all the other castle residents every evening. They had names and families. Or maybe it was because here, there was no fire to cover everything in its all-obscuring haze of smoke and cloak of ashes.

"None survive," Larke said, rising from closing a final set of eyes, his face revealing his sorrow.

"He went this way." Mirimel pointed up a steep cleft in the cliff face. "And he carried her. He must be terribly strong to manage carrying her while climbing that."

"And the wolves?" Ari asked, striding forward, his immobility and queasiness dispersed by Ispiria's trail.

"Some followed him, some went north and some went south. They seem to have scattered. I can't tell how many went with him. Perhaps six."

"Help me move these men, Larke," Ari said, crossing to stand at the feet of one of the guards. "We'll lay them out over there."

"We must hurry," Mirimel said. "These men are dead but my cousin, the gods willing, is alive. Sir Cadwel said he was sending men to tend to the bodies."

"They are soldiers of Sorga," Ari said, moving with Larke to take up the body. Ari recognized him as a young man who was engaged to be married. He'd come to Sir Cadwel not five days ago, asking his lord's blessing on the union. He'd probably volunteered to escort Ispiria back so he could return to his fiancée sooner. "I will not leave them sprawled in their own blood. It will take but a moment."

He didn't lie, for he and Larke made quick work of carrying the bodies to the side of the trail. Mirimel relented enough to go behind Ari and Larke, straightening each body and folding stiffened arms across their chests. Ari saw her shudder as she reached for one man's arm, only to find it almost completely torn off.

97

When they were done, Ari returned to Stew to retrieve his pack, bringing Mirimel hers. "You lead," he said to her.

She nodded, settling her pack on her shoulders before strapping her bow over it.

"Larke, you go second," Ari said. "I'll act as rear guard." He turned to Stew. "I don't know how long we'll be gone," he said. Ari felt a little silly, knowing Mirimel was listening to him talk to Stew, but it couldn't be helped. Maybe Larke could make her forget it. "Try to keep an eye out for us and stay out of trouble. I'm sure you'd be very tasty to a pack of wolves."

Stew shook his mane. Ari wished he knew exactly how much his horse understood. It seemed to him Stew understood just about everything. Ignoring the look Mirimel gave him, he gestured for her to lead the way up the trail.

They climbed what must have once been a streambed. The way was, as Mirimel suggested, quite steep. Ari thought he could manage to climb it while carrying Ispiria, but only if he had her thrown over his shoulder. He didn't much care for that idea. He added it to his list of the Caller's offenses.

After a long climb, Mirimel led them away from the dry bed at an angle, making for easier going. Ari was glad he'd brought the hawk guardian along. He could only rarely see signs of passage, and none of them near enough to each other for him to have any hope of following the trail.

The day wore on and they wound about the mountain, their ever-tightening spirals bringing them closer to the peak. They continued in grim silence until, near dusk, Mirimel raised her hand to halt them. "I can't make out their path well enough any longer."

She sounded bitter, disappointed in herself. Ari wanted to reassure her, but he was afraid his voice would give away his own frustration, for he wished to press onward. He could see, but couldn't discern the trail. Mirimel could follow the trail, but her human eyes betrayed her. He glanced at Larke, hoping the bard might have a way for them to continue, but Larke shook his head.

"We need to rest," Larke said in answer to Ari's unspoken question. "Even you, lad."

"Can't you lead the way, Larke? You can still see," Ari said. He didn't care that Mirimel heard. Let Larke take the memory from her if he felt Ari had compromised the secret of the Aluiens. Now that it was dark, his mind was full of images of Ispiria huddled somewhere, alone and cold, surrounded by Empty One wolves. He couldn't let her spend another night as a prisoner. "Do you have any means by which to track him?"

"How can he still see?" Mirimel asked, her tone sharp.

"Lad," Larke said, giving Ari a pained look as he nodded toward Mirimel. "Tracking has never been a facility of mine, I'm afraid. If I lost our way, which I very well might do, we'd only have to waste time backtracking come morning."

"Can't you call the Lady?" Ari asked, anxiety over Ispiria's plight leading him to abandoning all caution.

Larke's eyes went wide. The bard glanced at Mirimel, his face twisted with worry and warning. "You are throwing away your vows in a moment of desperation. I thought better of you, Ari." Larke's voice was touched with anger.

Ari winced, rebuked. Larke was right. Even though the bard could erase Mirimel's memory of the conversation, it didn't mean that speaking in front of her wasn't breaking Ari's vow to keep the secret of the Aluiens, but he had to find Ispiria. "I'm sorry," he muttered, trying to squelch his frustration. "But you're going to remove any recollection of what we say from her mind anyhow, so what harm is there?"

"He's going to what?" Mirimel asked, her tone moving past sharp into angry. "Is that what you were trying to do with all those strange gestures and tones when you found us in the forest?"

Ari and Larke turned from each other to stare at her in surprise.

"You remember that?" Ari blurted.

Larke groaned and rubbed his hands over his face. "Why do I always get the difficult ones?"

"It's because she can hear the hawks, isn't it?" Ari said. "Mirimel really does have magic, like I do, or Siara. That's why your spells don't work on us, why you have to keep casting them over and over."

"Aye," Larke said, sighing in seeming resignation. "Guardian Mirimel is descended from the original Hawkers. Their line's bred true in her. She has some small amount of magic, and that allows her to sense the hawks."

"So I truly can?" Mirimel asked, astonishment lightening the anger in her tone. "I've never been sure it wasn't all in my mind. If I can hear hawks, what can Lord Aridian do?"

Larke looked at him and Ari flushed, the bard's courtesy sparking more guilt for how Ari had just gave away Aluien secrets. "I'm just a little--" He floundered, trying to think of a way to say it that didn't make him sound a braggart. "You know, faster, stronger. That sort of thing."

"And the lad heals more quickly too," Larke said, a touch of mischief flittering across his face. "And he can see in the dark. He's a veritable super-human."

"I think she gets the idea," Ari said before Larke could continue.

Silence settled around them. Ari could hear the wind sighing through the pines and rustling the budding branches of the thin mountain aspens. He felt his face heat under Mirimel's scrutinizing gaze.

"Well, if he can see in the dark, he can set up the tents," Mirimel said. "I can't see well enough to, now we've stood about talking."

"Oh, and he's less pervious to heat and cold," Larke said, his tone light and his face cast into a helpful look.

"Good," Mirimel said. "Next time we're safe enough, he can be in charge of the fire."

"That's a marvelous idea," Larke said, setting down his pack. "He's excellent at gathering firewood. Unless you send him out with a pretty girl. Then he dawdles."

"I'll keep that in mind."

"I'm glad you two find this entertaining," Ari said.

"What?" Larke's tone was biting now. "Am I giving away your secrets?"

Ari couldn't answer that with any dignity, so he set up Mirimel's small tent. He didn't bother setting up his own. It was mostly for show. If Mirimel already knew that Ari didn't need a tent to stay warm, he didn't see any reason to bother unpacking it. When he was done with her tent, she seated herself in front of it. Ari laid out his bedroll to her right, sitting down to glare at Larke across the small open space where the bard was setting out food. It was approximately where they would have put a fire, if the woods weren't almost certainly populated by Empty One wolves who wanted to kill them.

"Why can't you erase what we said from Mirimel's mind?" Ari asked, curiosity rousing him from his near pout. "Ferringul made Siara forget. Well, she didn't forget him, but she couldn't speak of him. He did the same to me. Are Empty Ones stronger than you are?"

The look Larke gave him was withering, reminding Ari of Sir Cadwel. Ari realized that just because Larke couldn't take memories from Mirimel didn't mean he should be telling her any more than she already knew, but Ari sort of liked the idea of having someone aside from Larke and Sir Cadwel to talk to about these things. He hated always keeping half of his life hidden.

"'Tis a question of style, lad," Larke said, composing himself. "It's not mine to risk your mind."

"What risk to our minds?" Mirimel said, her wariness returning.

Larke frowned at Ari. "This is on you," he said, before turning to Mirimel. "You must think of a thought, a memory, as a blot of ink, lass. It isn't a well-contained thing, but one that reaches out and touches other thoughts, mayhap even altering them in some way. I never take anything from you, as young Lord Aridian so crudely put it. I merely suppress things. To truly take something, tear it free, can do unknown and irreparable harm." His tone was touched with sorrow. "I'm

101

afraid the Empty Ones aren't as concerned with subtlety as I am. I daresay they lean more in favor of results."

"And that Empty One could be doing things to Ispiria's mind right now," Ari said, fighting the urge to rise and pace. They weren't on a real trail, so pacing would be nearly impossible. There was barely enough space among the trees for them and the tent.

Mirimel's face was thoughtful. "If you know so much, whoever you really are--"

Larke held out his hands before him, palms toward her as if he could push away the mistrust in her tone. "I am meself, lass. Larke the Minstrel who's played for the Hawkers often enough over the years."

"Larke the Minstrel who can hide memories from a person in the confines of their own mind and who knows all about whatever that is." She nodded toward Ari, her expression no less suspicious. Ari winced. "And who obviously has greater knowledge of our enemy than we do." She glared at Larke until he nodded. "Then, Larke the Minstrel, tell me, why does this Caller want the stone the hawks had? Why was one little white stone worth the burning of my village? The destruction of the grand aerie? My family's death?" She sucked in a ragged sob, swallowing, but her eyes didn't leave Larke's face.

Ari wasn't sure how much Mirimel could see in the darkness that had descended on the pinewoods, but a look of pain twisted Larke's handsome features. "I don't know," the bard said.

Mirimel opened her mouth. A few sputtering noises came out. Abruptly, she stood, turning from them to stomp away into the trees.

Ari sighed. He should have asked after her kin. He was only thinking of himself and Ispiria. He'd seen the village. He knew how few tents Sir Cadwel had set up for survivors. Again, an image of the twisted and burned corpses in the front yard of the home where he'd first found Mirimel came back to him. Who could that be if not her family?

"I'll follow her," Larke said. "It's too dangerous for her away from us. While I'm gone, perhaps you could meditate on the meaning of the word secret?"

Ari nodded, grimacing. Larke was correct to reprimand him. Shaking his head, Larke followed Mirimel into the forest. Ari was glad the bard had thought of going after her before he had. He'd no idea what to say.

She couldn't have gone far, for Ari could hear Larke's voice drifting back to him, even quiet as it was. He couldn't make out the words, but Larke's tone was soothing. If Mirimel said anything, Ari didn't hear. He stared at the food Larke had set out in the middle of their camp, wondering if he had the stomach to eat. He wished they dared build a fire. Not for warmth so much as company. Larke's voice grew more distinct and Mirimel's joined in. Ari realized they were returning.

"I know why I want to find more hawks," Mirimel said as they reseated themselves. Even though the sun had set, Ari could see wet lines down her cheeks. He wondered if she realized his sight was that good. Her voice as she spoke was even. "But why do you want to? I only know for certain of one who escaped."

"Because I must secure the stone before the Caller can locate it," Larke said.

"You think the hawks will show you where it is?" Mirimel asked.

"No." Larke smiled. "I think they will tell me."

Her face turned skeptical and she shook her head. "Well, the one Lord Aridian sent to Sorga was locked in the cellar with me. She won't know anything."

"One came to Sorga during the battle," Ari said, picking up the threads of the conversation. "He might know. If he lives."

Two pairs of eyes turned to him.

"One made it to Sorga?" Mirimel asked at the same time as Larke leaned forward, saying, "How badly wounded was he, lad?"

103

"The hawkmaster tended him. He looked pretty bad to me, but Master Rellus said he might live."

Larke looked almost as if he would stand.

Ari frowned. "We can go see the hawk as soon as Ispiria is safe."

"Yes," Larke said, settling back. "Of course, lad." The bard looked over his shoulder in the direction of Sorga, worry on his face.

"Hawkmaster Rellus has no extra abilities." Mirimel emphasized the word extra. "But he's very adept. If anyone could save the hawk, he could."

"Aye," Larke said, although Ari didn't know what part of the statement the bard was agreeing with. "I guess there's nothing for it but to press on. The sooner we rescue Ari's fair maiden, the sooner we'll arrive in Sorga." Larke picked up a small loaf of bread, tearing it into three pieces and handing them round. "To a valiant rescue," he said, raising the bread as if to toast.

Bemused, Ari did likewise.

With a reluctant grimace, Mirimel joined in.

Little more was discussed that night, save who would stand which watch, although Ari knew Larke needed no sleep and could take them all. The bard went first and, as Ari half-expected might happen, Larke let them sleep till morning.

Ari awoke to the sound of Mirimel and Larke talking. He stretched, yawning. A protruding tree root jabbed into his left shoulder.

"You should have woken us for our turns." Mirimel was standing in front of Larke, looking a bit cross.

Ari sat up, rubbing his shoulder.

"You needn't have stood watch all night on your own," Mirimel continued.

"But, lass, I wanted you and Lord Aridian to get your rest. The young are always in need of it."

"I suppose you don't even require sleep," Mirimel said.

"Not noticeably so." Larke shrugged. "Although I do enjoy it from time to time."

Ari's memories of his time among the Aluiens were vague. He always assumed that was the result of the poison-induced fever he'd been in, but after what Larke had said the night before, he worried it was something they'd done to him when they suppressed his memories. He hoped they hadn't broken anything inside his head. He could recall, though, that Aluiens didn't need to eat, drink, or sleep. The Orlenia flowing through their veins sustained them. Many chose to, though, out of habit or desire and, he supposed, comfort. He stood, stretching again, a bit stiff from sleeping on the ground.

"If I asked you what it is you are, exactly, would you tell me?" Mirimel glared at Larke as if she could pry the information out of him with her anger.

"I am the bard Larke," Larkesong said. "Minstrel renowned." He swept off his yellow-plumed hat in a low bow. "And if you search back through your mind, you'll recall that you've known me your whole life. I come yearly to the Hawkers' village to have words with the hawks and bring my fine entertainment skills to your isolated community."

"That isn't really an answer," she said.

From where he stood, Ari couldn't see Larke's face, but the bard put his hat back on, giving it a slight twist to display the puffy feather to its fullest. "'Tis so an answer," Larke said.

"Then, it isn't an answer to the question I asked."

"The answer to the question you asked, lass, is no."

Mirimel frowned. She glanced past Larke at Ari, but he only shrugged. He wasn't getting involved. If Mirimel wanted information from Larke, she would have to get it out of him. Ari just hoped it didn't make her too crabby. He knew from personal experience how difficult it was to get Larke to tell you something he didn't want you to know. Ari suspected it pained the bard to keep secrets from his friends, but Larke must abide by the rules of the Aluiens.

Mirimel turned her glare back to Larke, but before she could pursue the matter, there was a rustling sound in the woods. Ari put his hand on the hilt of his sword, ready to draw. Mirimel whirled, her bow and an arrow immediately at the ready. Larke cocked his head to one side, as if listening. He raised a staying hand.

The noise grew in volume, and Ari deciphered it as the sound of someone approaching, and making no effort to hide it. Still, it must be someone familiar with the forest, for sounds of their approach were soft and infrequent. A moment later, Kimmer appeared.

Surprised, Ari let his hand fall from the hilt of his sword. He squinted up through the trees, trying to get his bearing. She'd come from farther up the mountain, not from behind. Could she have come searching for them and passed them in the dark? Was something amiss back at the village?

Mirimel lowered her bow, returning the arrow to the quiver at her waist. "Kimmer," she said, her tone melding worry and surprise. "What are you doing here?"

"Has something happened?" Ari asked.

"Yes," Kimmer said, excitement in her voice. "We found Lady Ispiria, and the evil one, the one who commands the wolves, he's not there. He left. We have to hurry before he comes back."

Ari started forward immediately. He didn't care that he was supposed to return and get Sir Cadwel and more men. Ispiria was near and the Caller was not. He couldn't turn back and leave her now. He must seize this chance.

He realized Mirimel and Larke weren't with him and turned to see them packing up their meager camp. Frustration flashed through him, but he went back and bundled up his bedroll, tying it to his pack and hoisting the lot of it onto his shoulders. "Where is she?" he asked, turning back to Kimmer.

"They have her in a cave. I left Peine to watch, in case the evil one comes back. We have to hurry." She didn't approach, waiting where she'd emerged from the trees.

Ari stared at her in astonishment. He almost asked her to repeat herself. Peine was somewhere in the woods?

"You can get into the cave from a small ledge near the peak, but there are wolves guarding her," Kimmer said. "Come on."

Ari frowned. He didn't like the idea of Peine alone near the Caller. He glanced at Larke. The bard shrugged and started forward, settling his pack on his shoulders. Ari followed a half-step behind.

Mirimel hurried to Kimmer, stopping in front of her. "What are you doing here?" she repeated in a low tone that did nothing to hide her displeasure. "And why did you bring Lord Aridian's valet?"

"I had to bring him," Kimmer said. "He caught me listening behind Sir Cadwel's tent." Her tone was defiant, but her face turned bright red as she spoke.

"Listening?" Mirimel shook her head. "Kimmer, that is not acceptable."

"Come down from your high and mighty perch, Mirimel," Kimmer said, turning away to push through a few low reaching pine boughs. "Just because Peine and I are a couple of years younger than you and Lord Aridian doesn't mean we can't help. We found her, after all, while you three were sitting around talking."

Ari scowled. Kimmer was right. They were sitting around talking. He should have kept looking last night. He didn't know why he'd let himself be persuaded to stop. Now Ispiria had spent another night alone in a cave with wolves.

With Kimmer in the lead, they pressed forward at a northern slant, abandoning the tracks they'd followed the day before. No one spoke. Ari didn't know if the others felt as grim as he did, but the combination of fear for Ispiria and tension over Kimmer's and Peine's behavior made talking impossible. Plus, the farther they traveled up the peak, the more pressing their need for stealth became. Ari wasn't sure how far they had to go, but the increasing steepness of their route made him think they must be near their goal.

Kimmer held up a hand and they halted. She pointed, and Ari could make out Peine crouched among the pine trees ahead, his back to them. His hair was disarranged and flecked with pine needles and brittle bits of leaves. Ari still couldn't believe Peine was there.

They started forward again, moving as quietly as possible. Peine turned to look at them. His face was pale, where it wasn't dirty. There were dark rings beneath his eyes. He looked fairly miserable. The eyes he raised to Ari's face were worried, almost fearful.

As well they should be, Ari thought. Peine was certainly here without Sir Cadwel's knowledge or permission. He'd snuck out of camp and he was shirking not only his duties, but his punishment. Ari frowned, trying to set aside his anger. He would talk to Peine about his behavior later. There wasn't any real discipline Ari could deal out now, and they had more important things to worry about than Peine's increasing rebelliousness.

Peine gave Ari an apologetic grimace before turning back to peer through the trees. They drew alongside him and, following Kimmer's lead, crouched down. The boughs of the pine trees grew low, forming a verdant wall, and Ari realized there must be an open space on the other side. He reached out and carefully pushed down on a branch, giving himself just enough room to peek through.

Beyond the pines was a gently sloped clearing. Early blooming wildflowers stood out as bright dots of color in the spring sunlight. Across the glade, north of them, a sheer cliff face rose. Squinting upward, Ari could see the jagged peak of the mountain, looking hewn off by the cliff. About halfway up the face was a ledge where two massive gray wolves lounged outside the narrow mouth of a cave. It was barely more than a man-height crack in the side of the mountain. If Ispiria was in there, Ari hoped it widened out somewhere.

He let the branch slide back into place and wended his way a few paces deeper into the forest, gesturing for the others to follow. When he halted, they gathered around him, their faces serious.

"You know for certain she's in there?" Ari asked in a low voice.

Kimmer looked to Peine, who nodded. "She crept to the mouth of the cave earlier. One of the wolves growled and she ran back in."

Ari didn't realize he was clutching the hilt of his sword until Peine's eyes flickered toward his hand, then back to his face. Taking a deep breath, Ari forced his muscles to relax.

"She looked well," Peine said. "I mean, scared, but she didn't look hurt."

Ari nodded. "And those are the only two wolves you saw? What of their master?"

"We saw the man earlier," Kimmer said. "He went into the cave, but he only stayed a moment. She came out after he left. As for wolves, I think those two are different from the two who were there earlier?" She looked at Peine.

"They are, but the other two aren't inside," he said. "A little while ago, those two came out of the cave and the two who were guarding left. I don't know where they went, but they didn't come close to me." He shuddered slightly.

"And we don't know how far back the cave goes or how many might be in there?" Ari asked.

Peine and Kimmer shook their heads.

Ari gazed down into the maze of fallen needles at his feet, trying to formulate a plan.

"I could go in, lad," Larke said. "It may be I can draw them out, and should I sustain some small hurts, well, I'll heal soon enough."

"Absolutely not," Ari said. Larke might be an Aluien, but he wasn't invincible. A fatal wound to an Aluien was still fatal, and Larke wasn't much of a fighter. "If anyone's going inside that cave, it's me."

Mirimel opened her mouth to speak, but Ari held up his hand.

"I'm not just charging in there. Hear me out. Mirimel and Kimmer, you will shoot the two on the ledge. Larke, you stay with them. If more come out, or those two come down, the three of you lead them away. Don't fight them, just run."

He held each of their eyes in turn until they nodded.

109

"Yes, my lord," Kimmer said.

Mirimel raised an eyebrow at that, but didn't speak.

"Peine, you'll come with me up the mountain. Once we're in place above the cave, we'll signal for the shooting to begin. When we're sure as many wolves as possible have gone after them, I'm going in."

Peine nodded.

"You stay above the cave. If any more trouble shows up, come in and tell me. Don't yell, and don't stay outside. I don't want you facing whatever it is alone." What Ari really wanted to do was to tell Peine to hide if more wolves or the Caller came, but he didn't want to belittle him by saying it.

"I'm not totally incapable, Ari," Peine said, darting an embarrassed glance Kimmer's way.

"You don't even wear a sword," Ari said. He didn't mean to make his friend look bad in front of a girl, but this was serious. This was life and death. At least Peine's interest in Kimmer explained why he'd followed her out into the woods.

"Here," Kimmer said, pulling out her hunting knife and offering it to Peine with an almost shy smile. "In case you need it."

"Thank you." Peine took it awkwardly and tucked it under his belt.

Ari was glad Peine hadn't accidentally cut through his belt and drop his pants. He wished Kimmer hadn't given over the knife. Ari was sure Peine would only hurt himself with it, but he wouldn't humiliate Peine further by telling him to give it back. "Are we all clear on the plan?" There was a low chorus of affirmation. "Let's leave our packs here." Ari dropped his to the ground. The others followed suit. Taking a deep breath, he turned back toward the cave.

Chapter 9

Crouching low, Ari led Peine through the trees, skirting the clearing at the base of the cliff. The two wolves on the ledge looked as if they were asleep, but Ari didn't trust that. He didn't dare cross to the cliff in the open, or climb the front side.

Time stretched out before him under the heavy pine boughs. He knew he and Peine were moving, but it seemed to take them hours to reach the side of the peak where it angled sharply up out of the trees. By the time they got there, Ari's nerves were taut as lute strings, though in truth, their passage was nearly as silent and swift as Ari could have hoped.

Ari was impressed with how much better Peine was getting at sneaking in the woods, and wondered if Kimmer had been teaching him. In a castle, Peine had no trouble sneaking. In fact, lately it was rare to find Peine in his room at night. In the past few months, since about the time of his fourteenth birthday, Peine had found the young ladies of the castle noticeably more interesting. When Ari had gently reprimanded him about his nocturnal stealth, Peine said all he and whichever lady he was with were doing was talking.

Ari paused at the base of the cliff, peering up. Scanning it, he could see the trail they must take. He was fairly confident Peine could make it. Were he alone, Ari might have chosen a more direct route, but Peine's presence deprived him of that option. Ari subdued his annoyance by reminding himself that he might not even know where Ispiria was if not for Peine and Kimmer.

Taking a deep breath and squaring his shoulders, Ari started up the cliff face, Peine a short distance behind. They climbed at an angle designed to take them around to a large rock Ari had noted earlier. It was to the north of and slightly above the cave. Ari hoped it would shelter them from the wolves' sight as they drew near.

The climb, like the walk, seemed to stretch interminably, focused as Ari was on the idea of Ispiria alone and afraid somewhere inside the mountain. Yet, when he finally reached the protruding rock and looked up at the sun, little time had passed. He couldn't see Mirimel, Kimmer or Larke from where he and Peine crouched behind the rock, clinging to the side of the mountain on a small ledge, but he knew they watched. Reaching above the edge of the rock, Ari waved.

No sooner did he lift his hand than two arrows flew through the sky. Ari jumped to the top of the rock so he could see the wolves. One arrow embedded itself deep in a wolf's eye. The creature fell dead even as it strained to stand. The other arrow, Ari assumed Kimmer's, shattered on the rock above the second wolf's head.

Ari jumped down onto the ledge in front of the cave, ready to kill the beast before it could sound an alarm, but when it opened its mouth to howl, a third arrow buried itself in its throat. The howl came out a gurgling murmur, even as Ari's sword was in his hand and descending. His blade cleaved through the creature's neck. Its head made dull thunking sounds as it bounced down the side of the cliff.

Ari looked back at Peine, who peeked over the rock with wide eyes. Ari nodded, indicating he was going into the cave. Below, he glimpsed Kimmer and Mirimel coming forward, bows at the ready, Larke a tall streak of yellow and blue behind them. Ari considered waiting for them to climb up. They hadn't planned to, but he'd thought they would be chased. It hadn't occurred to him that Mirimel would be able to slay both wolves so quickly. Ari smiled in grim admiration of her skills and ducked into the narrow cave. Let them follow if they would. He couldn't leave Ispiria there a moment longer.

Half crouching, his sword held before him, Ari crept into the darkness. Of his companions, only Larke would be able to see inside the cave without a torch. Ari was glad he didn't need one, for it would blind him to what lay ahead and give warning to those inside. He wrinkled his nose. The cave smelled like a neglected kennel. The walls about him were jagged. At one point, he had to turn sideways and squeeze through, leaving fabric from his doublet along with the clumps of wolf fur already claimed by the rough stone.

Sword before him, Ari crept farther down the tunnel. Color returned to his surroundings as his enhanced vision gave way to more normal sight. He realized a faint flickering glow came from ahead. The sharp tang of blood assailed him. His breath grew harsh. He hurried forward, abandoning stealth. Where was Ispiria?

Rounding a turn in the tunnel, he saw her. She sat on the rough stone floor in what looked like a small cavern, her legs pulled up tight against her. In front of her was a sputtering fire, the rent carcass of a deer sprawled before it.

Ari realized some of the bite marks were fresh, his mind struggling to take in details even as he longed to run toward her. She looked up, her bloodshot green eyes going wide.

She mouthed watch out, darting her eyes almost imperceptibly to his left.

Ari turned in the direction she looked as a massive form hurtled forward from somewhere just out of sight. With

113

nowhere to go in the narrow tunnel, he wrenched his sword up, bracing his palm against the flat of the blade so he could hold it across his body. He caught the giant claws of the wolf, but its snapping maw came on. Ari pushed, trying to throw it backward so its teeth couldn't reach his face. For a moment, they were suspended, its paws on his sword, its giant yellow fangs a finger-width from his eyes. Ispiria screamed.

Ari clenched his teeth. Bracing his feet on the uneven rock floor, he gave a massive heave, throwing the wolf backward. It didn't topple, instead twisting to the side to land facing him. Ari leapt after it, into the cavern. The space was larger than he'd hoped, giving him room to circle, allowing him the desperate luxury of swinging his sword.

A quick glance showed the cave to be blissfully empty of all but his assailant, Ispiria, and the dead deer. Ari thanked whatever gods dwelled in the mountains of Sorga that the cavern wasn't full of wolves.

The wolf circled toward Ispiria, but she scrambled along the wall until she was behind Ari. His sword wove before them in low arcs, daring the beast to attack. He lunged at it, not expecting to land a hit. It dodged away, farther from the cavern entrance.

"Once you can get to the tunnel, run," Ari said. He didn't look over his shoulder at her. He didn't dare take his eyes off the wolf.

"I'm not going without you."

Ari heard fear in her voice, but also resolve. Desperate to get her out of the cave in case he should fall, he tried a different tactic. "Mirimel and Larke are out there. You have to get them, tell them to come help."

The wolf lunged. Ignoring Ispiria's startled squeak, Ari swung, slamming his sword into the wolf's maw. It twisted away, avoiding the worst of the blow. A puckered line of open flesh appeared across its snout, made all the more gruesome by the lack of blood.

With a snarl, the wolf came at him again. Ari hammered it back. He knew it didn't feel pain the way a normal wolf would.

114

Nor would it tire. He would have to keep fighting until it was dead. He did his best, as he parried, to press it farther back in the cave. He knew he needed to get away from the dead deer and the fire before he tripped over them, and to open the way for Ispiria to escape.

"It'll be dark," he said, "but just keep going. Now."

Ari launched into a rapid series of attacks, pinning the wolf against the back wall. It may not know the pain a mortal animal would, but it seemed smart enough to know that it couldn't fight Ari as well if he cut off half its jaw. With that as his goal, he rained blows down on it. The wolf snarled, dodging away from his attacks. Ari heard Ispiria scurry down the tunnel behind him.

With a tooth-shattering snap, the wolf closed its jaws on the flat of Ari's blade. He pulled, trying to wrench his sword free. The wolf shook its head, almost dislodging the hilt from Ari's hand, or his shoulder from its socket, whichever gave out first. Ari tried pivoting the blade to snap open the wolf's jaws, but the beast clamped down even tighter. With a hissing sound, Ari pulled air through his teeth, forcing down the shadow of panic he felt building in him. If the wolf managed to disarm him, he wouldn't stand long against it.

Over their strange tug of war, it met Ari's gaze. He saw a deadly intelligence there. Not the mind of a man, full of arithmetic and literature, but a creature whose whole being was devoted to the art of the kill. This wolf gave a fierce yank, pulling Ari from his feet as he determinedly held onto the hilt of his sword.

Ari threw himself sideways as he fell, using his momentum to rotate the sword in the wolf's mouth. Now, though it still held the flat of his blade locked between its teeth, it no longer held it from the side. Rather, the point of Ari's sword was aimed directly down the wolf's throat.

Before the creature could realize the change, or capitalize on Ari's semi-prone position, he surged to his feet. With an inarticulate yell, he lunged toward the wolf. Both hands on the hilt of his sword, Ari shoved the blade through the back of its

115

mouth, splitting cartilage and bone. It tried to pull back, but met only unyielding rock behind it. Ari heaved, driving his sword into the wolf's brain.

As surprise cut through the curdling look of hatred in the wolf's eyes, their light faded. Its body began to shrink in on itself as it fell, its exceedingly accelerated decay revealing it to be a much older wolf than the two Mirimel had killed outside. The way it fell from Ari's sword, a rancid cloud of dust puffing up from it, made him think it had been long on this earth.

Too long, and now it was well gone. Ari stepped back, looking around for something on which to wipe his sword before he realized that all traces of flesh left on it had already shriveled away. He sheathed it, noting as he did so that the wolf's teeth had left deep dents in the dully-shining metal.

A quick glance told him there wasn't anything else in the cave, and no reason to attempt to put out the small fire. Nothing there would burn once the twigs fueling it were gone. The deer carcass would rot, but then it too would fade. Turning, Ari hurried down the tunnel. He was assailed by the sudden fear that the Caller might return, or more wolves. He had to find Ispiria.

He needn't have worried, for as he emerged, he found her and the others just about to enter. Ispiria dropped the makeshift torch she was holding and flung herself into his arms. She smelled like wolves and dirt and there was blood splattered across her green gown. Ari didn't care. He wrapped his arms around her, burying his face in her hair.

Nothing in his life had ever been as important as finding Ispiria alive. He drew in a shuddering breath. For the first time, he resented his Aluien-given gift of strength. He desperately wanted to squeeze her to him, to release all his fears in their embrace, but he knew he would hurt her. Instead, he clenched his muscles tight, his body straining against itself. Hearing the others move, he raised his head.

They'd lit a fire. He realized it would have taken Ispiria some time to make her way out of the cave in the total darkness, something they obviously planned to remedy.

Kimmer and Peine each held a torch, although Kimmer was even now tossing hers into the flames, Peine watching her. Mirimel had turned away, leaving only her profile visible to Ari. He saw her reach up with two quick swipes, drawing her sleeve across her face, and realized she was crying.

"We won't be needing this fire after all," Larke said into the silence. "Peine, be a good lad and help me put it out."

Peine, Kimmer and Larke began scattering the fire on the rock ledge, stomping out the coals. Mirimel carefully returned her bow to her back and crossed to Ari, gently touching Ispiria on the shoulder.

"Ispiria," Mirimel said, her voice soft. "Mother and Father are gone."

Ispiria turned and Ari forced his arms to open so the two could embrace. Ispiria clung to her cousin, dissolving into tears, and Ari saw anew the anguish on her face when she'd found her ancestral village burning. He swallowed, wishing there was something he could do, anything, to bring back all those people. If Mirimel was Ispiria's cousin, and Mirimel's family was dead, what did that leave either of them? Mirimel hugged Ispiria to her, but her face was composed now, a hard mask in place over her sorrow. She stroked Ispiria's hair.

"We should go." Ari's voice came out harsher than he wanted, and he cleared his throat. He looked around at all the sheltering trees and up at the sun, now past its zenith. "We aren't safe here."

Mirimel nodded. She stepped back from Ispiria, but reached out and smoothed her red curls back from her face.

"Where to, lad?" Larke asked. Everyone turned to look at Ari.

"Sorga," he said, after a moment's thought. He was sure Sir Cadwel had everything under control in the village. He didn't want to take Ispiria there to confront the ruin again, and the Caller was still about, somewhere. Ari wanted Ispiria safe in the castle. Even if much of Sorga's forces were in the village, it was still an unwalled semicircle of tents, not a castle built into

117

the embrace of the mountain. Ari would send Sir Cadwel a message letting him know that Ispiria was safe.

"Then Sorga it is," Larke said, leading the way back down the cliff face.

Chapter 10

It took them much less time to return to the mountain trail than it had to wend their way up the day before, but the sun was still too low for Ari's liking by the time they emerged from the trees onto the path. Stew and Larke's gray stood waiting for them, one on each side of a bedraggled looking Charger. The men Sir Cadwel had sent after them had removed the bodies, but there were still dark stains on the stone where they once lay. Ari tried to steer Ispiria away from them, waving Stew over.

Ari was a bit annoyed with Peine for leaving Charger on the trail unattended, but he felt he couldn't say anything because he and Larke had left their mounts. Of course, Stew and Larke's gray were capable of caring for themselves, whereas Charger was not, but Ari couldn't admit that to Peine. He'd already been reckless enough with secrets the night before.

"Thank you for waiting," Ari murmured to Stew before mounting. Reaching down, he pulled Ispiria up behind him. Peine and Kimmer followed suit with Charger, who looked tired and scared. Mirimel stood in the middle of the trail, seeming a trifle unsure. Ari frowned. They didn't have time for reluctance. They needed to get out of the mountains before dark or they'd have to dismount and lead their horses to be safe, slowing their pace to a crawl.

Larke crossed to Mirimel, issuing a low whistle to call his horse over. Ignoring the look of reluctance on her face, Larke picked the orange-haired hawk guardian up and put her on his horse. She pressed her lips together, thin lines of anger creasing the skin around her eyes.

Ari didn't care if or why Mirimel found it uncomfortable to ride with Larke. Getting Ispiria to safety as quickly as possible was more important than Mirimel's sensibilities. He turned Stew down the path, trusting Larke to act as rear guard. Ari's every sense was on alert. He expected the Caller to appear at any moment to reclaim Ispiria.

Setting as fast a pace as he dared, for the trail was steep and all three horses overburdened, Ari led them toward Sorga. The sun was a blinding ball of orange to their right when they finally spilled out onto the plain. Ari urged Stew into a canter, not caring if the others could keep up. He had Ispiria almost home.

The guards must have spotted them, for the outer gate started to swing open as they approached. Ari was glad to see they had it closed, and that the number of men on the wall was double what it normally would be, but he also felt a twinge of sorrow. He'd hoped never to see the day when the massive outer gates of Sorga were braced shut against the possibility of assault.

Ari saw one of the armsmen atop the wall waving a signal flag and knew that the second set of gates would be opening too, and that Sorga's master steward, Natan, would be waiting for them on the castle steps. He slowed Stew once they passed beneath the massive outer arch, allowing the others to catch up while they crossed the killing zone between the two gates. Ari wondered at the eight pyres, four on each side, before he realized they were for the men who'd been guarding Ispiria. He turned his gaze ahead, to the opening inner gate. He wished there was some way he could have kept Ispiria from seeing the funeral preparations.

True to Ari's prediction, Natan strode down the steps as their small group passed under the inner portico, castle folk spilling out behind him. "Ispiria," Natan cried. Cheers erupted from the crowd.

Stew stopped before the steps and Ari handed Ispiria down. She was crying again and it was all he could do to force himself to let go of her. Natan clasped her close, looking for a moment worn and old, showing his nearly sixty years as he never had before. Ispiria's ladies swarmed around her, taking her from Natan and herding her up the steps. Castle folk called her name, reaching out to her as she passed.

At the top of the steps, Ispiria's great grandmother, Lady Enra, emerged from the keep. Her nearly sightless eyes rested on Ispiria for a moment before lifting to look at Ari. Anger sparked in them and Ari blinked in surprised. He'd just saved Ispiria from the Caller. Why did Lady Enra look so angry with him? He recalled her absence at their departure. Had she not wanted Ispiria to go to the Hawkers' village? Didn't Ispiria go every year?

A groom approached and Ari slid from his horse. "See they get a good brushing," he said to the boy. "Take special care with Peine's Charger. He's had a rough time of it."

The groom nodded and led Stew away.

Ari was of half a mind to make Peine care for Charger himself, but he was worried Peine would be in too much of a hurry to do a good job. And, Ari admitted, he really didn't want to give Peine orders or deal out punishment. Especially not there, in the middle of the courtyard, in front of everyone.

Looking up the steps, he caught a glimpse of Ispiria's red curls before she disappeared into the keep in a sea of weeping ladies. Ari sighed. He probably wouldn't get to see her again until sometime tomorrow.

"I'm perfectly capable of dismounting unaided." Mirimel's voice was cold.

121

Ari turned to see Larke lower the hand he was offering her. The bard blinked, looking a little hurt. Maybe Mirimel was angry with Larke for not answering her questions, or for not waking her to guard, or maybe she'd decided she didn't like uncanny minstrels. Ari hoped the hawk guardian's animosity wouldn't grow into a problem.

"I see that bard who followed you and Cadwel about all autumn has turned up again," Natan said, coming to stand at Ari's side. "There's something peculiar about that one."

"That's what Sir Cadwel always says," Ari said. "The study?" he asked, for that was where they normally adjourned to when they needed to discuss their journeys and the business of the keep. Of course, it was Sir Cadwel's study and in the past, the knight was always there to lead any such discussions, but Ari didn't have a study of his own for them to use.

"I'll order some refreshments," Natan said, nodding. He turned and trotted back up the steps, returned to his usual vigorous self.

The others were all dismounted now and watching Ari, their horses being escorted to the stable. Waving that they should follow him, Ari headed inside. He nodded to the ragtag collection of castle folk lingering curiously on the steps, but didn't pause, not wanting to get involved in any questions.

He realized the people of Sorga would need a report. The men Sir Cadwel had sent to bring the bodies of Ispiria's escort back would have arrived yesterday with news of her capture. While it was obvious everyone was relieved to see her safely returned, they would want to know more detail about what had happened. Usually, Sir Cadwel delivered any important news when they all assembled for dinner. With Sir Cadwel in the Hawkers' village, Natan must be the one who did it.

Ari led the way across the stone foyer. The heavy wooden door to Sir Cadwel's study stood open, his great shaggy hounds, Canid and Raven, barely looking up from where they sprawled before the fireplace. All the two old dogs did anymore was soak up heat and sleep. Ari knew the kennel master was grooming up a new pair, but he didn't like to think on that. Sir

Cadwel loved the two old hounds. Natan once told Ari that before Ari's arrival drew him from his depression, there were weeks that went by when Sir Cadwel spoke to no one but them. Ari seated himself on one of the green leather couches. Peine, Larke, Mirimel and Kimmer followed his example, no one making a move to sit in Sir Cadwel's armchair by the fire. A book lay open on the seat, revealing detailed drawings of catapults mounted on great sailing ships. Ari had never thought about war at sea before. The books looked interesting.

"Here we are," Natan said, entering. He set a tray on the low table between the sofas, turning back to close the door. Sitting down with Larke and Ari, Natan poured himself a drink.

Ari considered mentioning food, but discarded the idea. There would be time for food soon enough.

"May I?" Larke asked, reaching for the small decanter of liquor on the tray.

"Be my guest," Natan said. "I'd serve you all, of course, if it didn't violate my basic tenet that I don't actually serve anyone." Natan leaned back in his seat, putting his feet up on the table, near the tray. Neither Ari nor any of the three across from them made a move toward the drink.

No one spoke. Ari cleared his throat. "What's been happening here?" he asked, feeling they had to start somewhere.

"A score of guardsmen came in yesterday with the bodies of Lady Ispiria's escort," Natan said. "I've organized the funerals for tomorrow. It took a little time to gather enough wood and build the pyres, but now that they're ready, there's no sense in delaying it. None of their families requested the burial service favored by worshipers of the Overgod, so we don't have to send for a priest. Funerals are best quickly done with."

Ari nodded, not having anything to say to that.

"As you can guess, they gave us the news of Lady Ispiria's capture and that Lady Civul is distraught, but well enough. The next time a large group returns from the village, they intend to bring Civul. Cadwel didn't want her riding with the bodies."

Ari was glad Ispiria's ladies had taken her away. He glanced at Mirimel, her face composed, and Kimmer, whose eyes were wide and a little scared. Maybe he should have sent them with Ispiria.

"We've sent Cadwel all of the supplies he requested, or sent riders to requisition what we don't have or can't make ourselves," Natan continued. "There hasn't been any sign here of whatever it was that attacked the Hawkers' village. I daresay the villains are holed up in the mountains somewhere. That's about all." He leaned forward, setting his empty glass down on the tray, his typical charming smile turning up the corners of his mouth. "Now, tell me who these lovely ladies in green are?" He turned his gaze on Mirimel. "Surely, you must be Lady Ispiria's kin?"

"Forgive me," Ari said, fighting not to blush. Natan had given him ample time to properly introduce Mirimel and Kimmer. Ari shot Peine a look. Peine was supposed to keep Ari from making these sorts of mistakes. Peine wasn't looking at Ari, though, his abstract gaze on the wall somewhere behind Larke's head. "That is Hawk Guardian Mirimel, Ispiria's cousin," he said.

Mirimel nodded, her expression unreadable.

"And that Hawk Guardian Kimmer." Ari gestured to the steward. "This is Master Steward Natan."

"Pleased to meet you," Natan said, holding each of their gazes in turn. Kimmer blushed.

Ari was a bit taken aback. He knew Natan's reputation, and knew the former lord and knight had been stripped of his titles for overly voracious fraternizing, but surely Natan had learned his lesson all those years ago? Besides, Mirimel and Kimmer were young enough to be his granddaughters.

Larke started whistling a tune, one Ari recognized as a somewhat inappropriate tavern song, and Natan dropped his gaze, pouring himself another drink before settling back into his seat.

"Does Cadwel know you've rescued his grandniece?" Natan asked, ending the somewhat awkward silence.

"No," Ari said. He hoped Sir Cadwel wouldn't be angry he hadn't kept to the plan they'd made. "We came straight here. Sorga was nearer." He didn't add that he also didn't want to take Ispiria back to the village, not wanting to remind Mirimel and Kimmer that their home was burned. It occurred to him that Kimmer must have found her kin among the few survivors, for she didn't seem too distraught. "We should send him a hawk at first light."

"We can't," Natan said.

"Why not?" Mirimel asked, her tone betraying concern.

"Surely the hawks here are unharmed?" Larke asked, standing.

"Sorry." Natan grimaced. "I didn't mean to spread panic. Do sit down. You're like a giant yellow and blue stork looming over me. They're fine."

Larke sat.

"Cadwel ordered us not to use them. He's worried whoever attacked the village might be on the lookout for them, ready to shoot them down. The hawk you sent made it, though. She's been laying eggs, by the way, if anyone's interested."

"She has?" Mirimel leaned forward in her seat.

"What hawk you sent?" Kimmer asked, her eyes narrowing.

"The one who hadn't clutched yet," Mirimel said. "I had her with me. Lord Aridian sent her to the keep after he found us."

"I didn't realize that," Kimmer said. "That's good news. What of the one who was injured? The one who came here to seek Lord Aridian?"

"The hawkmaster reported he's recovering," Natan said.

"How can we get word to Sir Cadwel that Ispiria's well?" Ari asked. He didn't like to think of Sir Cadwel not knowing Ispiria was safe for any longer than necessary.

"We're under orders to send no fewer than twenty men at a time into the mountain pass," Natan said.

Ari nodded confirmation.

"We'll have to ask for volunteers this evening," Natan continued. "They can leave in the morning. I don't know who'll be willing to go, what with the funerals to take place, but we'll find some few who wish to bear happy news for a change."

"Ari, I be needing to see that hawk, lad," Larke said.

"It'll have to wait till after supper, I'm afraid," Natan said, standing. "Now it's time for Lord Aridian to appear before his vassals and assure them that he shares their grief and that all will soon be well again in Sorga."

"Me?" Ari looked up in surprise. "Don't you make the evening announcements when Sir Cadwel is away?"

"I make them while you and Cadwel are away," Natan said. "You outrank me, boy."

"I don't mind if you do it." Ari glanced over to Peine, expecting his valet to have something to say about his duties as a lord, but he was still strangely silent.

"Definitely not," Natan said. "I'm not ending up with another duke who places all the tedium of running Sorga on me. Fulfill your duty, Lord Aridian. Reassure your people."

Ari sighed, standing. Natan was right, of course. That meant Ari would have to eat at the head table. He'd never eaten at the head table without Sir Cadwel there. He hoped no one would suggest he sit in Sir Cadwel's chair. The others stood too. Mirimel and Kimmer looked around, obviously not knowing where to go.

"You'd best hurry and change," Natan said. "I had water sent up to your suite as soon as we saw you coming. I'll send extra up for you," he added, turning to Larke. "As I recall, you're Lord Aridian's personal minstrel and prefer to stay in his suite, which saves me the trouble of ordering a room made up."

Larke nodded.

"What about us?" Mirimel asked.

"I'll show you to a room near Lady Ispiria's," Natan said. "If you'll follow me?"

Natan led the hawk guardians away, Peine trailing after. Ari would have gone too, but Larke caught his arm.

"I must see that hawk, Ari, the one who came in hurt," the bard said, his voice low.

Kimmer paused in the doorway, Peine halting behind her. "I'd like to see the hawks too," she said. "It's so good to know at least some escaped."

"Of course, lass," Larke said.

"Kimmer," Mirimel called from some somewhere out of sight.

Kimmer gave them a smile and hurried out. Peine stood in the doorway for a moment, looking between Larke and Ari. Before Ari could tell him to go on ahead, Peine turned away. The sound of his footsteps dwindled as he headed across the foyer. Ari turned back to Larke.

"I'll make the announcements at dinner and then we'll go," Ari said. As if in protest, his stomach let out a loud rumble. He hadn't eaten since the night before, when Larke had insisted on serving dinner.

Larke sighed. "Your gut is right, lad," he said, looking resigned. "The hawk is well enough, from the sound of it, and isn't going anywhere. Best we eat and I play and we make the noble people of Sorga forget some of their worries and sorrows. Then we can see the hawk. It wouldn't do for you to go running off during dinner. Not in troubled times."

Ari nodded and the two of them headed from the room. Troubled times, Ari thought. Under Sir Cadwel's direction, he'd been reading books of history. It was never good to live in troubled times.

Chapter 11

Dinner was even more awkward than Ari had anticipated. Natan did insist Ari sit in Sir Cadwel's chair. Ari felt extremely out of place standing in front of it making announcements, although Natan's whispered prompts helped. That part over, Ari expected the rest of the meal to go as normal, but to his annoyance, Peine didn't sit beside him as usual. It took Ari a moment of looking around, but he finally spotted Peine at a table with Kimmer and Mirimel.

Ari would have had them up at the head table with him, but he hadn't thought to ask and didn't want to do so in front of everyone. What would he do, walk over and ask, or send Natan? Either way, it would seem like an order and it would be awkward. Ari thought Peine could have warned him, though, while they were getting ready, but Peine had been uncharacteristically silent and had looked lost in thought.

Watching him now, sitting beside Kimmer, Ari worried that Peine was in love again. He'd been in love for a few days earlier that spring, and it had been awful. All Peine did was sit around, staring into space and sighing. Then, just about the time Ari had thought he might have to give up and say something, Peine had apparently fallen back out of love. Ari wouldn't really mind Peine's infatuation with Kimmer, except the timing was atrocious. The Caller was out there somewhere and Ari needed his friend helping him do whatever it was he was supposed to be doing as duke while Sir Cadwel was away. Peine was useless when he was in love.

Sitting there listening to Natan and Larke chat about people and places he'd never heard of, Ari could see why Sir Cadwel had insisted Ispiria stay in the keep. Dinner was much nicer when she was there. Normally, Ispiria sat next to Ari and Peine every night, with her great grandmother at the end of the table, but tonight neither of them appeared.

Raven and Canid had, however, flopping down under the table at Ari's feet. Just as Sir Cadwel did, Ari snuck them a few scraps. At least the shaggy gray hounds hadn't abandoned him.

At first, dinner was tense and silent. Ari couldn't help but look about at the half-empty room. He recalled what Sir Cadwel had said in the village. They'd lost men already, who were searching in small groups. Ari was ashamed to realize he hadn't asked how many or who, and he couldn't tell. Not with so many missing because they were off in the Hawkers' village or standing a doubled lookout on the walls of the keep.

As everyone ate, or half-heartedly pushed food around on their plates, Larke got up and began to play, walking seemingly at random throughout the room, weaving between tables. His songs were at first melancholy, matching the mood, but slowly lightened. The bard didn't rise to the level of full out frivolity, but he did move into happier songs, seeming to pull the mood of the room up with him. He then turned to a ballad of victory and honor, bringing back their sorrows. This time, though, sorrow was tinged with purpose and hope, no longer the despairing malaise of earlier.

With the keep in this improved mood, Ari left the dining hall. Having already noted that the hawkmaster wasn't there, he headed up the inner steps to the common wing. Halfway up, he became aware of shuffling sounds behind him. Someone was following, perhaps even two people. They treaded softly, but Ari could hear.

He turned a corner, stopping on the landing. The steps behind him continued. As they neared the top, Ari jumped out, grabbing for his pursuer.

In a flash of orange hair and green leather, Mirimel stumbled backward, one hand grasping for the wall, the other for her hunting knife. Ari reached out, trying to catch her before she could tumble down the stone steps, but he missed. Fortunately, Larke was behind her. His long-fingered hands clamped down on her shoulders, steadying her.

"Are you trying to kill me?" Mirimel asked, her voice low with anger. She jammed her knife, half drawn, back into its sheath. With a shake, she dislodged Larke's hands.

"I didn't know it was you," Ari said. "I'm sorry. I heard someone sneaking and . . ." He shrugged, letting his voice trail off. What was he thinking? He was in his own keep, in Sorga. He drew in a deep breath, fighting against his taut nerves.

"Sneaking?" Larke said, his insulted tone at odds with the amusement dancing in his eyes. "Me lad, were I sneaking, you would know it. Or rather, you wouldn't."

"I agree," Mirimel said. She gave Ari a forced-looking smile. "You're being a bit insulting. That was not sneaking."

"Where are Peine and Kimmer?" Ari asked, looking past them down the steps.

"Please, lad." Larke shook his head. "I don't need an audience. You may be in the business of giving away secrets lately, but I am not."

"I said I was sorry," Ari muttered, turning back up the steps. It didn't help that he knew Larke was right to reprimand him.

They trailed him up two more flights and down the hall to Hawkmaster Rellus's room. Ari knocked several times without receiving an answer. He hoped the hawkmaster hadn't gone to sleep early. If he had, they would need him to wake up. Ari didn't think Larke would be put off from talking to the little hawk much longer.

"Allow me," Larke said, reaching past Ari and pushing the door open.

Ari grimaced. It was very impolite to walk into someone's quarters. Very few doors in Sorga had locks, an arrangement made workable by a certain amount of courtesy. Inside, the room was dark, the faintest of glows coming from smoldering charcoal in the fireplace. "Master Rellus," Ari called, his nerves returning in force.

Behind him, he heard Mirimel slide her knife out. Ari was starting to reconsider not carrying one. It was the height of bad manners to go armed inside the keep, so Ari had left his sword in his rooms, but knives didn't count. A lot of people wore them. They were more of a tool, used for everything from eating dinner to trimming nails, although Ari hoped they were cleaned in between.

It occurred to him that he could solve several problems at once by carrying a knife. He could do away with the cutlery at the head table, which he despised. He didn't know why just they had to use all those fancy little forks and knives, although he supposed it had something to do with Lady Enra and Ispiria being ladies. More important than his dining woes, he would then be armed. Not to mention, if he ever did need to trim his nails while he was wandering around the castle, well –

"Ari," Larke hissed in his ear, breaking into his thoughts. "We must go in, lad."

Ari nodded, realizing he was stalling. He didn't want to walk into that dark room. At best, the hawkmaster was away and they were invading his space. At worst . . . Ari squared his shoulders and stepped forward.

Whistling came from the corridor leading outside and Ari stepped back out of the room just as Hawkmaster Rellus entered from the aerie tunnel. He halted immediately, even stilling the hands he was wiping clean on a rag. "My lord? Can I be of service to you?"

"Hi, uh, yes," Ari said, feeling foolish. He heard Mirimel sheath her knife.

"Mirimel," Hawkmaster Rellus said, coming forward with a smile. "I heard you were in the keep." His smile faltered, and Ari knew he must be thinking about the circumstances that brought Mirimel there.

"Hawkmaster," Mirimel said. She stepped past Ari, bowing from the waist. "You remember Minstrel Larke?"

Hawkmaster Rellus nodded. "Aye, always a pleasure to have such a talent among us. It even tempted me to dinner, but I've been taking extra care with my charges of late."

"We've come to see how the hawks are doing," Mirimel said, leading the way farther into the room. "Are there many eggs yet? How fares the one Lord Aridian brought you?"

"Perhaps you and your aerie would like a private performance," Larke said. He unslung his lute from his back.

"A good idea," Master Rellus said, turning back down the tunnel. "The hawks are agitated. Music might soothe them."

They followed him down the aerie tunnel and around the sharp corner that helped keep the elements out of Master Rellus's room. Ari inhaled deeply as they stepped out onto the ledge. The spring night was cool, but full of the smells of melted snow and fresh life. Ari smiled, finally finding some relief from the tension that filled him. He always felt better outside.

There was a weird chirping sound and a bandage-swaddled little hawk teetered to the opening of one of the cages.

"I'm coming," Master Rellus said, hurrying forward. "You know you can't fly."

He picked the hawk up, carrying him to the stone table in the center of the ledge. The other hawks came to the fronts of their cages to watch, some flying out to perch on spikes driven into the cliff face. One hung back, and Ari realized she was the hawk who'd carried his note to Sorga. She didn't come forward because she was sitting on her eggs.

The four of them gathered around the hawk on the table. Ari assumed the hawk was better because he was awake, but he looked terrible. One eye was missing and he had to hold out his broken foot at an awkward angle in the splint. His wings hung uselessly, thick with bandages. His remaining eye was bright, though, as he looked up at Ari.

"Hi little hawk," Ari said. He glanced at Larke, wondering what the bard would do.

Bringing his lute into position, Larke started to play. It was a soft, melancholy melody. Ari had heard it only once before, but he had a secret suspicion about it. Larke didn't sing the words then, or now, but the music alone was heartbreaking. Ari had nothing to back up his guess, but he thought the song was one of lost love, and he thought it was about Larke and the queen of Lggothland.

Ari was so caught up in the sorrow of Larke's music that he didn't notice until Larke stopped playing that Master Rellus's eyes had slid shut. The hawkmaster stood where he was, swaying slightly, his breath even.

"I didn't know you could do that," Ari whispered.

Larke winked. "Now, my little friend," he said to the hawk. "Please tell me the stone is safe?"

The hawk bobbed. It cocked its head to one side, looking Larke in the eye. Larke sagged. For a moment Ari couldn't tell if the bard was relieved or saddened, but then he smiled.

"It's here. He was bringing it here to you, lad."

"Me?" Ari asked, surprised. "Why?"

"You're to keep it safe, he says." Larke nodded toward the hawk cages. "They hid it in with the eggs, as they always do. He wants you to take it."

"So you truly can speak with them?" Mirimel's voice tinged with envy. "How?"

"Practice," Larke said. "Maybe someday I'll teach you."

Mirimel gave him a withering look. "I'd ask you not to taunt me where the hawks are concerned, sir."

Ari left Larke to get out of that one and went to the cage containing the female hawk and her nest. She looked up at him calmly, but he didn't want to reach in and pull things out from under her. "Hi. May I have the stone, please?"

Craning her neck, she rolled an egg out of the nest, pushing it toward him.

134

"That's very kind of you, but I don't want your egg. I think you should keep that. I just want the stone."

Ari hadn't realized a hawk face could so fully express annoyance until that moment. He looked over his shoulder at Larke. Mirimel was glaring at the bard. Catching Ari's glance, Larke shrugged at her and hurried over.

"She says it's inside that egg," Larke said after a moment, sounding unsure.

"Is it?" Ari asked.

"How is that possible?" Mirimel said, crossing to peer into the cage with them. "Are you sure? I'll not have you breaking eggs."

"That's what she says, lass," Larke said. "I'm just the interpreter. Can't you tell how she feels?"

"She's not upset," Mirimel said. "But what if she doesn't understand what we're planning to do? We can't just smash it. There could be a baby hawk in there."

The hawk's head darted forward, her beak dipping down to smash the egg. Mirimel gasped, reaching for it like she might push it back together again, but her hands stopped shy. There was no liquid in the egg, and, to Ari's relief, no baby hawk. Tentatively, he reached out and pushed the fragments aside. In the middle of the broken shell was a small white stone. It looked almost like an ordinary pebble, except it was perfectly round and flickered with an inner glow. It was as if somewhere deep inside of it there was a source of light.

Ari looked around at the hawks, who regarded him with gleaming eyes. Several bobbed their heads, as if encouraging him. He reached out and picked up the stone, thinking it would have fit perfectly inside the closed claw of the injured hawk. It was smooth, almost like glass, and oddly warm and heavy.

The hawks bobbed on their perches, releasing a strange cacophony of noises. Ari started to put the stone back, worried he'd upset them.

"They're happy," Mirimel said, looking around with wide eyes. "They're ecstatic. They feel fulfilled."

The hawks settled down, most of them returning to their cages, looking as if they were preparing for sleep. Even if he couldn't talk to them like Larke or sense their emotions as Mirimel, Ari could practically feel the sense of satisfaction radiating from them.

He stared at the stone in his hand, feeling an odd mixture of awe and disgust. He was holding something that was worth dying for, but how could one milky-white pebble be worth hundreds of lives? Shaking his head, he tucked the stone into the coin purse sewn into the lining of his doublet. He never kept any coin there, but surely, right over his heart as it was, it was the perfect place to keep the stone.

The hawk in her nest bobbed her head at them, chirping.

Larke turned back to her. "She wants us to dispose of the shell, so we don't upset Rellus."

"That's very considerate," Mirimel said, reaching out to scoop up the pieces. She looked around.

"Put them on the table," Larke said.

Mirimel looked as perplexed as Ari felt, but she complied. The bandaged hawk examined the shards, peering up at Larke.

"Step back," Larke said to the hawk.

He made an arcane gesture over the shards, speaking a few syllables in a low voice. A blue flame rose up from the table, surrounding the fragments. It reduced the shell to ash without scorching the table beneath it. Mirimel's eyes were wide in the dancing blue light. Even though Ari had seen Aluiens use the same flame to cremate the dead, he still felt a thrill of amazement at Larke's display. When the last fragment was gone, Larke waved his hand and the fire went out. Leaning over, he blew on the pile of fine white ash to scatter it.

Ari met Larke's gaze with raised eyebrows.

"Well," the bard said, "it's not as if there's any sense pretending in front of you two."

The little hawk chirped at Larke again.

"Yes, it's about time we rouse Master Rellus." Larke retrieved his lute from his back and resumed playing, this time choosing a song that, while soothing enough, was devoid of the boundless melancholy of the last. After a moment, Hawkmaster Rellus blinked, coming awake.

"As you can see, my lord," he said to Ari. "He's recovering well. Better than I'd hoped, truth be told."

"And he has your excellent skills to thank for it, I've no doubt," Ari said, smiling. Finally, something was going their way. They had the stone. The little hawk would live. They were all safe in Sorga. Maybe Ari didn't need to carry a knife around after all.

Later, as they left the hawkmaster's quarters after dutifully praising the little hawk and the new mother on her nest, Mirimel halted at the top of the stairwell, her stubbornness clear in the tilt of her head. "We need to talk," she said, looking back and forth between Larke and Ari. "Where we won't be overheard."

Ari sighed. It was late, and he was tired, and he'd been enjoying his newfound sense of optimism. He had a feeling Mirimel's talk was going to ruin that. "We can talk in my suite," he said, pushing past her to lead the way.

Chapter 12

"What if Peine's in there?" Mirimel said, stopping Ari before he could open the door to his sitting room.

"He won't be." Ari knew his friend. When Peine was in love, he was never around. "If he is, I'll send him for something."

Ari opened the door, leading the way in. His sitting room had a round table, where he and Peine sometimes ate, as well as a leather couch and two matching chairs set in a semicircle around the fireplace. It was completely dark inside. Mirimel stopped in the rectangle of light spilling in from the corridor.

Leaving her and Larke to light the fire, Ari crossed to the door to his sleeping chamber. It too was empty and dark, the fireplace inside unlit. Ari supposed that if he needed a fire to keep warm he would be annoyed, but as it stood, he shook his head indulgently at Peine's lack of attention to duty. To be thorough, Ari checked the other two rooms off his sleeping chamber, Peine's and the bathing room, and even opened his wardrobe and pushed the clothes around.

Returning to the sitting room, where Larke and Mirimel sat opposite each other in the two armchairs by the now lit fire, Ari crossed to the other side and repeated his inspection in the unused duchess' quarters. The duchess' quarters were actually larger than the duke's, having the addition of a nursery and a whole room for hanging dresses in, instead of just a wardrobe. As always when he entered them, Ari couldn't help but pause before the large, cloth draped canopy bed that would someday be Ispiria's. He forced down a blush.

"I take it we're quite alone?" Larke said when Ari returned.

Ari nodded, sitting on the sofa. He felt a little odd with one of them on each side of him, as if he was some sort of centerpiece. "What did you want to speak to us about?" he asked Mirimel.

"You didn't know they could hide the stone inside an egg?" she asked, looking first at Larke and then Ari. Larke shook his head.

"I didn't even know there was a stone," Ari reminded her.

"I knew there was a stone, but not about the egg," Mirimel said. "I've only seen it in the fall, when they take it out and pass it among them. When the bards come to play at the festival . . ." She trailed off, glancing at Larke, surprise rounding her eyes.

"As I said, lass, you've known this talentless old husk of a bard for quite some time."

"It never occurred to me to wonder that you never age," she said.

Larke winked.

"But I thought your magic doesn't work on Mirimel, because she has magic of her own," Ari said.

"I said it doesn't work as well, lad," Larke said. "In a few years, I daresay she would have caught on, once the timeless self-absorption and confusion of youth left her. The real question is, would she have confronted me or would I have gone on my merry way, returning every year, not knowing that one among the Hawkers could see the truth?"

"Self-absorption and confusion?" Mirimel repeated, her voice tart.

Larke grinned.

140

"My point being." Mirimel had obviously decided not to pursue the bard's words. "The Caller seemed to know that the stone would be in an egg. He broke them all. He may even have timed his attack for after clutching season. How could he have known?"

"Maybe he just thought it was in the nests," Ari said. "He might have broken the eggs while searching, as we first thought."

"Or out of malice," Larke said, his face serious. "Ruin and sorrow are his daily want."

"But every egg was smashed," she said. "Every single egg."

They sat back. After a moment, Ari ventured, "Does it matter? How he knew, that is."

"I don't know," Mirimel said. "I'm just trying to piece this together. I want to know why my home was destroyed."

Ari looked at Larke. Surely, after showing Mirimel the blue fire of the Aluiens, Larke couldn't mean to keep what he knew of the stone from her. The bard sighed.

"When I said I didn't know why the Caller wants the stone, that was in its way true," Larke said.

Mirimel frowned at him.

"What we do know is that there were once three stones. Three, to meld body, soul and deed. Although, some say it's body, heart and deed. The most ancient passages about the stones are in Old Wheylian, so it's open to interpretation."

Ari hoped that didn't get back to Sir Cadwel. He'd be stuck inside all summer, learning the no longer spoken script of Peine's great ancestors.

Mirimel when she opened her mouth.

"But one of the stones has long been missing," Larke continued before Mirimel could speak. "No one knows where it can be found and no magic can seek it out, rendering the two others useless. That's why I said I don't know why the Caller and his master chose now, of all times, to attack your village."

Ari's eyes narrowed. He didn't recall Larke saying the Caller had a master before. Was it a slip, or a hint? He knew the bard tried very hard to obey the rules of his people, even if they chafed him.

"That's really all I may say, lass," Larke said. "My people are very sensitive to me breaking our laws. Especially when it comes to Ari. There are those among us still looking for an excuse to correct what they see as the great wrong we did in saving him."

Ari recalled Larke using that same phrase last winter. As it did then, his mind shied away from what correcting him might mean. He was quite sure he didn't want the mistake of saving his life to be fixed. "What about you, Larke?" he asked, it occurring to him that the Aluien must have ways of punishing their own. "They won't do anything to you for telling us about the stones, will they?"

Larke looked into the fire, his lips thinning as he pressed them together. When he turned back to Ari, there was no spark left in his eyes. "I'll worry about myself and my people, lad. You have enough trouble with the Caller abroad."

Ari didn't care for the sound of that. He shifted on the couch, the leather creaking in the silence. He couldn't think of anything reassuring to say to Larke, and he couldn't unknow things Larke had told him. A popping sound came from the fire as one of the logs split.

"What are you going to do with the stone?" Mirimel asked. "Maybe we could use it to lure this Caller out, so we can kill him. Why wait for him to come after it again when we could battle him on our own terms."

"That would be a great risk," Larke said. "What if we fail and the Caller takes the stone?"

"You said one of the stones is lost forever, so what does it matter?" Mirimel said. "We have to find a way to put an end to him. He will pay for what he's done." Her face was set, her jaw clenched.

"We can think on it, of course," Ari said. He stifled a yawn. He was pretty sure the two of them could have that argument somewhere else. For his part, he had no intention of letting the Caller take the stone, yet Mirimel made a valid point.

It would be better to lure their enemy to them, now that they knew he was out there, than wait for him to strike. "For now, I'm going to go find Natan and ask him to lock it away with the tithes."

"I don't think that would be wise, lad," Larke said. "I don't think you should tell anyone where it is."

"Surely, you don't mistrust Natan?" Ari asked, surprised. Natan was Sir Cadwel's master steward. He was in charge of all of the daily tasks of the keep. He used to be one of the king's own knights.

"It isn't that," Larke said, shaking his head. "'T'would just be safer if only you knew the location of the stone. In fact, barring the three of us, I don't know as you should even tell anyone 'tis found. Outside of this room, only Sir Cadwel knows the stone is what the Caller seeks."

"But, Civul brought us that message from the Caller, offering to trade Ispiria for the stone, so she knows, and surely the guards around her heard her speak of it, and the medic . . ." Ari's voice trailed off at the amusement on Larke's face.

"Did they, lad?" the bard asked. "Do the guards, or medics, or even Lady Civul, out of who's mouth the words came, really know anything about the Caller or the stone? I daresay if you ask them, they'll not be having any idea of what you speak."

"I see," Ari said, trying not to frown. He rubbed his forehead. "You made them all forget about it."

"You're sure that doesn't do anything bad to them, you mucking about in their heads?" Mirimel asked. "Because I tell you, Kimmer's gotten dumber of late."

"Mucking about?" Larke looked offended. "I am a master of precision. An expert on extraction, a delicate delver into the-"

The door opened, revealing Peine. They turned to look at him and he stopped, one foot still in the corridor. "I'm sorry," he said. "I didn't know you were in here, having a private conversation." He looked down, but not before Ari saw the hurt on his face. Peine pulled on the door, shuffling backwards.

"We aren't," Ari called, saddened by his friend's obvious feelings of exclusion. "Peine, come back."

"Yes, my lord," Peine muttered, coming in a few steps and standing there, staring at the floor.

"Well, I best be going for that walk," Larke said. "Always nice to walk before bed. That's what I say. Were you coming too, Hawk Guardian Mirimel?"

Mirimel shot a glance at Peine and nodded, ignoring the arm Larke offered her as they left. Ari was glad they were going. He was tired and he didn't have any answers to Mirimel's questions. He just hoped they wouldn't seethe in his head, keeping him awake. Although, her questions were better than dwelling on the Aluiens correcting the mistake they made by saving him, or what they might do to Larke for giving away their secrets, or how Ispiria was recovering from being kidnapped and imprisoned by the Caller.

"I'm glad you're here," Ari said, rising and heading toward his sleeping chamber. "That conversation wasn't going anywhere anyhow."

Ari stopped, realizing Peine was still standing near the door to the hall, not following him. It wasn't that Ari actually needed any help getting ready for bed, but he and Peine usually talked. Well, Peine talked, emptying Ari's head of any worries of the day by filling it with chatter about who said what about whom, and who got angry and who threw the cook's favorite stewpot in the midden, or spilled wine on whose dress.

"You really weren't interrupting anything," Ari said, worried that Larke and Mirimel leaving had only made Peine feel worse.

"I'm sure I was, my lord."

Ari blinked. He couldn't see Peine's face, angled as it was toward the floor, but his friend didn't sound sad. If Ari didn't know better, he'd say Peine was angry. "Shall we ready for sleep?" Ari asked.

"Whatever my lord wishes."

Ari suppressed a sigh. He was sure now. Peine was angry. Why under the moon and stars, Ari didn't know, but he definitely was. "You're angry with me."

"It's not my place to be angry with you, my lord." Peine lifted his chin, scowling. "I'll go find someone to assist my lord in his evening preparations. I find I'm feeling indisposed."

Ari wasn't sure what indisposed meant, but two long strides took him across the room. He grabbed Peine's arm as his friend reached for the door. Peine tried to pull away, but Ari only tightened his grip. "What's going on, Peine?"

How long had Peine been angry with him? The funny looks in the pinewoods, Ari realized. Those looks weren't because Peine was afraid of what Ari would say to him for sneaking away from Sir Cadwel. They were Peine trying to hide his anger. Peine's recent disregard of his duties took on a new light. Was he even in love with Kimmer, or was it only anger driving his negligence of late? Ari recalled the way his friend had looked at the blonde hawk guardian, sure it was with infatuation. Ari couldn't believe he'd misinterpreted Peine's feelings about Kimmer, but he had certainly missed his friend's anger.

Peine looked down at Ari's hand on his arm. "Using your superior strength to force me to do as you say, my lord?"

"What do you mean?" Ari said, his gaze narrowing. The emphasis Peine put on it, superior strength, made Ari think Peine wasn't just referring to the fact that he was a swordsman and nearly two years Peine's senior.

"You shouldn't have sent Larke away," Peine went on, his voice seething with ire. "How will you order him to erase my thoughts if he isn't even here?"

"That's enough," Ari said, his tone hard. He dropped his hand from Peine's arm. Peine obviously knew something. Ari wanted to know how, and he was starting to get annoyed with his friend's venomous tone. "What is it, exactly, that you're talking about?"

"We heard you, Ari," Peine said, his voice suddenly more normal. Anger slid from his face as hurt returned. "I heard you.

We were going to come to your camp, but then we heard the three of you talking. You're stronger and faster and all that. Larke said so, and Mirimel knows. You just met her, Ari, and she knows. I'm your best friend."

Ari sighed, scrubbing a hand through his hair. So that was what Peine was upset about. Maybe he should call Larke and ask him to fix things.

"And I heard what else you said, that I saw things that very morning and Larke took them right out of my head. Kimmer and I talked about it. We can't remember whatever it was. All we saw was you killing a couple wolves. I don't know how he can do that. I'm not sure I even care. How can you let him do that to me? Why didn't you tell me about the things you can do?"

Ari didn't know what to say. He recalled how upset he'd been with Larke when he finally realized the bard had kept him from knowing things. Important things. Was it really right to let Larke keep taking Peine's memories away? "I swore a vow."

"That didn't seem to stop you from talking to Mirimel," Peine said, a little of his anger returning.

"But it should have."

"Fine. I'm sick of being angry with you anyhow. Call Larke in and make me forget. I don't care. Just remember, we'll never really be best friends, Ari, because I don't even know you."

Peine pushed past Ari and fled into the sleeping chamber. The door to Peine's room slammed shut. Ari stayed where he was, his hands clenched at his sides.

Peine wasn't right, was he? They were friends. No one ever knew everything about someone else, did they? Ari had promised the Aluiens he wouldn't tell people about them.

Of course, he hadn't told Peine anything. Peine had overhead it. Did not telling Larke that Peine overheard them count as breaking his vow?

Ari shook his head. Of course it did, because he didn't actually vow not to tell people. His vow was to protect the secret of their existence.

Was his vow to the Aluiens more important than his friendship with Peine? How could he weigh that? Peine was his best friend, but Ari had given his word of honor.

He looked toward the door, knowing Larke couldn't be far. Sorga wasn't a big place. Even if he couldn't find the bard, Larke would be back at some point, sprawling out on the sofa to sleep. Or pretend to sleep. Ari was never all the way sure which it was.

He took a step toward the door, his thoughts tumbling over each other. Peine hadn't overheard anything about the Aluiens, he realized. Keeping them secret wasn't the same as keeping his extra speed and strength secret. He stopped, grasping at that thought. His abilities were his secret. He hadn't promised anyone he wouldn't talk about them. Of course, if people asked how he got the way he was, well, he wouldn't be able to answer that, but Peine could know that he was different without knowing why. He wanted Peine to know.

Ari turned back toward the sleeping chamber, crossing through it to knock on Peine's door before pulling it open.

"Is he here?" Peine asked, standing. "Will it hurt?"

To Ari's surprise, Peine wiped his face on his sleeve, blotting up tears. "He isn't coming," Ari said. "Peine, you're my best friend. I should have told you that I'm stronger and faster than a normal man. And I don't get cold. That's why I'm always opening the windows. Why not have fresh air all the time when you don't need to stay warm?"

"Because then it's freezing in here and I do get cold." Peine sat back down on his bed. "He's really not coming?"

"I'm not going to tell him," Ari said, although he realized that might not be true. He should probably tell Larke that Kimmer had heard them. If he did, would Larke insist on making Peine forget too? "But you can't ask me why I'm different, or how Larke can do what he does. I'm sorry, but I made a vow. I can't tell you, on my honor."

Peine looked thoughtful. "I guess I understand. Thank you for not telling Larke."

147

He went silent again, looking down. Ari searched his mind for something to say. He wanted things to be like normal between them.

"Does Sir Cadwel know?" Peine asked.

"He does."

"Is that why he chose you to be his page?"

Ari shook his head. "He didn't know then. I didn't know then. It was just luck."

"I guess you're luckier than the average person too," Peine said, smiling a little.

"I think I am," Ari said.

"Does the king know?"

Ari nodded.

"What about Prince Parrentine?"

"He knows too," Ari said. "And Princess Siara, but not anyone else. Not even the queen." Ari added that because he knew it would make Peine happy to know something that the queen didn't know. "You know you can't tell anyone, right?"

"I know," Peine said, his face solemn. "I won't tell anyone."

"Not even Kimmer, because she might not remember for much longer."

Peine's eyes went wide. He nodded. "What about Ispiria?"

"I can't tell Ispiria," Ari said, her name bringing back all his worries about how the kidnapping may have effected her. "I told you, I have vows to uphold. I can't just tell people about this, Peine. And she'd want to know how. She'd never see my word of honor as a good enough reason for not telling her everything."

"And she'd be right. She's going to be your wife, Ari. You'll have to tell her. She should know. What sort of a life will you two have together if you keep things from her? Especially really big things like this."

Ari sighed. Maybe he should have called Larke, but he wouldn't change his mind now. He couldn't do that to Peine, even if Peine would never know. "I'm going to sleep," he finally said. He closed the door to Peine's room, hoping his friend wouldn't be too insulted he did it.

Ari was tired. He'd slept on the ground, killed a giant undead wolf, rescued Ispiria, recovered the stone and had an argument with his best friend. He just wanted to get in bed and shut his eyes so he could have a little rest and quiet.

He shook his head, recalling he needed to write a message to send to Sir Cadwel in the morning, and the message needed to be delivered to Natan to give to the men who volunteered to take it. Ari had made the announcement at dinner. He was sure someone would be setting off first thing in the morning.

He glanced at Peine's closed door. No, best to leave Peine alone for now. Ari would write a quick note to Sir Cadwel, leaving it on the desk for Peine to take to Natan in the morning, and then, finally, he'd be allowed to sleep.

Chapter 13

Ari opened his eyes, trying to figure out what had woken him. He looked around his darkened room, but no one was there. He glanced at his wardrobe, where the stone rested in one of his doublets. Nothing seemed amiss.

A faint scratching sound came from his bedroom door. Was someone trying to get his attention? Maybe Larke, finally returned for the night? Usually, the bard was quite willing to wake him up without any pretense at subtlety. Straining his ears, Ari could hear Peine breathing, asleep in his room.

The scratching sound came again. Ari rolled silently from his bed. Even through the heavy rug, he could feel how cold the stone floor was. He crept toward the door, his eyes going to his sword where it hung, sheathed, beside his wardrobe.

"Ari?" Ispiria's voice whispered.

Ari's shoulders sagged, tension draining out of him. "Just a moment," he whispered back. Walking over to his wardrobe, he pulled on breeches, shucked his nightshirt and donned a tunic. He tugged the laces tight before cracking open the door.

"Ispiria," he greeted, smiling at her. She looked well enough. Her eyes were wide, but not with fear. There were no lines of pain or sorrow etched around them, or her lips. He cleared his throat. "What are you doing here? Is all well? If anyone sees you . . ."

He shook his head. He didn't even want to think about how much trouble they'd be in if anyone saw her. He kept his voice low so he wouldn't wake Peine. A quick glance over her shoulder told him that Larke wasn't in the sitting room.

Ispiria's hair was a jumbled mass of curls, their normal bright red color darkened to nearly black by the lack of light. She narrowed her eyes, peering up at him, and he guessed she could hardly see anything at all. She had a shawl wrapped about her, and Ari blushed to see her high-necked nightgown peeking out from underneath.

"I wanted to talk to you," she said.

"In the middle of the night in my rooms?" he said. He tried to put censure in his voice, but it was difficult. He was too happy to see her. He wondered if he should invite her in so they could sit. Darting a glance at the only place in his room to sit, he came out instead. He closed his bedroom door quietly, and firmly, behind him.

"Well, I want to talk to you now," she said, letting him take her arm and lead her to the couch. He started to sit next to her, but changed his mind and moved to a chair by the fire instead. "And you're in your room, so I can hardly talk to you anywhere else, can I? I mean, that would just be silly, because you certainly wouldn't hear me."

Ari took up the poker and stirred the fire until the coals gave off a little more light. "But, couldn't it wait till morning? How are you feeling?" She looked well, and sounded like herself. He'd been afraid her experience with the Caller might have changed her. Dampened her.

"I'm well enough." She gave him a bright smile. "And I'm here, so we may as well talk."

"That's true," he said, putting the poker aside. She was there, now, in his sitting room. It would be their room someday. The common area linking their suites. Ari was suddenly very conscious of the emptiness of the room around them.

She looked at him with warm green eyes. "I was just wondering if you'd found the stone yet."

Ari fought not to jerk backward in his chair. "Pardon?" he asked, trying to keep his tone normal. How did Ispiria know about the stone? Had she learned about it during her summers with the Hawkers? Even so, how did she know it was missing? He restrained himself from glancing toward his room, where it was hidden in the doublet he'd been wearing.

"The stone the Caller is looking for," she said, her tone so nonchalant, it made her words all the more startling.

"You know his name?" Ari asked, although he supposed Caller was more of a title than a name.

"He told me." She sounded as cheerful as always, like they were talking about a picnic. "And he said you would trade the stone for me or I would die. Isn't that awful? Me, for just a stone? I mean, I'm a person. That's why I wasn't very worried. I knew you would trade a stone for me."

"I . . ." He struggled to find something to say. Larke's warning not to tell anyone they'd found the stone rang in his head, right alongside Peine's words about not keeping secrets from Ispiria. "We couldn't trade the stone for you. We didn't even know where it was. That's why I had to come get you instead. You're right, I would have traded it."

Of course, Larke and Sir Cadwel wouldn't have let him, and he still wasn't sure if he really would have, but he clearly remembered wanting to. He hated telling her half-truths, but Larke's warning, coming as it did from an Aluien, carried more weight in this matter than Peine's advice. Advice Ari still had to think on for a while.

"But don't you have it now? Surely you've been looking for it?" She leaned forward, her eyes narrowing. "I just want to see it, Ari. I want to see this stone that's worth my life."

"I wish I could show it to you, but I can't," he said, hoping she would hear the truth in his words and not sort through them for his deception.

"I want to see it as soon as you find it, Ari," she said, her voice demanding and tinged with anger. "Promise me. I know you keep your promises."

"As soon as I find the missing stone, I'll show it to you." In his mind, he was saying those words about the stones that were truly missing, not the one in his room. After all, how could it be the missing stone when he knew right where it was? He felt awful, though. His words were all but lies, and what she said about him keeping promises only made him feel worse.

"Thank you." She slouched back into the couch. "I feel so much better. I think I'll be able to sleep now."

"You couldn't sleep before?" he asked, frowning.

"I wanted to. I'm very tired," she murmured, her eyes sliding shut. She pulled her feet up onto the couch, tucking them under her. "But all I could think about was that stone. That silly stone. I have to have it, Ari. I just have to." She barely got the last few words out, nestling down onto the couch as sleep overtook her.

Ari stared at her beautiful face, serene now, his insides twisting. Something wasn't right. That didn't sound like Ispiria to him. Unable to sleep because of a stone? And what she said at the end, she had to have the stone? No, that didn't sound like Ispiria at all. Where was Larke when Ari needed him?

He stood, uncertain. Should he leave Ispiria there alone and seek the bard? Somehow, that seemed irresponsible, but he needed Larke. Ari frowned. This was his sitting room. The sitting room of the Lord of Sorga, right in the heart of the keep. Where was safe if not there?

Retrieving a blanket from his bed, he covered her, tucking it in around her shoulders. She was so beautiful. It tormented him to think the Caller might have done anything to her mind. With a slightly shaking hand, he smoothed her curls back from her face, his eyes on her lips.

Straightening, Ari crossed to the door. He could wake Peine to watch over her, he knew, but then Larke wouldn't be able to help as much, or, if he did, he'd erase Peine's memories, or put him to sleep first, or something that would compromise

Ari's resolve not to let his best friend be magiced anymore. Ari would just have to find the bard quickly and return, although he had no idea what he feared would happen to Ispiria while he was away.

Ari made his way from his rooms and down the stone steps leading to the foyer. Trying to appear casual, he nodded to the guards who stood on either side of the keep's closed double doors. The notes of music he could hear slipping out of the great hall reassured him that he wouldn't have to hunt for Larke for long.

In spite of the late hour, for Ari marked it as just past the mid of night, there were quite a few castle dwellers still awake. Ari took in the sorrow that filled the room, crossing to where Larke stood. The bard played softly, one foot resting on a bench. People sat in small groups or alone, many with tankards in hand. To Ari's right, two women were crying.

Eight funerals, Ari reminded himself. That was how many they must hold tomorrow for the men who'd volunteered to escort Civul and Ispiria back to Sorga. The first would begin when the sun rose, a time not that far distant. Those funerals didn't even include the men who'd already died while searching for survivors in the pinewood. Ari dreaded the arrival of their bodies, which he knew might well be tomorrow.

Somewhat to his surprise, he spotted Mirimel seated near Larke. She was leaning back against the wall, her feet propped up on a chair she must have taken from the head table, a tankard of ale cradled in her hands. Her face was unreadable. She didn't lift her eyes to look at him when he passed.

As Ari reached Larke, the bard's music trailed off. No one seemed to notice. Their thoughts, Ari knew, were on their own concerns. He leaned close to Larke, lowering his voice to a whisper he was sure no mortal man could hear. "Something's wrong with Ispiria. I need your help."

Larke nodded, gesturing to catch Mirimel's attention. "I'd not leave her alone right now," the bard said in response to Ari's questioning look. "She's more distraught than she appears. The lass just lost her home and family."

Ari squelched his annoyance. He didn't want anything to inhibit Larke from doing all in his power to help Ispiria. Mirimel was even worse than Peine, because Larke couldn't take memories from her. Still, he couldn't argue with Larke. Mirimel was already coming to see what they wanted, and their sympathy was her due, for she'd lost everything she had.

"Yes?" she said, reaching them. "What brings you down to the mourning room, Lord Aridian?"

Her face was composed and her words lacked inflection, but Ari could sense a harshness behind them that bespoke of someone holding thinly to the decorum of normal behavior.

"I need you and Larke to come with me, please," he said. He didn't want to mention Ispiria to Mirimel where others could see, afraid her composure would break.

She gave a curt nod, gesturing for him to lead. Having Mirimel follow him reminded Ari of having her ride behind him. He could all but feel the heat of her anger. He wondered how long she could stay so angry about what the Caller had done to her people before sorrow overtook her.

Ari led them back to his sitting room, pausing outside to whisper, "Peine's sleeping. Try not to wake him, please." He let them in, gesturing them toward the couch before closing the door carefully behind them.

Mirimel stopped halfway across the room to turn and glare at Ari. "What is my little cousin doing on your couch?"

"Something's not right with her," Ari said.

"What do you mean?" Mirimel asked, fear pushing some of the anger from her tone. She moved to stand behind the couch, Ari following. "What's not right with her? She looks perfectly well."

Larke knelt down beside Ispiria, laying a long-fingered hand on her forehead. "Aye, lad," he said, looking up. "You were right to get me. He's been messing about in there. Why didn't I think to check?" Larke shook his head. "And I call myself a thinking man." His tone was bitter with self-recrimination.

"Who's been doing what, exactly, to Ispiria?" Mirimel said, her voice rising. "Speak plainly, bard."

Ari noticed her hand was resting on the hilt of her hunting knife. He didn't think she even realized it. He cast Larke a surprised look, but the bard was focused on Ispiria.

"The Caller, lass," Larke said, his own tone touched with annoyance. "Who else would I be meaning? Use your mind, girl."

Mirimel scowled at him.

"Can you help her, Larke?" Ari asked. How could they be thinking about getting into a fight when something was wrong with Ispiria?

"I can sense his compulsion, but I can't remove it." Larke leaned back on his heels. "He has it too twisted about in there. I need to find the key to unraveling it. I don't want to go yanking at the wrong things. What's it a compulsion to do? Do you know? Do we have time?"

Ari struggled to focus on Larke's words through the pain that clutched at him. Something was wrong with Ispiria. Something Larke couldn't just fix. They hadn't saved her from the Caller. His evil was still in her mind.

"A compulsion?" Mirimel said. "What does that mean? What has he done to her?"

"It's a pressure toward or away from an action, lass." Larke looked back down at Ispiria, his face intent. "It's a way to control a person's thoughts and actions. What did she try to do, Ari lad, that made you realize it was here?"

"She asked to see the stone. Did she know about it, Mirimel?"

"I don't think so. I don't know. That's all? Did he tell her about it? Maybe nothing's wrong."

"She said she needed it, that she must have it," Ari said. "She wouldn't sleep until I promised to show it to her as soon as I found it." He winced as he said it, for lying was even worse when you had to confess that you'd done it.

"You didn't give it to her?" Larke asked, his blue eyes going wide.

157

"No."

"You can't let her have it, lad," Larke said. "I can't tell what suggestions he's put in her mind, but I don't doubt they include bringing the stone to him once she has it."

"So Ari must keep lying to her," Mirimel said, casting Ari a bitter glance.

"I don't know if I can live with that." Ari scrubbed a hand through his hair. "I can't lie to Ispiria like that."

"You can and you will, lad," Larke said. "But it won't be enough. She'll grow more desperate, more insistent. Lying will only buy us time." He stared at the wall behind them for a moment before sighing. "His work is beyond me, but I know someone who can give me the key to unraveling it."

Standing, he crossed to a window, tucking back the curtains and unlatching the frame. Cool spring air blew in. Larke leaned his head out, a trilling whistle leaving his mouth to drift into the night sky. He repeated it twice before stepping back, an expectant look on his face.

A few moments later, a wren flew into the room, alighting on Larke's outstretched hand. Ari looked between the bird and Larke in surprise. One little brown bird looked much like another to Ari, but he was almost positive he'd seen this one before. A dew-drenched morning came to mind, the previous fall, when Ari and Sir Cadwel had ridden out of the capital to practice jousting. Larke had been sitting in the clearing they'd used, that wren perched on his finger, singing to him.

Carefully, Larke came back to kneel beside Ispiria. He held the wren out, close to her face. It cocked its head to one side, regarding her with serious black eyes. Larke stroked its head with one finger, trilling to it. He sounded almost like a bird himself. After a few moments, he brought the bird up to his face, looking intently into its eyes. It dipped its head.

"You'll be swift?" the bard asked it.

The little bird chirped. Ari watched, bemused, as Larke brought it back to the window and sent it out into the night, closing the glass and curtains behind it.

"Don't tell me that wren can understand you like Lord Aridian's horse can understand him?" Mirimel asked, her tone a mixture of skepticism and annoyance.

"I'm afraid not," Larke said, turning back to them. "He's just a simple wren." He raised his hands as if to ward off their disbelieving looks. "He's the Lady's wren. She's worked with him." The hesitant way the bard said worked made Ari think it meant more than simple training. "I've placed images and ideas in his head. He can't understand them, but he'll carry them in his mind to the Lady."

Relief washed through Ari. Surely the Lady would know how to undo the Caller's evil.

"And what will this lady do?" Mirimel asked. "Will she help Ispiria?"

"The Lady," Larke said, adding a little emphasis to the title. "She will undoubtedly be able to tell me how to help Ispiria."

"What should we do until then?" Ari asked, looking down at her. Red curls spilled over the arm of the couch. "Do you think the Caller let us have her back, Larke? He left and put only a few wolves to guard her in the hopes we would free her, didn't he? It was a trick."

"Aye, lad, and we obliged him. I didn't even question our fortune. I was so eager to return to Sorga, to speak to the hawks."

"But how did he know that?" Mirimel asked, frowning. "How did he know we didn't have the stone to trade for her, or that if we returned to Sorga, you could ask the hawks? Only knowing those things would make his actions sensible. He had her, after all. Did he not know any of that, he very well should have kept her. If he knew it, why take her?"

They were all silent while they thought about that.

"Maybe we really did rescue her? The compulsion could be a fallback plan," Ari said. "Maybe Sir Cadwel did something that called him away, or he thought he'd found the stone, or--"

"Enough," Mirimel said, holding up a hand.

Ari studied her. Fatigue and sorrow put more age on her face than her seventeen years warranted. Her lips were pulled down at the corners and her blue eyes were sunk in dark pits of charcoal-tinged skin. Even her hair hung limp, as if it could barely muster a curl.

"Sleep will bring us more clarity," Ari said. He refrained from adding that they wouldn't get much of it, as the funerals would start at first light. "What do we do for now, Larke, about Ispiria? Until you hear from the Lady."

"I can put a counter compulsion on her, if you two aren't minding. My work isn't as highhanded as our enemy's, so I can't tell you how well it will be working." Larke looked thoughtful. "And, with your permission, I shall suppress the memory of tonight in the lass's mind, so, should she be inspired to seek the stone again, she'll start over at the beginning and not be taking any sterner measures as of yet."

"And I'll take her back to her room," Mirimel said.

"Larke will have to go with you," Ari said.

"The lad's right," Larke interjected. "It's best done in her room, so she won't have any memory of being out of it, and you'll want me to make sure no others see her, or you, coming and going."

"Fine," Mirimel said. "I guess if I'm in this mess, you bewitching a few more people can't make it any more sinister."

"Bewitching?" Larke said, looking hurt.

Ari watched, feeling a bit wretched about it, as they woke Ispiria and led her away. Larke kept up a soothing monologue, one Ari knew from experience was invading Ispiria's mind and keeping it from being fully awake. He didn't feel at all right about what they were doing to her, but what choice did they have?

Sighing, he closed the hallway door behind them and returned to his bed to find what sleep he could. Come morning, he must be Lord of Sorga in Sir Cadwel's absence. That duty had never before seemed as unpleasant as it did now, but the people of the keep needed him to be their duke. Never had he realized that honor would have him presiding over so many funerals.

Chapter 14

Ari woke to the sound of someone entering his sitting room. Whoever it was, they were making no effort to be stealthy. He stifled a groan. Could this be the same night? Was there a conspiracy not to let him sleep? There was a knock on his bedroom door.

"Lord Aridian?"

It was Natan's voice. Ari sat up in bed. "Come in." He pushed himself to his feet, trying to gauge the time. Natan entered, fully dressed and looking worried. Ari could hear Peine stirring in his room.

"I'm sorry to wake you so early, Ari. There's a bit of a situation in the courtyard. I tried to work it out, but it requires the ruling of the lord of the keep."

"What time is it?" Peine asked, sticking his head into the room. He raised a hand to his mouth, covering a yawn.

"About an hour before dawn," Natan said.

"What sort of situation?" Ari asked, going to his wardrobe to look for something to wear.

Peine hurried past him. "I have your second best finery ready," he said, his tone anxious.

Ari knew he was supposed to wear his most lordly clothes when he presided over the funerals, but his best doublet was ruined and there hadn't been time to repair it. Peine was undoubtedly upset, worrying that Ari's attire would offend the castle folk, but Ari didn't think anyone would notice or care.

"It's Melaina, Gremble's wife." Natan sat on the edge of the bed as he spoke, looking as weary as Ari felt. Ari racked his brain, coming up with a face and the knowledge that Gremble was one of the dead guards they were to honor today. "She tried to sneak his body out of the keep under the guise of going to the farms to collect straw."

"In the dark?" Peine asked, holding up Ari's doublet.

Before letting Peine put it on him, Ari took it, turning away for a moment to circumspectly transfer the stone to the doublet's coin pocket. If Natan or Peine noticed, they were too polite to ask about it. Probably, they simply thought he was transferring his coin and found it amusing he should be so concerned with money now that he was heir to Sorga.

"Who knows what she was thinking?" Natan said. "Maybe she thought the guards would be easier to fool at this hour. She told them there wasn't enough straw for the funeral pyres, but the back of her wagon was full of chests and parcels, so they started searching it. She said they were to trade for the straw. They appear to be some of her possessions, and her children's. Gremble's body was hidden under them."

"The children are with her?" Ari asked, finishing tugging on his breeches. He grabbed his boots. "Where was she going?"

"She wants to take Gremble south to her village, to be buried in one of those cemeteries the followers of the Overgod build." Natan shook his head. "Whoever came up with that ridiculous notion deserves to wind up in one. Why would you want to keep fields full of bodies like that, trapping their souls in the ground?"

"Don't they believe burying them will allow them to all meet in that after realm their priests are always speaking of?" Ari glanced at Peine for confirmation, receiving a nod.

Although a Whey, Peine was also the youngest son of a noble and had served as a valet in the capital. Peine knew more about the religion of the Overgod than Ari did. It was more favored among the nobility of the land than the common folk, who preferred to stick to the Old Wheylian ways of praying to the gods that inhabited the world around them.

"Well, after realm or not, the rest of his family thinks that if he isn't properly burned, his spirit will be trapped by his body and he'll be forced to haunt them," Natan said. His voice deepened when he spoke of haunting, revealing his bias for the old ways. "I told Melaina that Gremble belongs to his house, as does she, but she won't desist. She wants your ruling on the matter."

Ari nodded, turning to lead the way from the room.

"Natan is right," Peine said, hurrying along at Ari's side. "A woman belongs to her husband's house. With Gremble gone, Melaina is beholden to his family."

Ari nodded again. Peine stopped when they reached the sitting room door, not accompanying Ari and Natan any farther. Ari was glad, as Peine was still in his nightshirt. As they descended the steps into the foyer and crossed to the massive double doors leading from the keep, Ari tried to decide what Sir Cadwel would do.

A wagon stood in the courtyard, the parcels in back pulled aside to reveal Gremble's corpse. He'd been cleaned and dressed in his finery, making him look all the more gruesome to Ari. Two guards stood by the pair of horses hooked to the wagon and two more by the bed. Melaina was between the wagon and the steps, her arms around her three young children. She glared up at Gremble's parents, older brother, and sister-in-law.

"Lord Aridian," she said as Ari trotted down the steps. "My lord, you must help me. Surely you will see reason. I must be allowed to take Gremble to be properly buried."

Before Ari could descend the final step, Gremble's family surrounded him. They all spoke at once, giving Ari a general impression of grief and anger. He held up a hand and they trailed off.

"Melaina," Ari said, looking over their heads. "You know you were given into this family when you married. You know Gremble is a son of their house." He gestured to Gremble's father and brother. "Why should you think I will side against the king's laws?"

"Because everyone knows your kind heart, my lord." She sounded near to tears. The two little girls clinging to her skirts were already weeping but Gremble's son, a boy of about nine, looked between Ari and Melaina with a face pinched by his struggle not to cry.

"What is it you have to say that will appeal to my heart when my head knows the law?" Ari asked. He tried to make his tone kind.

"Gremble wished to be buried by a priest of the Overgod, in a proper cemetery," she said, pulling her shoulders back. "He wishes to ascend into the after realm of the Overgod, the holy land reserved only for true believers. If . . ." Her voice trembled. "If he isn't given proper burial, he'll never be allowed into the after realm and I'll never see him again." She burst into tears, squeezing her children to her.

"You won't be getting any outlandish Overgod funeral when you go," Gremble's mother said. "Not if we have any say in it, girl, so what do you care?"

Melaina only cried harder.

Ari scrubbed a hand through his hair. "A man has the right to make that choice," Ari said. "Is there any here who can confirm Melaina's claim? Did Gremble wish an Overgod burial?"

"He only mimed a care for that Overgod of hers," Gremble's mother said. "He was just like any other boy chasing after a girl, my lord."

Melaina looked at them, her face crumpled with sorrow. "He was a believer."

Gremble's father leaned over and spat.

"My father did believe," Gremble's son said, pulling away from his mother.

Gremble's brother cleared his throat, casting a sheepish look at his family. "The boy's right, my lord," he said. His face hardened at his family's exclamations. "I don't like it any better than the rest of you, but Lord Aridian is right. A man has the right to make that choice, and I know Gremble. He may have started out as a man trying to win a girl, but he came to believe. He spent hours--" He stopped, clearing his throat again. "Hours trying to convert me. He said he wanted our whole family to convert, so instead of our spirits returning to the fire of the earth as they ought, we'd live on in that after realm. I just wish he was right, so we could see him again."

"You see, my lord?" Melaina said, her voice triumphant.

"If it was Gremble's own wish, we must honor it," Ari said.

Natan frowned, looking displeased with the decision.

Ari took in Melaina's relief, the anger of Gremble's parents, and the quantity of possessions piled around the dead man in the back of the wagon. "How far are you going, Melaina? You seem to have packed a great many things."

"To my village," she mumbled, dropping her gaze to the ground.

"And how long were you and the children planning to stay there? Does an Overgod funeral take a long time?"

"No, my lord," she said, not looking up, confirming his suspicions by her demeanor. She didn't mind making Gremble's family angry with her because she didn't have any intention of coming back.

"I know you're headed south, away from the mountains," Ari said. He couldn't recall exactly which village she'd once called home, but from Sorga, nearly everything was south. "But even in those peaceful lands, it's not wise for a woman and children to travel alone. I'm going to send some guards with you."

167

"That's very kind of you, my lord," she said, looking up, a hint of desperation in her tone. "But I'm sure we'll be safe. All the trouble's been in the mountains. We shan't go near them."

"No, I won't hear of you going alone." Ari was more sure than ever that she didn't intend to come back. It was one thing to honor Gremble's wishes, but quite another to take the children from the family. Especially since, as far as Ari was able to recall, Gremble's brother hadn't yet sired any. "Natan." Ari waited until Natan met his gaze before continuing. "Please pick two men to accompany Melaina. Advise them that they should take special care not to let any of them out of their sight for even a moment. I don't want to compound the grief of Gremble's death by losing his wife and children."

Natan cocked his head, seeming to take in Ari's carefully selected words. "Yes, my lord," he said. He gave Ari the barest of winks before executing a crisp bow and hurried away.

"You're too kind, my lord," Melaina said, her voice bitter.

Ari scrutinized the hard lines of disappointment and anger marring her face. He felt bad for this young widow. He knew her family had sent her from her home in the south, willing to place her so far away because she came without a dowry to offset the additional expenses she would incur her husband's family. He was sure she and Gremble had formed a true attachment, however, and now even that small comfort was gone.

There wasn't anything he could do about it, though. The law was very clear. A woman went from being in the keeping of her father's family to being in the keeping of her husband's, and any issue of the union were members of his family. Knowing the law didn't make Ari feel much better about his decision. He comforted himself with the thought that now, with fresh grief to guide her, was not the time for Melaina to be making such hasty decisions about her future or her children's. Maybe in time, when calm and reason prevailed, some other agreement could be reached.

Ari waited with Gremble's glowering family while Melaina reorganized the possessions in the back of the wagon. He was glad the children were small enough that they could all fit in the seat with her. None of them would have to ride in back with their father. She lifted up the littlest girl, then the next, but when she reached for her son, he stepped back.

"I don't want to go," he said.

Beside Ari, Gremble's family stirred.

"But we have to take Daddy away," Melaina said, holding out a hand to him. "You have to come, to say goodbye."

"I want to stay here and fight with Lord Aridian," the boy said, turning pleading eyes to Ari. "I'm big enough. I'm going to kill those wolves. Daddy was a guard. He would want me to fight them for him."

Fresh tears leaked from Melaina's eyes. She took a step toward him. The boy scooted backward. She shuddered, looking as if her self-possession was about to slip.

Ari realized he had no idea of the child's name, and made a mental note to ask Peine later. "Your first duty is to your mother and sisters now," Ari said. He walked over to the boy, placing a hand on his shoulder. "What your father would want is for you to protect them on the journey south."

The boy looked at the hand on his shoulder before tilting back his wide-eyed face to look up at Ari. He gulped. "Yes, my lord."

"And you'll do a good job of it?"

"Yes, my lord."

"Good lad," Ari said, trying to sound like Sir Cadwel. He patted the boy on the shoulder and pushed him toward his mother. Melaina scooped him up, putting him in the wagon with his sisters. She cast Ari a grateful glance before walking around to the other side to take her seat there. Ari stepped back by Gremble's family and their stiff silence.

Natan returned with two mounted soldiers. One was an older fellow, Serel, and the other, to Ari's surprise, was a younger man about Melaina's age. Ari cast Natan a questioning look and received another wink in reply. A page came out of the castle and hurried up to Natan, drawing him away.

Ari stayed, waiting until the wagon was moving, the little boy turning to wave, before retreating up the steps and back into the keep. The sun was still below the horizon, and he wanted to get something to eat before the great hall filled up. It would be hard enough to eat now, knowing the day that lay before them. He didn't know if he'd be able to stomach anything at all once the hall was filled with mourners.

Peine was waiting for Ari outside the large arched entrance, dressed in his own finery. He looked paler than ever. Ari couldn't tell if it was because Peine's naturally light Wheylian complexion wasn't complemented by his dark formal clothes, or because of the sorrows of the day.

"What happened?" Peine asked as they entered the great hall. "Did you let Melaina go? Didn't that make Gremble's family furious? I had one of the pages take the message for Sir Cadwel to Natan."

There were a few people already in the hall, alone or in small groups. All of the usual chatter was missing, replaced by low whispers or blank silent stares. Ari nodded at Peine's words, glad Peine had noticed the message Ari'd scribed the night before, for he'd forgotten about it.

Setting aside his usual habit of eating at one of the lower tables in the morning, Ari led the way to the head table, where Sir Cadwel's chair was, and where Ari and Peine ate dinner most evenings. He thought it might look reassuring to the people if he was up there, and he didn't want to chance sitting below and having anyone join them. Ari sat in his usual spot, to the right of Sir Cadwel's. He looked across the room at the side table where the cooks were assembling food, unsure if he really wanted any.

"I did let her go," Ari said, once he and Peine were seated in the relative seclusion of the head table. "And Gremble's family was furious. So was Melaina, for I sent two men to guard her and insure that she and the children return. I think she didn't intend to."

"What?" Peine said. "She's lucky you're so perceptive. If she ran off with the children, Gremble's family could ask to have her branded a thief and put a price on her."

Ari hadn't even thought of that. He was just trying to correctly implement the king's law. He looked around, wondering when Ispiria would be down. She was usually an early riser. Then again, even if Larke had hid her memories of her late night visit to Ari, she would still be extra tired, wouldn't she? She would probably sleep as late as she could. He wanted to see her, though, to make sure she seemed herself.

"Ari." Peine's voice was loud in Ari's ear. "You aren't listening to me, are you? I asked, do you want me to get you any food?"

"I can go myself."

"I'm aware that you're physically capable of getting food. I'm just worried you aren't mentally capable of it."

Ari frowned at him.

"Don't look at me like that. You have a long day ahead. You have to preside over every funeral. Well, except Gremble's, I guess. And I know you're worried about if you did the right thing about Melaina. I'll just go get us something to eat. You wait here. Maybe Ispiria will come sit with you. She should be down soon. She always is."

The last few words of Peine's chatter trailed off as he walked away, not seeming to mind that he was carrying on a conversation with no one. Ari leaned back in his chair.

On the heels of Peine's reminder about the funerals came a wish that Ispiria would be too indisposed to come down. If Ari was expected to witness each one, so was she. Ari didn't want her to have to watch people she knew being burned. True, that was the fate of most all who died in Sorga, but it seemed grimmer to Ari now, after witnessing the village. He wondered what the priests of the Overgod would do about something like the village. The people were already burned, their souls released back to the fire of the earth, so how could the Overgod priests trap them and save them for their after realm?

To Ari's relief, Natan came striding in, breaking into his grim musings. Natan, Ari noticed for the first time, was wearing his finery as well. The handsome master steward strode the length of the hall, coming to stand across the table from Ari.

"You do realize you're going to have to learn to sit in it someday," Natan said, glancing at Sir Cadwel's chair.

"Someday is not today," Ari replied a bit sourly. "Have you already eaten?"

"In fact, I have. Do you wish to come see off the men taking news of Lady Ispiria's safety to Cadwel, or shall I do it?"

Ari scrutinized him, trying to figure out if it was some sort of test. There was no real reason for him to go. He was trying to eat breakfast. Peine was headed back with food. Sir Cadwel didn't see off every contingent that set foot outside the keep. Natan's face was expressionless, giving Ari little to work with.

"Yes," Ari said, standing. He wasn't sure if seeing the men off was required of him or not, but they were going into a dangerous situation and he was their lord.

He followed Natan, whose face had lightened from expressionless to pleased. "I won't be long," Ari said to Peine, who was just then arriving with their food.

They headed back outside. Ari stood on the steps, making a slight show of looking over the score of men before him. Their faces were grim and all were weathered. Older men with more to fight for and less to lose.

"Your number should protect you from ambush, so don't press your mounts for undue speed," Ari said. "Dying by riding off a mountain cliff will make you just as dead as being killed by wolves."

The men nodded.

"You have your message?" Ari asked, focusing on their commander, denoted by his position in front of the others.

"Aye, my lord. We're to tell Sir Cadwel that Lady Ispiria is rescued and give him your note." He patted his breast, indicating he'd secured the parchment in his doublet.

Ari wondered if he should have added to it, to tell Sir Cadwel about the compulsion the Caller had put on Ispiria, but he discarded the idea. All Sir Cadwel needed to know was that she was safe, the details of her rescue, and the details of Peine's bad behavior.

Ari hoped his friend wouldn't be in too much trouble. Sometimes, when provoked, Sir Cadwel could be harsh. Ari also hoped that Larke would find a way to cure Ispiria soon, for her sake and to alleviate the need to burden Sir Cadwel with any more worrying news.

"You're bringing Sir Cadwel good news," Ari said, forcing a smile. "He'll be happy to see you. May your journey be swift and safe."

"But not too swift, my lord," one of the men called, his tone amused. The rest chuckled.

Ari smiled, waving them toward their mounts. He didn't mind the man's words. He knew he hadn't really needed to warn veteran soldiers like these about not riding too fast on the mountain trails. He stayed on the steps until they mounted and headed out, falling into formation as they went.

Ari returned to the dining hall, leaving Natan to start preparing for the first funeral pyre to be lit. The hall was fuller now, although still lacking Ispiria, and the food Peine put in front of him was cold. Ari glanced around at the grieving people of Sorga, his eyes ending on Ispiria's empty seat. He pushed his food away.

Chapter 15

Ari stared into the flickering fire. It was the last of the funeral pyres that had been lit that afternoon, and even though it was full dark now, it still blazed brightly. Each pyre was large, ensuring that it would last for nearly a day, leaving nothing left but the low pit in which it was set and a pile of ash. Tomorrow, the pits would be filled and the killing ground between the outer and inner gates of Sorga raked clean.

Ari had done his best, speaking before the lighting of every pyre, as the lord of the keep ought. He worked to make each speech different from the last and to make his words personal, but it was a difficult task. It was only a few short months now that he'd dwelled among them. Not since his arrival the fall before had he felt so keenly that he wasn't from Sorga. Ari hadn't grown up among them. Many of them, he barely knew. The seven they burned today, he never would.

He watched, mesmerized, as cinders floated into the night, wondering if the soul was freed as soon as the still form atop each pyre crumpled in on itself, or if a man's life force couldn't return to the fire of the earth until it was carried into the air in individual sparks. Unbidden, Gremble's face rose in Ari's mind.

175

Had he done the right thing, letting Melaina take Gremble's body away to be buried in the ground?

Ari didn't believe in the Overgod. He knew he wasn't an expert on the secret workings of life, but he felt his time among the Aluiens gave him more insight than most. Ari knew that a man's soul was trapped in his body. When an Aluien was created, a human was, in essence, killed. He or she was brought to the point of death and then beyond, revived by the Orlenia. If the soul wasn't trapped in the body, why would it stay when death came? There would be no revival, Orlenia or no, because the soul would already be gone.

And what of Empty Ones? They were brought beyond death and their souls didn't depart. Their spark of life remained to animate them. It was crossing over that line, the one between life and what came after, that imbued both Aluiens and Empty Ones, and Ari, with superior strength, accelerated healing, and more.

Contemplating the pile of ash beneath the flames, Ari's mind turned to how these semi-immortal beings died. Young Empty Ones died in a gruesome spurt of accelerated decay, but when the oldest died, they disintegrated into ash. The Aluiens used magical blue fire to cremate their dead. Was that all that waited for anyone, Empty One, Aluien or man? The ashes of death?

The fire writhing before him, Ari wondered if the Orlenia and the fire of life deep inside the earth were the same thing, but that, he realized, was a question he would likely never have answered.

Ari sighed, pulling his eyes away from the blaze. The killing ground was still full. He could see Larke walking about, speaking with people in soothing tones. In his wake, they were calmer, less distraught. Ari wondered if the bard was truly that gifted in his craft or if he was using some sort of Aluien magic. Mirimel must have wondered as well, because she trailed along behind him.

Ari didn't think a single person had returned to the keep yet, save Ispiria and her ladies. Her grief was a bitter thing, tears pouring from her eyes all day, until they were swollen nearly shut and as red as the flames. He wished he could go to her, that he had some comfort to give. He knew she blamed herself for these men being dead, even if no one else did. If anything, it was Ari's fault. For some reason, the Caller had thought Ari could bring him the stone. Had the Caller known the hawks wanted Ari to have it? But had they even wanted that, before the attack?

Glancing over his shoulder, he could see the windows of Sorga set into the mountainside. Rather, he could see a smattering of them. Most were dark. He didn't see any light coming from the nobles' wing, but that didn't mean for certain that Ispiria was asleep. More likely, it meant the curtains were drawn tight. He hoped she slept, though, for her sake.

Movement high up on the wall of the keep caught Ari's eye and he turned fully from the fire, squinting. Something was moving in the night. Ari suppressed a surge of panic, starting forward. He couldn't make out what it was. It was too far and there was too little light, even for his vision. It was a flickering of dark on dark near the western edge of the keep. Near the aerie.

"Larke, Mirimel," Ari called, trying to keep the alarm from his voice. He quickened his pace. Ahead of him, he saw them turn to look at him. They started toward him, but he waved them in the direction of the keep, breaking into a jog. He was sure of it now. Something was moving in the aerie. An ear-splitting avian shriek cut through the night.

Larke's body jerked with the sound. Mirimel started running, Larke a half-step behind her. Ari struggled to catch up to them, the startled faces of the castle folk an indistinct blur as his long strides cut through their ranks.

They sped through the inner gates and up the steps of the keep, the riotous calls of angry and hurt hawks raining down from above. Ari realized everyone in Sorga was following them, but there was no help for it. They had to get to the aerie.

In spite of Larke's height, Mirimel was still in the lead. She took the steps three at a time, Ari and Larke behind her. As

177

soon as he reached the top, Ari could see that Master Rellus's door was open. A hawk came streaking out, screeching. It dove at them, then whirled, speeding back into the room.

Mirimel skidded to a halt just inside Master Rellus's room. Larke dodged around her, not slowing. She reached a hand out in front of her, taking a tentative step, and Ari realized that she couldn't see beyond the light spilling through the doorway. Still in the hall, he grabbed the nearest torch from its sconce and hurried to her, holding it high above his head.

"Thank you," she said, heading across the room.

Ari nodded, even though he was following her.

Mirimel hurried down the hallway leading out to the aerie, but astonishment slowed Ari's steps. Ahead of him, he could hear Larke cursing. The bard never cursed, but expletives broad and colorful in nature flowed down the hall in elegant, well-modulated, anger-drenched tones. Hearing the sound of running feet in Master Rellus's room, Ari turned back, relatively sure from Larke's reaction that, while something terrible had happened, there was no immediate danger. Behind him, he heard Mirimel let out a low cry.

The two guards who were stationed on the steps that evening came running across Master Rellus's room, followed by a sea of castle folk. They skidded to a halt when they saw Ari emerging from the tunnel, people piling up inside the room and spilling back out into the hallway. Ari could see that all eyes were on him and the torch.

"Something has happened to the hawks," Ari said, loud enough to carry. He turned to the two guards. "No one is to come down this tunnel, save Master Rellus. I'll call you if we need you. Get some more light in here so people can see." He handed one of them the torch, waiting until they nodded before hurrying away.

The aerie ledge was a star-drenched gray, but Ari knew the heavens provided enough light for Mirimel to see at least somewhat because she knelt in a mess of broken eggs before the cage which once housed the female hawk she'd saved. Hawks crouched on ledges around her, silent now, statue-like observers. Mirimel cradled something in her arms. Larke stood behind her, his hands resting on her shoulders, but as Ari stepped out into the night, the bard whirled to face him.

"Who knew?" Larke demanded. "Who knew they hide the stone in their eggs?"

Larke's self-control was slipping, the illusion he used to hide his true self giving way with it. His eyes glowed with the pale blue light of the Orlenia. Alone in their cavern home, Aluiens all glowed, the power that infused them spilling forth in a joyous display of light, but when they walked among humans, they took pains to hide themselves.

"The Caller knew," Mirimel said.

Ari couldn't see her face, but her words were ragged. He felt ragged himself, almost ill. Those were the last eggs of the season. All of the baby hawks for that year were gone, wantonly destroyed.

"The Caller was not here," Larke said. "I would know. There's no way something that foul could come so near without me sensing it. Ari, did you?"

"Would I be able to?" Ari asked, surprised. He reached up to touch the amulet the Lady had given him. It was warm against his chest. Would it be cold if the Caller was near? But no one was here now. How near would an Empty One need to be to alert Ari or the Lady's gift?

"Yes, of course," Larke said, his tone impatient.

"Larke." Ari had never seen Larke angry before, and he didn't want to antagonize him, but he was worried Master Rellus would arrive soon. "Your eyes are glowing."

"My eyes?" Larke closed them, drawing in a deep breath. When he opened them again, they were a mortal blue. "Thank you, lad," he said in a more normal tone.

Peeking out from his cage, the bandaged little hawk made a chirping sound, cocking his head at Larke.

"What does he say?" Mirimel's voice was tattered around the edges. She stood, placing something on the central table, and Ari realized she'd been holding the hawk she'd saved, the one her father had locked in the cellar with her. The hawk was flat, her head twisted around at an impossible angle. Mirimel drew in a deep breath, resting one hand on the body, gently smoothing the feathers. Ari lifted his eyes from the hawk to Mirimel's face, amazed all over again at how calm she could make herself seem.

"He says--" Larke blinked, looking between Ari and Mirimel, his face lined with worry. "He says their attacker had her face and hair covered. They can't identify her."

"Her?" Ari said sharply, tension filling every muscle.

"Aye. They're sure of it. Too small to be a man, not the right shape. Whoever did this was a she."

Silence descended on them. Ari looked up at the moon, hoping with all his being that it wasn't Ispiria. It couldn't be. Even if the Caller had planted ideas in her mind, she wouldn't do this. Ispiria wouldn't murder unborn baby hawks. He thought back, trying to estimate how long she'd been gone from the funerals. He wanted to tell himself he was wrong, but he knew she'd had enough time.

"We need a plan," Ari said, speaking before either of them could voice what he was thinking. He didn't want to hear Ispiria accused aloud. Once they were done where they were, he would go find her and ask her where she'd been. "And I'll need to tell the people something. There's no way to hide this."

"I'd be a month trying to clean up this memory," Larke said, nodding.

Ari thought for a moment. "I'm going to tell them that this is over a stone," he said, raising a hand to forestall Larke. "Not a magic stone. Just a highly valuable one. This attack, and the one on the village, were all over a very valuable stone that the Hawkers have long kept in secret, guarding it for the Lord of Sorga. At least that's pretty much true." Ari sighed. He hated lying. It was all true, though, or at least half-true. The Hawkers had been guarding the stone for the Lords of Sorga, in a way, for the hawks had given it to Ari. The Hawkers just hadn't known they were guarding it. "And then I'm going to tell them that I've given the stone to Natan for safekeeping and he's locked it away in the castle stores." Although Ari had never seen the storeroom in the short time he'd been living in Sorga, he knew there was a locked room somewhere in the keep, where all the money was kept. Only Natan and Sir Cadwel had keys. "Then, we'll see who comes for it."

"But won't that put the stone in danger?" Mirimel asked. She still stood with one hand resting on the dead hawk.

"We won't really put it there. We'll lie." Ari grimaced, but there was no point in lying about intending to lie.

"Won't Natan want to see the stone?" she pressed. "Can we trust him?"

"There will be no more giving up of secrets," Larke said. "Trust him as I do, we're not showing Natan the stone."

"Mirimel's right," Ari said, deflated. It had seemed like a good plan when he'd thought of it. "He'll want to see the stone, and I don't know if I can deny him. It would hurt him too much to feel he's not trusted."

"We'll give him a stone," Larke said, a smile flickering across his face. He glanced around for a moment, then reached down and retrieved a small pebble. Muttering to himself, he made a swirling gesture around it, glowing Orlenia trailing from the tips of his fingers. Suddenly, in place of the stone was a large sapphire.

Mirimel's lips parted, surprise infusing her face. Larke winked at her.

Ari shook his head. "I can still see the stone underneath your illusion."

"Of course you can, lad, and were she to try, Mirimel could as well, but I assure you, Natan cannot."

"But won't the traitor who did this know that's not the real stone?" Mirimel asked. She looked from the dead hawk to the smashed eggs. "They'll know it isn't a sapphire."

"I don't mean for anyone save Natan to see it," Larke said. "You can't go waving it about. Keep in mind, we don't actually have a giant sapphire." He frowned at them, the dour expression strange on Larke's face. "No one else is to be seeing it, and when we're through, Natan won't recall he did either."

"But . . ." Ari paused, his mind fleshing out the full extent of the plan. "Won't we be putting Natan in danger? I think it's fairly common knowledge that only he and Sir Cadwel have keys to the treasure room."

"So warn him, lad," Larke said. "Natan is perfectly capable of seeing to his own welfare."

The little hawk made his strange chirping sounds again, a noise that seemed too gentle to come from the mouth of a bird of prey. They all turned to look at him.

"He says our plan is sound," Larke translated. "He also says some of the hawks suffered minor hurts that need tending and they would like me to cremate the mother and the eggs." The lines on Larke's face deepened as he spoke.

"Where is Master Rellus?" Ari said, looking around, although he knew the hawkmaster wasn't there.

"I don't know," Larke said. "But I've the feeling we should find out."

"I'll go make my announcement and send out a search for him," Ari said, squaring his shoulders. Larke handed him the sapphire. Ari almost dropped it, surprised he could feel the facets of it when he knew it was really a rounded pebble. "That's amazing."

"Finally, some appreciation," Larke said.

Ari shook his head.

"Lord Aridian," Natan called from somewhere out of sight down the tunnel.

"Best hurry, lad," Larke said.

Ari looked around the silent aerie, sadness settling on him. "I'm sorry I didn't keep you safe," he said to the hawks, before turning and heading back down the tunnel to Master Rellus's room. It was time to try to look reassuring while he lied to his people.

Chapter 16

"Lord Aridian said we wasn't to let anyone go down there but Master Rellus." The uncertain voice of one of the guards reached Ari as he headed back into the tunnel.

"I doubt he meant to include me in that statement," Natan said, sounding annoyed.

Ari rounded the corner, entering the firelight that warmed Master Rellus's room. A quick glance didn't reveal the hawkmaster, but the room and the hall beyond were filled with castle folk.

"It was a hastily given order," Ari said as he drew closer. He nodded to the two guards he'd left at the entrance to the aerie tunnel. "Thank you." He stopped just inside the tunnel, aware that everyone was watching him. He wanted to talk to Natan alone. He found himself shifting from foot to foot, clenching the fake sapphire tightly. Should he order everyone away or try to walk through them? He couldn't bring Natan out to the aerie. Larke was probably using that magical blue fire out there.

With a slight shake of his head, Natan turned to face the room. "Everyone to the great hall," he called. "Lord Aridian will be addressing us all shortly in the great hall, where everyone can hear at once." People must have thought it was a good idea. Word was passed and Master Rellus's room began to empty. "You too," Natan said to the two guards at the end of the tunnel. They looked to Ari.

"Please find out where Master Rellus is and bring him to the great hall as well," Ari said to them, ignoring Natan's raised eyebrows. They nodded and left.

Natan stood by Ari's shoulder until they were alone. Ari used the time to carefully work out what he wanted to say. He knew misleading someone was almost as bad as lying, but, for the sake of his conscience, he was determined to lie as little as possible. When the last curious pair of eyes in the hallway turned and headed down the steps to the main level, Natan broke the silence.

"Ari, what's going on?"

"Someone attacked the hawks in the aerie," Ari said. He held out the stone. Natan's eyes went wide. "The hawks in the village have long guarded a secret treasure. At least, we thought it was a secret. The one who flew here the morning that the Hawkers' village was attacked--"

"He was carrying that?" Natan interrupted, his voice tinged with awe. "It's amazing."

"I need you to lock it away somewhere safe."

Natan pressed his lips together in a frown. "I can lock it in with the tithes. That's about as safe as we can make it. There's only one key, and I keep it on me unless I'm asleep." Natan patted the breast of his doublet, indicating where he kept it.

"Sir Cadwel doesn't have one?" Ari was surprised. He'd always thought there were two keys.

"You know our great lord and master," Natan said. "He likes it better when he doesn't have to manage anything."

Ari didn't think that was quite fair. Yes, Sir Cadwel traveled a lot, leaving Natan to run everything, but the knight saw to his duties as Duke of Sorga when he was in the keep. It occurred to Ari that what Sir Cadwel did in Sorga may not be the source of Natan's continued complaints, however. It might have more to do with the fact that Natan would never be in tourneys or go on quests or any of that. He'd been stripped of his knighthood, after all.

"Will you take this and lock it away for me?" Ari asked, keeping his internal revelations to himself.

"At once," Natan said. He held out his hand and Ari dropped the fake sapphire into it, feeling slightly guilty at the awed look on Natan's face as he held it.

"Natan," Ari said to stop the master steward from leaving. "I'm worried that whoever smashed the eggs will come after it again. In fact, I hope they do, so that we can catch them. I'll make it public that it's locked away, but I'll probably be putting you in danger when I do so."

Natan nodded, not appearing very worried. "I'm the perfect man for the task, my lord. I'll meet you in the great hall."

"Right," Ari said, grimacing. He wasn't relishing the idea of what he had to do next. He followed Natan from the room, almost stopping in surprise when he heard fleeing footsteps on the stairwell in the hall. Whoever they were, they trod softly, but Ari's ears could pick out the sound. If someone was coming up, why did they run back down? Could they hear Natan and him talking from there? Ari clenched his fists, realizing his hesitation had already cost him the chance of going after whoever it was.

He and Natan parted ways where the inner stairwell emptied into the foyer, Natan to descend into the bowels of the keep and Ari to cross to the great hall. Stepping inside the massive room that was the heart of Sorga, Ari surveyed the gray stone walls, the rough dark wood beams and the tension-filled faces illuminated by thousands of flickering candle flames. He took a deep breath, raising a hand to silence the murmuring crowd. Before he could speak, his eyes caught sight of a body laid out on a wood plank table. One of the guards he'd sent looking for Master Rellus hurried forward.

"My lord," the guardsman said. "I was just coming to find you. We found the hawkmaster outside with that hawk

185

guardian and carried him in here." He lowered his voice. "I think he's been poisoned, my lord."

"Thank you," Ari said, nodding. He walked down the tunnel that opened in the throng of castle dwellers, the guard following. Ari was acutely aware of hundreds of worried eyes, all fixed on him.

Master Rellus appeared to be unconscious. He rested on someone's cloak on top of the table, his breath ragged and shallow. Kimmer sat beside him, holding his hand. On his other side was the castle physician. The physician's countenance was grave, but Ari knew that to be his normal expression.

"Bartel," Ari greeted the dour gray-haired little man. "What happened?"

"My lord," the physician replied, giving a quick bow. "I have had little time to examine the patient, but my opinion is that he was almost certainly poisoned."

This sent a murmur through the crowd, and Ari realized he'd undone all of the guard's care in imparting the information.

"Where was he found?" Ari asked, turning to look at the guard.

"I found him, my lord," Kimmer said. The eyes she raised to Ari's were dark with worry, her round face pale under her blonde hair. "When we were all outside, one of the hawks came to me and he was so upset. He acted like he wanted me to follow him, so I did. They're awful smart, Sorga hawks, so I thought I'd better. He led me to Master Rellus, all slumped down just off to the side of the inner gate, in the shadows. I called for help, and some guards came and carried him inside." She stopped talking, sounding almost breathless from the effort, and bit her lower lip, dropping her eyes to the hawkmaster's face.

Ari stood for a moment, thinking. He knew everyone was waiting for him to tell them what was going on and what to do. He had to put some words in order in his head and get them out, and make sure he sounded sure of himself when he did it.

"I came looking for you after they carried him in here," Kimmer blurted, breaking the silence. Ari realized he hadn't stopped staring at her but he'd been too deep in thought to notice when she looked back up. "But I didn't find you, so I came back."

He frowned and she dropped her gaze again. That seemed like an odd thing for her to say. His mind went to the stealthy footsteps on the staircase moments ago. How long had she been back? Kimmer was capable of walking with stealth. More so than Ispiria. In the castle, though, Ari would rank Peine as the best at sneaking. Peine, who was still of slight enough build to be mistaken for a woman, especially in the dark by hawks.

Ari didn't like that thought at all. He was almost ashamed to even have it. Peine was acting so odd lately, though. In fact, Ari realized that he hadn't seen Peine in hours. Worry shot through him like lightning hitting a tree.

"Peine?" Ari called, trying to keep the fear from his voice.

"Yes, my lord?" Peine said, pushing his way forward through the crowd. He came to stand before Ari, looking up at him expectantly.

Relief dulled the intensity of Ari's worry, although he realized that finding Peine in the great hall didn't prove anything. Peine looked like himself, though. His dark hair was neatly in place, his face composed. He didn't look guilty or disheveled or in any way incriminated. He was, however, obviously waiting to see why Ari had called him over, and there was absolutely no possibility that Ari was going to ask his best friend where he was when the eggs were smashed right there in front of everyone.

"Uh, go make sure Master Rellus's room is ready for him," Ari said, settling on a plausible enough reason for calling Peine forward. "And see if Larke and Mirimel are still out on the aerie ledge caring for the hawks. Tell them what happened and that Master Rellus is being brought up. I want Larke to look at him. And have someone make a stretcher and bring it here."

187

"Yes, my lord," Peine said, looking undaunted by the list of tasks. He bowed and hurried away, pulling a few people aside to give them orders in a low voice.

"My lord," Physician Bartel said.

Ari turned to face him, taking in the deeper than usual frown lines.

"May I ask why you see fit to request a wandering entertainer look in on my patient, my lord?" Bartel said, his voice brittle with affront.

"Because Minstrel Larke is well traveled," Ari said, keeping his own tone firm. "He has a vast store of knowledge that may be useful to you, and some small healing skills of his own. I ask that you give him every courtesy and I'm sure he will give you the same."

"Yes, my lord," the physician said, the lines on his face not relenting. "I shall gather my things and take myself to Master Rellus's room. I trust he will arrive there shortly." He bowed slightly before thumping past Ari and out of the room.

Physician Bartel's exit was slightly marred by the arrival of two guardsmen with a makeshift stretcher. He had to step aside to allow them to pass down the narrow corridor formed by the crowd. Ari assisted the guards in moving Master Rellus onto the stretcher, using his strength to make the transfer as smooth as possible. Kimmer hampered them all somewhat by refusing to let go of Rellus's hand, but no one said anything. Ari watched, along with the rest of the castle folk, as they took the hawkmaster from the room.

All eyes turned back to him, and Ari realized the time had come. He must tell the people of Sorga something. They looked at him with faces full of worry, but also hope, making him feel that much worse. He stepped up on a bench, although he was already one of the tallest people in the room. Even their breathing seemed hushed as they waited for him to speak, to explain to them what had happened and reassure them. He hoped he could.

"You all know that someone attacked the village of the Hawkers, burning it to the ground." There were nods and murmured affirmations. "We have since learned that the villain who led the attack had one simple motive, greed."

He paused, clearing his throat, his mind fumbling through what he wanted to say. "This greed is for a certain priceless stone. The Hawkers have long kept it hidden in their village, most of them without even knowing it." That created a stir. Ari waited for silence to return, using the time to form his next words. He wanted to stick to the truth as much as possible. "Most of you also know that a wounded hawk arrived in Sorga on the morning that the village was attacked. He was carrying that stone."

Again, the crowd fluttered, low voices of surprise and curiosity mingling like the rustling of wind-stirred fall leaves. As before, Ari let them talk. He'd rather have more time to think about what to say next than get his speech over with quickly. All too soon, they settled down. A room of eyes, dancing with reflected candlelight, looked up at him.

"Somehow, a member of the enemy infiltrated Sorga." Ari swallowed, certain he'd just told his people a lie. He didn't think anyone had infiltrated, but rather that someone had been corrupted. He didn't want the panic that admission could bring. "They broke in under the cover of our grief, poisoned Master Rellus to keep him away, and snuck into our aerie to search for the stone."

This drew anger from the crowd, battering down curiosity and worry alike.

"The intruder was not caught, but also did not get the stone. This valuable stone, although protected by the hawks when in the Hawkers' village, was not with the hawks here. In fact, it is locked safely away in the storeroom."

Ari scrubbed a hand through his hair, feeling the weight of duty upon him. How much simpler would his life be if he was one of the people filling the great hall, not the one standing on a bench, delivering half-truths and lies to those who looked to him for leadership? He wished he could just tell everyone the truth, but the truth wouldn't lead them to any greater

189

satisfaction. Ari didn't himself understand why the Caller wanted the Hawks' stone.

He needed to offer his people something, though. If he couldn't supply understanding, he would try to give comfort. "I don't know why this enemy has sprung up, intent on destroying those we love," he said, keeping his tone even, but pitching his voice to carry. His mind went to the battles Sir Cadwel had him read about, too many of them fought for even more obscure and stupid reasons even than greed. "It seems like the world will always breed this kind of avarice. It seems like someone without the basic cornerstones of humanity always comes along to disrupt the peace we build. Someone who interprets contentment and prosperity as weakness. But we are not weak, and we will not let these attacks on Sorga go unpunished. You know Sir Cadwel will not. You know he will seek out any enemies of Sorga and bring them to their knees, and so will I. What we cannot mend, we shall at least avenge."

Ari's voice rose as he spoke. His final words were met with applause and cries of agreement from the crowd. He drew in a shaky breath. He hadn't intended to make an impassioned speech. Standing in front of a hall full of expectant eyes, though, seemed somehow to focus all of his fears and grief. His heart broke out through the words leaving his mouth, telling his people what was contained inside it. Telling them that he and Sir Cadwel would make this right.

As right as they could, at least. He stepped down from the bench, deflated by his thoughts. They could never make it all the way right. People were dead. A great number of them, and now the last of the hawks of that year were too. On top of all that, he had to go somehow ask Ispiria if she was the one who'd destroyed them.

Ari did his best to smile as he left the hall, people slapping him on the shoulder and reaching for his hands as he went. When he got to the entrance, he turned back to face the room. "It's been a hard day for us all," he called out over the din. "The sun is long since set. Get dinner on the tables."

There was more cheering, as if he'd said something important. Resisting the urge to shrug at them all to indicate his confusion over their response, Ari left the great hall. He hoped they would eat and then sleep and that tomorrow could be almost like a normal day. He was starting to feel as if he hadn't gotten a normal day in quite some time.

Before that could happen, though, he had to go see Ispiria.

Chapter 17

Ari weighed the various possibilities in his head as he crossed the foyer. The way he saw it, the Caller had plenty of time to corrupt Peine, Kimmer or Ispiria. Any one of them might be the one who'd smashed the eggs. That was part of the evil of the Empty Ones. They didn't need a willing tool. They could tamper with a person's brain and make him or her do things they didn't want to do. Things they may not even remember doing.

As much as Ari might hope that out of those three possibilities, it was Kimmer, he had to face the fact that the Caller had Ispiria in his control for over a day and she'd already tried to get the stone once. Still, Peine had been acting very odd, although he'd rarely been out of the sight of other people. Kimmer had, Ari realized, but she seemed the least strange of the three and he wasn't sure if even an Empty One could make a hawk guardian smash hawk eggs.

Of course, he realized as he trotted up the steps, the egg smasher might be someone else entirely. He always thought of Sorga as very secure, but how secure was it? He paused before turning down the corridor toward the rooms Ispiria shared with her great grandmother. Shaking his head, he started forward again. No, that thought was too confusing. He needed to start with what he already had. He would find out where Ispiria had spent her evening since leaving after the last pyre was lit, then he'd worry about Peine and Kimmer. Once he eliminated them, he could seek other possibilities.

Ari stopped outside Ispiria's rooms, only a few down from his own, and knocked softly. A rustling sound came from inside and, moments later, a maid opened the door. She blinked once in surprise before composing her face into a mask of politeness.

"May I help you, my lord?" she asked, curtsying.

"I would like to speak to Lady Ispiria, please," Ari said, trying not to sound worried. He didn't know what he would say or how he would say it. Ispiria would want to know why he wanted to know where she'd been. He really didn't want to have to tell her he was worried her mind was corrupted and she was a poisoner and a hawk murderer. That was not a conversation that would go well at all.

"Just a moment, my lord," the maid said, closing the door.

Ari waited, clenching and unclenching his hands at his sides, trying to sort out the murmuring voices inside the room. A few moments later, to his surprise, Ispiria's great grandmother opened the door.

"My lord," Lady Enra said, her face folded into hard lines. Though her eyes were milky with age, they locked onto his. "They tell me you wish to speak to my great granddaughter at this hour of the night."

"I realize it's late," Ari said, suppressing a grimace. "But it's an urgent matter." Indeed, he hadn't spared the time much thought. Now that she mentioned it, he realized he was being a bit rude. He'd have to wait to talk to Kimmer in the morning, he supposed, but hopefully he could still put his mind to ease about Ispiria.

"No matter is that urgent to a lady," she said in a crisp voice. "I'm sure it can wait until a reasonable hour in the morning."

"Uh, well, yes." He didn't want to wait until morning. He would worry about it all night. He couldn't frame a polite disagreement, though. "My lady, it really is urgent."

"Ispiria is sleeping," she snapped. She started to slide the door closed.

"For how long?"

Lady Enra paused, frowning. "I daresay until she wakes, although I find your manners impertinent, to say the slightest, young man."

"No, that is, how long has she been sleeping?" He was surprised at the animosity radiating from Lady Enra. He cast back in his mind, wondering when it had started. She ate dinner at the head table almost every night, but he rarely spoke to her. Usually, he, Peine and Ispiria talked a lot and the old woman sat in silence at the end of the table.

"Since she returned from the funeral rites hours ago. Such sorrow is exhausting to one of her delicate nature. It's something I strive to shelter her from. Good night, my lord." She closed the door, not very gently, leaving Ari standing in the hall, gaping in surprise.

He blinked a few times, gathering his thoughts. At least he knew Ispiria's great grandmother thought she'd been in her room when the hawks were killed. Ari wished he could feel more reassured by that, but he knew how adept Ispiria was at sneaking out.

Realizing he wasn't going to get anywhere further with that line of inquiry until morning, Ari turned and headed into his sitting room. He'd hoped Peine would be there so he could eliminate his valet from the list of suspects, but his rooms were empty. He considered going to check on Master Rellus, but Larke was already with him and, more than likely, Peine would have any news there was when he returned. Ari walked over and stirred up the sitting room fire, staring into the flickering flames.

He wondered what Sir Cadwel was doing. Hopefully enjoying a relatively pleasant evening. The knight would know by now that Ispiria was safe, and Ari wouldn't send news about the attack on the aerie until morning, so Sir Cadwel shouldn't be worried. For now.

The door opened, drawing Ari's gaze from the flames.

Peine came in, smiling and closing the door softly behind him. "Larke says Master Rellus is going to be well. He started to recover soon after we brought him up. Physician Bartel seemed surprised." Peine lowered his voice. "Do you think Larke did something magic to save him?"

"I have no idea," Ari said, scrubbing his hands through his hair. "Peine, don't take this the wrong way, but where were you when the hawk eggs were smashed?"

"I was looking for Kimmer."

Ari could tell by the way the smile left Peine's face that he was offended.

"I was near you, though," Peine continued. "I saw you call out to Larke and Mirimel and all three of you went running. Everyone else started to follow and I got held back. I guess I'm not tall enough to be that fast. Yet."

Ari nodded. "I'm sorry," he said, hoping Peine could tell he meant it. "It's just, you were up in the mountains. It's possible you've been exposed to the Caller and you don't remember it. He can do things like that, like Larke can. He can make people do things they don't want to and don't remember doing."

Peine turned his gaze in the direction of Ispiria's suites. "I see," he said. "I understand." He pursed his lips. "Um . . . did you ask where Ispiria was? I mean, don't be angry, but if what you just said is true, we know he had her, and--"

"I did ask," Ari said, cutting into Peine's babbling before it could become too frantic. It almost made him smile, how worried Peine was about suggesting that it might be Ispiria, even after Ari had half-accused him. "But I didn't get a very good answer."

"Can't Larke tell?"

"A little." Ari shook his head, realizing that was an inadequate response. "He can tell that the Caller did something to Ispiria's mind, but not what, exactly." Ari locked eyes with his friend. "I don't want it to be Ispiria. If she poisoned Master Rellus and smashed those eggs, even if she doesn't remember doing it and didn't mean to do it, if we let her find out, she'll be mad with grief."

"Then we won't let her find out," Peine said, squaring his shoulders. "Or anyone else."

Ari nodded, but he didn't feel as confident that they could accomplish that as Peine sounded.

"But, Larke said this Caller person did something to her?" Peine asked. "When? I mean, when did he find out? Didn't he fix it?"

"I found out, and Larke confirmed it. It was last night. I couldn't tell you then because Larke was here and I didn't want him to do anything to you."

Peine nodded, his face serious, but not upset.

"Larke couldn't fix it yet, but he will." Ari hoped his friend would be content with that. He didn't feel like working through a lengthy explanation, balancing truth and vows.

Peine looked thoughtful, but he nodded again. "What did you mean, that you didn't get a very good answer from Ispiria?" Peine asked, crossing the room to stand on the other side of the fireplace, holding out his hands to the warmth. "Did she say she didn't know where she was?"

"No." Ari hesitated. He didn't want to say anything mean about Ispiria's great grandmother. "Lady Enra came to the door and she said Ispiria was sleeping."

Peine grimaced at him. "I see."

Ari cocked his head at his friend, wondering what that meant. He thought he'd kept any hint of Lady Enra's ire out of his reply. "What?"

"Well, it's just, she wouldn't be the best person to ask," Peine said, shrugging. He turned back to the fire.

"Why not?" Ari asked, starting to get a bit annoyed. Why did he always feel like everyone else knew five times more about everything than he did?

"You really don't know?"

Ari shook his head.

197

"Well, I suppose it's my job to tell you these things."

He didn't go on. Ari's hands twitched. He wanted to reach out and shake the information out of Peine. "What?" he said again, his voice hard.

"Lady Enra hates you," Peine said, shrugging. "Pretty much everyone knows it."

"She hates me?" Ari pulled back in surprise.

"Oh yes." Peine nodded. "She dictates her letters, you know, since she can't see well enough to write anymore, and she's written to Sir Cadwel seven times now asking him to forbid you to pursue Lady Ispiria's hand."

"Seven times?" Ari ran some quick calculations. He hadn't even known Ispiria for six months, and he'd been away for most of them. "Seven?"

"And been to see him quite a few times as well. It's only since he told her to stop wasting his time coming down to his study railing about you that she started writing him about it."

"But--" Ari sputtered. "Why?" He knew he wasn't perfect, and that he'd started life as a commoner, but he was the heir to Sorga and he'd won the fall tourney and, well, people liked him. Aside from people who were trying to kill him, and Prince Parrentine when they first met, Ari hadn't met anyone who hated him.

"Well, her personal maid, who takes her letters." Peine leaned forward and lowering his voice. "She said that Lady Enra says that the lords of Sorga have taken everything good in her life and destroyed it. Her eldest daughter, her youngest daughter, her granddaughter, and now you want Ispiria." He straightened, his voice returning to normal. "And now her whole village is burnt down. I know that probably doesn't have anything to do with you and Sir Cadwel, but I hear she's sure it does. She says the lords of Sorga are cursed to bring pain and suffering on their families, and that there's no way she will ever let you and Ispiria wed. I heard she even planned to take Ispiria to the Hawkers' village this summer and keep her there."

Ari stared at him.

"Why did you think Ispiria couldn't go to the spring tourney with you?" Peine asked. "You really believed what she told you about not being able to organize her ladies and her dresses in time? Ari, that's ridiculous. It's Ispiria we're talking about. She doesn't even care if she has ladies and dresses."

"The spring tourney," Ari said. He winced. He was entered into the spring tourney. He was supposed to leave for the capital in two days. There was no way he could leave, even if he wanted to, which he didn't. Keeping Sorga safe and finding the Caller were much more important tasks than winning the spring tourney. Still, he was disappointed. He wouldn't get to compete or to give Prince Parrentine and Princess Siara their wedding presents. He would have to send a messenger to them and to the king.

"Peine, remind me in the morning--"

"To send someone to bring Prince Parrentine and Princess Siara their wedding gifts and to take a message to each of them and to the king?" Peine grinned. He gestured to the writing desk standing to one side of the fireplace. Ari realized it was set out with parchment and paper.

"I don't know what I'd do without you," Ari said, walking around Peine to get to the desk.

Peine hurried after him to pull out his chair, but Ari beat him to it. He seated himself with a hint of triumph. He'd asked Peine a hundred times not to pull out chairs for him. Ari wasn't, as Sir Cadwel put it, a soft-handed lordling incapable of buckling on his own sword belt. He could pull out his chair.

"I wrote down the proper address for each letter," Peine said, pulling over a piece of parchment. "I know you can never keep all the titles straight."

"Thank you," Ari said. "But, I can write to Siara and Parrentine together now that they're married, can't I?"

Peine frowned. "I'm not going to pass on gossip, Ari," he said, "but I think you should write to them separately."

"But a wedding must mean they've reconciled their differences." Unbidden, Ari's mind called up the moment when King Ennentine told the prince that he must marry Princess

Siara. Parrentine hadn't been very happy about the idea. He'd just suffered a grievous loss, however, and Ari held hope that he would move past it in time. Siara loved Prince Parrentine. Ari was sure her love would win in the end. "I'm writing them one letter," he said, pursing his lips. In this, he wanted to let optimism triumph.

"As you see fit, my lord."

Ari rolled his eyes. Calling him my lord was how Peine said he thought Ari was making a mistake. He shrugged, pushing forward with the letters. Blocking out all thoughts of Peine or the Caller or even Ispiria, Ari concentrated on writing. It wasn't his best-honed skill, so he had to be very careful while he did it. Peine stayed quiet, although he watched over Ari's shoulder the entire time.

"There." Ari leaned back from the table and set the quill on its stand.

Peine moved around to stopper the ink.

Ari reached for some fine sand, sprinkling it over the ink to speed it in drying. "I'm going to go ready for bed. Can you seal them once they're dry? Tomorrow morning, ask Natan who would be best to send. You'll need to go down with him to the storeroom to get the gifts. They're locked away with the tithes." He frowned, not liking to be reminded of what else was locked away down there, his worries descending on him in a landslide of doubt. "We'll want someone exceedingly trustworthy. Sir Cadwel said the wedding gifts cost enough to feed an army for a month. In fact, maybe we should send several men. Natan will know what's best."

He looked to Peine for an answer, receiving a gaping yawn instead. "And then you should get some rest, too," Ari said, standing.

"I will," Peine said. "I just have a few more duties to see to. Are you sure you don't want me to help you?"

"I'm quite capable of undressing myself."

"Yes, but are you capable of properly stowing away your second best doublet and trousers?"

"I think so," Ari said, heading for the door to his bedroom. "But I'm sure you'll redo it anyhow."

"Of course I will," Peine said, turning back to the desk to rummage in the drawer where they kept sealing wax. "Have a good sleep, Ari."

"You as well," Ari said, smiling. He was glad at least one thing was back to normal.

Ari didn't sleep well. His dreams were a jumbled mess. He saw the little wren Larke had sent to the Lady, its mind full of the bard's message about Ispiria. It flew through clouds and fire and snapping wolf jaws before a long-nailed hand closed around it, squeezing it flat in a puff of downy feathers. Ispiria appeared, a never before seen look of evil cunning on her face as she mixed a dire brew of drugs and wine, twirling about a small cauldron in her bedroom, red curls flying. It boiled and frothed and she laughed a shrill screeching laugh. Flames and soot danced up her walls, devouring her curtains, but she didn't care. Then she poured the frothing concoction into a wineskin and ran off to find Master Rellus. Lastly, Ari saw the face of the Lady, repeating over and over her message that he must beware the called.

Ari tried to ask her who the called were. Was it the wolves, was it Ispiria? He started awake as Ispiria leapt up behind the Lady, wrenching back her head to pour the poisoned brew down the old Aluien's throat.

His hand flew to the amulet beneath his nightshirt, his breath ragged. The amulet wasn't cold. It lay like any normal metal against his chest, the same temperature as his skin. Ari let his hand drop. His sheets were tangled about him, his forehead coated in sweat.

Getting up, he padded over to his washstand and poured himself water, gulping it down. Setting the glass aside, he examined his amulet again. He didn't know for sure what it reacted to, or how to interpret its warnings, but it was completely inert. He could hear Peine's quiet breathing in the room beyond, somehow soothing.

Ari returned to bed, straightening his sheets before getting in. He knew he needed to set his worries aside and get some sleep. He wasn't a child, to let bad dreams bother him. He did wish, though, that he'd been a little firmer with Ispiria's great grandmother. He would sleep better if he'd gotten to look Ispiria in the eye, so he could know for sure the egg smasher wasn't her.

Chapter 18

Ari slept well the rest of the night, recovered enough from his nerves by morning to be amused at Peine's daily ritual of trying to treat him like a lord. Peine had their breakfast sent up, so it was waiting for them as soon as his friend deemed Ari presentable enough to be allowed to eat it. Sitting down at the table with Peine, Ari even forwent his normal protest that it didn't matter what he wore to eat in his own rooms. He also decided not to mention that he would have preferred to eat in the great hall where people could be reassured by seeing him and where he might see Ispiria.

He wanted to talk to Ispiria about her great grandmother. He couldn't believe she'd been hiding from him that Lady Enra didn't like him. She had to know he'd find out eventually. Hiding something like that was almost like lying. Ari felt guilty that, deep inside, knowing Ispiria was hiding something from him made him feel better about all the things he'd said, and hadn't said.

After he confronted Ispiria about her great grandmother, he would have to ask her where she was when the eggs were smashed. That thought stole Ari's appetite and he set down his spoon.

"Finally had enough porridge?" Peine said, looking up from his ham and fried potatoes.

"Porridge is good for you," Ari said, trying to regain the happy level of normalcy he'd felt only moments before. "Have you arranged the messengers yet with Natan?"

"Ari, it's only just past dawn. You always wake up so early, I practically have to get the cook out of bed so he can feed you. I'll do it after breakfast."

Ari knew the cook got up quite early, so he mustered a smile.

"We'll go talk to Ispiria after breakfast, too," Peine said, setting down his utensils. "I just wanted you to get a good meal before the troubles of the day begin."

"Maybe today won't be troubled," Ari said, although he didn't really see how that could happen. They didn't know who'd smashed the eggs, grief for all those who'd died filled the keep, and the Caller and his wolves were still out there somewhere.

"Maybe." Peine pushed back his chair. "I'll go see if Natan is up yet. He usually is."

Ari poked at his porridge while Peine gathered up the parchments from the desk and crossed to the door. No, Ari didn't see how this day could go any better than the last few. None of their days would go very well until the Hawkers' village was rebuilt and the Caller was dead.

At the door, Peine made a chocking sound. Ari's head jerked up. Peine was silently sliding the hallway door closed. The sealed messages Ari had penned the night before were scattered on the floor at his feet. His face was white, his eyes wide. Ari stood, sending his chair skidding backward.

"What?"

"Shh," Peine hissed. He cracked the door open, then shut it again. He leaned his back against the wall.

"What is it?" Ari demanded in a loud whisper. "Should I get my sword?"

Peine shook his head.

"Peine?" Ari asked, his worry mounting. What could Peine possibly have seen in the hallway? "You have to tell me what's going on. Whatever it is, we can fix it. Just tell me."

"No," Peine said, his voice breaking. "You can't fix this, Ari."

To Ari's surprise, Peine raced past him. Ari turned to see his friend flee into his bedroom, slamming the door behind him. Then, to Ari's bewilderment, he heard Peine start to cry.

Glancing between Peine's closed door and the door to the hallway, Ari crept toward the latter. What was in the hallway that had upset Peine so much? Visions of those he knew and loved dead and dismembered swam through Ari's head. Was the Caller in the keep? Where was Larke?

His hand shaking, Ari cracked open the door. All he saw was an empty hallway. Carefully, he stuck his head out. He looked left and right. Nothing. He tiptoed out and looked down the steps. He could hear people below, talking as they crossed through the foyer and into the great hall for breakfast. Everything seemed normal.

Still sneaking, although he had no idea why, Ari returned to his suite, closing the door softly behind him. He scooped up the letters, looking them over on the off chance they offered some clue to Peine's behavior, but they were just what they should be. He set them back on the desk. Treading softly, he went to Peine's room, tapping on the door. He could hear Peine crying.

"Peine," Ari called. The sobs grew muffled. "Peine, what happened?"

Ari waited, his heartbeat slowing to an almost normal rhythm. He did his best to be patient, but he mind started to range over the doings of the day. He needed to check if there were more men willing to take another message to Sir Cadwel. He needed men to send to the king. He wished now he hadn't let two of them go off with Gremble's body. It would soon get to the point where he didn't have enough men to put a double guard on the walls, because everyone had to sleep sometime.

Fortunately, a score had come in with the bodies of Ispiria's fallen escort to make up for the score that Ari had sent with the news of her rescue.

Realizing his hands were clenched and he was grinding his teeth, Ari decided to try once more before leaving Peine to whatever was bothering him. Clearly, it was private. Nothing was amiss in the hallway. Ari simply didn't have time to wait for Peine to decide to open the door.

"Peine, I'll go talk to Natan about the messages. You stay here until you're feeling more yourself."

"No," Peine called.

Ari could hear him scramble up from the bed. The door was thrown wide. Peine appeared, his face blotchy red against an overly white background.

"Don't go in Natan's room," Peine said, tears trickling out of the corners of his eyes. "Not right now."

"What is going on?" Ari used his firmest tone. If something was wrong with Natan, Ari needed to know. There was only so much coddling he could give.

Peine looked down. "Kimmer's in there, with Natan."

"In Natan's room?" Ari remembered how Natan had looked at Kimmer and Mirimel when he'd first met them. He fought down a blush.

"I saw her sneaking in," Peine said. "How could she do this to me? Why is she sneaking into Natan's room so early in the morning? Why sneaking? I mean, a woman should never go alone into a man's quarters, but the sneaking makes it so much worse. If she were doing anything irreproachable, she would have knocked and called out, and he would have come out into the hall. She wouldn't have gone in. How could? She . . . we. . ." Peine sputtered to a halt. He stepped back from the door, sinking down to sit on the edge of his bed. Resting his elbows on his knees, he lowered his chin to his hands. "I should have known that once we got here, to Sorga, she'd find someone else. What's a lowly valet who can't use a sword compared to Natan?"

While Peine was ranting, Ari's mind was turning, thinking, rearranging. He discarded his embarrassment at the idea of Kimmer and Natan together. He ruthlessly pushed aside his worry over Peine's obviously broken heart. What remained was a sudden fear for Natan.

Ari whirled, grabbing his sheathed sword as he ran back through his room. He crossed the sitting room in four great strides, bursting into the hallway. He could hear Peine scramble after him. Ari leapt down the hall, skidding into Natan's door even as he tried to fling it open. Behind him, he heard Peine's shocked protest.

Throwing the door wide, Ari tumbled into the room. He stumbled forward, taking in Natan's still form sprawled on the floor, blood pooled around his head. Careening about, not fully regaining his balance, Ari slammed into Peine, sending his valet flying backward to land with a thump in the hall.

With his free hand, Ari grabbed onto the doorframe to steady himself. Letting go, he reached down and pulled Peine up. "Get the physician, and Larke, if you can find him." Ari buckled on his sword belt so he could have both hands free. "Get someone responsible to the coffers. Someone who won't take anything if the door is open." Ignoring the slack-faced look of shock Peine was giving him, Ari ran down the hallway. He didn't slow as he hit the stairwell, plunging down the steps four at a time.

The gray stone walls of Sorga were a blur. He sped to the bottom of the keep. He was aware of people calling out to him, but he didn't slow. He all but jumped down the final flight of steps.

There were two guards outside the room where Ari had Natan put the fake gemstone. One was slumped by the door, the other halfway to him in the long hall. Both had arrows through their chests. Ari snarled in frustration, trying not to take in their faces as he passed. He didn't have time right now to stop and think about them as people he knew.

Why were they even there? The room wasn't normally guarded. He hadn't told Natan to place guards. Ari was furious with himself. He should have known Natan would take the initiative to order extra guards. The chief steward was accustomed to being in charge.

Skidding to a halt at the end of the hall, Ari dove into the room. Chest and drawers were upended. Chaos abounded.

No one was there.

Ari spun. He could hear footsteps pounding down the stairs. He stepped out of the room and shut the door. The key stuck out of the lock. Ari wrenched it around, locking the door, almost bending it in the process. He yanked it out and stuck it into his doublet beside the stone.

Some coins spilled out from the room, scattered as if kicked, but he didn't bother to collect them. Four men trotted out of the stairwell. They were all cooks, three holding knives and one a long-handled spoon. They skidded to a halt when they saw him.

"Peine said--" one started, but he stopped when his eyes fell on the guard closest to him.

"Take care of these men," Ari said, although he was relatively sure they were beyond care.

Pushing past the cooks, he bounded up the steps. In the foyer, he slid to a stop in front of the great double doors, already open for the day, a guard to each side. "Have you seen Hawk Guardian Kimmer?" he asked. "The blonde one?"

"Yes, my lord," one said. The other nodded. "She asked to go out just a short time ago. My lord, we saw you running. What's wrong? Is the keep in danger?"

Ari drew in a deep breath. "Kimmer is the traitor who poisoned Master Rellus and attacked the aerie. You," he turned to one of them, "stay here in case she tries to come back in." He turned to the other. "Spread the word. Put out a search, but don't panic. She's just one person. And don't pull any men from the outer wall. I don't want to see those gates open." He pointed across the courtyard to the inner gates.

Ari waited for an answer before stepping outside. He did his best to appear calm, ignoring the commotion erupting behind him in the keep. He knew it would be only moments before guards swarmed out, throwing the courtyard into turmoil. He looked up, scanning the battlements. Where would she have gone?

Turning, he spotted her in the far east tower where it stood against the cliff-like arm of the mountain that reached out to embrace Sorga. The low-hanging sun hadn't yet risen high enough to illuminate the easternmost towers, sheltered as they were by the mountain, but Ari's keen eyes could pick her out.

As he crossed the courtyard, he could see both guards' heads getting lower, one after the other, and guessed they were descending the stone steps that wrapped around the inner wall of the tower, departing the ramparts. He quickened his pace, wondering why they were leaving her alone up there. What if she scaled down the outside? Then they would have to open the inner gates to go after her. Was this all an elaborate trick to undermine their defenses?

The two guards appeared in the dark archway leading into the tower from the yard. One stayed there, glancing up nervously, but the other hurried toward Ari. Behind him, Ari could hear the searchers spreading out in the courtyard. He lengthened his stride, even though he was torn between calling them to order and finding out what the guard jogging toward him wanted.

"My lord," the man called as Ari drew close enough. "Hawk Guardian Kimmer sends a message to you, my lord." The man waved his arm behind him in a vague gesture toward the tower top.

Ari glanced back to see the searchers nearest him pause. He waved them forward with him, all of them coming to a halt as they met the oncoming guard halfway across the courtyard. The man made a quick bow.

"What message? You left her alone up there? She's the traitor."

"So she said, my lord."

Ari nodded for the man to continue, hoping the action hid his surprise. Why would Kimmer climb a tower and tell the men on top that she was a traitor? He raised his gaze from the guard's face, trying to keep an eye on her. She was standing with her back against the outer wall, facing him. As he watched, she slid down it and out of sight.

"She's dying, my lord," the guard said. Behind Ari, a murmur rose from the gathering crowd. "She says she poisoned herself and that she'll only talk to you, alone. Says she has the cure, but she won't take it until you talk to her. She looks bad, my lord."

"I best get up there, then," Ari said, starting forward.

"She has her knife and her bow, my lord," the guard called as Ari walked past him.

"I have my sword," Ari said, not slowing.

The guard who'd stayed at the entrance to the tower looked at least as worried as the one who'd delivered Kimmer's message. He stepped aside when Ari approached.

"Don't let anyone up until I say so," Ari said, striding past. He caught the man's affirmative as he started up the stone staircase.

Inside the tower, it was much darker and cooler than without. Ari's feet were a muffled drumming on the stone steps. He wound about the tower once, coming up in a room that stood on level with the ramparts at the top of the deep inner wall. Sunlight and concerned faces filled the doorway. He gestured the guards back, wishing they would keep to their positions along the wall, worried Kimmer was a decoy.

Ari started up the second set of steps, slowing as he neared the top. There was nothing comfortable about sticking his head out of the top of a staircase where he knew someone waited who wasn't afraid to kill and wasn't on his side. Taking a deep breath, Ari launched himself up the final steps, bursting into the morning air.

He needn't have worried. Kimmer was slumped against the wall opposite him. A quick glance showed her knife sheathed at her side. Her bow lay on the ground near her, within reach, but not drawn and leveled at him as he'd feared.

Not that she looked well enough to draw it. Between them stood a brazier of coals that the guards used to warm themselves during long nights at watch, or to ignite burning pitch during harrowing times of war. Heat shimmered above it, blurring Kimmer's face, but not obscuring its unnatural pallor. The young hawk guardian's blue eyes were closed. Her shoulders drooped. Her arms lay listlessly at her sides. Ari wondered if he was already too late.

"Lord Aridian," she whispered, her eyes fluttering open.

"Kimmer. Take your antidote. You have my word we'll talk after."

"I'd rather talk now." She pushed herself upward against the wall. She held both arms out, bracing herself against the gray stone.

"As you like," he said, holding back the feelings of sympathy that threatened him. However wretched she looked, she was still a traitor, poisoner and murderer.

She closed her eyes. "I'm sorry. I had to do the things I did."

Ari folded his arms across his chest. He didn't answer. There was no reason to make things any easier on her, even if she was dying.

"This winter, I was out scouting. He came to me. The Caller. He showed me things, inside my mind. Images of what would happen to our village." She shook her head, opening her eyes to meet Ari's. "Horrible images. I begged him not to do it. I offered anything. He wanted the stone. I tried to get it, my lord. I really did, but the hawks put it away in the fall, and I couldn't find it." She drew a shuddering breath.

Ari scowled, keenly aware of the stone pressed against his chest, hidden in the coin pocket of his doublet. "You should have come to Sir Cadwel." Before she spoke, he knew her answer. He knew what it was like to have a compulsion placed on you.

"I couldn't. I couldn't tell anyone. I tried not to go back into the woods, but somehow I had to go. I had to confess my failure." She raised a shaking hand to her face. "He was so

211

gentle. He stroked my cheek and he told me he knew I'd done my best. He said I was a good helper, a good little spy for him."

Ari wanted to look away from the pleasure shining in her eyes as she repeated the Caller's praise, but he didn't.

"He said that if I stayed good, a good girl, he would reward me." Her hand fell back to her side. "He said that when spring came and the hawks put the stone into one of their eggs, he would come for it, but he wouldn't hurt my family. Not mine, because I was a good helper."

Ari turned his head away, not wanting her to see the disgust on his face. She made a choking sound, drawing his eyes back. He wasn't sure if she was laughing or crying.

"He did spare them, my lord. My family is alive, and I kept them that way. I did a good job. I almost got you for him, too, but who knew you'd be able to fight off four of his wolves at once? I would have brought more, if I'd known then what you really are."

"You lured us into the woods so we could be attacked?" Ari asked. His eyes narrowed. "How many others did you lure out before I came along?"

A guilty flush brought new color to her face. Defiance squared her shoulders. "What difference does it make?"

"And you spied on us in Sir Cadwel's tent," he said, realizing it must be true. "Peine caught you, so you dragged him out into the woods to spy on us more. You told the Caller that we didn't have the stone and that Larke needed to return to Sorga to find it. You poisoned Master Rellus. You smashed the eggs. The only surviving eggs of the year. A whole season of hawks, dead."

Ari didn't know when he'd raised his voice. Kimmer was staring at him with wide eyes, fear flickering in her gaze. At some point, he'd uncrossed his arms. His hands were balled into fists at his sides.

"But it was all for nothing," she said.

He didn't know if the sorrow in her tone was for her failure to find the stone, or the evils she'd committed in pursuit of it.

"You have the stone here, in the keep." Her eyes flickered in that direction. "Somewhere safe, no doubt. Obviously not where you said it was. I was a fool to believe that."

He glowered at her over the glowing brazier.

"And since I didn't get it for him, he'll kill my family now. All of them." Her blue eyes glared at him from the chalk-white of her face. He could see she was shaking now, the poison she'd taken eating away the last of her strength. "You're going to let them die."

"I'm not giving up the stone, Kimmer. You know I can't do that. It has to stay here where it's safe. I'll send a message to Sir Cadwel to guard your family, but I can't trade it for them."

"So it is here," she whispered. She pushed herself off the wall, taking three steps toward him before the brazier between them stopped her. Her breath was shallow, her eyes hungry.

Ari winced, realizing he shouldn't have confirmed it for her. Especially not if she was going to survive. Looking at her, he wasn't sure she would, even with the antidote. She was covered in sweat, her breath ragged. Her slender body was racked with tremors. "Take your antidote, Kimmer. We can talk more when you're well."

"Will you lock me up, my lord?"

"Yes."

Her hands shaking so much she could barely accomplish it, she untied a pouch at her waist. She reached inside, pulling out a red powder. "For my family," she said, and threw the powder onto the coals.

Ari jumped forward, flinging out his hands, but there was no way to grasp the red dust. Kimmer slumped sideways, crumpling. Crimson smoke billowed up from the brazier. Ari toppled it, spilling hot coals across the stones of the tower, but individual coals continued to smoke. Thin lines of red threaded their way up, meeting above him to add to the cloud. They converged as they rose, the smoke cloud growing. Ari suppressed a frustrated shout, sure it could be seen from anywhere on that side of the mountain.

Ignoring the hot coals, he dropped to his knees beside Kimmer. "What have you done?" he roared.

She didn't answer. He grabbed her by the shoulders, shaking her. Her head wobbled from side to side with each jerk of his arms. Ari yanked her up, bringing his ear down to her mouth. She wasn't breathing.

In the distance, a wolf howled.

Ari let Kimmer's body slump back to the stone floor. There were burned spots on her clothes, but the coals had stopped smoking. He didn't know if the powder was used up, or if the cold gray stone of the tower had stolen all of the coals' heat, but it didn't matter why the smoke had stopped. The signal had been sent.

A second howl answered the first. Ari stared down at Kimmer's white face. His horror at her death slammed into his anger at her betrayal, leaving him numb. He cradled his head in his hands for a moment, fighting at the sick feeling in his gut, before pushing his fingers through his hair.

Squaring his shoulders, he stood. More howls rose from the mountains around them. Ari walked to the edge of the tower ramparts. The howls merged into a violent cacophony, growing closer. He looked down into the courtyard at the mass of people there. He had failed them. The wolves were coming to Sorga.

Chapter 19

From where he stood in the tower, Ari could see that most of the castle folk were in the courtyard now. Hundreds of faces looked up at him. Some were worried, some confused, and already some were filled with fear. Larke and Peine were notably absent. Sir Cadwel was deep in the mountains. Natan was in who knew what state. Ari drew in a deep breath. Ispiria burst from the keep, red curls bright in the morning sun, her upturned face joining the others.

"Assemble the guard," Ari called, making sure his voice was loud and strong. He knew from the battles Sir Cadwel had made him read about that chaos and fear were as much their enemies as the wolves. "The entire guard. If anyone's still asleep, get them up." He raised his voice to a Cadwel-like bellow as the raucous calling from the mountains grew louder. "Women and children into the keep. Now!"

Startlement at his final shout chased some of the fear from their faces. The courtyard erupted into motion. Ari could see Ispiria, green eyes wide, struggling to keep sight of him as her ladies all but dragged her away. He wished he could go to her. He wanted her to smile at him and laugh away the fear growing in his gut and tell him he could do anything. The maw of the keep swallowed her up in a jumble of curls.

The soldiers of Sorga were filling the courtyard. Ari tried not to let his despair at how few men he had show on his face. There were still some on the outer wall, after all. A double guard of two score men. The ones on the inner wall were all below, following his order to assemble. Nearly one hundred and twenty faces looked up at him from a mass of Sorga brown.

Silence fell inside the courtyard. The howling of wolves echoed off the hard rock of the mountains that embraced them. A glance over his shoulder told Ari that a messenger was racing across the killing zone from the outer wall. On the top of every tower, the blue and white hawk-adorned banner of Sorga snapped in the breeze.

Ari struggled to organize his thoughts. Sir Cadwel's voice filled his mind with the old knight's drills, lessons and stories. Ari ran through them like a list, pulling out all of the things Sir Cadwel had told him to do in a siege.

"You've all heard tales of the strange wolves that attacked the Hawkers' village and Lady Ispiria's escort." The men nodded, looking up at him expectantly. "They're coming here now. I need you to set aside any wonder you have about how or why, any ideas you have about wolves being no threat to a castle full of men. They are brutal, they are cruel, and they will kill everyone you hold dear if they breach our fortifications."

He gazed down at them, assessing the effect of his words. Grim faces looked back. Ari didn't know how convincing his speech was, but the twenty men who'd brought in the bodies of Ispiria's escort had undoubtedly spread word of the state of the Hawkers' village. Even if the men couldn't comprehend how wolves could do such things, they already had proof that they would.

"Oil brigade deploy," Ari ordered.

A group of twenty peeled away from those before him, running for their equipment. Ari knew the Caller liked fire, but he also knew Empty Ones could burn. If the fire was hot enough, they would die. As much as he could avoid it, Ari would keep his men from engaging the wolves. In hand-to-hand combat, he didn't think they stood a chance. They would shoot at the wolves and repel them from the gate, but not do one-on-one battle with them.

"Gatesmen, open the gate. Keep it open until I say otherwise."

Another contingent of twenty broke formation, scurrying to do as he ordered. To Ari's relief, the men below him almost imperceptibly relaxed. There were no murmurs of wonder at his orders. No tentative looks to the left and right as the men tried to ascertain if their neighbors thought him as incompetent as they did. He felt his gut unclench a fraction.

The inner gate swung open. The men of the oil brigade, well trained, were already returning to the courtyard, burdened with the oil soaked cloths of their trade. Horses were being hooked to carts and barrels of oil loaded in. They would seed the killing zone, creating a deadly inferno to be released on their enemies should they breach the outer fortification.

"Eleventh contingent, into the keep." He chose them because they'd been on the inner wall all night. "Be ready to bar the doors if needed, but take what rest you can. You're on relief. Send out the--" Ari hesitated. He needed to meet with the master steward to organize those within the keep, but Natan didn't have an assistant. He wasn't a very good delegator and, Ari knew, Natan didn't like to admit he was old enough that it might be time to train up someone else. "Send me Peine," he said, deciding that his friend would do well enough. Everyone really knew what to do. They just needed someone to get them started.

There were firm nods as another block of twenty men hurried away. Sixty faces, three contingents, still looked up at him. Ari counted himself lucky that all three of them were trained in archery. Most of the men he had in the keep were. He wasn't sure why Sir Cadwel had arranged it that way, except that their archers were better suited to shoot from castle walls than in forests and mountains. They weren't trained for the terrain around the Hawkers' village, as Mirimel and Kimmer were. As Kimmer had been, he corrected himself, not looking toward where her body sprawled.

"The rest of you will take up position on the outer wall." Ari had to shout now to be heard over the spine-piercing howls of the wolves. He held up a hand to keep them from leaving. The messenger he saw running across the killing zone trotted into the courtyard, his slow pace showing that he'd already noticed their signs of preparation and realized his message was moot. "Send the men who are there back." The two contingents who were there had been there all night. Ari would order them to rest, putting the returning oil brigade on the inner wall.

"Light the pitch. Ready your bows. Do all you can to keep that gate secure. They are wolves, so they won't be able to scale the walls. They won't bring siege engines. If we keep the gate, we beat them." He paused, looking them over, meeting their eyes. "If the gate falls, drop the reserve gate and get back here as fast as you can. You are not to engage them."

This order brought the murmurs and covert glances Ari had feared.

"Listen to me. They are not ordinary wolves. Sir Cadwel feels it takes twenty men to slay even a small group of them." He could see this reminder argued his point well. Everyone knew Sir Cadwel had increased the number of men allowed to traverse the mountain trail to a score at a time. "And this won't be a small group. If they break the gate, fall back. No feats of valor. Staying will only make it so we can't light the killing zone. Understood?"

He scrutinized them, counting up the grim nods. He felt the tension in his shoulders mounting. Beyond the walls, he could hear the wolves baying and yapping. He dared a glance from the men, looking out over the plain. Something dark was massing there. Lithe forms flowed from the east and west, coming out of the mountains to join the undulating cloud of fur and fangs that converged on the grasslands.

"Go," Ari ordered, pointing. He didn't tell them to run, but his urgent tone must have conveyed it. He watched them, pleased that they kept formation in spite of their hurry. Formation, he realized, was nothing in itself to men deploying across the killing zone, but it represented everything that was important. It showed training, discipline and strength. It even bespoke, he felt, of a faith in him and his orders.

Ari watched, caught in an odd lull of inactivity, as his men crossed to the outer wall and the two contingents there formed up to jog back. The oil carts were almost to the outer wall now, the killing zone nearly primed. The howling mass on the plain writhed, but didn't yet advance. The streams of wolves pouring from the mountains to augment the main force trickled off.

Ari gripped the edge of the tower ramparts, wishing he could be on the outer wall to meet the charge. If Sir Cadwel were there to give orders, or even Natan, he could be. He could be with the men of Sorga, lending them the courage of his presence as the attack came, flinging up his sword and voice in defiance of those who dared accost their home.

Not that he'd be much use atop the wall, he admitted, his shoulders sagging. Giving him a bow would be a waste of arrows, and he couldn't stand and fight once the gate fell, for the same reason he'd so adamantly told his men. If the outer wall was breached, their hope was in the killing zone. They couldn't beat these wolves with swords. After all, look what had happened to the Hawkers.

He just hoped the thin reserve gate would give his men the time they needed to get back to the keep. It should. That was what it was made for.

Turning, he took in the high mountains. Always, Ari thought the mountains of Sorga were a thing of great beauty but today, he resented them. If they weren't so massive, he could light a signal fire for Sir Cadwel. If they weren't so tall, he wouldn't need hawks to summon Sir Cadwel home. But if the burning of a whole village couldn't be seen from the keep, there wasn't enough here for Ari to burn to get Sir Cadwel's attention.

His thoughts jumped to sending out riders, but he knew that was hopeless. He didn't have enough men to break through the Caller's line. From the moment Kimmer had sent that signal, they were trapped. The howling came so soon, from so close, Ari was sure the Caller and his minions had been lurking about them, just waiting for confirmation that they were near their goal.

Maybe, though, he could get a hawk through.

"Ari," Peine's voice called from the courtyard below.

Looking down from the cliffs above them, Ari saw Peine, Larke, Mirimel and Ispiria on the castle steps. Fresh anxiety assailed him. Why was Ispiria out of the keep? He'd ordered her inside. He glanced down at Kimmer's body. Would Peine be able to do the tasks Ari needed of him once he knew?

Ari shook off the immobility of his worry. If Peine couldn't organize the castle folk, Ari would find someone who could. He would also order Ispiria back inside, no matter how she looked at him with her big green eyes. This wasn't a game.

Crouching, he hoisted Kimmer's body over his shoulder, grimacing at the limp way her head flopped back. He trotted down the steps, laying her inside under the stairs. He would have to send someone for her. They would need to clear the space beside the stable, remove the accouterments of the practice field. In a siege, that space was where they must dig out a deep cool place in the earth to house the bodies until they could be properly burned.

"What are you doing out of the keep?" Ari asked Ispiria as he crossed to them. He frowned, as much at his overly harsh tone as at her.

She lifted her chin, pressing her lips together. "I am here to talk to you, Lord Aridian, about converting half of the great hall into an infirmary. As principle lady of the keep, it is my duty to oversee those preparations." She frowned at him. "And you can't just tell me what to do, Ari," she added, her tone aggrieved.

"It's her job," Peine added. He sounded normal enough, but his eyes kept darting past Ari toward the entrance to the tower, where Kimmer's body lay.

"Fine," Ari said. He was sure they would need an infirmary, and he didn't really care what Ispiria was doing, so long as she was doing it inside the keep. "You are responsible for that."

She nodded. Emotions flickered over her face, from annoyance to pride, but they ended in a loving look. Springing up on her toes, she kissed him.

Ari was about to put his arms around her, forgetting where they were and what they were doing, when she dropped back to her heels and hurried away. He half-reached out, but restrained himself from catching hold of her and dragging her back.

Larke cleared his throat. "Natan will live." The smile Larke gave Ari didn't quite reach his eyes. "He's still groggy. I have him in an inner room where he can't hear what's going on out here. I'm afraid he won't be much use to anyone for days, lad, but he should fully mend in time."

"It's better news than I'd hoped for," Ari said, the memory of all the blood pooling on the stone below Natan's head coming back to him. "Thank you."

"'Tis my pleasure, lad."

Three pairs of eyes looked at Ari expectantly.

"Peine, I need you to help organize the keep," Ari said. "I need foodstuff arranged properly in case we can't get in supplies for a while. Talk with the head cook about it. He'll know what to do. We also need him to keep meals available in the great hall, because the men will need to eat when they can. Bring in the cots from the barracks for Ispiria's infirmary. Pick ten of the other pages to put in charge of that. Ask the guards in the foyer what they need for sealing the keep. I'll want everything in place. Can you do this?"

Peine's face was white, even his lips. His eyes were wide. He met Ari's gaze, and while there was fear there, there was also determination. "I can do it."

"Good," Ari said, reaching out to clasp him briefly on the shoulder.

Peine nodded and hurried away.

"And us, lad?" Larke asked, nodding toward Mirimel.

Ari could hear the strain in the bard's voice, see the conflict on his face. Larke wasn't supposed to get involved with human wars. Larke was also supposed to be keeping the supernatural nature of the Caller and his beasts out of human memory. Larke, Ari thought, was not having a good day.

"Go first to the hawks, please. Ask for a volunteer. We need to get word to Sir Cadwel to return with the rest of the men." They nodded. "Then, both of you, please stay in the great hall. Do what you can for the people. Keep them calm." He looked at Larke as he said it, before turning to Mirimel. "And if anything goes terribly wrong, take Ispiria and the other women and the young ones into the inner keep. They know where. We have a widows' safe. Once it's sealed, it can only be opened from the inside."

"I should be on the walls," Mirimel said. "A wolf an arrow, I promise you. You need me, Ari."

Ari scrubbed a hand though his hair. She probably could guarantee him a wolf an arrow. "That's what makes you the best guard for Ispiria and the others." She frowned, but Ari cut her off before she could speak. "Mirimel, you are the one person who I can trust to both protect Ispiria and make her do what needs to be done. She won't want to go to safety." He looked her square in the eyes, pleading with her. He hoped she saw his sincerity and not the small prejudice corner of his mind that thought women should be in the castle where it was safe. Even ones who could shoot as well as Mirimel could.

Mirimel bared her teeth at him in a scowl. She pivoted away, stomping up the steps and into the keep.

"You'll be hard-pressed to smooth that one over, lad," Larke said, shaking his head.

"Do you want her on the walls?"

Larke blinked at Ari in surprise. He cocked his head to the side, a startled look flashing across his face before being replaced by an expression of deep thought.

Behind him, Ari could hear the two contingents from the outer gate forming up, each twenty men strong. In his peripheral vision, he could see the oil carts by the stable, the horses being unhitched. He took a deep breath to steady his patience. "Larke, I don't really care what your answer is. Just go do what I asked you to do, please."

"Heh?" Larke blinked at him again. "Oh, aye, sorry lad. Sometimes, I forget how urgent the world of men is."

"Right now, very urgent." Ari turned his back on Larke. He ignored the bard's offended huff, glad he could hear Larke walking away. "Thirteenth and sixteenth contingents," Ari greeted the men. "Get something to eat immediately and take what sleep you can. That's an order. Oil brigade, man the inner wall. Ready the pitch. Stock the arrow pots. Go."

They jumped to follow his orders. Men streamed past him into the keep, while others climbed the towers, spilling out onto the walls and popping up on the tower tops. Ari crossed to the base of one of the left hand towers. He would have the best view from one of the towers flanking the portico, but he knew those were filled with the gatesmen and he didn't want to be in their way. If the inner gate needed to be closed, he didn't want anything impeding them.

He trotted up the stone steps, glad he hadn't chosen the tower where Kimmer's body was. He'd have to put one of the contingents to work digging soon, thirteen or sixteen, but not until after they'd slept. Ari was halfway up the tower steps when a terrible high-pitched wail slammed into him, deafening even inside the tower. Ari took the remaining steps in three great leaps.

Bursting out into daylight, he was assailed by the same cry, even louder. When it stopped, the silence nearly hurt. Several men from the oil brigade manned the tower top. Ari moved to stand with them at the ramparts, their gazes turned outward, toward the grasslands. Raising their muzzles, the mass of wolves on the plain before Sorga howled a third time.

This time, when their terrible cry ended, they burst into motion. As they raced toward the outer wall, they solidified into individuals. Ari worked to hide his dismay. He would guess their number at five hundred. Five hundred Empty One wolves, nearly invulnerable to mortal men, storming toward them.

He suppressed a shudder, keeping his face a mask in case anyone wrenched their eyes from the sight before them to look at their leader. For the first time, Ari entertained the idea that they might all die. Half a thousand wolves strong, a wall of fur and fangs roared across the grassland, surging toward Sorga in an unstoppable wave.

Chapter 20

Ari watched as the wolves crashed against the outer wall. From where he stood on top of one of the inner towers, he couldn't see the ground where stone and fur met, but he could hear their terrible howling. Unlike human soldiers, they didn't spread out along the wall. They funneled to the gate. He could hear the pounding of their massive bodies as they flung themselves against it.

From the top of the wall, his men rained arrows down on the wolves. Ari realized he should send an order for them take careful aim. They were used to human targets, who would be slowed by injuries. With the Empty One wolves, any shot that didn't kill would quickly heal. Even now, several of the beasts staggered back, using their jaws to tear arrows from their bodies before returning to the fray.

Ari rested his left hand on the hilt of his sword, clenching the cool metal until it hurt. Against his chest, the amulet the Lady had given him was like ice. Ari wondered what else he was forgetting. What else he should be doing. He didn't want to undermine the men's confidence in him, but maybe he should gather some of the old veterans in the keep and ask them for advice. If there was any with advice to give. With the last real war the kingdom had seen ending over twenty-five years ago, few of the men on the walls were old enough to have fought in it.

"My lord?"

Ari turned to see the young leader of the gatesmen standing behind him. The man made a quick bow.

"Shall we assemble the catapults, my lord?"

"Yes," Ari said, wincing inwardly. There was at least one thing he'd forgotten. He looked about the yard. The catapults used twenty-five years ago had long since been dismantled. "Out of what?"

"We've been drilled on how to make two catapults out of the garden shed and part of the stable, my lord." The man's round face looked as nervous as Ari felt. "And more out of the rest of the stable, and other things out of the barracks, such as a reinforced gate for the keep, my lord."

"Ah, let's just start with the two catapults. That won't keep your men from being ready to close the inner gate, will it?"

"No, my lord." He bowed as he turned toward the tower steps. "We can do both, my lord."

Ari nodded, his gaze returning to the battle. He ground his teeth. He felt so powerless standing there on top of a tower on the inner wall. He turned to the man next to him.

"Go tell them to take more careful aim with their bows, and spread the word here too. You can't slow the beasts, only kill them. Aim for the eyes and ears, or their throats when they howl."

"Yes, my lord." He jerked a quick bow and hurried away, calling out Ari's message to others of the oil brigade as he went.

Ari watched him head off through the killing zone at a run, his path seeming a bit random to anyone who didn't know where the lightly dusted over lines of oil-soaked cloth were. Atop the outer wall, the men let out a roar as they upended a pot of burning pitch onto the wolves before the gate.

There was a heinous shriek. Three wolves fled, coats on fire. Two fell to the ground, writhing, and started to disintegrate. One disappeared into the mass of others. Still, the pounding against the gate continued. It wasn't, Ari realized, as if the grisly deaths of their comrades would demoralize the rest.

"What . . ." a guard standing next to Ari began. "I mean, my lord, what happened to them when they died? Did they burn that fast?"

"They rotted. They decay as soon as they're dead."

Ari was aware that the man was looking at him like he was crazy, but he wasn't going to explain any further. How under the moon and stars he and Larke were supposed to keep a whole castle full of people from realizing something very odd was going on, Ari didn't know. Right then, he didn't care.

Something flew through Ari's peripheral vision and he turned his head. Larke, Mirimel and Master Rellus stood at the stone rail of the aerie. A hawk spiraled upward, obviously trying to gain enough altitude to fly over the peaks behind them without venturing out onto the plain. Ari held his breath as it spiraled up and up. It curved once more around, heading toward the mountainside.

The hawk burst into flame. Mirimel let out an anguished cry, but the hawk was silent as its fiery body plummeted downward, bouncing off the side of the mountain. With so much fire, Ari hoped it had died instantly, for its sake. He lowered his gaze. The hawk was their first casualty.

Maids scurried into the courtyard with water and bread, passing it up to the men on the walls. Ari realized he'd barely eaten breakfast, but he wasn't hungry. He glanced up at the sun. It wasn't yet lunchtime. Peine was sending food out early. Ari was glad for the reassurance that somewhere in the castle, people were being productive, not just huddling in terror.

Ari found himself pulling apart a hard roll, his eyes locked on the outer wall, and shoved some of the pieces into his mouth, not wanting to toss away food. The man he'd sent out had long since returned. The archers were taking more careful aim now, shooting slower. Since the bodies of the wolves decayed, there was no way to tell how many had been slain. The mass outside the gate didn't seem to be diminishing.

Overhead, the sun crept across the sky. Before them, the wolves pounded at the outer gate. The drumming sound their bodies made against the metal-reinforced planks mingled with their interminable howling. Behind him, the catapults were completed. The gatesmen set about arming them, filling their bowls with a mixture of metal scraps and pitch that they would hurl over the wall and into the enemy. Time stretched on endlessly. Ari felt exhausted, and he hadn't even done anything yet.

"How long have we been up here?" he finally asked, hoping one of the guardsmen around him would know.

"I'd guess near five hours, my lord," a man said, squinting up at the sun.

Five hours. It hardly seemed possible. Ari loosened the grip he had on the hilt of his sword, his hand nearly numb from clenching it. He stretched, then ordered the men to do the same. Soon, he would rotate the guards. Five hours sleep wasn't much, but the men holding the wall must be exhausted. They would need to be relieved.

A lone figure descended the wall and raced toward them across the killing zone. Ari curbed his impatience, wondering what message the man could have. From where he stood, nothing seemed to have changed. The man came through the gate and was directed upward, but Ari came down to meet him. It felt good to be moving, and he wanted to spare the runner the climb.

"My lord," the man panted. "We're nearly out of arrows, my lord."

Ari frowned. He could send more arrows, but they'd only held back a third. If he sent enough to make a difference, they wouldn't have any left. Yet keeping the outer gate was imperative.

There was an ear-splitting crash, sending Ari racing back into the tower and up the steps. The outer gate had burst open. Wolves poured in. Atop the outer wall, Ari could see two men hacking at the ropes that suspended the reserve gate. Others flowed from the towers, struggling to push the wolves back with long pikes. The reserve gate crashed down, but at least twenty wolves were inside. His men couldn't stand against them.

"Get me my horse," Ari yelled into the courtyard, hoping someone would listen. "No saddle, just bring him."

He darted down the steps. Bursting into the sunlight, he saw Stew trotting over. Ari grabbed his mane and pulled himself up. "Signal the retreat," he called, even though the men already knew they were to return once the gate was breached. Stew, taking the initiative, was heading for the inner gate, moving as fast as he could in the somewhat crowded courtyard. As they passed through the inner gate a horn blared, the signal for retreat.

Stew sped across the empty space between the walls. Ari knew they were going fast, maybe faster than they ever had before, and he didn't have much of anything to help him keep his seat, but all he could think about was how stupid he was.

His orders were standard, the right tactic to use, but his enemy was not. Why hadn't he realized that if the outer gate went, enough wolves would get in before the reserve gate dropped to kill half of his men? Yes, with human attackers the same thing would have happened, but a small number of a mortal enemy would be easily slain. Not so for the wolves. Ari couldn't believe he hadn't taken that into consideration when choosing his strategy.

Long cracks appeared on the reserve gate. It had nowhere near the strength of the real thing, made as it was simply to buy time to retreat. His men were fighting for their lives. They weren't making any progress toward the safety of the inner wall.

Brown uniforms swarmed the wolves inside the yard, but men were dying. Some of the wolves were too, though not enough. Not fast enough. Five guards surrounded one, using their pikes to hold it down and impale it until it died. Another sprouted so many arrows, even an Empty One wolf couldn't take them all, and it fell in on itself in a cloud of foul dust, but there were too many human bodies on the ground.

Afire with rage, Ari and Stew slammed into the fray. Stew was a thing possessed, his high-pitched whinny cutting across the wolves' angry snarls as his front hooves smashed into one, flattening its head. Ari leapt to the ground, sword in hand, unsure when he'd drawn it.

He charged four wolves who had a group of men pinned against the trembling gate. With two mighty swings, full of the all of the power of his Aluien-given strength and manmade rage, he chopped two of the wolves in half. The other two turned to face him, ignoring the guards, who immediately set to stabbing them in the flanks.

One launched itself at Ari. He let it come, his sword braced before him. It slid down the blade, not seeming to care if he impaled it, so long as it could get its jaws to his face. Ari let out a roar, wrenching the wolf around with all his strength and slammed it into the second one before that one could attack him too. He smashed the impaled wolf down on the other, then wrenched his sword free, the blade tearing out organs in its wake.

The beast started to disintegrate, the other one rising from beneath it and shaking off dusty remains. It turned hate-filled yellow eyes on Ari. The men behind it charged en masse, seven swords chopping into its spine. Ari saw surprise overtake it, just before death.

Turning, he charged the next wolf he saw. Stew was riding down another, stopping it from attacking a group of men who were trying to carry off their fallen comrades. Ari swung his sword in a blur of anger, splitting open the wolf's skull as it dove at him. Another sprang up in its place.

They knew he was there, now. They were disregarding the easy prey of his men, surrounding him. There were eight left. Ari could see a trail of men heading for Sorga, obeying the horn, but all those most able were forming up, surrounding the ring of wolves. Ari backed toward the throbbing gate. The wolves let him, seeming leery of getting too close.

Three grew bold at once, charging Ari. His men roared, slashing at the other five. Ari dove to the side, out of the range of one wolf, hitting the ground hard. The one to his left soared over him, and Ari raised his sword, disemboweling it. Organs sprang out, hitting Ari in the face, strangely dry.

Ari could hear men screaming in agony, but the middle wolf was upon him, others surely circling around. He got his sword between himself and the wolf, but the angle was too awkward to do more than keep it at bay. He needed to get back to his feet. Somewhere close, Stew gave a shrill cry of pain.

Ari was pinned to the ground, pressed up against the gate. He could hear it cracking. He batted at the wolf with his sword, hoping to at least cut off its jaw and paws, even if he couldn't get enough space for a killing blow. Another barreled in, trying to catch his sword arm in its mouth.

There was a loud twang, and another. Ari's first thought was that the gate was giving out, but the wolf above him reared up, its skin pulling back in decay to reveal a gleaming skull before that too started to crumble. Ari jumped to his feet. Another twang, and the wolf trying to grab his arm fell dead.

Riding on Larke's gray, Mirimel sped past, loosing another arrow. Ari darted forward, decapitating one of the remaining wolves with a sweeping overhand swing. The gray wheeled, bringing Mirimel back. Only two wolves remained. She pointed at one with her bow, and Ari attacked the other. It took him two swings to her one arrow. Her earlier words echoed in his mind.

Stew trotted forward, blood streaming from his neck, but his eyes alert. Ari hesitated to mount, but Stew butted him impatiently.

"Come on," Mirimel yelled, the gray turning again, heading back toward the keep.

Sheathing his sword, Ari hauled himself up onto Stew, but he didn't go. Nearly fifteen men were still there, searching through the bodies. "Do any live?"

"None of these," one said heavily, straightening.

"We're almost done checking, my lord," another man said, coming away from the area where he'd searched. "You best ride back."

231

"Done here," another called.

"Form up when you're finished," Ari ordered. "Yell if you find anyone alive."

Stew shook his mane. Those who were done searching stood in nervous silence, quickly joined by others. Outside, wolves howled. The reserve gate let out another loud crack. Mirimel stopped halfway to the keep, looking back.

"All the rest are gone," the final searcher said.

"Head out," Ari said. "I recommend you run."

He stayed a moment more, looking down at the torn bodies. He knew the men were thorough. He knew Sir Cadwel had taught them a system for checking the dead. Ari wasn't worried they'd missed anyone who could be saved. He just couldn't bring himself not to look, to take in the faces of the fallen. The men who'd died to defend Sorga that day. His throat tightened, sorrow burning behind his eyes.

Stew shook his head again and turned back toward the keep. Ari didn't try to stop him. They caught up with the running men, but didn't pass them. Mirimel galloped in front of them, her orange hair streaming back like a banner until she disappeared behind the inner wall. The inner gate was poised half-closed. Ari was glad they were prepared to shut it.

Twining one hand firmly into Stew's mane, Ari twisted, straining his neck, wanting to keep an eye on the bulging reserve gate. It bent inward, a wolf-dam about to burst.

They were two thirds of the way back when it did.

Chapter 21

The howling was deafening. A flood of gray and black fur poured through the rent gate, thrusting the timber inward to slam against the walls and topple to the ground. Ari thought one or two wolves may have been crushed when it fell, but the others were undaunted. Not a single beast cared if or how its compatriots died.

Ari felt the tension in Stew, but the brown made no effort to pass the running men. Stew knew, Ari thought, that there was no way Ari would pass under the inner wall without them. The guardsmen were running flat out, their heads down. Ari didn't bother to urge them to greater speed. The mad howling behind them spoke more eloquently of the need than he ever could.

Archers appeared atop the wall, Mirimel in their center. They didn't shoot yet, bows at the ready. The roaring wave of wolves boiled forward. Ari gave up looking behind and bent low over Stew's neck. He imagined he could feel the heat of the wolves' breath upon him, even though he knew their breath was ice cold.

The men running with him dashed through the nearly closed gate. The metal wrapped wood bruised Ari's knees as Stew followed, squeezing in. It slammed shut.

"Hold the portcullis," Ari bellowed, waving at the gatesmen on the wall. "Wait till they're here and drop it on them." The men looked startled, but nodded.

Ari jumped down from Stew.

A page rushed forward, his eyes round.

"Find the Minstrel Larke and the stable master," Ari said. "Have them see to Stew's neck."

The boy nodded and ran off.

Ari patted Stew on the side. There were four long gashes down his neck, blood still trickling from them. "They'll fix you." He patted Stew again, hoping it was true. "I have to go."

Ari headed for one of the towers. Injured men from the outer wall were staggering around the courtyard, but women were coming out to lead them inside. A quick glance told him that no one was sleeping anymore. Every able-bodied man was on the walls. He would have to correct that, he knew. He wanted the men who'd been on the outer wall inside, resting.

He trotted up the tower steps, but didn't go to the top. Instead, he came out on the ramparts atop the wall, joining Mirimel where she stood in the center, over the gate. She had her bow drawn, an arrow ready. Ari tried to take a rough count of the wolves as they barreled toward them.

Fewer than three hundred, he thought, but barely. The first wall hadn't even cost them half, and Ari only had one wall left. His mouth curled into a grim smile. Now, though, they were in the killing zone.

"Men from the outer wall." Ari had to bellow over the howls. "Inside, now. Eat. Rest yourselves. We'll need you soon enough." Ari could hear them obeying. The first of the wolves were nearly to them now. "Are the catapults ready?"

"Yes, my lord," one of the gatesmen called.

"Is the gate soaked down?"

"Yes, my lord."

"As soon as the first of them hit the gate, drop the portcullis and launch the fire." He raised his voice louder still, shouting, "Be ready to get down," to warn the men on the wall that the catapults would soon be deployed.

Ari held his breath. Each great leap brought the beasts bounding closer. Each time they bunched their bodies, he was sure their next lunge would reach the gate.

Wolves slammed into the gate with enough force to send a tremor through the stones on which Ari stood. Arrows flew, Mirimel's dropping one massive creature to the ground. The portcullis slammed down, impaling three. With a swish that seemed to suck up all the air around him and replace it with heat, the catapults sent two flaming masses of tar and jagged metal sailing over the wall.

"Down," the gatesmen yelled.

Most of the men dropped behind the protection of the battlement, as they'd been drilled to do. Ari hesitated, watching as the balls of flame arced into the sky, raining down on the wolves. A sheet of fire burst up where they hit, running both away and toward him. Ari flattened himself, grabbing Mirimel on his way down.

A boom louder than the slamming of wolves into the gate hit them, rocking the wall. Those few men who hadn't gotten down were thrown from the battlement. Heat billowed over the top of the ramparts they crouched behind. Mirimel turned stunned eyes on Ari.

"You could have warned me," she gasped.

"I said be ready to get down," he said, but he knew it wasn't much of an excuse. Mirimel didn't know why it was so important to get down. Then again, he specifically recalled telling her to stay inside the keep. He stood, eager to see the damage they'd wrought, pulling her up beside him.

Below, the killing zone was awash in fire. Heat beat at Ari's face, but he didn't care. Wolves writhed on the ground, their skin bubbling, their fur gone. Exultation shot through him. They'd won.

Ari heard a faint sound, like someone inhaling. It grew louder, raising the hairs on the back of his neck. Wind rushed from behind him, blowing his hair forward into his face. The heat of the fire receded. The bright flames diminished, dropped, sputtered. A figure came striding through the fire, toward the keep. The flames raced toward it, converging on it, coming to form a ball in its cupped hands.

All about them, charred wolves struggled to their feet. Ari could see that only a little over a hundred remained, but he had the chilling realization that a hundred would still be enough. They were almost out of arrows, they were almost out of fallback positions, and they were almost out of time. He wished he had horses, after watching Stew's success at riding them down, but Sir Cadwel had nearly all of their mounts.

Along with the others on the wall, Ari watched in stunned fascination as the remaining wolves seemed to shake off the effects of the fire. Their eyes reformed, the gelatinous streams they'd become sliding back into place. Fur sprouted to cover blackened skin. They bared their fangs. The figure, the Caller, Ari was sure, raised his arms, flames flickering in his hands. Below the gate, an enormous black wolf threw back its head and howled.

There was a twang, and one of Mirimel's arrows embedded itself in the giant wolf's neck, dropping it to the ground. Behind Ari, people moved inside the courtyard, some rushing to help those who were blasted off the wall. On the battlement, there was silence, the men around him gazing down at the reformed wolves in terror.

The Caller lifted his voice in a high-pitched call, his wolves joining in. Even though he was too far away to clearly make out his face, Ari felt like the Caller met his eyes. Swinging one arm down, their enemy sent a white ball of fire flying toward the gate.

"Down," Ari yelled. He reached toward Mirimel but this time, she was already ducking. "Down," he shouted again, as men still stood in stunned silence. Ari pulled down anyone he could reach.

The fireball slammed into the gate. The inner wall shook. Men flew from the battlements, crashing into the courtyard below. Human screams joined the raucous howls. There was an ear-shattering boom as the inner gate exploded, showering the courtyard with debris. Wolves streamed in.

"Seal the keep," Ari shouted as loud as he could. "Seal it now."

People were struggling to get inside. The guards at the massive double doors, one with blood streaming down his face, started to tug them shut. Ari leapt from the battlements, sword in hand, smashing into the wolves below with a knee-jarring thud. His only thought was to buy the men at the castle door enough time to shut the keep.

The inner reserve gate slammed down, crushing several of the beasts under it. Men swarmed out of the towers, meeting the attacker. Two wolves were on the steps, jaws pulling at the great double doors, wrenching them back open.

Ari swung left and right, trying to aim killing blows, deflect attacks, and make his way to the keep steps all at the same time. He was swimming in a sea of claws, teeth and fur. A sharp pain shot up the back of his left leg. He spun, decapitating the wolf who'd just missed his hamstring.

Larke stormed out of the stable on his gray, a bandaged Stew beside them, hooves flashing. The bard stood in his saddle, his hands weaving. He pointed at the wolves wrenching open the doors. One was immediately surrounded in blue flame. It cried out, writhing as it burned. Larke's gray and Stew charged up the castle steps, their sharp hooves knocking back wolves. The doors to the keep boomed shut.

The courtyard was chaos. At least thirty beasts had made it in before the reserve gate was dropped. Ari swung his sword as fast as he could. Sweat beaded on his forehead, trailing down his face and threatening his grip on his hilt, but no matter how fast he swung, all around him, the men of Sorga were dying.

Wolves were dying too. Many of the men had grabbed up long-handled pikes, better than swords for them to attack the wolves with. Mirimel and several other archers still stood on the wall, each carefully placed arrow doing precious damage. Barely paying attention to what he was doing, focused as he was on the battle as a whole, Ari split the skull of another beast.

Soon, though it cost them dearly, there were only a few left. Ari charged one while his men surrounded the others, impaling them until they died. Ari severed the spine of his, immobilizing it. Feeling the strain in his muscles, he lifted his sword again, bringing it down to cut off the beast's head. The look of hatred in its eyes didn't fade until its skin shriveled away, decaying.

The courtyard reeked of carrion. Dusty puddles of what were once wolves lay everywhere, men fallen around them. A glance told Ari that Mirimel had turned back toward the killing zone, where he knew at least seventy more wolves remained. Now that the desperate battle in the courtyard was over, Ari became aware of a strange absence of sound. There were no wolves pounding at the reserve gate. Far from relieved, a chill shot through him. Looking around, he didn't see Larke and the horses anywhere.

"Get the wounded into the barracks," Ari called, his voice hoarse. "Shore up the gate." Not sheathing his sword, he entered one of the towers, forcing himself to jog up the steps.

Coming out onto the wall by Mirimel, he looked down to see the remaining wolves watching the gate in eerie silence. The Caller strode closer. He still had a ball of fire in one hand. He smirked up at Ari, raising his arm. Mirimel launched an arrow at him, but a neglecting flick of his empty hand sent it spinning away.

There was a strange thundering sound, Ari realized, distinguishing it from the pounding in his head. The Caller narrowed his gaze, aiming his second ball of fire at the reserve gate. His wolves started to howl. The thundering grew, becoming so loud that Ari raised his eyes from the spectacle below.

Out on the plain, streaming through the smashed outer gate, came Sir Cadwel on Goldwin, followed by a hundred and sixty mounted men. The Caller howled, whirling to face them.

Ari yelled a warning he knew wouldn't reach them, realizing the fireball was now aimed at Sir Cadwel and his men, instead of the gate.

Mirimel wrenched back the string on her bow, arrow in hand. The Caller's arm dropped. The twang of her bow releasing filled the air. Ari held his breath, watching the arrow speed away from them. With an echoing thud, it slammed into the Caller's descending hand, coming out the other side.

His fire disappeared in a puff of smoke. He grabbed onto his wrist, turning back to face them. Rage contorted his already deranged features. His lank gray hair stood out from his head. Twisting his lips into a feral snarl, he started running.

Sir Cadwel and his men crashed into the remaining wolves, hooves and swords flying, but the Caller spurted out from the side of the fray, heading for the sheer cliffs embracing the killing zone.

"More arrows," Ari called. "Get that gate open. Bring up some rope. We've got to get down there." The reserve gate, quick to drop, wasn't as easy to raise up again.

Sir Cadwel and his men were riding down the wolves, trampling them. Some of the beasts tried to flee with their master, but the warriors of Sorga chased them down. The old knight, Ari saw, wasn't wielding his greatsword. Instead, he had a flail, a chain with a massive spiked ball at the end. He was using it to send wolves flying, crashing to the ground, so that the horses could trample them.

Ari skidded down the first rope that was set, joining the fray. A strange pool of gray at the base of the gate caught his attention, and he realized it was the melted remains of the portcullis. He could see the Caller, miraculously scaling the sheer stone of the mountainside. Ari hacked at wolves, trying to break free of them to reach his enemy, but there were too many.

Fighting overtook him, pulling his mind from the Caller. The brief respite atop the wall hadn't fully restored his strength and he needed all of his concentration to kill wolves and stay alive. He could only imagine how the other men felt.

A giant beast got past his guard, bearing him to the ground, but the men around them stabbed at it, killing it. Ari struggled up from its rotting body, charging a wolf that had its mouth wrapped around the sword arm of one of the guards. Bringing down a massive overhand swing, Ari cut it in half, severing its rear from its front. Looking up from its crumpling body, he paused.

There were no more. Around them, there was silence. Not of men, for some groaned and some cursed. The reserve gate creaked, halfway up and tied in place. Somewhere inside the courtyard, a woman was crying. But there were no more snarls. No howls. No wolves left at all.

Sir Cadwel tossed his flail to the ground, grunting as he dismounted. Goldwin hung his head, blood on his muzzle, his sides heaving. Sir Cadwel crossed to Ari, his face hard as he maneuvered around the fallen.

Ari realized he was still holding his sword at the ready. He stuck it into the ground, wiping a hand across his forehead to push back the hair that was plastered there. Salt stung his eyes.

"I heard you were trying to have a fight without us," Sir Cadwel said. The lines on his face were etched deeper than usual, emphasized by sweat and dust.

"It wasn't my idea, sir." Weariness filled Ari. All around him, men were dead. Ari could feel his whole body trembling. He was worried that, soon, it would turn into shaking. Behind Sir Cadwel, a horse came forward from where it stood at the base of the outer wall. Ari could make out a man, with someone small riding in front of him. "Who's that?"

"Our intrepid messengers," Sir Cadwel said. "Come, I'll hear your report in my study." He glanced around. "There's much to be done."

Ari nodded, pulling his sword free and sheathing it. He fell in beside Sir Cadwel. They ducked under the half-raised reserve gate. As they crossed the courtyard, Sir Cadwel's bellowing voice brought order. People scurried about, purpose replacing despair.

Relief washed through Ari. The real lord of the keep was back. No one could restore the dead, but Sir Cadwel would make everything right. As right as it could be.

Not to mention, with Sir Cadwel there, Ari would be free to pursue the one task foremost in his mind. He would take a brief rest, put together some provisions, and get Mirimel. She would track the Caller down, and Ari would kill him.

Chapter 22

They had to wait while the doors to the keep were unbarricaded. Sir Cadwel kept up a steady stream of commands. Men were dismantling the catapults and more of the stable to create temporary gates. Others collected the fallen, while another group tended the injured, readying them to be taken inside. The walls were manned by anyone who could fletch an arrow, that task occupying the men as they kept guard. A contingent was sent to ready a massive pyre. After a battle, comrades left this realm together, in one enormous blaze.

They started a picket line in the killing zone for all of the uninjured horses, just outside the inner wall. Those in need of extra care would stay in the remains of the stable. Ari noticed that neither Stew nor Larke's gray were led out. He pushed a shaking hand through his hair, hoping Stew hadn't sustained more injuries.

"Where's that bard?" Sir Cadwel said, after bellowing an order directing a group of pages to start bringing up fresh water and keep doing it until infirmary, soldiers, stable and picket line were supplied. The doors to the keep creaked as they started to open.

"He might be in the stable," Ari said, since the last time he'd seen Larke, he was with the horses. Mirimel came jogging through the ruined inner gate, angling toward them. Ari hadn't realized she'd left the ramparts.

"Where's the blonde hawk guardian?" Sir Cadwel asked, nodding toward Mirimel. "I see you couldn't keep Mirimel inside with the women."

"I did send her there," Ari said, unsure if Sir Cadwel's hard tone was a censure on her, or him, or the toil the day had taken on his keep. As for where Kimmer was, he thought that better told as part of his report.

"Come," the knight said, for the doors were finally open.

He led the way to his study. Even from halfway across the foyer, Ari could hear Canid and Raven inside, scratching at the door and whining. Sir Cadwel shot him a surprised look. Ari knew the hounds slept in the study when Sir Cadwel was away. They wouldn't sleep in his quarters without him. Natan had to shut them in, or they would paw at the doors of the keep all night, trying to get out to seek their lord.

"Did Natan leave them locked in here all day?" Sir Cadwel asked, throwing open the door to their enthusiastic greeting. They wriggled like puppies, shoving their muzzles into his hands. Ari winced at the pile of wood scrapings on the floor and tried to ignore the mess the dogs had been forced to make. "Where is Natan?" Sir Cadwel asked, eyes narrowing.

"My lords." Ari turned to see Peine crossing the foyer, wiping his hands on a kitchen cloth. "It's good to see you back, Lord Cadwel. May I fetch you anything? We have hearty stew and fresh bread. Lord Aridian, I believe, hasn't eaten since breaking his fast, and noontime has come and gone."

Ari was relieved to see Peine looking and sounding like himself. Confident beyond his years, his mind not muddled by love, anger or fear. He looked tired, and stress pulled at his features, but he looked like Peine.

"Ari," Mirimel called, striding into the keep. "The Caller's gone. He escaped."

Ari didn't know if it was the content of her announcement or the hot anger in her voice, but a strained silence fell on the foyer.

Sir Cadwel scowled. "We were just about to discuss his pursuit, Hawk Guardian Mirimel."

His tone was cold enough to make even Mirimel hesitate, her mouth falling open.

"Come," Sir Cadwel said, waving her over. "Peine, bring us food and get someone in here to clean up this mess. Find me that bard, then find me guardsman Serel and Gremble's son. They should be together. I'll want them to wait in the great hall until I send for them. Post a page outside in case I need anything else."

Ari frowned. Serel was the old guard Natan had sent with Gremble's wife, along with the younger guard, Wenten. Why were he and the boy back? Ari hoped it wasn't more bad news.

"Yes, my lord," Peine said, bowing. As if that example of normalcy was all that was needed, motion returned to the foyer. Wounded men were being brought in, and food out. The debris of the barricade was nearly cleared away. Canid and Raven walked on either side of Sir Cadwel as he stalked into his study, their long bodies pressed up against him. Mirimel hurried across the foyer, closing the door behind her at an inpatient gesture from the knight. As Ari had suspected, the door was a crosshatch of canine claw marks.

Sir Cadwel moved to stand by the mantel, staring at the unlit logs for a moment before turning to face Ari and Mirimel. Canid and Raven plopped down at his feet. "Hawk Guardian Mirimel." The old knight's voice was as hard as his face. "I'd appreciate it if you would endeavor not to spread panic among my people. I think they have enough to trouble them."

"Yes, my lord." Mirimel looked and sounded meeker than Ari would have thought her capable of.

"Sit," Sir Cadwel ordered, pointing at a couch.

Mirimel complied without protest, her face turned down toward her clasped hands.

"Lord Aridian, report."

Ari opened his mouth, starting his story from the moment he'd left Sir Cadwel in the Hawkers' village. The knight let him talk, accepting a bowl of stew from Peine without looking at him. Peine set another bowl on a small table near Ari before slipping back out. Ari ignored it, since he couldn't eat and talk. Behind him, he could hear the mess the dogs had made being cleaned up.

Larke came in, giving Ari the impression, from the corner of his eye, of a piece of parchment someone had scraped nearly raw, leaving it almost too thin to pen another message on. The bard slumped down next to Mirimel.

By the time Ari was up to the point where Natan got hit over the head, he was sure his stew was cold. To his surprise, he was hungry. He hadn't been before, stress overwhelming his appetite, but telling everything to Sir Cadwel was almost like making it better. Much of the tension left his shoulders, unclenching from his gut. The throbbing in his head lessened. Sir Cadwel's face was a grim mask, however, and Ari worried what it was like to be the lord. Ari could pass all of his worries on to Sir Cadwel, but to whom could the old knight give them?

"You tended Natan?" Sir Cadwel asked, breaking into Ari's monologue and turning to Larke.

"Aye," the bard said, sitting up from his distracted slump. "He'll recover."

Sir Cadwel waited, as if expecting more, but Larke returned to his own thoughts. The knight looked at Ari, who shrugged and continued his tale. When he finally reached the point where Sir Cadwel arrived, the knight gestured him to silence.

"You examined the Caller's trail?" he asked Mirimel.

"He made his way up to a narrow ledge that runs along the arm of the mountain." She leaned forward. "If I could get up there, I could track him, my lord."

Sir Cadwel nodded. "The horses?" he said, his eyes moving to Larke.

"We lost some." A dim light seemed to fill Larke's eyes, and Ari realized that his will was worn thin indeed. He was barely managing to maintain the illusion that kept mortals from realizing that he was glowing. "Some will need a lot of luck to survive, but most will be well. Stew shall recover, and Goldwin's merely exhausted and scratched."

"And your gray?" Sir Cadwel asked when it became obvious that Larke wasn't going to say more.

"He's in a terrible state." Larke's voice cracking at the edges. "But I can save him. I'm sure of it."

Ari wished Larke's tone was as firm as his words. He looked through his mind for something to say, trying not to think about how upset he'd be if Stew was dying.

"He's very brave," Mirimel said, putting a comforting hand on Larke's arm.

The bard nodded, his gaze on nothing.

"Ari, ask whoever Peine left outside to fetch Serel and the boy," Sir Cadwel ordered. "We'll have their story next while you eat."

"Yes, my lord." Ari crossed to the door to give the order. He unbuckled his sword and stood it in the corner. Coming back, he took up his bowl and sat on the couch opposite Larke and Mirimel. As soon as he sank into the yielding green leather, he was assailed by how long he'd been on his feet.

Ari spooned food into his mouth. Serel and the boy came in. Gremson, Ari recalled, relatively sure that was the boy's name. He remembered Peine telling him it was a new trend, adding son to your name to make your son's. Ari had asked Peine what happened when people had more than one son. His friend's slightly bitter reply was that younger sons didn't matter as much and didn't need names that paid homage to their fathers. Peine himself had two older brothers. That was why he'd been sent to the capital to become a gentlemen's gentleman.

"My lords," the old guard Serel said, bowing. He pushed gently on the back of the boy's head, reminding him to do the same. With wide eyes, the child complied.

"I'd like your report now," Sir Cadwel said. "How came you so fortuitously to rally us from the village?"

Ari realized Sir Cadwel must not have asked for explanations when Serel had reached them. He was exceedingly grateful his mentor was more a man of action than reflection. Another might have wanted the full tale before setting out, and Sir Cadwel had arrived just in time.

"Well, my lord." Serel regarded Sir Cadwel with eyes creased in a perpetual squint. "There ain't much to it. Lord Aridian sent us, me and Wenten, with Gremble's widow, to keep her safe on her journey." He winked at them over the boy's head. "Well, this one snuck out at night and saddled up Wenten's horse and up and took off, my lord."

The boy looked down, his face red.

"I left Wenten with her and the two girls and their cart, it carrying that certain burden, and set out after him. I caught up to him this morning, coming up on the keep. I think he'd stopped on his own, on account of that hell-spawned noise."

"I had to come back to avenge my father," Gremson said, looking up. "I wasn't afraid, my lord."

Ari could tell by how hard the boy had to swallow to keep from crying that he had been very afraid. Ari didn't blame him.

"Well, my lords," Serel continued. "I took one look at them creatures massing before the keep and galloped us into the mountains. I figured, with all them down here, not many could be left up there, and I figured, since I'd barely been gone more than a day, that you might still be up there, Lord Cadwel, not knowing what was going on down here. No hawks and the keep surrounded and all. I can't say as it was more to come for you or to get me and the boy away from them monsters, but head for Hawkers we did."

"And we're glad for it," Sir Cadwel said. "You have rendered Sorga a fine service. Invaluable. I'm sure Lord Aridian and I will be able to find a suitable reward for you."

"I don't need no reward other than that bastard's head, sir." Serel looked as if he might spit, but then obviously thought better of doing so in his lord's study.

Ari wished that Mirimel hadn't announced in the center of the keep that the Caller had escaped. Many people may not

248

even have realized it, or who their real enemy was. Most would have been happy with the destruction of the wolves.

"I'll take that into consideration," Sir Cadwel said. "Thank you for your report. I'm sure you can find someone in the great hall to tend to the boy. Your conduct was exemplary."

"Thank you, my lord," the old guard said, standing tall. He bowed, backing from the room. A hand on Gremson's shoulder pulled the wide-eyed boy after him.

"I'm not in trouble?" Ari heard the boy ask as the page outside swung the door shut.

The only discernable reply was the old guard's chuckle.

"Now, Ari." Sir Cadwel sank into his favorite leather chair, setting aside the book that lay in it. Canid and Raven wriggled toward him, lying on his feet. "You have that twice cursed stone safe, I presume."

"Yes, sir," Ari said, reaching for it where it rested inside his doublet. It occurred to him that keeping it there during the battle may not have been the smartest thing, but he'd put it there when he'd dressed that morning and then forgot it.

"Give it to Larke," Sir Cadwel said.

Ari nodded, leaning forward to hand it to the bard across the low table. Larke's worried expression didn't change. Mirimel took it, pressing it into the bard's hand.

"Hm?" Larke said, looking up. "What's this? Oh, the stone. Ari, the hawks said you were to have it."

Sir Cadwel shook his head. "That's well and fine, but Ari's going on a mission and I don't think he ought to take it with him. I assume that right now, no one knows where it is?"

"I don't think they do," Ari said. "Not even Peine."

"Fine, then they won't know Larke has it either," Sir Cadwel said. "Off with you, bard. Go tend to your horse."

"Right," Larke said, springing up. He tucked the stone in his garish doublet, the colors slightly dimmed by dust. Three long strides took him across the room and from it, pausing only to swing open the door. "Just send someone for me if you need me. I'll be ready. Always willing to help. No complaints from me . . ." Larke's voice trailed off as he crossed the foyer. The page closed the door again.

Sir Cadwel shook his head. "I hope the beast makes it. That cock's tail of a minstrel is obviously quite fond of him." Sir Cadwel cleared his throat, and Ari wondered if the same thoughts were going through the knight's mind regarding Goldwin as Ari had about Stew. "As for your mission, we obviously won't be getting any help from him."

"I'm going after the Caller now, sir?" Ari asked, hoping Sir Cadwel meant to send him immediately, even if Larke couldn't go too. He sat forward on the couch, filled with renewed vigor at the idea.

"Aye, you're going after him, but tell me first about Ispiria."

Ari's spark of energy left him. "There's nothing beyond what I told, sir." His shoulder's slumped. "Larke did his best, and he sent that wren, but it hasn't yet returned. She hasn't tried to get the stone again, but she hasn't truly had time. I don't know what the Caller's enchantments are doing to her mind."

"Well, I'll keep an eye on her, lad, and so will Larke. All the more reason to keep him near. She has no idea where the damnable thing is, and you won't be here for her to ask. I'd set Guardian Mirimel to watch her, too, but she must go with you."

Ari smiled in relief. He needed Mirimel with him. He needed her tracking skills, and her bow. All of the wolves who'd attacked with the Caller were dead, but he may have held some back, or maybe he could make more. Ari wasn't very clear on how Empty Ones were made, or how long it took. The Caller could be out there in the mountains building a second army right now.

"That is, if you're willing to volunteer, lass," Sir Cadwel said.

"I am, my lord." Mirimel's tone was firm, her posture purposeful.

Ari marveled at her poise. She'd had days of battle and death. Her village was destroyed and her family dead, but her shoulders were unbowed. Her gaze as she met Sir Cadwel's was unwavering.

"How soon will you be ready?" Sir Cadwel asked, looking from Mirimel to Ari.

"I'm ready now," Mirimel said, standing. "We'll need a ladder."

Chapter 23

After leaving Sir Cadwel, who insisted Mirimel take the time to gather provisions, Ari hurried up to his rooms. He changed as fast as he could, putting on serviceable garb and washing his face and hands. Taking up his pack, he shoved a change of clothes in and headed back toward the foyer, his eyes lingering on the door to Natan's room as he passed. He hoped Larke was correct in thinking Natan would be well.

Entering the great hall, Ari saw Peine ladling out stew and waved him over. Ari could easily secure provisions for the journey himself, but he wanted to tell Peine where he was going, and to say goodbye. His friend handed the ladle to a nearby kitchen worker and hurried across the hall, wiping his hands.

"Did you eat?" Peine asked as soon as he drew near.

"Yes," Ari said, smiling a little at his friend's worry. "I ate the whole bowl, thank you." He glanced around, making sure no one was standing particularly near, and lowered his voice. "Mirimel and I are going after the Caller. We're leaving as soon as I gather provisions."

Peine nodded, lines of worry creasing his forehead. He looked down, fidgeting with the dishcloth he had tucked into his belt.

"Peine, you can't come with us," Ari said, heading his friend off.

"No, it isn't that." Peine grimaced. "I learned my lesson last time, and besides, there's too much needing my attention here, what with Natan unwell. I just, I wanted to ask you something." He went back to fidgeting.

"I don't really have that much time," Ari said when Peine didn't show any sign of continuing.

Peine pulled his shoulders back, looking up. "Did she say anything about me? When you were in the tower, before she, you know, died. Did Kimmer say anything?"

Ari took in his friend's stricken face. He wished Kimmer had said something, anything that he could pass on, but she hadn't. "She didn't have time. She poisoned herself. She wanted me to know she did it to save her family. That's all she said."

"I see." Peine dropped his gaze again. "I just thought . . . I mean, that night, in the woods . . ." Peine leaned closer, whispering. "We kissed, and we. . ." He twisted the dishcloth so tightly that Ari thought it would tear. "Did she ever really care about me, Ari? It was all a lie, wasn't it? Just a lie to keep me from telling you what she'd overheard."

Taking in the misery on Peine's face, Ari wished the code of conduct he strove toward, the knight's code, didn't include not lying. It seemed cruel not to make up something to comfort Peine. A little lie wouldn't hurt anyone. Kimmer was dead, after all, so she wouldn't care. Ari sighed. Lately, he and the truth were having trouble getting along.

"I don't know. She didn't say anything about you. I don't think she was evil, though, and you're a good judge of people, Peine. I think that if you thought there was honesty between you, then there probably was."

"Maybe." Peine released the dishcloth, reaching out to take Ari's pack. "I'll go get you some provisions. Ispiria's coming," he added, looking behind Ari. "Good luck with your farewells. You know she doesn't like you going on dangerous missions."

As Peine hurried away, Ari turned to see Ispiria coming up behind him. She was smiling, but she too looked terribly tired and her dress was dirty. Ari was sure many of the stains on it were from blood, and realized she'd been tending the wounded, as she'd said she would.

"We won," Ispiria said, reaching out to take his hand. "Have you come for your victory kiss?"

Ari felt his face heat. "Uh, I came to tell you I'm going on a mission." He winced at the way her face fell.

"But we won." She pulled on his hand. "Let's not talk here."

She led him from the great hall, across the foyer and into the stairwell. Ari wondered if he should hold back, not sure where she was going. The only place the staircase they were on led to was the wing of the keep where their rooms were. Halfway up, she stopped on the deserted landing. He told himself he was relieved.

Turning to face him, she took both of his hands, rose up on her toes, and kissed him. Ari felt the barest flicker in his conscience as he pulled his hands from hers so that he could wrap his arms around her. He'd been fighting all day. He was going on a dangerous mission. All he wanted was to kiss Ispiria. Just kiss her, not break any vows about her honor. His lips never leaving hers, he lifted her up, putting her on the next step so that she was almost as tall as he was. He pressed her more tightly against him, well satisfied with the results.

A noise in the foyer below caused them both to start, jumping away from each other. Ispiria looked almost as guilty as he felt, but she smiled.

"I guess that's what they mean when they say some good comes from even the most dismal things," she said, but Ari could see that smiling was hard for her. He wished she didn't have to endure all the suffering and death that the day had brought them. She stepped down onto the landing. Bridging the space their guilty jump had left between them, she put her arms around him, laying her head against his chest. "What is this mission you must go on?"

"We have to go after the leader of the wolves." Ari didn't want to use the Caller's name, unsure if she would remember it after whatever Larke had done to her. "He escaped."

She snuggled closer. "Have you found the stone yet?" she asked, sending a wave of dismay through him. "I think it will be best if you take the stone with you. That way, if he catches you, you can trade it to him for your life." Her voice took on an overly cheerful tone, the tiredness and sorrow of the day leaving it. "That would be best, don't you think? You should bring him the stone." Her arms tightened around him, giving Ari the impression of a vice. "He will have it," she hissed. "You will give it to him."

He drew in a ragged breath, smoothing her curls with a trembling hand. He couldn't stand to hear Ispiria speak that way, in malice-drenched tones. He was glad he couldn't see her face.

"Ari," Peine's voice called in the foyer. "Lord Aridian?"

"I have to go," Ari said, pulling lightly at her arms.

She leaned back, glaring up at him, but didn't release him. Her eyes were narrow, her mouth twisted like she'd just bit into something revolting. "Bring him the stone, Ari. I know you have it. You can't fool me. Don't make him have to hurt us again."

"I have to go," he repeated, wrenching her arms off him.

"Do as I say," she said, raising her voice.

Ari fled down the staircase, leaving her standing on the landing with her fists clenched at her sides. To his relief, she neither followed nor kept shouting. He ignored the few curious glances that met him as he crossed the foyer, realizing her parting demand had made its way down the steps.

"I have your pack ready, my lord," Peine said with a half bow, straightening to glare around the foyer at anyone who was watching Ari instead of working. All around them, people hurried back to what they were doing.

"Thanks," Ari said, taking the proffered bag.

256

"What did she want you to do?" Peine asked, lowering his voice. "Stay here?"

Ari shook his head. "I have to go. Keep safe."

He hurried outside, hoping Mirimel and the ladder she'd asked for would already be out there so he wouldn't have to go back in. He didn't want to risk another encounter with Ispiria. Slinging the pack over his shoulders, he pushed a shaky hand through his hair.

"Sir Cadwel said to send you through," one of the guards at the bottom of the steps said, pointing toward the killing ground.

Ari nodded, but turned aside to his right, where the half torn down stable stood. He had one more goodbye to say before he could go.

The stable doors were thrown wide and Ari could see Stew as he approached. One side of Stew's head and neck was swaddled in bandages, but his eyes, ears and mouth looked untouched. The bandages reached along his back and wrapped around both forelegs. His stall was within the large square of sunlight that poured in through the open doors. He started to shake his mane at Ari's approach, but stopped, flicking his ears instead.

"How do you feel?" Ari patted Stew's neck on the uninjured side. "You were very brave. Larke says you'll be fine."

Stew whickered softly.

"Next time, get someone to put your armor on you before you start fighting," Ari said, ignoring the fact that he was the one who'd called for Stew without even a saddle. "That's why you have it, after all."

Stew snorted at him.

The side of the stable nearest the castle was completely torn down, but Ari's eyes were drawn in the other direction. Stew, too, turned toward the scene at the south end of the stable, resting the side of his head against Ari's chest.

Larke's gray lay on a heap of straw in the large stall at the end, usually used for foaling. The stall door was swung wide, and Ari could see the stable master crouched at the gray's side, changing out bloody compresses. Larke knelt in the straw by his horse's head. The bard was bent double, leaning low over the gray's ear. No one else would be able to hear what Larke was saying from so far away, but Ari could make out enough to know the words weren't in the Lggothian or Wheylian tongue.

Ari didn't know if it was an incantation or a wish the bard murmured, but all of Larke's attention seemed focused on it. The horse's sides heaved, each breath seeming a labor. Ari caught himself holding his own breath each time the gray breathed out, willing the horse to inhale again so that he could too.

Stew nudged him and Ari pulled his eyes away. The stable was full of injured horses, but all of the others stood. Ari knew that when a horse was too injured to stand, that usually meant the death of it. He was sure that, for any other horse, they would have eased his passing and moved on. Well, any other horse aside from Goldwin or Stew.

"I'm going after the Caller," he told Stew in a low voice.

Stew looked at him with worried eyes.

"Mirimel is coming with me."

Stew didn't look reassured.

Ari let himself stand with Stew a moment longer, soaking in his horse's strength. They were a strange dichotomy, these animals. They held nearly unparalleled strength and endurance. Ari had seen Stew crush an Empty One wolf's skull into dust. Yet, they could be so breakable.

Ari wondered what it was like in the kingdom of the Questri, far away across the northern range. Did the horse king have some sort of throne? Were there horse cities? Most of all, he wondered if those few Questri who came south to serve the Aluiens missed their home. Did Stew, Goldwin and Larke's gray dream of where they were from? Ari tried to picture endless rolling plains with herds of valiant Questri galloping across them. He hoped more than ever that Larke's gray didn't die. Not here. Not so very far away from home.

Sighing, Ari stepped away from Stew, giving him one last pat. "I'll be back as soon as I can." He turned and heading out of the stable. Squaring his shoulders, he purposefully left thoughts of sorrow behind him.

Ari was impressed with how much progress they were already making toward a temporary gate. He crossed the courtyard and walked under the archway cut in the thick wall, appreciating anew how well-built the defenses of the keep were. They just needed stronger gates. The gate would always be the weak point. Maybe they should have three of them.

A giant pyre was being built in the center of the killing ground. Many of the dead were already assembled there, but bodies and mourners were still scattered across the space. Women and youngsters walked between unattended corpses, searching for those they knew. There wasn't as much wailing as Ari expected. He swallowed down his own anguish, realizing the faces he could see were streaked with tears. The women of Sorga wept, but they wept in silence.

Pages were hard at work raking, erasing blood and the ashes of Empty One corpses. To Ari's left, the picket area was already raked clear and the horses were in line, troughs of water and feed set out for them to be led to in rotation. Grooms brushed them down, inspecting them and caring for wounds too small to warrant the attention of Larke and the stable master.

He could see Mirimel and Sir Cadwel waiting for him a third of the way down the killing zone. Beside them, two men were setting up a ladder so that Ari and Mirimel could climb to the top of the cliff that formed a natural wall on that side. Canid and Raven sat nearby, watching Sir Cadwel for orders. By the time Ari reached them, the ladder was set up and Mirimel already climbing it, a pack strapped to her back.

"My lord," Ari said in greeting as he drew alongside Sir Cadwel.

Sri Cadwel nodded, but his eyes were on Mirimel. She stepped off the ladder, bent low to scrutinize the ground. Straightening, she turned back to them.

"His trail is clear enough and it looks like a fairly easy path leading along the ledge." Her impatient eyes fell on Ari.

"Don't do anything too heroic," Sir Cadwel said, turning to clasp him on the shoulder.

"Ispiria tried to get the stone again," Ari said in a low voice.

"I'll keep an eye on her, lad." Sir Cadwel looked up at Mirimel. "Safe journey to you both."

"Thank you, my lord," she said.

"My lord," Ari repeated, bowing.

He climbed the ladder, feeling it was a bit awkward to do with a pack and aware that everyone was watching him do it. There was a narrow ledge at the top, on which Mirimel waited. She pointed to the rock below their feet.

"His trail is clear, even if I hadn't watched him go. We'll have no trouble following it." She hosted her pack more firmly into place and set off down the wall.

Ari looked down, waved, and turned to follow her. As much as he tried, he couldn't see the trail of which she spoke. He would have to ask her to show him, once it tuned away from the wall. As things stood, he felt a bit foolish, for their path was along the cliff above the killing ground, and everyone seemed to have stopped working to watch them.

"Good hunting, my lord," a woman called.

"Bring us his head, my lord," another yelled.

Ari waved at them, trying to convey his willingness, although he knew there was no way he could bring back the Caller's head. It would disintegrate too quickly. To his relief, Mirimel turned, leading him through a steep walled cleft in the cliff face. The cool shade of the fissure surrounded them and they left the sounds of Sorga behind.

Chapter 24

If Ari had realized how long it would be before he saw Sorga again, he would have stopped for a moment and taken in the soaring walls of the keep, Sir Cadwel's weathered face, and all of the views of home, but the Caller had only a few hours head start on them. Ari had no idea that, twelve days later, he and Mirimel would still be tracking, still be following, never once having sighted their prey.

Ari scratched at the scruff growing on his face. He hadn't thought to bring anything to shave with. One of these days, he reflected, he really should get himself a knife.

"Our mistake was stopping that first night."

"We were exhausted," Mirimel said from behind him. "And you hadn't learned to track yet. I keep trying to tell you, some of us can't see in the dark."

Ari grunted. It was an old argument. Nearly twelve days old. The Caller didn't need to rest. He didn't need to sleep. They would gain on him, getting closer and closer, but then the need to rest would overtake their human bodies, and while they slept, he would keep going.

He wasn't moving fast. Either he didn't know they were behind him or he didn't care. They could tell he sought something, for he was wending his way back and forth across the mountains in broad sweeps. What he was seeking, they could only guess at. Ari just wished they could guess right so that the knowledge could help them get out ahead of him.

"Not that you've learned to track very well," Mirimel said, pulling Ari from his thoughts. She pointed to his left, where the Caller's trail broke away from the direction he was idly walking in. "You have to pay attention, Ari."

Ari fought down his annoyance at her acerbic tone. He told himself, for probably the thousandth time, that she wasn't angry with him. She was angry with their lack of progress. With the Caller. With the world, maybe, but not really with him.

"Rabbit," Mirimel snapped.

Instantly, Ari lifted the bow he carried, pulling an arrow from the quiver at his waist and loosing it almost before he could even register the little form fleeing between the trees ahead of them.

"Nice shot," Mirimel said, passing him to collect the rabbit.

They had a rule. Whoever shot dinner didn't have to dress it. At first, this meant Ari spent a lot of time borrowing Mirimel's knife and getting bunny and squirrel blood all over himself every evening, but under her tutelage he was becoming a much better shot. They took turns wearing the bow and quiver. Ari just had to make sure that, in his enthusiasm, he didn't draw with too much vigor, pulling the string back too far and breaking it. He'd already done so several times and Mirimel was running out of replacements.

"I wonder if it will transfer to the longbow," Ari said. The longbow was what Ari needed to master for shooting in the king's tourney in the fall.

"With a little practice." Mirimel scooped up the carcass, pulling the arrow out and cleaning it off in the dirt before tying the rabbit at her waist. "It's basically the same thing, after all. I wish I had your speed."

"You're much faster with a bow than I am."

"I used to be." She gave him a rare half-smile. "But you are now. After only a few days of practice. It's almost sickening."

Ari shrugged. It was true, he seemed to learn martial skills very quickly. Of course, he hadn't tried any non-martial ones. He'd been practicing shooting for months now, though. The difference was that Mirimel's advice was better and made more sense than what others had told him. That, and that there was absolutely nothing else to do while they followed the Caller's trail each day.

He pulled out another arrow, aimed for a spot on a tree up ahead, and shot. The spot he chose was low. Ari had learned early on that Mirimel didn't take kindly to him putting her arrows so high up in a tree that they didn't have time to climb up to get them.

"He turns aside here," Mirimel said, stopping to point out the subtle indentations and compressed leaves that Ari wouldn't have been able to pick out twelve days ago.

Ari passed her, retrieving the arrow. It was almost exactly where he'd aimed. Looking up the deer's path they followed, he could see the Caller's tracks returned to it just ahead. Mirimel drew alongside him, but she kept looking back.

"Look." Ari pointed to the tracks. "That's his footprint. I don't think we should waste time following a detour. These tracks are getting very fresh, aren't they?" Ari hadn't thought about it until he said it, but the footprints on the trail ahead were deep and crisp. Little time had passed since the Caller made them. Ari's heartbeat sped up. He lowered his voice. "How old do you think they are?"

Mirimel looked up the trail, then back at the tracks leading from it. "A few hours. No more than half a day, but don't you want to know what he was doing?"

"Not as much as I want to catch him."

She chewed on her lower lip, thinking. Ari rolled his head from side to side, trying to loosen the tension in his neck. They were close. Closer than they'd been since they'd left Sorga. Why was she pausing?

"I'll go see what he was doing and then catch up," she said.

"No, we'll both go." Letting them get separated seemed like the worst possible idea, and he could tell from Mirimel's tone that she wasn't going to back down. Best to go see and get back as quickly as possible.

"I'll lead," she said.

Ari knew that was Mirimel's attempt to be nice. What she meant was that they needed to go fast, not waste time, and he still couldn't track well enough to lead them swiftly. They only followed him when they were on a trail, like the path made by deer they were following, or when it was too dark for Mirimel to see anymore. She pushed her way into the underbrush, moving quickly.

The trail led them to a nearly man-height opening, a dark line cut in a rising cliff. Ari grabbed her arm, pulling her back behind him. She gave him an irritated look, but didn't argue. He hid his smile. It was always best to annoy Mirimel when it was time to be quiet.

Ari drew his sword and crept forward, more sensing her behind him than hearing. He paused outside the cave, but could discern nothing. Ducking slightly, he stepped inside, pausing for his eyes to adjust. It was the wrong time of day for light to reach in. Mirimel wouldn't be able to see a thing.

Nor would she want to. Ari sheathed his sword and pulled the edge of his dirty tunic up over his nose. The cave reeked of death. Fur and blood were spattered everywhere. Ari tried to focus on the jumble of tracks on the cave floor, but his attention kept going back to the mess. He heard stone hitting stone and turned to see Mirimel sparking a candle stub.

She stepped up beside him. Her only observable reaction to the carnage was to wrinkle her nose at the smell. Bending low, she held the candle close to the ground, stepping lightly among the dead. Ari stayed where he was. As far as he could tell from the odors he could sort out that weren't blood and decay, this was a bear den. The torn furry remains, then, were most likely bear.

Mirimel straightened, gesturing him out of the cave, her frown thoughtful. Joining him, she blew out her candle. "He went this way," she said, taking point once again.

"He killed a bear?" Ari asked as they hurried back toward the path.

"He killed three cubs," she said.

"Three cubs?"

"Let's be quick. I want to check the tracks you spotted up ahead on the trail. There were bear tracks, but I didn't think anything of it."

The way back was faster. More of the branches were already bent, forming a path through the underbrush that even Ari couldn't lose. Back on the deer trail, Mirimel stopped, pointing out the large bear prints mirroring the Caller's. Mirimel set a rapid pace up the path.

"You see how the bear's tracks are sometimes over his?" she asked. "That's because the bear follows him. Closely from the looks of it, but he's not running."

"Bear cubs would be constantly beside their mother this early in the spring. It's what he's been searching for." The realization left his mouth as it came to him. "He used up all of the wolves. He took her, the mother bear."

"How do you make an Empty One? How long does it take?"

"I don't know."

"I suppose that bard wouldn't tell you."

"I've never asked." He wished she wouldn't be so hard on Larke. Who knew what arcane punishments the Aluiens had for those who broke their rules?

"As if asking would help. That bard is insufferable. He--" She stopped, holding up a hand.

"What?" Ari whispered the words, suddenly feeling the need to.

"The bear tracks turn aside here." She turned to face him, biting her lower lip. "Ari, give me my bow and quiver."

265

He unbuckled the quiver, handing it to her. After she had it on, he passed her the bow. She put an arrow to it, turning slowly to scan the woods around them.

"What is it?" Ari asked, keeping his voice low.

"I don't know," she said, still scanning. "The bear tracks turn aside and his go on. I can see them up to that turn." She pointed with her arrow toward a large boulder that redirected the path. "I feel like someone is watching us. Don't you?"

Ari strained his senses. Surely, if something was near, he would hear it. Beyond the usual sounds of the forest, like the hammer of woodpeckers and the trill of songbirds, he could usually hear well enough to pick out the sounds of squirrels running along the branches above, or birds rummaging in the dried remains of last year's pine needles on the forest floor, looking for bugs. Yet now, there was only silence. All he could hear, he realized, was their breathing and the beat of his own heart.

"Where are all the birds?" Ari put a hand to his chest, pressing the amulet the Lady had given him against his skin. It was ice cold.

Mirimel turned slowly, scanning, until she was facing him, looking back down the trail.

The Caller stepped out onto the trail behind her.

"Behind you," Ari yelled, even as Mirimel pointed her bow toward him.

"Duck," she cried.

Ari dove to the side, wrenching his sword free. Mirimel's arrow sped past him, right through the spot where he'd been standing, hitting the bear behind him with a thunk and a roar.

Ari glimpsed the snarling beast out of the corner of his eye, but he was already lunging past Mirimel, charging the Caller. The Caller's long stringy gray hair was plastered to his head, oily and slick. He wore dirt-colored rags, his skin matching them so well that it was hard to tell where cloth ended and flesh began. The only parts of him that weren't a mirage of dirt were his mad blue eyes and the ball of fire dancing in his right hand.

He raised his hand, and Ari realized he wasn't going to make it. He was running flat out, but the Caller would throw his fire before Ari could reach him. Ari bunched his muscles, ready to throw himself to the side. Another arrow whistled past him, right at the Caller's face. The Caller jerked away, but the arrow cut a deep gouge through his forehead, taking off a chunk of his scalp. He threw back his head and howled.

Mirimel screamed, a sound full of pain rather than fear. Ari whirled, charging back down the trail toward her. Why had she shot the Caller instead of the bear?

Her left arm hung limp, blood flowing down her back from a large claw mark. She faced the bear, her hunting knife raised. It swung at her with both massive paws and she jumped back, the bear lurching after.

Ari could hear the Caller striding up the trail behind him. Skidding to a stop beside Mirimel, Ari lashed out at the bear. He struck near the shoulder, trying to cut off a front leg, but he didn't manage to cleave all the way through. It snarled, swinging at him with both front paws, although the nearly severed one only jerked awkwardly. As he parried, Ari could see the wound already growing closed.

Mirimel darted to the left, hammering her hunting knife into the bear's side. The creature didn't seem to notice, swinging at Ari again. He blocked, trying to ascertain where he could strike a killing blow. Mirimel wrenched her knife free. Ari knew the Caller was behind them. He risked a glance over his shoulder.

Mirimel slammed into him, knocking them both to the ground. A ball of fire smashed into the bear. It howled, clawing its way toward them. They rolled apart as it toppled, trying to land on them to crush them with its weight and blazing fur.

Ari jumped up, spinning to stab the bear in the back of the head, severing its spine. Mirimel charged past him, her hunting knife held low, Ari a step behind. He wished she wasn't so fast, and so impetuous.

The Caller let her come to him. He was strapping something to his hands. Ari couldn't see what until Mirimel reached him and he raised one, slapping her knife aside with it. They were claws. Metal gloves that gave him long-bladed claws.

With the return of the blow he'd used to knock her knife away, the Caller backhanded Mirimel across the face, sending her flying. Ari, half a step behind her, didn't slow as he slammed into the Caller.

They both flew backward. It was like running into a wall. Ari barely kept his feet.

The Caller grinned, crouching low. He lifted his nose, sniffing. "You smell familiar, boy." His voice grated like old hinges. "You smell like a man and woman I killed years ago." He sniffed again. "And you smell like fear."

Ari raised his sword, ready to ward off the blows he knew were coming, but his mind was assailed by memories of his dream. He saw the fire, and the wolves. He saw the Caller, and the two dead bodies sprawled in the farmyard dirt. The Caller lunged forward, claws raised.

Ari knocked one aside, but the other raked down his chest. He felt the chain on his amulet snap. It hit the ground with a dull thud. Four hot lines of blood seared across Ari's chest. He brought his sword back around to strike.

The Caller made an arcane gesture, his clawed fingers tracing lines of light in the air. His eyes dropped to the amulet, his grin revealing pointed teeth. "Now that trinket's out of the way," he said, his voice taking on a more soothing tone. "You and I can be friends, boy."

Ari couldn't bring himself to strike. He felt his sword arm relax. His blade lowered.

"I like friends," the Caller said. "Friends who bring me gifts."

Ari felt dizzy. He wanted to raise his sword. The Caller had lowered his guard and his ice-blue eyes were smug. It was the perfect time to strike, but Ari couldn't muster the will to do it. Rage filled him, but he couldn't force it past the wall of indifference the Caller's magic was building.

"Do you know what gift I most want, boy?"

"The stone." Ari heard himself answer as if listening to someone else.

"Do you know where it is?"

Ari willed himself not to nod. He could feel the strain in his neck. He clenched his teeth over the affirmative that threatened to burst out. Larke had said Ari could see through illusions not because of the amulet, but because he possessed magic of his own. Ari was sure that if he tried hard enough, he could beat the Caller's spell.

"I asked you a question, boy." The Caller came closer. His breath reeked of death, like the inside of the bear cave. He placed the tips of one clawed hand under Ari's chin, tilting Ari's head back so their eyes met. "Do you know where the stone is?"

The claws dug into Ari's neck. Pain stabbed through him, scattering his thoughts and splintering his resolve not to speak.

"You're a stronger man than your father. I'll give you that. You must take after your mother. She took longer to kill."

Rage shot through him. He opened his mouth, curses of defiance on his lips. "Yes, I know where the stone is." Ari snapped his mouth back closed, aghast. With the pain of his parents' murder devouring his insides, how could those words leave his mouth?

The Caller smiled. It was such a smug smile, Ari thought he could muster the strength to tear it from the Empty One's face with his bare hands. The metal claws slid from his chin and up his face, the other set coming to join them, almost as if the Caller clasped Ari's skull in a cage.

"I knew we could be friends." His ice-blue eyes filled Ari's world. "You'll get the stone for me, won't you, Aridian?"

"Why do you want it?" Ari managed to ask, gasping with the effort. The Caller's claws tightened about his head, squeezing it, but it felt almost good. The claws were holding his head together, because the pressure of not agreeing to get the stone filled his mind like it would burst.

269

"My master is making a set." The smile slid from the Caller's face, replaced by a thoughtful look. "But if I kill you, he may not need it."

Thoughtful was replaced by surprise and the Caller jerked back, swinging a clawed hand down. Ari saw a spray of orange curls as Mirimel was flung away again, her hunting knife protruding from the Caller's calf at the bottom of a large gash. Warmth rushed through Ari's body and he gasped, not quite sure when he'd gone as cold and still as marble.

He wrenched his sword up, his first movement clumsy. The Caller knocked the blade away. Ari pressed forward, swinging again, more sure this time. The Caller parried with one claw, reaching out to strike with the other. He stumbled, blue eyes darting down to look at his leg.

Ari swung again, his intent not actually to strike a killing blow, but rather to cut off one of the Caller's hands. When the Empty One brought up his claws to block, Ari twisted his blade, severing the wrist below the metal glove. The Caller howled as his left hand skittered away across the path.

He tried to step back, staggering again. Anger and pain contorted his dirt smeared face. Ari realized Mirimel must have severed a tendon and it couldn't heal as long as her blade remained.

Ari pressed his advantage, but the Caller took a different tactic, lunging forward instead of away. He drove the four long blades on his right hand at Ari's face. Ari twisted aside, getting in a deep cut across the Caller's ribs as they passed. The Caller shook his leg, trying to dislodge the knife.

Ari glared at his enemy, gathering his anger. The Caller's words about his parents, the dream he'd had about the people at the farm dying, the people of Sorga and the Hawkers. Larke's horse, Kimmer and Ispiria. He pulled it all to him, watching as the Caller lunged, pushing off with his good leg.

The Caller let out a blood-curdling yowl as he attacked. Coiled into a spring of rage, Ari launched himself at his enemy. Point first, he jammed his sword into the Caller's outstretched clawed hand, cutting through metal and bone alike. Using the force of their joint charge, he pressed the blade farther, the hand splitting in two as metal surged through it to plunge into the Caller's chest.

The Caller snarled. Ari drove the blade deeper, twisting it to widen the hole. The Caller threw back his head and howled, thrashing. Hilt in both hands, Ari lifted the Caller's body, then slammed it into the ground. He tore his sword free, pulling it out through the Caller's side, breaking his ribs and popping them from his flesh. There was a terrible crunching sound as Ari's boot slammed down on the Caller's shattered chest, pinning him.

The Empty One fell silent. Dazed blue eyes looked searchingly up at Ari. Putting the point of his sword under his enemy's jaw, Ari drove it home, severing the Caller's spine. With a jerk, he snapped off the head, sending it flying.

"If I thought you could feel pain, I would have made sure you took longer to kill," Ari snarled.

The corpse below his foot disintegrated and Ari stepped back. He drew in a deep shuddering breath. He forced his jaw to unclench. It was over. The Caller was dead. The Empty One who'd murdered the people of Sorga and killed his parents was dead.

Chapter 25

Ari stood in the middle of the deer trail, catching his breath. Mirimel's knife glinted in the scattering pile of dust that was once the Caller, his amulet nearby. Sheathing his sword, he bent and picked them up. He tucked her knife under his belt and looked about. Spotting a pile of orange curls a few paces into the trees, he hurried forward, tying the broken chain of his amulet beside her knife.

Mirimel lay on her side, facing away from him, wrapped around the base of a tree as if she'd hit it. Ari knelt beside her. She was breathing, he could see, but not conscious. He reached out and gently rolled her onto her back.

With her face relaxed, worry and anger no longer hardening it, she looked more like Ispiria than ever. Two large bruises spread across her pale skin and blood trickled from the corner of her mouth. Ari ran light fingers down her side, noting where her ribs were most likely broken, and she flinched without waking. The wounds on her shoulder raked from front to back, blood caking her tunic on both sides, but they had mostly stopped bleeding.

Ari pushed a hand though his hair, recalling his vow to learn more about healing and wishing he'd followed through on it. Not that he'd had time. Shaking his head, he carefully scooped her up, holding her limp form against his chest.

His indifferent skills aside, they weren't going to stay where they were. He may not know much, but he should bathe her wounds in clean water. Not to mention, since the dead bear was a freshly made Empty One, its half-burned corpse was showing no sign of the accelerated decay that normally marked their death. It was going to rot in the middle of the trail, and Ari didn't feel like staying around to witness it.

He carried Mirimel back the way they'd come, recalling a stream not too far away. The dead rabbit hanging off her belt flapped with every step, keeping a macabre tempo with Ari's walk. At least he'd have something to make them for dinner without having to leave her alone to find it.

By the time he located the stream, made a fire, cleaned her up as best as he felt a combination of decency and necessity allowed, cooked the rabbit, bathed in the stream, and ate, he was starting to really worry. No one truly understood head wounds, but it was common knowledge that when people didn't seem inclined to wake up from them, something was wrong. Ari stared into his small flickering fire, feeling exhaustion in every limb, and wondered if he should put it out and start carrying her home.

After watching her lay unmoving and expressionless for a few moments longer, he decided they'd better head home. He scuffed out the fire and wrapped up the last bit of the rabbit. Dumping out her things, he put them inside his pack, rolling hers up and adding it. He had extra room, having changed to his spare set of clothes and left his torn and bloodied ones by the stream, but it was still a tight fit. He slung her bow over it and put on her quiver. Her knife he sheathed at her side.

Lifting her gently, he cast about for a glimpse of the lowering sun, checking his direction. If he pressed hard and didn't lose his way, he should be able to make it back to Sorga in four days. Their journey out had been circuitous because of the Caller's search, but Ari hoped he could find a much more direct route back, for Mirimel's sake.

After two days of Ari trying to find their way through the mountains, Mirimel still hadn't woken. The bruises had spread across her face, nearly encompassing it. Her eyes were sunk in black circles. Whenever fatigue got the better of him and he was forced to stop, Ari would dribble water into her mouth with a damp cloth, but he didn't know if it was doing any good. The wound on her shoulder was growing infected and he had no way to clean it, no salve to place on it. He cursed his lack of knowledge and his ineptitude hourly.

He had to constantly remind himself not to squeeze her too tight, for fear of damaging her ribs. Every time he looked down at her, he wanted to crush her to him and beg her not to die. He'd never felt so powerless. He pushed himself as far as he could go each day, into the night, but in his heart he knew he wasn't even sure of their path. Mirimel was the one who knew how to find their way home.

He heard the rain first, his ears picking up the gentle patter of it around him before his body registered its touch. He groaned, glancing over his shoulder at the storm clouds. A spring rain could last for days. He plodded forward, scanning for some form of shelter. At least someplace he could put Mirimel, even if he had to stay outside.

Spotting a jagged ridgeline rising above the trees, he angled toward it. As he'd hoped, it rose abruptly from the forest floor, as did many of the higher points. Unlike the slow symmetrical rise of the Wheylian mountains that ran north to south, the northern range was a jumbled pile of hewn off stones and the occasional peak. It was as if, sometime in the distant past, someone had taken the mountains and shaken them.

Leaning over Mirimel in a vain attempt to shelter her from the rain with his body, he followed the cliff, relief filling him when he found shelter. A jut of stone stuck out, creating a natural roof. He'd been hoping for a cave, but the overhang sheltered them from the rain quite well, and a cave most likely would have been occupied. Ari had seen enough enraged bears for one spring.

He set her down carefully and darted out to gather what wood he could before it was all soaked. It was difficult to find enough while still keeping her in sight, but he created a moderate blaze. The heat it gave off reminded him of how cold she must be. Cushioning her as best he could with the packs, he placed her near the fire.

His sword resting on his knees, he sat cross-legged by her feet, watching the world for danger and pondering what he would do if the rain didn't stop soon. Would it be better to carry her through it or wait? He looked around, wondering if he could fashion something to cover her while they walked, to keep her dry.

Ari didn't realize he'd fallen asleep until a gentle hand shook his shoulder. He jumped up, grabbing for the hilt of his sword and nearly knocking Larke down. Letting the sword fall, he clasped the bard in a rough embrace.

"Lad, you're crushing me."

Ari stepped back, embarrassed. "Larke, thank the gods," he said, reaching down for his sword and sheathing it. "How far are we from the keep? You've got to help me. Mirimel . . ." He let his voice trail off, unsure what to say about Mirimel. She lay where he'd left her, her head lulled away from them.

"She isn't asleep?" Two long strides took Larke around the fire and to her side. He gasped as he knelt beside her, cupping her chin in his hand to turn her face toward him. His other hand trembled as he reached to brush her hair back from her forehead. "Ari, this isn't good."

"I know," Ari said, turning to stare out into the rainy night. He cleared a throat that threatened to close with tears. "I didn't know what to do. I'm sorry, Larke. All I could do was try to bring her home."

Behind him, he heard Larke draw in a deep breath. "I know you did your best, lad."

Larke's words only made Ari feel worse.

"Here's what I want you to do." The bard's voice was firm now.

Ari turned to find resolve on Larke's face.

"Get the pot from my pack." He pointed to a large bundle on the ground.

Ari hadn't even noticed it, but Larke must have set it down before waking him.

"Fill it with water and put it on the fire. I'm going hunting for some herbs and any dry kindling I can find. Set up my tent and get out my clean clothes. Put them by the fire to make sure they're dry. Not too close, mind. We don't want to burn them."

Ari nodded, kneeling by the pack and pulling it open. A stab of hope shot through him, so strong it made him dizzy. Larke would fix this. He would make Mirimel better.

"Mind my lute," Larke said.

Ari nodded again, his hands shaking as he untied the instrument from the back of Larke's oversized pack. He set it carefully aside before going back to his rummaging, pulling out Larke's cooking pot.

"And lad," the bard said, rising from Mirimel's side.

Ari stood too, holding the pot.

"Did you kill the Caller? Did he pay for this?"

Ari's lips curled in a grim smile. "He paid for it all."

"Good." Larke gave a sharp nod, striding out into the darkness.

Ari set the pot out beyond the overhang, the raindrops filling it setting a nearly musical accompaniment to his rambling thoughts as he put up the tent. He found Larke's change of clothes, well-crafted in subdued shades of brown. Ari supposed they were better for sneaking, though the bright blues and yellows Larke normally wore were no less of a disguise, in their way. In the caves of his home the bard wore white, as all Aluiens did.

Ari put the water-filled pot near the fire, placing the lid on to keep out floating ashes, and sat down to wait for Larke's return. He wasn't long, coming back with more wood and a bundle of roots and branches, which he proceeded to clean, chop and crush in various ways. He bundled some in compresses he made using his blanket, which he was shredding into strips as he went, added others to the pot, and put some aside.

"Can't you fix her with magic?" Ari asked, interrupting Larke's ongoing muttering about spring being a terrible time to hunt down herbs.

"Aye, some," Larke said, not looking up from his work. "I can augment the process, but I think the process may need some extra encouragement. I'm almost done here. Take her tunic off and we'll get her shoulder cleaned up."

Ari gaped at him.

"Ari?" Larke asked, seeming to note Ari's complete silence.

"Do what?"

"Her tunic, lad." Larke frowned at him. "We have to examine her shoulder."

"I can't take her clothes off," Ari said, choking on the words.

"They work the same as a man's, lad," Larke said. "I'm sure you'll be able to figure out a way."

"But, do you know what's under her tunic?" Ari could feel the heat in his face. "I'll cut the shoulder of her tunic away."

"I reckon that what's under her tunic are her smallclothes, which you by no means shall be removing." The corners of Larke's mouth twitched. "Do you mean to be telling me you'll not be helping me change her into clean clothes, then?"

Ari leapt to his feet, blood surging to his head. He swayed slightly, little sparks momentarily clouding his vision. "I'm going to go get more firewood." Larke's chuckle chased him as he fled the camp.

When he came back later, soaked to the skin and positive enough time must have passed for Larke to be finished, Mirimel was dressed in Larke's clean clothes and sleeping inside his tent. Larke sat by the fire, looking exhausted. Even from outside the tent, Ari could see that the bruises on Mirimel's face were faded and hear that her breathing was stronger. Ari felt a moment's awe for the bard's skills.

He also felt a little guilty. Not only for leaving Larke to do everything, but for not staying behind to guard Mirimel's honor. Not that it needed guarding from Larke. Though he looked like a man only ten years her senior, the bard was over twice her age. He was also a noble and magical being, not actually even human.

"She looks much better," Ari said, coming to sit by the fire. He set down the bundle of somewhat dry wood he held. "I'm sorry I left."

Larke waved a hand in dismissal. "Sometimes I forget how very young you are, lad."

"And she's Ispiria's cousin." Ari wasn't sure why, but the fact that Mirimel and Ispiria looked so much alike made the idea of sneaking peeks at Mirimel nearly naked even worse.

"Consider it forgotten."

"Did she wake?"

"No." Larke's face seemed to age with the admission. "I'm sorry I wasn't there to help you, lad. I followed as quickly as I was able."

"You had something important to take care of. I understand." He hoped Larke's words meant his horse was well enough to leave, as opposed to the alternative.

"He's one of my oldest friends." Larke gazed into the fire. "Over twenty years we've traveled the lands together, watching history make itself."

"He's well, I hope?" Ari asked, worried by how glum Larke seemed.

"Oh, aye, he's better now, lad." Larke's eyes went to the tent. "And I wouldn't make the choice differently if I could, but I'll never forgive myself if the lass pays the price."

"But she'll get better now, won't she?" Ari asked. "You're here now."

"It's hard to say, lad. She's already much healed, as you can surely see. Her shoulder wounds are clear of infection. Her ribs have mended. Even those ugly welts on her face are faded, but

279

she didn't wake. It's always hard to tell with a blow to the head. Did the Caller do all of that? I'd swear the cuts on her shoulder are from an animal."

"A bear. It clawed her. The Caller hit her in the face, and knocked her into a tree. I think that was what broke her ribs. She shot him in the head, though, and stabbed him."

"And you finished the job, you're quite sure?"

"He's nothing but dust."

Larke nodded. "I'll have to take my satisfaction in that, and I do. So will Cadwel and all of Sorga. If she doesn't wake by morning, you go back to them. I'll stay and tend her."

"I can carry her back."

"I fear quiet rest is our only hope."

"As if anyone could rest quietly with you about," Mirimel said from inside the tent.

Her voice was rough and thin, and she dissolved into a fit of coughing. They both jumped up, almost running into each other in their haste to look inside the tent.

Mirimel peered up at them through sleep-caked eyes. "Water," she croaked.

They both turned. Ari grabbed up his water skin. Larke produced a cup, ducking into the tent to kneel at her side. He put an arm behind her, helping her to sit up. Ari held out the skin. Larke handed Mirimel the metal cup, taking the water from Ari to pour her some before returning it. Larke kept one arm around her shoulders, wrapping a long-fingered hand about hers to steady them as she raised the cup to her lips.

"Thank you," she said once the water was gone.

Larke took the cup, handing it to Ari as well. Ari put the cup and water skin back with the packs, returning to sit at the entrance to the tent. It was a tent fashioned for one person and very crowded with Mirimel stretched out in it and Larke kneeling beside her, holding her up. Ari pulled his knees to his chest, trying to fit into the entrance. Mirimel was looking around, obviously assessing the situation.

"I feel like someone broke my ribs." She lifted a tentative hand to her face. "And my jaw."

280

"The Caller did," Ari said. "You don't remember?"

"I remember the bear." She dropped her hand to her bandaged shoulder. "I stabbed the Caller in the leg?" She sounded unsure.

Ari nodded. "He got you once. I thought you were out cold, but you crawled back and stabbed right through the ligament in his calf. Then he hit you again, but you left the knife in there, so it couldn't heal. If you hadn't, we would have lost."

She frowned. "It's all a blur. I remember him hitting me once. After that, I was too dizzy to stand." She went silent, rubbing her eyes. When she lowered her hand, she locked her gaze on Ari. "I don't remember the rest, but you got him, didn't you? Please tell me he's dead, Ari." Her voice was low and intent.

"We got him. He's very, very dead."

Mirimel smiled, and burst into tears.

Larke pulled her to him, holding her close and murmuring soothing sounds that Ari didn't think were in any language, magical or otherwise. He stroked her matted orange curls, meeting Ari's gaze. Ari tried to express his concern with his eyes. Larke gave him a reassuring smile.

"I'm sorry," Mirimel said eventually. She pulled away from Larke, wiping her face on her sleeve. "I didn't mean to cry."

"Everyone cries, lass," Larke said.

Ari nodded his agreement.

"Even you? Is your horse better? Will he live?"

"He's well."

"May I have more water?" Mirimel asked, looking at Ari.

Ari hurried to get it. He was only gone a moment, but when he returned, Mirimel looked much more composed. Larke sat back against the wall, no longer holding her up. She was sitting on her own. The hand she held out for the cup Ari offered her was nearly steady. She drank the water down, handing it back.

"Do you want more?" Ari asked.

"No." She shook her head. "I do have a few more questions, though."

They both looked at her attentively.

"We're in the woods, it seems to me."

They nodded.

"And no one else is here."

They shook their heads.

"Exactly who, then, put me in these clothes?"

Ari looked at Larke. Mirimel followed his gaze. Larke cleared his throat, suddenly looking anywhere but at her. Mirimel's eyes narrowed.

"Ah, I was about to go refill this," Ari said, shaking the water skin and jumping up. As fast as he was, he still learned several new expletives.

Chapter 26

Mirimel insisted she could walk the next day, although she had to take frequent rests. Larke hovered around her, constantly asking her if she was dizzy or nauseated and trying to look at her eyes. She mostly ignored him, and when she did address him, it was with calm indifference.

Even at her slow pace, Mirimel's expert guidance had them out of the forest and standing before the newly constructed temporary gates of Sorga in two days. Ari had been taking them in a direction that was generally correct, although it would have brought them out onto the plains much farther southeast than expected.

It was a pleasant two days for Ari, with more archery practice and the occasional tall tale from Larke, when he wasn't busy pestering Mirimel. Spring was fully upon them. They weren't hunting anyone and no one was trying to kill them. After the first morning, Mirimel even started treating Larke like normal again, or maybe even a bit nicer. She seemed nicer in general, although sad, and Ari could tell that most of her anger had finally left her.

They reached Sorga in the early evening, spurring an instant party. Ari was happy to see that Natan was up and about, not even bandaged anymore. He had some sharp words for Larke about how the bard had cut away a large section of his hair to suture his head, but everyone could tell they were in jest. Larke came back with some quips about not letting young girls into your rooms. Ari noticed the bard was careful about who he said them in front of.

Stew, too, was much improved, although he had some nasty scars that Larke said would fade, and Peine seemed himself. What Ari was most happy about, aside from the fact that he was home and their enemy slain, was seeing Ispiria. She seemed so much herself and so wonderfully normal. Ari wondered if Larke had fixed her before he'd set out to find them, or if it was just a result of having the Caller dead.

Finally, the party dwindled down. Larke, who still looked more worn than usual, begged to end the music early, and Ari found himself alone at a table with Peine and Ispiria. Mirimel had long ago retired, saying she needed a bath and sleep in a real bed more than she needed another mug of ale. Ari didn't drink ale, but he agreed with her about the bath. Everyone was being polite, but he knew he smelled. He was surprised Peine hadn't dragged him away hours ago.

As if reading his mind, Peine stood up. "I'm going to order water sent up for you, Ari. I think everyone's done congratulating you for now. I'm sure there'll be an even larger party tomorrow."

"Thank you, Peine," Ispiria said. She wrinkled her nose at Ari. "I'm more glad than anyone that you're home, Ari, but I think dirt is actually falling out of your hair onto the table. And what is that beard? Did you do that on purpose? I know there aren't mirrors in the woods, but aren't there at least pools of water to look in or something?"

"I didn't remember to bring any shaving tools," Ari said, trying to muster up as much dignity as he could.

"That's what happens to him when he goes off without his valet," Peine said, grinning. "I'll expect you shortly, my lord." He gave a bow and left the hall.

"I'm glad everything is back to normal," Ispiria said.

She took Ari's hand, which wasn't really that dirty. He'd washed up in a stream just that afternoon, before they came down out of the mountains. Not that he could recall the last time he'd washed his hair. Ari smiled at her, but he could see sadness in her eyes.

He squeezed her hand. "What is it?"

"I wish so many people hadn't died," she said, her voice low.

"Me too."

"All for that silly stone," she said, her gaze abstract. "I never did find it. It was very bad of you not to bring it to me."

A chill ran through him. He knew that a compulsion stayed even after the caster died, but he'd been hoping that since she couldn't take the stone to the Caller anymore, the compulsion wouldn't have any hold on her.

"Do you still want it?" he asked.

She looked thoughtful. "I do, but I can't think why. Isn't that silly? Why would I want something that I don't want? I am very sorry I yelled at you, though. I don't know what came over me."

"It's all right." He resolved to talk to Larke about it in the morning. He wondered if the wren had returned. How long did it take for a bird to fly halfway across Lggothland and back? "I'm sure you were just tired and worried."

"I was, and then you left and I was even more worried than ever. I'm so glad you came back. I couldn't bear it if the last time I saw you all I did was yell at you." She leaned toward him, bringing her face so close the tip of her nose touched his. "Well, not exactly all."

"No, not exactly," he said, tilting his head to kiss her.

She let him for a moment before pulling away, giggling. She made a face. "Ari, I demand you shave that beard immediately." She let go of his hand, smiling at him.

285

"I will, immediately." He stood, but didn't leave, a bit reluctant to go.

She made shooing motions, laughing.

He bowed before walking away.

***

Ari had no idea what time of the night it was when Larke shook him awake. He groaned, wondering what could possibly be wrong now. Surely they'd killed everyone who wanted to bother them for at least the rest of the spring.

"Ari, the Elders are coming." Larke's voice was a mixture of fear and awe that brought Ari fully awake.

"Who?" Ari asked, sitting up and throwing back the covers.

Larke paced to the window and back again, looking almost frantic. "The Elders. The real Aluiens. Undoubtedly to clean up my mess. I did the best I could, Ari. What more could one man be expected to do?"

"Clean up your mess?" Ari said, not liking the sound of that. "What are they going to do, Larke?"

"I don't know." The bard slumped onto the end of Ari's bed, propping his head on his hands. "I really don't. I have to go." He jumped up, all but running from the room.

Ari pulled on breeches and a tunic before going to the window to peer out. It looked as if the moon rested on the ground, far out on the plain. As Ari watched, the glow grew, getting closer. The distance and the radiant aura of light made it impossible to pick out individual figures.

"Ari, what is it? Did I hear Larke?" Peine said, sticking his head out of his door.

"Larke says the Elders are coming to clean up his mess."

Peine's eyes went wide. "What does that mean?"

"I don't know, but I don't like it. Get dressed. I think maybe you should hide."

"Hide? Where?" Peine ducked back into his room, not shutting the door.

"Make your bed." Ari didn't know if they could fool these Elders, or if they should fear them, but he'd rather err on the

286

side of caution. "Make it look like you haven't been here for weeks. If anyone asks, I'll say you're away visiting your family."

Ari turned back to watch the glow. He could pick out movement now, inside the arc of light growing on the plain. Horses, he thought, and riders in long flowing robes.

"Ready," Peine said.

Ari dropped the curtain. Peine looked disheveled but determined. "Where should you go?" There was no way Peine could get out the front gate without being seen.

"The widows' safe," Peine said, after a moment's thought. "We checked over the stores during the battle. How long will they stay? Do you think that if I lock it, they'll be able to open it?"

"I don't know." Ari racked his brain for another idea. It was a sound plan. It was also the best they could do. "Come on."

They hurried through a strangely silent keep. Ari guessed the night to be fairly young. The quiet was unnerving. The guards in the foyer slumped in place. A white glow was seeping in under the barred double doors. Peine started to falter, slowing, but Ari grabbed his arm and pulled him along, down into the bowels of the keep where the widows' safe lay hidden.

Ari fingered his amulet. Larke had already repaired it for him. He wondered if it was protecting him from the somnolence the white glow seemed to create. What if they took it from him, these Elders? Would it matter? He'd nearly resisted the Caller without it. Larke and the Lady had often told him he had magic of his own. That was why Larke could never truly keep Ari's memories from him.

As they neared the last turn before the hallway where the safe was hidden, Ari could hear low voices ahead. He pulled a stumbling Peine against the wall, his friend blinking at him in surprise. Peine shook his head as if to clear it, his gaze gaining focus. Ari inched forward along the rough stone and peeked around the corner.

Larke and Mirimel stood in the corridor before the widows' safe, their hands searching the wall for the hidden catch.

"Didn't Ispiria show you how to open it?" Larke's voice was full of urgency.

"I didn't stay in the keep, if you'll recall. You're the one who's good with secrets. Can't you figure out how to open it?"

"I know how," Ari said, pulling Peine around the corner with him.

"Ari, lad." Larke looked between him and Peine is surprise. "What brings you to this lovely hallway this fine night?"

Ari raised an eyebrow at Mirimel. She frowned. "It's his idea. He says they're probably coming to steal the Caller and his deeds from our minds."

"I don't know what they'll replace it all with, lad," Larke said. "Whatever it is, it won't be the truth, as it were."

"Are you sure you don't want that?" Ari asked Mirimel, scrutinizing her. Her face was a sallow yellow, nearly healed. He could see the bulk of the bandages on her shoulder under her tunic, but what really concerned him were the lines. There were lines of sorrow around her eyes that he doubted would ever leave.

"Larke says they can't bring back the dead. However they change people's memories, my family will still be gone. We killed the one who did it. I don't want to lose the truth of that. I don't want to lose the truth of any of what happened."

"Ari, lad, if you could open the safe, please?" Larke tapped the wall in an urgent rhythm.

Ari ran his hand over the stone until he found the catch, pressing it. When the door was closed from the outside, it would open with the press of a hidden system of levers. When it was locked from the inside, it could only be unlocked from the inside.

An entire portion of the wall swung out, revealing a vast dark chamber. Inside were provisions, candles, bedding, water and more. It was designed to hold all of the women and children of the keep for nearly thirty days. More if they were careful. The only trouble was, as of yet, there was no back way out. Some work had been done on a tunnel, but it wasn't often undertaken.

"How will we know when to open it?" Peine asked, stepping in.

Mirimel followed him. The two of them looked alone and small in the doorway, darkness spreading out behind them.

"You know the signal?" Ari asked, referring to the series of taps that would let the women of the keep know to open it, were they inside.

Peine nodded.

"Light a candle, lass, and we'll be closing it," Larke said. He kept looking up the corridor. "Hurry."

Peine and Mirimel made quick work of lighting two of the candles placed by the door, each taking one. Ari waved as Larke swung the open section of wall back into place. As soon as it was closed, the bard started tracing symbols on the wall, muttering to himself. His fingers left blue streaks that faded almost before Ari could see them.

After a few moments, Larke stepped back, looking satisfied. "Come. Let's go greet our guests. We don't want them to find us down here."

"You're going to let Mirimel remember everything?" Ari followed Larke toward the stairwell. "Is that because it would be too much work to keep the memories from her, since she has magic of her own?"

"I doubt her touch of magic could protect her from the will of the Elders."

They trotted up the steps.

"Then why not let them take the memories from her?"

"Why did you bring Peine down to the safe?" Larke asked, glancing back over his shoulder at Ari. "And what is it he knows that you want him to keep knowing? Have you been telling him secrets, lad?"

"No," Ari said, a little offended at the suggestion. "I just haven't been telling you what secrets he's found out. There's a difference."

"A slight one."

"You didn't answer me about Mirimel."

"No, lad, I didn't."

Larke strolled across the foyer, shedding his illusion as he went, until he was enveloped in the radiance of the Aluien, all color leaching from him in the intensity of the glow. He lifted the heavy bar, which took two normal men to move, setting it in the corner where it stood during the day. With both arms, he flung the double doors wide.

The courtyard was filled with a nebulous blue-white glow. At the center, a tall man bestrode a white horse. His face was unlined and somehow more angular than a normal man's. Long white hair spilled down the back of his flowing robes. There were more shimmering Aluiens arrayed behind him, at least a score of them, but their features were an indistinct glow. Ari's eyes were caught by the depthless black irises of their leader. The Elder showed no inclination to let them go.

Larke dropped to his knees on the foyer floor. Ari found himself following suit without even meaning to. Bowing his head, he at last freed himself from the Elder's gaze. The glow of the Aluiens was everywhere, enveloping them in silence and light.

"Rise, Larkesong." The Elder's voice held the sound of wind as it whispered through forest branches and across grassy plains. It held notes Ari didn't think could come from a human throat, and it blended them together into music. "Rise, for we have heard of your troubles, and we are arrived. We have woken from our sleep and crossed these which were once our lands. We have come north, to this place men call Sorga, to help you. Rise, my son, for we are here, and we shall make all things right."

Chapter 27

Ari stayed on his knees, head bowed, as Aluiens streamed around him into the keep. They moved in silence, light seeming to float off of them like mist from a lake. It snaked about the keep, filtering through seams and cracks like smoke. Ari couldn't have said in what exact way, but everything the light reached seemed to change.

"My Aridian."

Ari looked up to find the Lady standing before him. She reached out, a delicate hand touching his cheek.

"Come, show me where your dear Ispiria is. I would like to take special care with her."

"Yes, Lady," Ari said, standing. She seemed smaller than ever. He felt almost embarrassed that he'd grown more, that he loomed over her.

He led the way up the staircase to the nobles' corridor, aware that Larke followed them. Aluiens drifted about the keep, flittering into rooms and back out again. They all seemed to be this white haired, black eyed, angular type, like their leader, and each wore an expression of inhuman calm that Ari found vaguely disturbing.

He stopped at Ispiria's room. The door was already open, glowing beings moving about her sitting room, but the Lady and Larke walked onward. Ari turned, confused, and followed after them. They walked toward Sir Cadwel's door, Larke leading the way. An Aluien drifted up to them, tilting its head in inquiry, as if loath to use speech.

"I will care for this one," the Lady said. Her voice was musical as well, but it was the music of life. It was the fullness of an ancient Wheylian lilt, rich and melodic. Not the inhuman harmony of the Elders' tones.

"What about Ispiria?" Ari whispered after the Aluien had floated away in a silent swish of white robes.

"She will be fine under their care," the Lady said. "They will cleanse her mind as they reshape it. I must insure they leave Cadwel alone."

"Reshape it?" Ari ran a hand though his hair. "What do you mean?"

"They will not harm her," the Lady said.

She opened the door to Sir Cadwel's sitting room. Leaving it open, she crossed to his sleeping chamber, pushing open that door as well. Larke followed. Casting a worried glance toward Ispiria's room, Ari went with them.

"They are taking away the Caller and his wolves," the Lady said, moving to stand at Sir Cadwel's side. "They are leaving a new memory in their place. I wish for Sir Cadwel to know the truth of it all."

Sir Cadwel lay in his bed, Canid and Raven sprawled on either side of it. The lines of care on his face were eased by sleep, the thick scar on his forehead dimmed in the glow the Lady and Larke gave off. He would have looked peaceful, if it weren't so disturbing to Ari that they could walk into his room, talking, without him or his hounds waking.

"You're sure Ispiria will be well?" Ari kept his voice low, feeling like the sound of it was an intrusion into this world of light and melody. His mortal voice fell flat and hollow from his lips.

"They will take every care with your love, Aridian," the Lady said.

Ari blushed. "What are we doing with Sir Cadwel?"

"Please seal the doors," the Lady said to Larke.

The bard nodded, returning to the sitting room and closing the door to the hallway. He sketched some of the same signs Ari had seen him use earlier on the widows' safe before returning to the bedroom to repeat the process on that door.

"Will that truly keep them out?" Ari didn't mean to belittle Larke, but the strange angular beings walking through the keep seemed much more powerful than the bard, or even the Lady.

"I haven't the strength to bar their way, lad, but I possess the subtlety to discourage them from wanting to take it."

"Larkesong is adept at spells of guile," the Lady said. "In that realm, he surpasses even me."

"Guile?" Larke repeated, looking hurt.

The Lady smiled at him. She placed a hand on Sir Cadwel's forehead. "Wake, master of Sorga."

Ari was worried that Sir Cadwel would jump up, reaching for a weapon, but his eyes opened slowly. He blinked once, looking about him. "My lady," he said, nodding. "This is interesting company to wake into." He sat up. "If you'll give me a moment, I'll dress."

"No, my dear Cadwel. Stay abed. They will expect you to sleep till morning."

"They?" Sir Cadwel leaned back against his headboard. Ari envied how his mentor could look so stern, seem so commanding, when he was sitting in his bed in his nightshirt with two glowing people standing beside him. "Please explain."

"Only the Lady would warrant a please," Larke muttered to Ari.

"May I?" the Lady asked, gesturing to a large armchair that stood in the corner of the room, near the window.

Sir Cadwel nodded. Larke, with what Ari thought was great daring, sat on the end of the bed. Ari stayed standing by the door. While the Lady situated herself, Sir Cadwel looked down at Raven, frowning.

"You haven't hurt them, have you?" Sir Cadwel asked, gesturing to the old hound where he lay beside the bed.

"They're but asleep, oh noblest of knights," Larke said.

"Would you mind stopping that?" Sir Cadwel asked, squinting at him.

"Pardon?"

"That infernal glowing. Dim it down, bard. I can hardly see."

"Ah, yes, of course." The aura around Larke diminished, although it didn't retreat entirely. "Pardon my exuberance."

"Thank you. Now, what is it you need to tell me, and who has put my hounds in such a sleep that they don't wake for intruders?"

"The Elders have come," the Lady said. "Led by the Khan Dar himself. The council woke them from their sleep. Only they have the power to erase from memory what the Caller has done."

"Erase from memory?" Sir Cadwel sat up straighter. "Is that possible? So many people, so much death. The hawks. The gates." He shook his head. "Who is this Khan Dar?"

"He is our leader."

"I thought the Aluiens were governed by a council." Sir Cadwel looked to Ari, who shrugged.

Ari had thought they were governed by a council as well.

"Our people are, yes," the Lady said. "But we also have a leader. The Khan Dar, he is called. It is an ancient title. It means the One Who Shapes. It is he who preserved the last of the Aluiens. He who struck the bargain with the heart of the earth, that the Aluiens might carry on past their time. Normally, he partakes of the deep sleep. All of the ancient ones do. This preserves them. It is only in times of great need that they awaken."

"Like when an Empty One raises an army of wolves, destroys an entire village, and ravages my keep?" Sir Cadwel said, sounding bitter.

"The loss of your people grieves me," the Lady said. "You know it would be my way to hunt down all Empty Ones and

294

put an end to them. Letting them roam free can only bring turmoil, and the type of disaster that has befallen your people."

"I know, my lady," Sir Cadwel said. "Forgive me. I suffer when my people die."

"There is nothing to forgive. Your noble heart is what makes you so great a man."

Sir Cadwel looked away, clearly embarrassed.

"Why will everyone be dead, then?" Ari asked. "If they don't know about the Caller, what will they think happened? Why will they think the Hawkers' village burned? Almost all of the hawks are dead. Our gates are smashed."

"Some material things shall all be restored. The Elders have this power. Your gates are already mended, the stable rebuilt. By morning, all signs of war will be erased."

"And everyone will be alive again?" Ari asked, taking a step toward her, joy shooting through him.

"No, my Aridian."

Ari looked down, deflated.

"Even the Elders do not have the power to restore the dead."

"What story have they crafted?" Larke asked. "What is it they whisper in the ears of the sleepers?"

"A dire tale, full of every bit as much hardship and sorrow as the truth," the Lady said. "From somewhere deep in the mountains, a plague came, swift and deadly. It killed man, horse and hawk alike. It was brutal and cruel, feeding on those in their prime. Sir Cadwel rode out to contain it, taking the men of Sorga with him. They succeeded, but they too succumbed. Only those kept safely isolated in the keep were spared, mostly the women and the children."

Silence settled over them. Ari turned the idea over in his mind. Would people believe it? He supposed they must, for to them, it would be as if they'd lived it. All the trouble, death and pain the Caller had brought, recolored in the light of random misfortune. Of course, to most of those in the keep, the Caller had been simply that. In many ways, the truth and the lie would be the same.

"So we burned the town?" Sir Cadwel asked. "Often, when there is plague, the only recourse is to burn."

The Lady nodded. "Already, Elders are there, insuring the strength of this new truth."

"And they'll all believe it?" Ari asked, awed. He could hardly comprehend a lie of the magnitude the Elders proposed.

"By now, they already do," Larke said. He shook his head, looking troubled.

"But, what of the wounded? What of all the supplies we used and the infirmary Ispiria set up and everything?" Ari asked.

"Part of the viciousness of the plague is the deep lesions it causes," the Lady said. "Long ragged open wounds, they are, and so brutal they almost look like the bites and claw marks of giant beasts."

Ari was astonished by the cavalier nature of the lie. His mind sought more objections, though he realized what he truly objected to was the fabrication itself, not the details of it. He had the sinking certainty that any disagreement he could imagine had already been thought of and overcome by the powerful minds of the Aluiens.

"I don't like it," Sir Cadwel said.

"I don't think they care," Larke replied.

"What about the stone?" Ari asked. Mortified, he realized he didn't even know where it was, the strange little rock that had started their troubles. He'd been so caught up in saving Mirimel and coming home, he'd forgotten to ask Larke or Sir Cadwel what they'd done with it.

"The Elders have little interest in the stone," the Lady said. "I have convinced them that it should be left with you, as the Sorrecia Hawks wish it."

"But the Caller said his master sent him," Ari said, feeling almost panicked. He didn't want the trouble the stone seemed to bring. "Won't he try again? This will happen all over."

"Who knows that you have this stone?" the Lady asked. Her question cut into Ari's growing worry.

"You," Ari said, gesturing around the room. He glanced at Larke. "And Mirimel."

"I deem it safe enough," the Lady said. "The Caller failed. Those seeking the stone shall know it wasn't with the hawks by now. They may suspect you, but they won't attack Sorga on a mystery and a thought. No, they will try trickery first, to find it and perhaps even win it. Subtlety is their way."

"You're sure of this?" Sir Cadwel asked. "I think it would be better if you took the damnable thing."

"Sorrecia died to give the stone to Aridian," the Lady said, her tone firm.

"I suppose there are worse places to keep something valuable than Sorga," Sir Cadwel muttered. He exchanged a worried glance with Ari. They both knew, like it or not, they would do as the Lady asked. "I take it there's nothing I can do about this daft plague idea either?"

"I am sorry, Lord Cadwel," the Lady said, standing. "It is the will of the council. Even I could not keep this thing from being done. Now, you must stay abed and feign sleep. Aridian, Larkesong and I must go out to them. The time will soon come for our bard to hear his punishment."

Ari looked at Larke in surprise.

"Punishment?" Sir Cadwel said, scowling. "I don't see how any of this is his fault."

Larke stood, but his shoulders were slumped and his face worried. "It isn't just this mess. I've been rash too many times. I can't always count on lenience."

"What will they do?" Ari asked.

Larke glanced at him with a shrug.

"I shall not permit them to be too severe," the Lady said but, for the first time, even she sounded uncertain.

"Let them take my memories," Sir Cadwel said, swinging his feet to the floor. "I'll stand beside you first and have my say. You've committed no crimes."

"'Tis kind of you, old friend," Larke said. He raised a hand, his glow brightening. "Don't think I'll be forgetting the offer." He traced a symbol in the air. Sir Cadwel's eyes slid shut. Larke stepped forward and tipped the knight back into bed before he could fall, arranging the sheets around him.

"They come," the Lady said. She moved to the door, making a sweeping gesture. Larke's symbols flared back to life before disappearing. Opening the door, the Lady crossed the sitting room, repeating the process. Larke followed her, Ari trailing behind. He carefully shut all the doors after him.

As they walked down the corridor, a glowing being appeared at the top of the steps, beckoning them with a gesture. It waited for them, following them down. Ari felt strangely like a prisoner being marched to his trial.

In the courtyard, the Aluiens were once again mounted. Larke's gray was there too, saddled and looking well. The Khan Dar walked his horse forward, coming to a halt before the steps. Riding, he was at eye level with them where they stood, except for the Lady, who was only half Ari's and Larke's height. The Lady and Larke knelt. Ari copied them, trying to hide his shock that anyone would make the Lady kneel.

"So this is your precious one," the Khan Dar said. "Your Thrice Born." He slid from his horse, coming up the steps to walk in a slow circle around Ari before moving to stand before the Lady. "It is an interesting specimen, I grant you, my child. I can see why it beguiles you."

"Yes, Khan Dar," the Lady said, her voice sounding small.

Out of the corner of his eye, Ari watched the Khan Dar place a long fingered hand under her chin, tilting up her head. "You should not let yourself become so attached to your playthings, child." His smile was benign.

"Yes, Khan Dar."

"You are young. What would be troubling in an Elder is merely endearing in you."

He released her, coming to stand before Larke.

"Larkesong, your transgressions are many."

"Yes, Khan Dar." Larke's voice cracked.

"There are those on the council who call for your disbandment. They demand a return of the sacred Orlenia flowing in your veins."

298

Ari sucked in a hard breath, fighting down fear. This was the punishment Larke faced? What would happen to him? Would losing the Orlenia kill him or, worse, leave him an Empty One? Maybe he would turn back into a man, but a lost and empty man twenty-five years out of his time. Ari darted a glance at the bard. Larke's head was bowed, his shoulders squeezed up around his ears, as if he expected a blow to fall.

"I find this demand to be harsh, and not in keeping with your talents," the Khan Dar said.

Relief filled Ari. Larke's shoulders relaxed.

"We gathered you in, made you one of us, for your art, your music. You are the most gifted human musician to ever stride across these lands. That is why we preserved you. Your skill, your depth of knowledge, cannot be lost. You are a valuable piece of our collection, culled in the prime of your life before any of your abilities could diminish."

"Thank you, Khan Dar," Larke said.

"But you do not add to our glory as you should. You traipse about. You mingle with humans. You divulge the secrets of our ways, rather than safeguarding them. This cannot go unpunished."

"I understand, my lord."

"You shall return with us now and devote yourself to your studies. To the purity of music. You shall do this fully, not setting foot outside our caverns again until the sun has set on this human land a thousand times. Perhaps this shall give you perspective. Perhaps it will aid you in gaining the separation from the trifles of man that you so clearly lack and remind you that we exist to further the scope of knowledge, not to trifle in the passing troubles of humans."

"Yes, Khan Dar," Larke said, folding himself onto the ground.

Ari watched Larke out of the corner of his eye, sad for his friend. Larke loved the world. He would be miserable locked away for a thousand days, even if it was in the Aluiens' cavernous home. Ari would miss him.

"My lord," the Lady said, looking up. "Khan Dar."

"Yes, child? You wish to plead for your bard? My punishment is not overly harsh."

"Your will is just, Khan Dar. It is a punishment that must be served, but one I wish to share. It is my fault, my poor influence, which has directed Larkesong's hand. Give him leniency. Allow me to assume some of his chastisement."

"You ask this knowing you, my first child, are also my favorite." The Khan Dar's angular face molded itself into a gentle expression. "I shall grant you this thing. You may assume as many as three hundred of his sunsets, child, but those you take, you must take in the deep sleep."

"My lord?" the Lady asked, sounding startled. "You know I do not partake of the deep sleep."

"I do know, child, and I can see the effects on you. You look distraught, weary. I would not have you squandering yourself. You shall set your playthings aside and partake of the deep sleep. Do if for your bard, or for me. The reason is your choice. The action is mine."

"Yes, Khan Dar," she murmured, lowering her head.

"Thrice Born," the Khan Dar said, his voice turning harsh.

"Yes, my lord." Ari looked up, the Elder's hard tone making him worried he'd done something wrong. Had they discovered Peine? If they had, Ari would say it was all his idea. He wouldn't admit anything about Larke.

"You have been told of the plague?"

"Yes, my lord."

"They tell me we should allow your memory to remain, that you are a true servant of our people."

Ari nodded, his throat too tight to speak.

The Khan Dar gazed long into his eyes. "You shall live this lie, Thrice Born. You shall uphold it. Swear this to me now."

"I--" Ari choked on the words. He cleared his throat. He didn't want to swear it. It was such a vast lie, and he'd never be able to uphold such a vow. Sir Cadwel knew the truth, and Peine, and Mirimel. He glanced at Larke, who was sitting up once more. Larke nodded. Ari took a deep breath. "I swear it, Khan Dar."

"Yet, you hesitate."

Ari's mind raced, skittering from thought to thought before slamming into a convincing reason for his slow reply. "A cart went out, my lord. It had a woman and her children, and her husband's body. They bear witness to the truth."

"Is this what troubles you, Thrice Born?" Ari nodded, for now that he thought of it, he was troubled. "We stopped this cart, turning it back. It moves slowly, but will arrive here in time."

"What of anyone they already met, my lord?" Ari asked, genuinely worried. If he had to help maintain this facade, he didn't need anyone coming to accuse him.

"I do not claim myself an expert on humans, but I feel any who hear both rumors will conclude the truth to be in the plague."

"You are wise, Khan Dar," the Lady said.

Larke shot Ari a look that begged him to stop talking.

"Thank you, child," the Khan Dar said, nodding. "Come, the night fades. Our work is complete. We shall leave the Thrice Born to his people."

"Yes, Khan Dar," Larke and the Lady said.

Larke stood, offering her his hand to help her up. He hurried down the steps, bringing her small white horse to her and helping her to mount before seeking his gray. Ari was pleased to see Larke's horse looked well indeed. Ari waited until the Khan Dar and the other Elders turned their mounts away, drifting out of the inner courtyard in a sea of light, before standing. The Lady waved to him, a sad smile on her face.

"My lute," Larke said, his voice loud. "I'll just be a tick. A short moment. You all carry on. I'll catch up in no time."

The Elders ignored him as they seemed to float across the killing zone. In their wake, Ari's eyes fell in awe on the magically restored gate. Once they passed beyond the outer wall, Larke slid down, coming up the steps to Ari.

"That went somewhat better than I'd hoped," Larke said, smiling.

"I didn't know that getting you to tell me secrets could make them . . ." Ari let his sentence trail off. He didn't even want to say it.

"It's one of the few punishments my people have, lad." Larke's smile disappeared.

"What would happen to you?"

"It's only been done twice. Both went mad. One flung himself from a mountaintop. The other drowned herself in the sea."

"I'm sorry. I didn't know."

"Anything I said or did was my choice, and I knew." Larke put a hand on Ari's shoulder. "Don't worry on it, Ari. No real harm's been done."

"Why is it a punishment for the Lady to go into this deep sleep?"

"Our Lady doesn't like to leave the world behind, lad. She doesn't like to miss anything. And," he lowered his voice, although no one was near. "She has theories about the sleep. She says it changes them. That it makes them feel less. Care less. It's hard to say if it's true, but she fears that. She doesn't want to become disengaged from the world she loves."

"I hope nothing bad happens to her."

"Don't worry. I'll take as few days from her as I can bear." He grimaced. "Locked away in that cave for three years."

"I really am sorry, Larke."

"Nonsense." Larke fumbled in his tunic. "Here, lad. I made you something while I was caring for yon steed of mine."

Ari took the small bundle. Holding it in his palm, he carefully folded back the soft cloth, one of the ones Larke used to clean his lute, to reveal a delicate stone wildflower hung on a silver chain. It was perfectly sculpted from opaque green rock, each petal a work of art. He looked up at Larke in mingled awe and surprise.

"It isn't the quality of the Lady's work, I know," Larke said. "I don't have the skill to weave in so many charms, but it will keep the wearer's mind free of Empty One ideas. It's the best I could do in the time I had."

"It's beautiful. Um, what do you want me to do with it?" He couldn't imagine Larke actually expected him to wear it. That would be exceedingly strange, even for Larke, and Ari already had the amulet the Lady had given him.

"Give it to Ispiria." Larke looked amused. He closed Ari's hand over the stone. "Not that I think my meager skills warrant it, but I recommend it as a betrothal gift. That way, you can count on her always wearing it."

"Oh." Ari blinked a few times, reordering his thoughts. Of course Larke didn't want Ari to wear it. He opened his hand again, taking in the delicate beauty of the piece. "It's perfect. She loves green. Thank you, Larke."

"The least I could do, lad," Larke said, smiling. "The least I could do." He walked back down the steps to his gray, mounting.

"What about your lute?" Ari asked, tucking the necklace carefully away inside his tunic. He wondered where the stone was, but he didn't ask. Sir Cadwel would know.

"Wouldn't you know it, it's right here, tied to my saddle." Larke pulled it free from between his other belongings, striking up a travel song. His gray turned toward the gate, unguided.

"Goodbye, Larke," Ari called.

"Until we meet again, lad." Larke paused in his playing to wave. "Don't forget to get Peine and Mirimel out." Music swirling along behind him, the moonlike glow of the Aluiens before him, Larkesong rode away.

Ari stood long on the steps, night settling around him as the light of the Aluiens faded on the horizon. His mind ranged over the enormity of what they'd done. They'd reshaped the history of Sorga. All to keep themselves secret. Ari wondered if secrecy was truly worth it, and he wondered how he would go through the rest of his life alone in knowing the truth.

Not alone, he corrected himself. Sir Cadwel knew the truth, as did Larke and the Lady. So did Peine and Mirimel. He winced, shaking off his reverie. He'd left them locked in the widows' safe long enough. They were surely worried. They would want to know what had happened, of course, and he would have to tell them. He frowned at the irony, that his first act in protecting his vow would be to break it, but not telling Peine and Mirimel the false story would wreak havoc on the lie the Aluiens had made.

He didn't even feel guilty about telling them, he realized as he trotted down the inner steps. He felt no pull from his conscience at breaking his word. He paused for a moment, considering this. It had to do, he concluded, with the nature of his vow. The Khan Dar had all but dragged the words from him. Ari didn't think a vow made under coercion truly counted. How could you promise with your heart when the promise was forced upon you?

Shrugging, he hurried to the safe and knocked out the code. He had time for thinking later. Now was the time for getting Peine and Mirimel out.

He brought them to Sir Cadwel's sitting room and woke the old knight. Once Sir Cadwel was settled on the large couch in his sitting room, Canid and Raven at his feet and Peine and Mirimel seated in two heavy chairs, Ari told them what had happened, filling Peine and Mirimel in about the lie.

They took it better than he'd hoped, though he could tell Mirimel was at least as upset as Sir Cadwel about Larke's punishment. Sir Cadwel, Ari knew, didn't want to wait three years before taking Larke to task for putting him back to sleep. Ari didn't know why Mirimel was quite so upset about it, but he did notice she was wearing a necklace of her own. What looked to be a small stone hawk, wings spread wide, peeked out from the top of her green tunic. Ari saw her hand stray to it more than once, but he pretended not to be looking.

Ari put the necklace Larke had given him in a secret compartment in his writing desk, but decided to keep the hawks' stone, which Sir Cadwel returned to him, on his person at all times. Ari was sure they would both be safe hidden in the secret drawer, inside his desk, in his sitting room, inside the keep, but he felt it was his duty to personally guard this stone that had cost so many lives.

His first inclination had been to give the necklace to Ispiria immediately, but he couldn't ask her to marry him until she was sixteen, which wouldn't be until fall. He really didn't think Empty Ones would be menacing them between now and then, and he had his own amulet to warn him if one did. He wanted to take Larke's advice and not make the necklace a casual gift. Since he didn't want to explain to Ispiria why she should wear it all the time, and he certainly wouldn't make any progress by ordering her to, he would have to do it right and make it special.

Slowly, over the course of the summer, things returned to normal in Sorga. The Hawkers' village was rebuilt. The royal wedding presents were delayed, waiting for Ari to take them in the fall when he went to the autumn tourney. People recovered as best as they could from the loss of those they loved. The days grew long and hot and Ari returned to practicing and learning. Life in Sorga was once again as it should be.

The End

ABOUT THE AUTHOR

Summer Hanford grew up on a dairy farm in Upstate New York. She earned her bachelor's degree in experimental psychology and went on to do graduate and doctoral work in behavioral neurology.

Turning away from long hours spent in research, Summer returned to her childhood dream of writing fantasy novels, although she enjoys turning her pen to science fiction, Regency and adventure as well. She is now a faculty member of the AllWriters' Workplace and Workshop and has launched her first fantasy series, Thrice Born, with Martin Sisters Publishing Company. To learn more about Summer visit www.summerhanford.com.

Made in the USA
Middletown, DE
10 May 2016